I0678137

James P. McDonald

Unbound and Determined

Book Three of Home Summonings

Infinity Limited Group Publications

Copyright

James McDonald. Unbound and Determined, Book Three of Home Summonings. Print Edition.

Infinity Limited Group Publications.

First Edition, V1.0

ISBN: 978-0-9960504-5-6

Cover Art by: Aleksandra Shiga www.gorillaconcept.com

Edited by: Neila Forssberg, Red Adept Editing

For the wife who is still putting up with my endeavors.

Other Works

Prologue

NORA STARED INTENTLY at the card she had received from Miss Tee. Her mother suspected she'd continued her visits to the hidden estate and had made sure Nora hadn't had free time for months. She still was unsure why her mother had originally pushed her along the path to meeting Miss Tee and learning Greyson's journey. She was more unsure of why, after almost two years, her mother now forbade it.

Nora had snuck out to sit on a rock next to the frozen stream. The chill in the air sent a shudder down her spine as she took a deep breath. Cracks were forming in the ice, and the flow of the water underneath had carved out a small channel. Needing running water for the incantation, she punched a hole through the thin ice. The trickle of water was less than she'd hoped for, but it would have to do. She dropped her offerings of a handful of earth, a feather, and a lit match into the hole.

She had read the words to herself many times but still had no idea who they would call. Would whoever it was answer?

"I beseech thee, Lelia. Please grant me your counsel."

A gentle breeze stirred through the dead woods.

Silence.

Should I read it again? Were the offerings not enough?

Anger welled up inside her. Was this some ridiculous test of Miss Tee's?

Nora had wasted enough of the precious free time she''d been given. If this was the best Miss Tee could deliver, maybe she was a fraud, and maybe Nora's mother was right. She wasn't sure which option was a more disturbing thought.

Nora watched the hole ice over before she gave up. She followed the animal trail that cut through the forest and led back home. At the edge of the woods, but before crossing the glen to home, Nora heard a barely perceptible voice call to her.

"Nora."

Looking around, she thought the woods might be getting to her, but then the call came again. "Nora. This way."

The only thing in sight was a gash in the nearby hillside barely large enough for Nora to slide through. She glanced around, measuring each step as she placed one foot in front of the other until she stopped in front of the crevice. "Hello?"

The darkness of the cave was broken by a pair of piercing white sclera without irises, as if the Cheshire Cat waited for her. "You summoned me?"

The hair on her neck bristled. "Lelia?"

A vaguely human form took shape in the darkness. "I am sometimes known by that name."

"Um, Miss Tee sent me."

Lelia's seemingly sightless eyes narrowed to slits. "And what is it you seek?"

Nora's heart pounded so hard it threatened to jump from her chest and find its own way home. "I... I don't know."

The eyes flared in the darkness and closed, leaving no sign of the figure. "Maybe you should have considered that first."

"Wait. Why would she send me to you?" Nora stepped forward into the cave, but it was empty. Unequipped to go any farther, she backed out of the cave and sprinted home, thankful to be alive but unsure why.

FOUR MONTHS PASSED. The beam from Nora's flashlight cut deep into the darkness of the cave, and the chilly atmosphere wrapped her in a cooling blanket against the blazing summer heat. In the few chances she'd had since the encounter with Lelia, she had explored the cave to its ends. It ran about two hundred yards before branching into a couple of paths, but neither of them stretched much further.

She had not had the courage to use the enchantment again.

Nora's efforts to return to Miss Tee's estate had been useless as well. The gateway wasn't presenting itself to her. Had the old woman given up on her? Had Nora's failure in the woods caused Miss Tee to lock her out? Had she died?

Nora's mother would be gone for a few days and had left a list of chores that couldn't be completed in twice that time. Nora extinguished her light and headed for home. With each step, she shed the remaining vestiges of hope she'd held for finding out more about Lelia and what she could learn from her. It was time to give up on the fruitless task of chasing Lelia and Miss Tee or learning Greyson's story. She needed to move on with her life as her mother wanted.

By the time she reached home, Nora had already mentally started on her mother's list. First, she would tackle the...

Her thoughts trailed off as she reached the house and saw a familiar small envelope tucked in the door. Nora's name flowed across it in Miss Tee's delicate handwriting.

Ire rose in her chest and threatened to spill over. She was not at the old woman's beck and call. She snatched the note and debated throwing it in the fire but instead put it in her desk before stomping off to resume the day's chores.

NORA TOSSED RESTLESSLY in her bed, the note refusing to leave her thoughts. Who was Miss Tee to leave her waiting and wondering? What could the old woman want now? The first rays of sunlight were reaching over the horizon when Nora gave up and threw the sheets aside, staring at the ceiling.

Yes. I am done with this. She would burn the note, then she would be able to sleep.

"Fine," she said to no one.

She turned on the small lamp, which sat on the desk next to her bed, and retrieved the note. The fine paper was smooth in her hand. She rubbed her eyes and sighed. "I should at least know what she has to say for herself. Maybe it's even an apology."

She broke the small red wax seal and read aloud the single word written on the enclosed card.

"Tempus."

She furrowed her brow. "What does..."

Nora's room shrank away. When the world solidified again, her bed disappeared beneath her, and she dropped to the floor of Miss Tee's study.

Miss Tee sat in her chair with a cup of tea in hand, looking down at a book. A figure cloaked in fabric darker than night stood facing her. A pair of sclera glared from underneath the hood. Nora sat on the floor in between the two and crawled backward until she felt the wall behind her.

The voice that came from under the hood reminded Nora of a lightning strike. "What is the meaning of this?"

Miss Tee looked up from the book in her lap.

Nora wrapped her arms around her knees, trying to make herself as small as possible.

Delicate hands drew the hood back to reveal a stunningly beautiful woman with alabaster skin and hair as dark as her cloak. She stared at Miss Tee. "I am talking to you. I asked why you have summoned me here."

Miss Tee sniffed. "Lelia, I sent this young woman to apprentice with you."

"And why would I agree to this?" Lelia asked.

"You know what she has been studying?"

"Yes, and this does not answer my question. Why should I not put her out of her misery now, and spare us all the effort? Have we not been down this road before?"

9

Miss Tee closed her eyes and appeared to debate her answer. "She is not her mother's child. But she will become so unless we help her."

"I'm right here," Nora croaked, waiting to discover if she would have to fight for her life.

Lelia slashed her glare to Nora. "And you wish this? Do you know what you ask of me? Do you understand what I ask in return?"

Nora yelped and looked for somewhere to hide.

"She wishes to continue her studies," Miss Tee said.

"I need to hear this from the girl." Lelia glided the few feet to Nora and grabbed the sides of her head, lifting her off the floor. She gazed into Nora's eyes as she spoke. "Tread carefully, girl. If you call upon me again, be prepared to become my apprentice or cease to exist." She looked at Miss Tee. "And you shall never summon me again, or you will face my wrath."

Lelia vanished before Miss Tee could reply.

"Who or what was that?" Nora was soaked in sweat. "And why would I have anything to do with her?"

"If you are to pick up where Greyson left off, you must learn to embrace your power. Use it. Control it. And you must learn the ways from which your mother has sheltered you. Lelia is one of the few left who can do this for you, but she is a demanding taskmaster. And there is no going back, no quitting." Miss Tee closed the book and laid it on the side table. "Are you ready to resume your studies, or do you wish to relinquish to another?"

"I... I don't know."

The old woman pursed her lips and replaced her cup in its saucer. "It is unfortunate, but as you wish."

"Wait." The deeper Nora became involved with Miss Tee, the more she thought her mother might have a point. Her mother wanted her to have a normal life. If Miss Tee were right, it didn't matter what she did because she was hurtling toward something in her future. Should she give herself over to another? Could she? Who else was there?

She closed her eyes and nodded. "Let's get started."

"Certainly, dear. You'll find the next chronicle on my desk. Run along."

Unbound and Determined, Chronicle III of Greyson Forrester

MELANIPPE'S ARROW WHISTLED for the three seconds it took to find its intended target. She was rewarded with a tortured howl that warbled between rage and agony. The breath of the creature she'd struck cast a large cloud in the frigid air of the Canadian winter.

I shuddered as an enormous mottled brown lycanthrope broke from its cover to thrash on the ground, his wound spraying a fountain of blood. "I didn't even see it in the trees."

The Amazon kept her next silver-tipped arrow trained on the beast as it fought, attempting to shift back into its human form. "You shouldn't be out here in the open. The energy barrier is weakening, and the new one isn't yet ready. You aren't in shape for combat if it were to come to the gates. A lucky shot for them could be… unfortunate. Besides, shouldn't you be preparing for the ritual?"

"I am." I was doing everything in my power not to think about the ritual, including watching the wounded Werewolf. Fur was reabsorbed into its skin, and it shed a couple of hundred pounds of muscle after rolling into the magical wall powered by the Earth's telluric energy, sending blue arcs into the woods. The actions were enough to drain the inner beast, leaving a muscled middle-aged man, naked except for the tattoos that covered most of his body. He reached down and ripped the arrow from his side with a tortured cry.

Irika, the Nubian Amazon who'd been serving as Priscilla's aide for many years, stuck her head out of the trapdoor in the roof and made a come-hither motion with her finger. Where Priscilla was firm and had a way of just appearing at the right moment, Irika was a stalker, not letting me out of her sight until the rite was completed. Her single-mindedness was crushing my ability to focus, much less meditate and prepare. Why couldn't she have stayed back in the office where she usually prowled?

Oh yeah, it had been destroyed.

"I needed some air to clear my head." I returned her narrow-eyed glare and held up my hand, signaling her to give me a minute. Though she dipped below the lip of the hatch, I Sensed her hovering nearby. But she gave me enough room to turn my attention elsewhere.

Even standing behind Mel, I could sense from her head and body movements that something was drawing her attention.

"How many are out there?" I asked.

She made a motion toward the wounded man limping back into the woods. The blood running down his leg was leaving a strong trail. "He makes the fifth pack I've seen. Can't be sure which one without getting a better look at his markings. It's unusual for two packs to be in the same territory at once, so it's a good bet they've all been brought here as ground troops. If the full packs are here, that's at least fifty of them, probably many more."

So far, our small fortress sanctuary had held for the week since the packs had started arriving, but they were breaching the barriers at a rapid pace. My bet was that this barrier would run out of energy by nightfall. At best, we had another day before the beasts were scaling the walls. "What are they waiting for?"

13

She shot another arrow into the branches. The lycan looked as though it was almost nine feet tall when it limply fell from the tree and crashed to the snowy ground. The broken shaft of the arrow stretched from its twitching neck, leaving a splayed naked body as the beast faded away.

"A different pack. That makes six. They must be doing reconnaissance while they wait for someone… or something." Mel had already nocked a fresh arrow and was taking aim. "Do you really think this will work?"

I was out of options. The previous attempts had failed, and Brighid was becoming too strong since she had attached to Drea's body. Brighid's body, however, was failing and wouldn't be able to hold Drea's essence much longer. "It has to."

"HOW MANY ANGELS does it take to get on my last nerve?" I asked.

"I love this kind of joke. How many?" Melvin smiled with glee, his *Magnum, PI* Hawaiian shirt flapping in an invisible breeze. He must have been watching '80s TV shows again. "I don't know. How many angels does it take to get on your last nerve?"

"One." I poked him in his thickly muscled chest.

His brow furrowed. "I don't get it."

My sour mood wasn't really his fault. I sighed and rubbed my temples. "Do you have the device?" Since I'd returned from the underworld, acolytes had been hunting us, hunting me. Then the lycans had started attacking, and we believed they were working for the Erebites. Wynn had passed along a message that LeGasse wanted my head, but the Regent had managed to keep me on the active list. Longbow wasn't out to get me, not yet.

14

The angel paused. "Heph cleaned it up and made a few modifications, but no one has used this thing in millennia. And this was never the prescribed use."

"So we're voiding the warranty," I snapped. "Did he have anything else in his workshop or a better idea?"

"Excellent question." Priscilla stood in the doorway with her arms folded. She was dressed in a short white ceremonial gown, and her hair was loose, streaming across her shoulders.

Melvin stared at the floor. "No."

I rubbed the back of my neck. "Look... Melvin."

The angel stared back at me with droopy eyes as if he were a puppy being punished.

"You weren't able to undo this with your power. The Anubian rites were a catastrophe." I realized I was rubbing my hand where it had been desiccated during the ritual. Magic could only do so much. My injuries from my last trip to the underworld were more than physical, and I was taking a long time to recover. I was developing a resistance to the restorative potions, and healers had been working overtime to help me. I'd barely made it out with the furball and Drea, who was riding along in Brighid's body. I hadn't done much to let my body rest since then.

Priscilla's voice trembled as she fought to sound as though she were in control. "Are you both certain about this? There is no other way?"

"I'm out of ideas." I swallowed. "Unless we can find some of these other lost devices, and we've been looking for months. I haven't found out where the armory is or how to get in even if we found it... if it's still there."

15

Melvin nodded. "I've failed to find the other devices from the book. Even Hephaestus has only limited knowledge."

The Amazonian queen's eyes glazed over, and she stared past me. "This is even riskier than your prior attempts. Not only for them, but you as well."

"I know." I shuddered, sending a jolt through my nerves. "If we only had more time…"

"But we do not." Priscilla locked her gaze onto me. She held me responsible for the body swap between Brighid and her granddaughter, Drea. Unfortunately, Drea didn't have much time left. Brighid's body wasn't made for that kind of spirit. Brighid, on the other hand, was taking full advantage of the power of her new shell. "More precisely, they do not."

It was my turn to look away.

"Walk me through this one more time. And I wish to see the device." She motioned to the hallway, and two women strolled into the room. Priscilla had brought the two shamans in to assist in the ritual. One was a local. The other, Tellia, had been with us for months. Like almost everyone in the Veiled world, she and Priscilla had a history.

Carefully, I poured the mixture made from Hephaestus's recipe into a set of vials. "Elixir of Spirit. Drea and Brighid drink this first, strengthening their energy, making it more cohesive, and loosening the hold on their bodies at the same time. Then I close the circle."

RAPID GUNFIRE ERUPTED outside of the thick stone walls. Mel screamed for everyone to get to the top of the two-story keep as she rang the alarm. I wished Melvin hadn't flown off so quickly.

16

He could have at least enjoyed the show if we were going to be slaughtered.

Five people stood at the edge of the barrier in defensive positions, waiting for the gate to be opened. All but one wore Longbow heavy armor, and they fired sporadic gunshots into the nearby woods. The Dagda stood a head taller than everyone in furs and plate armor, and I arrived in time to see him swing his staff in a high arc and bring it down to crush the skull of a lone charging Werewolf.

"Open the barrier," Priscilla yelled.

A gap shimmered in the pale-blue energy of the wall, and the group rushed through. Another lycan charged and mostly made it through the closing barrier. Its twitching back legs lay outside the wall, lopped off by the closing energy field. The flash of a blade belonging to one of the Longbow team sent its head flying, putting it out of its misery.

Irika tipped a ladder over the top of the wall, allowing the party to ascend the small fortress.

The first one over the top grunted with a familiar voice. "Werewolves in Canada. I hope this isn't a repeat of last time." Special Agent Girard Wynn peeled his helmet off.

Melanippe shoved him down as a flurry of small-arms fire peppered the keep, barely slowed by the barrier. The field was weakening more quickly than we'd expected. "You might want to keep that on until you get below."

I waved at Mel as she climbed back into the turret, which provided some protection but gave a wide field of view, and closed the hatch.

"Not that I object to the support"—Priscilla's hands firmly rested on her hips—"but why are you here? And how did you locate us?"

"I called them." Onyx cradled her helmet under her arm. "You hadn't checked in."

"And I found you." A short, solid woman with a thick French Canadian accent stuck out her hand. "Agent Aurelie Dube, Montreal office."

Priscilla turned, leaving the woman's hand floating in midair. "Might we speak in private, Girard?" She walked into a side room without waiting for his answer.

Wynn nodded and followed, closing the door behind him with a thud.

Grunts and sighs came from the rest of the group as they removed their helmets. Raines and Hicks nodded, exhaustion barely covered by the grime on their faces. I pointed to the small kitchen at the end of the hall, knowing both were looking for liquid caffeine. Dube turned and followed them down the hall.

I was most shocked by the last of the party. Inquisitor Delacroix tossed his helmet and balaclava onto a shelf and ran a hand through his hair. It had been his sword I'd seen flying on the battlefield. He leaned against the wall. "Great view, but the neighbors leave something to be desired."

"Yeah." I motioned to the kitchen. "The amenities make the place, though."

The Dag had already found a spot in the corner of the makeshift galley and snored loudly.

Raines and Hicks were worshiping the coffeemaker, praying for something hot to come quickly.

Dube was the only one who looked as if she was fresh and ready. She sat at the table, reloading spent magazines.

I stretched my hand across the table. "Hi, I'm—"

Her look stopped me cold. She stood and folded her hands in front of her. She was a little over five feet tall, and my best guess put her in her early fifties. Her brown hair was streaked with silver and cut in a precise bob. Her thick accent held thinly veiled contempt as she spoke in a flat tone. "Mr. Forrester, I am well aware of who you are. I have studied your file quite intently. Sorcier, strength unknown, but rated high to exceptional due to youth and restricted abilities through magical bindings. Sometimes conseiller for Longbow field operations, currently inactive due to fitness for duty and inquiry into a recent operation that resulted in high casualties and significant damage to multiple key operational facilities."

"You forgot pariah from his own home."

"Yes." Her grim and condescending smile chilled me. "Some portions of your file are incomplete, but I am aware of your juvenile history. We will have plenty of opportunity to fill those gaps later, but if you will excuse me…"

I didn't need to look at Raines to feel her warning glare as I blocked my newest fan's path. "Usually, I don't get the warm welcome until you get to know me."

She tilted her head and looked up into my face. "Mr. Forrester, I have no doubt of your charms, based on the way your friends run to your side even when you do not ask it of them. And we see where this has gotten them. It is as if someone were actively

19

helping you drive away or destroy everyone close to you. No, Mr. Forrester, I do not believe I wish to be in that club. I'll skip it and go straight to casual observer to watch you crash and burn." She leaned forward. "I simply hope you do not take any more good people with you when you go."

ONYX HELD BACK a flow of tears until she was outside the room Brighid and Drea shared. No one was sure if having them stay in such close proximity to each other was the best idea, but Brighid was growing stronger, and her power was melding with the power Drea's body held. Attempts at separating the pair had sped up deterioration of Brighid's body, and Drea's condition worsened in hours. Brighid's body was now confined to a wheelchair as she wasted away.

I wasn't sure what to expect when Onyx locked eyes with me. Embers of pain and rage about her adopted older sister flared into infernos as she grabbed the front of my shirt, lifted me off the ground, and slammed me into the wall.

She shook as she screamed at me. "Fix this. It's your fault. You fix this now." She dropped me to the ground.

Her Amazon training must have been going better than I knew. I wrapped my arms around her, and she shuddered. "None of this would have happened if you hadn't come back," she said in barely a whisper.

I knew she was at least partially right. She and Raines had been kidnapped and tortured, twice. Drea was on death's door. Even restoring Brighid to a body and bringing her back to the material world had left her in someone else's juiced-up body and half-insane.

On the plus side, we were all about to be turned into wolf chow by a bunch of pissed-off lycans. At least that was one way to fix the problem.

But I had a really bad feeling that if we got out of there in one piece, I would have a bigger problem with my part-time employers.

I half-waited for a blade to slide between my ribs as I pulled Onyx in closer. "I'm doing everything I can. I'm happy to see you, but you shouldn't have come."

I gasped as she threw a tight punch into my kidney and backed away. Red streaks ran down her cheeks where she hadn't been able to hold back the floodgate of tears.

"I had to see her one more time in case your cure finished killing her. And from the looks of things outside, you need all the help you can get."

I swallowed and tried to catch my breath. "You're in the middle of your training. You need to get back. As soon as the ritual is done, we have a way out. I have a plan."

"That's worked out so well." She turned and stalked down the hall.

WYNN MOTIONED FOR me to join him in the small bunkroom just off a side hallway. Wynn sat crouched on the edge of one of the lower bunks that took up most of the meager space. The air was heavy with sweat and tinged with something that left a coppery taste in my mouth.

"How bad?" I looked at a small pile of bloody bandages that lay on the other end of the bed along with empty packages that had held fresh dressings. Large swaths of red-tinged white shone through rips in his shirt and pants leg. I was pretty sure at least some of the blood wasn't his.

"Had worse." He winced as he struggled to look up at me. "A couple of hours of sleep will help."

I looked at the wound. "I've got to ask…"

He shook his head. The unspoken question was enough. We both knew what would need to be done if he'd been infected. "Small-arms fire and a rough trip. It's not a bite or a scratch. I'll be fine."

I sat on the bunk across from him. "How'd you find us?"

"Officially, Aurelie sent me a report about a lot of significant movement of lycans into the region. Since we had the first major encounter with them years ago when you were first with us, she came on board to monitor the packs. We're here to investigate why divergent packs are gathering."

"And unofficially?"

The old soldier in him sighed. "Onyx called Beth when you didn't report in, and she called me. We knew roughly where you were headed to attempt the ritual. It didn't take much to figure you might have unwanted company. I called Aurelie, and we all met up in Calgary. We tracked a small pack for two days until they attacked us last night. We took out most of them and followed the last one here this morning."

"But who is she, and why is she here?" Just the thought of the Canadian agent being here had me worried. "She seems to know a lot about me, and I don't think I'm going to be on her Christmas card list."

"I know her." Wynn swallowed. "She's an anthropologist that found out about all of this by accident. It's been hard for her to adjust to this world, and she isn't very trusting. It doesn't help that most of what she sees are the most predatory of the Veiled world. Give her time. You'll grow on her."

I wasn't so sure. At the moment, I felt like a specimen she wanted to dissect and throw in a jar.

"Things are pretty rough right now for Longbow," Wynn said. "Hell, the world in general. With the way things went down with the raid and the Erebite ritual, two-thirds of the southwest is still trying to recover. Anyone who can leave has. The meteorite cover story is holding, but enough people in the know are holding Longbow responsible, and that means it rolls downhill. Lucky for you, the Regent is still a fan. You stopped an apocalypse and saved his ass in the process. You can come back to work when you're ready."

I nodded. I wasn't sure I wanted to work with them as long as the self-righteous true believer LeGasse was still in charge. "I need to fix things here first. And I'm still pretty banged up." We both knew that was an understatement.

"Understood." He winced as he nodded. "But things are getting worse. I need you when you're ready. This big of a group of lycans from different clans is making people nervous and drawing a lot of attention."

"What do you know about the Weres? They picked us up a couple of weeks ago. Thought we'd lost them until we holed up here."

Wynn's phone beeped. "I'll let Aurelie fill you in with the briefing." He stood and shuffled out the door, waving off my offer to help. "Let's go."

THE LIGHTS DIMMED in the small hall and makeshift briefing room. Everyone except for one of the shamans, who was on the roof standing guard, was packed inside the cold stone walls.

Wynn leaned against a table to steady himself.

"Hello all." The small female agent stepped into the dim lights. I felt like a student showing up late for class and finding out I had finals. "For those of you I haven't met, I am Longbow Agent Aurelie Dube. I am here in support of the operation to gather intelligence on the seven packs of lycans that have flocked to these woods. How much do you know at this time?"

Mel spoke up. "I've spotted markings from six different clans. There's a seventh?"

"Excellent, yes. It's unusual for multiple packs to occupy the same region, at least without conflict. It appears these packs have been brought here for a reason. Something to do with whatever you're doing here."

Priscilla's stony face set the tone. "We have worked in partnership with Longbow many times, and often with the people in this room. Why don't you tell us what you know, and we will fill the gaps we can?"

An insipid smile framed Dube's face. "As you know our procedures, you know that—"

Wynn coughed, wordlessly giving the anthropologist an order.

Her pursed lips clearly showed her disagreement. "Very well." She nodded to Wynn. "There are two packs from the Fang Garrison and a third from the Blazing Claw motorcycle gangs. We followed reinforcements from Blazing Claw to find you. The forth

24

is a local commune pack. Agent Wynn, I believe you may have interacted with them in prior operations. The fifth is a feral pack from the Yukon wilderness. They all appear to have been brought in as contract muscle and disposable troops."

"By whom?" Priscilla asked.

Sigils for each pack were added to the projector display against the wall as she spoke. "Whoever hired them. I don't know, but the next two packs tell me they're investing a great deal in finding you. The sixth lycans are from a pack consisting of well-trained former guerrillas from Central America, known as the Loco Lobos. They travel globally and work as mercenaries. They are likely in place to keep order and handle the delicate work that the cannon fodder cannot."

"The seventh tribe. Go on," Priscilla said.

Dube coughed lightly and nodded to Wynn. "We do not have a name or a sigil for the seventh pack. They are more like ghosts than Werewolves. They don't have a formal known territory and are instead spread around."

"Then how do you know they even exist?" I asked.

Wynn cut off Dube before she could answer. "We've had a few dealings with them. Very different from any other tribe we've ever seen. They come from the San Fran area and were very savvy professionals that were turned. They now run some very questionable operations and are very much behind the scenes. We've seen indications that they're the ones managing the operation."

Priscilla crossed her arms. "How many are we facing out there?"

"Locally, I estimate about sixty," Wynn said. "That's a lot to pack into such a small area." The slide changed to a map of North America with the normal range of each pack outlined. "But they have reserves nearing three hundred that could be here in under twenty-four hours."

Several people muttered under their breath.

"What's your plan?" Melanippe asked.

Dube raised the lights and motioned to Wynn. "This is your circus."

Wynn tried to stifle his limp as he stepped to the center of the room and looked at me. "What's the plan?"

A small gasp came from Dube. "You said—"

Wynn raised his hand and motioned for her to be quiet. "Grey? Priscilla? What's your plan?"

I nodded. "Do the ritual and port out of here. But the portal won't open as long as the energy barriers are up, not that they'll hold much longer."

"How long do you need?"

I shrugged. "A few hours. The preparations are almost done, but the ritual has to happen at midnight. Ideally, tomorrow night."

"Can it be done tonight?" Wynn knew the stakes. He cared about Drea and feared Priscilla as much as he cared for her. "You have a little over five hours."

The shaman looked at me and nodded solemnly. "I believe so. The moon is close enough in phase."

I rubbed my hand, still feeling the injury from the last attempt. "The ritual shouldn't take more than a half hour, once we start. I don't know how long it will take Drea and Brighid to recover, but as soon as it's done, we grab everyone, drop the barrier, and use the portal in the room down the hall. It'll put us out at another sanctuary."

Priscilla nodded. "It's well protected, and we have healers and medical teams readied."

The alarms rang. The sentry shrieked out something that sounded like "Help."

Wynn drew his weapon. "Get on it. I don't think we can hold out another day."

NIGHT HAD FALLEN, and a light snow drifted from the skies. Two groups of Weres had shifted into their full form and were crashing fallen trees into the energy barrier as battering rams. A few others were throwing smaller trees the size of telephone poles against the field. Every blow yielded a shower of sparks and blue flashes.

The Dagda frowned. "They're doing a damned caber toss to bring down the field. And they aren't even doing it right."

"It's effective enough." Priscilla scanned the barrier with a set of high-tech goggles. "At this rate, we have an hour. Maybe two."

Wynn motioned to Raines and Hicks. "Let's slow them down a little." He opened a case holding a sniper rifle.

Priscilla placed her hand on top of his. "That will do as much damage to the barrier as they are. It is meant to slow energy and goes both ways. Melanippe has a cache of arrows that are less affected and do less to weaken the field. Try out some of the new explosive ceramic tips. They are silver-infused. There are similarly enchanted throwing knives as well. Save your weapons for when it falls."

Raines took a handful of arrows from Mel and pulled out her own collapsible bow. It was a gift from Mel, and the two of them had been practicing before we'd gone on the run.

Raines's first shot landed in the thigh of a Werewolf that had been throwing trees. The trunk fell back down on the lycan with a crack and sent the beast limping into the woods.

Six more Werewolves charged out of the woods with a gigantic trunk of a lodge pole pine. The root base shook on the end like a charging octopus until it met the barrier in a concussive splash of light and a thunderclap. The trailing ends of the shattered roots smoldered on our side of the barrier. The field had collapsed for a moment, and when it re-formed, it had left the forward three feet of the trunk inside the barrier.

Seeing the field was collapsing, the packs began a deafening, haunting howl. One of the more feral lycans threw itself high into the air, bouncing off the field and landing with a third of its body singed and smoking.

I reached for the Sig in my shoulder rig and wished I had my Colt. It was stored back in my lab along with some of my other gear. Mel had wanted everyone equipped with the same weapons to make it easier to share magazines and ammunition.

"Get the last barrier up." Priscilla tightened her grip around the hilt of the blade on her hip.

The tall shaman that had kept watch shook her head. "It's not ready. It's still charging. It—"

The queen of the Amazons grabbed my arm. "Get it up *now*."

I LANDED SOLIDLY at the base of the ladder. Irika, Wynn, Onyx, and The Dag were close on my heels. With the bare thought that I needed to manifest the change in my adaptable skinsuit, I Pushed the Leviskin into light armor to allow myself enough flexibility to slow down any glancing blows.

"What do you need?" Wynn asked.

I pointed to a large piece of quartz lying just inside a trail of white, black, brown, and green sand that ringed twelve feet outside of the stone walls. "Where you see one of these crystals, slide it up to where it touches but doesn't break the line. There should be twelve in total. This one's last. I'll start the ritual. Run back here when you're done."

I Sensed the crystal wasn't fully aligned and charged, but it didn't matter. This was supposed to be for emergencies in case the portal failed when we dropped the outer barrier. We needed any time it could give us. I plunged my left hand into the Earth and put my right onto the crystal, pulling as much energy from the telluric current that powered the place as I could get to flow through me.

I lost myself in the moment, but part of me still sensed the small-arms fire ricocheting off the wall behind me. Something stung my arm, and I fought to keep my focus. I had to be ready.

I dared breaking my meditation long enough to steal a glance. Holes were opening in the outer barrier. They were sealing up before anything got through, but we had minutes left before it collapsed entirely.

The Dagda's voice resonated as it dug through my subconscious. "Just a few more seconds. Be ready."

I couldn't look around to see if he was talking to me or someone else. Sweat ran in rivers down my back as I fought to keep focus.

The outer barrier failed, sending a surge of the Earth's energy rushing into me and into the stone. But at the same time, a frigid wave of air threatened to break my concentration.

"Now, lad," The Dagda shouted. "Do it now."

I Sensed the connections were complete, and it took all of my strength to slide the stone forward. It was connected to the telluric current, and moving all of the energy to close the switch felt like pushing an entire mountain forward.

I shut out the snarls and howls that rushed closer. *Half an inch. Another half an inch.*

"Dammit, boy. Hurry up."

The chunk of crystal hummed and whined as it contacted the barrier and brought it to life. It threatened to pull me into the Earth with it. It felt so warm, so soothing.

A scream of pain coupled with a powerful hand pulling me away from the crystal. I snapped back to consciousness. Irika dropped me to the ground and spun toward the cry with her drawn bow.

A half-dozen Weres collided with the new barrier and were instantly incinerated. Another dozen or so dead and injured lycans were spread along the field in front of us as the rest retreated.

"Onyx!" Wynn was screaming.

A lycan missing an arm danced and howled in pain until an arrow caught him in the throat, dropping his quivering form to the ground.

Onyx knelt on the ground, the rest of the lycan's claw and arm protruding from her chest like the branch of a gnarled tree. Pale and splattered with blood, Onyx looked at me vacantly and fell over on her side.

"IS SHE BREATHING?" Priscilla shook as we lifted Onyx's limp body over the railing. The Dagda had been able to stop most of the bleeding with the touch of his magic staff, but we were afraid of what would happen if we removed the claw. Now partially shrunken and returned to its human state, the claw's grip had tightened around Onyx's insides.

"Barely." Wynn was covered in blood. "Where's your infirmary?"

Priscilla stared at the wound. "The other side of the portal."

"We've got to go," Wynn snapped. "Get everyone below."

I watched as the remaining lycans charged back into the woods. "We can't. Not yet."

Wynn grabbed me. "You might be able to help Drea and the other one. But if we don't go now, Onyx is dead."

I pushed him back. "You don't get it. I just activated the field. It's at its strongest. I couldn't shut it down right now if every wizard, Werewolf, and fae in the world was trapped in here with us. If I bring that field down right now, everything for a mile will be incinerated, including us. It's why they all turned around. It'll be at least an hour before it stabilizes enough to where I can bring it down. And once it's down, that's it."

31

Wynn slumped to the ground. "I hate this magic bullshit."

"Dag." I swallowed. "Tell me you can do something."

"I can't heal her with the hand inside, and it's too dangerous to remove unless it lets go on its own accord." He shook his huge-bearded head. "And besides, you need to consider the rest."

"What do you mean?"

The eyes that had seen millennia of battles and countless dead still wept for each loss. "The wound. If she survives, you need to be ready in case she turns. It might be better…"

"I won't accept that," Priscilla snapped. "If we can treat it quickly enough, we can stop the infection. If not, we can temper it."

The howling and baying from the woods changed its tone. What I'd thought was celebration turned to panicked cries. Pocked gunfire echoed through the woods.

Priscilla looked at Wynn. "Yours?"

He shook his head.

After a few minutes, the forest around us went quiet for the first time in a week.

Wynn scanned the woods with night-vision goggles. "Something is coming. One person, maybe. None of the other hot spots are moving."

Priscilla pulled her own set of goggles to her eyes. "Get ready."

A lone figure in black emerged from the woods and stalked to the edge of the barrier. He stopped, looked around at the ground, and looked up at us on the wall. He waved then vanished and reappeared on the far end of the roof.

I summoned energy into my hands. Everyone else had already drawn weapons.

"I'm here to help." His hands went up, and he slowly raised his mask.

"Eric?" I asked.

It was Onyx's sometime boyfriend, the being who had helped pull me out of the underworld. And I had no idea how he had just gotten through the barrier.

"There's a cavern underneath," he said as if he'd read my mind. "Your shield only goes down about ten feet. I was able to use the gap as a stopover." He knelt down and kissed Onyx's forehead. "Sorry I'm late."

Her eyes fluttered slightly, and she managed a small smile.

"Can you get her out of here?" Priscilla placed her hand on his shoulder. "And get her to my people for help?"

He nodded. "I can get her out the same way I came in. I've eliminated all of the lycans in the nearby forest, but more are on the way. I will take her to safety and then return."

"No." Priscilla's glassy stare was locked onto Onyx. "Take care of her."

Eric gently lifted Onyx's head. "Stay with me, love. It will all be better soon."

With a small rush of wind, they were gone, leaving behind a thickening pool of blood.

33

"IT'S MY FAULT." I stared at the dried blood on my clothes and shaking hands.

Everyone else had gone below except for Delacroix, who had volunteered to take a watch. He'd been kind enough to dismiss Irika, my new shadow. I hadn't been ready to go below and face the accusations.

"Yes." His accent was thick and syrupy. "And no. People are lost in combat. You were responsible in as far as what you asked her to do, but she was a warrior."

"You speak as if she's already dead."

"You saw that wound as well as I did. It's a miracle she wasn't killed outright."

Bile bubbled up and burned the back of my throat. "Why are you here? I understood the rest coming, at least somewhat. Are you here to observe? Report back to whoever?"

He shrugged. "I'm here to help you. You'll need your strength and power for this to work. I wish to loosen the bindings further. One, maybe two more sessions should completely free you."

"Is that a good idea? After each time, it's taking longer for me to get control of the power. This is delicate work."

He placed his hand on my shoulder as he looked down at me. "It's up to you."

"And if I lose my mind this time? Completely lose control?"

He patted the hilt of the large scimitar that hung from his side. Powerful energy hummed at his touch. "I have this for any need that may arise."

"Let's meet halfway. Give me a little more to tap into, but something that will give me more control, less juice."

"Agreed." He knelt in front of me and locked his eyes on mine. "I think I have the trick for that."

"I'm ready."

We'd already been through this process a half-dozen times, so I knew what to expect. He recited a prayer low under his breath. "Breathe deeply," he said when he was finished.

The world around us faded away. A shadowy form, slightly resembling the Inquisitor in his robes, examined and plucked at the flowing, multicolored ribbons of energy that streamed in and around me. With each touch, he released a melody of light and tone. The number of tendrils surrounding me were far fewer than when the first ones were released months ago, but the ones remaining were strong and deep in tone and color.

After playing a small symphony, the shadowy figure seemingly found what he searched for. He touched and broke the band with a trumpeting crescendo.

The world phased back into view. I leaned against the wall for support as a flood of symbols accompanied by a frantic soundtrack battered my senses. I could feel much more of the world around me—the slight smell that escaped through the cracks from the kitchen, the grinding of the Earth as it supported the weight of the fortress, my heart willing to free itself from my chest.

I fell to my knees.

Delacroix panted as he sat down. "That should do it."

I spewed a geyser of bile and the residual black oil of the broken bindings over the wall. The Inquisitor took a step back, out of the spray. "Yeah. That did it," he said.

AURELIE DUBE STARED intently across the open field, where a hundred lycans postured and shrieked. The sweet smell of overcooked barbeque mixed with singed fur wafted over us as smoke rolled from the funeral pyres where the Weres had piled the bodies of their slain pack mates.

Melanippe and The Dagda discussed our dwindling defensive options as the Werewolves grew in number. They hadn't focused on the fortress yet, but when they did, none of us had high hopes.

"I don't understand how they got here so quickly," Dube mumbled.

I wondered the same thing. Unthinkingly, my newly freed Senses stretched to figure it out. The residual energy from a nearby portal drew my attention. Then I Sensed another portal, and another. I picked the freshest one and focused on it. The gateway felt cold but not quite lifeless.

Who had opened them? How? After the incident in the desert, the Veil was much harder to move through, and all but the most developed portals were quiet. It had taken our team almost two days to get the one below ready, and we even had a fixed place and a key scroll to connect with on the other end.

I could only determine that the portals had materialized around several locations. They weren't fixed spots, or even temporary, so

36

whoever had opened them had ridden through and remained on this side. With the Veil's current disruption, these had taken a lot of power and control to open.

I felt around until I thought I had found them all. "I count about two dozen portals having been opened in total nearby. Nine are still fresh, I'd say less than four hours old."

The Dag tried to whisper in his booming voice. "How many are out there?"

I felt around, but there were too many too count, and too many energy signatures, and something else. "I can't start to give a count on the lycans. But there are twelve of… something else. I can't sense what or who, but I'm betting they're the ones who opened and navigated the portals."

He shook his head. "Can you do anything about the… security gap that Eric used?"

I felt around until I found the opening. It was directly underneath but seemed small. I'd have to look to be sure. "Maybe." I closed my eyes and felt around the gap. Symbols flew before my eyes. I had a rough idea of where it was. I'd never opened a portal before or shadow-walked to a place I didn't know, or at least not to one I couldn't see.

An equation unrolled a map in my mind's eye.

With the symbols fixed in my consciousness, I sketched out a hasty circle lined with the images. "Be right back." I stepped into the circle. "I hope."

The transition was slower than usual. The world around me faded and was gradually replaced by a cold, damp darkness. Half a breath into materializing, I dropped about a foot and stumbled on hard earth. I must have materialized in midair.

The wave of my hand produced a small fireball that cast shadows onto glistening walls. Footprints, presumably Eric's, stood a few inches away. Another depression held a footprint and a small amount of blood. It must be where he and Onyx stopped on the way out.

The chamber was larger than I'd imagined. It was about twenty feet long and a little wider at the middle. A small creek flowed from a crack in the wall, forming a small stream that exited on the other side. The high-water mark went to the ceiling.

Seeing nothing useful, I scratched out another circle and returned to the surface.

Happy to be breathing and aboveground, I quickly described the chamber. Since escaping the underworld, I'd become a little claustrophobic.

"Flood it?" The Dag asked hopefully.

"If we had a lake, sure. I don't think we've got time to move enough dirt and rocks to fill it now either."

"We brought some explosives. Implode it?" Dube asked.

"Filling the hole with debris might work." I looked over the edge and estimated the cavern's location. "The cavern starts under the keep and goes beyond the barrier. We'd be just as likely to breach the field and maybe damage the foundation."

"Fire, then?" The Dag asked.

"It won't last long, but it could buy us a few minutes," Wynn said. "Maybe throw in a few Claymores for the first party that comes through."

I nodded. "And maybe we'll get lucky, and they won't figure out it's there."

THE FIRST WAVE hit a little after eleven. The energy of the blast jarred me out of my meditation before it reached the barrier. I was as prepared for the ritual as I would have the chance to be.

Everyone from the keep, except for Drea and Brighid, were on the top of the fortress. Twenty of us stood against hundreds of lycans, not to mention other unknown forces.

A large, sizzling, electric-blue ball floated on a lazy arc before splashing against the barrier. Residual energy oozed down the side in trails of sparks.

I traced the path of the ball back to its source and confirmed my suspicions. An image formed in my mind. Six hooded figures stood around a catapult made from the local trees. I Sensed the cold flowing from them. They poured energy into a holding field and prepared to launch another barrage.

"Dark Mages," I confirmed to my team.

"Whose?" asked Priscilla.

My head ached as I tried to sharpen my focus. "Can't tell. I can feel the cold flowing from them, though. Winter, if I had to guess. They feel like mercenaries. Not true believers."

That knowledge actually made me feel slightly better. It meant they were less likely to take risks. And if they had provided the ride in for the lycans, they would also be the way out. They were also much less likely to look for or find the cavern. Everyone on both sides knew that enough brute force and time would bring the barrier down.

Wynn and I had taken about an hour to set up a combination of artillery and magical traps in the cavern. If anyone attempted to come in that way, at least it wouldn't be a surprise for us. And if forces broke off to explore the cavern, it would thin out their numbers and slow them down for a while.

The queen of the Amazons stood defiantly in her battle gear. "We can hold them back if necessary. Greyson, go get ready."

"HOW MUCH LONGER?" The voice of The Dagda echoed off of the damp concrete walls. "I'm not rushing you, but I'm uncertain how much longer we can hold out."

An involuntary gasp escaped my lips from the pain as I bent over to pour the line of salt, creating a wide circle. I felt as if I'd cracked my still-healing ribs when I had pushed the stone into place. Just what I didn't need to throw off my concentration. I couldn't risk taking any of the usual potions or measures to dull the pain, because doing so would dull my power and control as well. A single small gap in the circle left enough space for the three of us to enter.

"It's ready," I said. "Are they?"

He grunted. "I'll let them know, and I'll ready the defenses, just in case."

The barrier had held so far but was showing signs of weakening. The attacks had picked up in pace, and the throb from whatever the mages were throwing echoed through the building every few minutes.

I turned all of my focus back to the task at hand. Since Drea's essence had been taken by Drake using the Anima Arca, Brighid's body, even though she was a powerful witch, wasn't strong enough to embody the soul of an Amazon. And Brighid was growing stronger from within Drea's body. I was worried she would soon be unable or unwilling to relinquish the power it gave her.

For weeks, I had been too broken, too injured to be of any help. Priscilla had enlisted all of her extensive resources to find a solution, and we had tried everything. But I knew this was something primordial and fundamental. Even the power of merely ancient gods wouldn't be able to fight it.

It had taken weeks to get the materials I needed for our last, desperate hope. Brighid wheeled Drea into the room in a small wheelchair. Brighid's body was weak but otherwise seemed in fair shape. I hoped she would be strong enough to survive the ritual.

I waved to Irika. She nodded in response and mouthed a blessing for luck before closing and barring the door. I didn't have time to be thankful she was leaving me to the rite.

I conducted a short invisible orchestra, and with a whisper, the candles and braziers sprang to life, casting a pale glow over the room. We would be shielded by the enchantment from those looking for a sign of this kind of power and from anyone looking to disrupt it.

I opened the first case and withdrew the Anima Arca. It held an unused crystal we had recovered in the underworld. The second case held Melvin's delivery, an enchanted silver Rod of Asclepius. For what it had cost, I just hoped it would deliver as advertised. If it worked, the rewards were priceless.

I looked at the two women I loved so dearly and knew that even if the ritual succeeded, one of them could die. Maybe all of us. "Let's get this going."

Two heads bobbed in assent.

DREA STOOD WAVERING in the center of the ring. Brighid helped hold her steady as I closed the circle. A second Push of Will locked the three of us inside of the ring, keeping any loose energies safe. Tellia observed quietly from the corner. Cool and reserved, she'd been guiding all of our efforts for months as we worked to return the souls to their proper homes, and she stood ready if needed.

I handed each of them a vial of elixir. "Drink this. It'll make it easier."

Drea gripped the handle of the Anima Arca with one hand as she raised the vial of potion to her lips with the other. Her skin flushed as the potion coursed through her veins and gave her strength. It wasn't the exact blade that had taken her soul, but it was close enough. However, it was the blade that had put Brighid into Drea's body, which should have made it easier to coax Brighid out. Opening my Sight, I saw each of their auras glowing brightly in the dim room.

"This will hurt." Brighid firmly grasped the handle of the rod. Slowly, the silver snake came alive and unwound from around the rod. The tail coiled up, winding around her arm and seizing its grip. She gasped as a small barb shot from the tail into her flesh.

Drea held the other end of the rod as the snake coiled around her arm. Its mouth opened, exposing a pair of needlelike fangs as it poised to strike.

The Anima Arca blade became translucent, and Drea firmly but gently plunged it into her own body. The crystal took on a soft glow as Brighid's essence trickled into it.

Thousands of years ago, this healing rod drew out the life of the condemned to save lives. The rod would drain the donor and transfer all of the life energy into the recipient. I hoped that with the elixir we'd created, the soul would follow.

I waved my hands over the length of the rod. "Open the gates to the river of life."

In a quick strike, the snake's fangs buried themselves deep into Drea's arm and began to draw her life force into her rapidly emptying body.

In a terrifyingly beautiful dance of energy rivers, Brighid's essence filled the crystal in the dark blade as it left Drea's body, and Drea's own energy replaced it. Brighid's weakened body slumped against me as the energy drained away.

"No no no no no." I couldn't be sure who shrieked from inside of Drea's body as it thrashed. I struggled to hold onto them both as Tellia pushed her way into the circle to help. Drea's eyes rolled back into her head as the silver serpent tightened its grip in the struggle. The shaman caught Brighid's body as she slumped to the floor.

The shaman froze, wide eyed, as we all felt the energy building and fighting within Drea. A banshee's cry escaped her, and a wave of power burst from Drea's body, knocking me back.

"A little help," I yelled at Tellia, shattering her from her absorbed state.

She waved her hands around and felt the aura. "There's a conflict within."

"Really," I snapped. "Tell me something I don't know."

The crystal in the Anima Arca dimmed as it emptied back into Drea's body. Emerald and violet eddies and currents fought through the middle of the now-translucent serpent. Drea and Brighid's bodies convulsed on the floor.

"They are lost." The shaman was hyperventilating. "We must go. Now." She dropped Brighid and broke the barrier, tossing something into the air as she fled for the door.

"Get back here!" I yelled.

A warm pulse took several seconds to spread through the chamber.

The serpent erupted into a shower of silver fléchettes.

44

Rivulets of red beaded all over the shaman's white gown, throwing her forward. Her head and arms thrust outward in a moment of agonizing ecstasy.

A coppery taste filled my mouth.

Tellia's mouth froze in a scream as her body took on an ethereal glow. Then she faded out in a shower of fireflies.

I looked down. Beads of blood increased across my chest. Silver glinted in the places where my armor had caught some of the fragments. A crystal shard, tinted in red, glinted from my belly and burned as it vaporized and cauterized the wound.

Priscilla burst through the door as I collapsed, face forward, onto the stone floor. I didn't even think to try to break my fall. I couldn't see as unsteady hands rolled me over and checked me for signs of life.

It sounded like a faraway echo when someone yelled for a med kit. "We're losing them."

Then there was merciful quiet.

A GENTLE WIND swirled around me and cleared a buffer of air inside of the murky bluish haze. A shadow swam past my peripheral vision and darted away.

A small girl in a sundress skipped out of the fog. "Hello."

"I… I know you," I said.

"You remember, do you?" she asked. "Good. Excellent. Do you remember from where?"

I strained to remember. I knew her face, her voice. "The underworld. You led me…"

"Yes." She held out a small hand. "You saved me, and I in turn helped you."

Her small hand felt very familiar in mine.

She pulled me deeper into the blue-gray haze. Hollow voices echoed around us. Dim, diffused light cast shadows all around.

I was a little nervous. "Where are we going?"

She squeezed my hand. "Hold onto me tightly. We're almost there. I wouldn't want you to get lost."

The soupy haze swallowed everything below my waist, and the end of my arm disappeared in the mist. The occasional squeeze of my hand reassured me it was still there. More concerning were several times something unseen brushed against my legs and caused me to do an involuntary dance, which was rewarded with a giggle. I tripped more than once, but the girl's strong and steady hand helped me stay upright.

I could barely breathe or see the end of my nose in the oppressive fog. A screech sent a chill through me. "What—"

"Shhh," the girl said in a quick reply.

A whooshing sound was followed by the thunderous crack of what I imagined to be a hundred-foot-long bullwhip.

"Gamóto." She nearly yanked me off of my feet in the mist as she started to run, dragging me along in her impossibly strong grip. "Too late."

Pain blinded me, and I barely heard the sickening crack coming from my left arm and ribs as a giant club drove me into the air like a golf ball.

Surprisingly, the girl clinging to the arm was not a rubbery mass of splintered bone and torn muscle. She landed solidly on her feet and pulled me erect from where I had crashed into hard ground. A thick, muscled mass wrapped around my leg, crushing and dragging me simultaneously over rocky terrain. Fighting the pain from my broken arm and the pressure around my leg, I shook as I grabbed the blessed silver blade with my good hand and swept it through the mass.

A piercing warble sounded from high above us, and the mist shook with the reverberation. The girl helped pull the severed tentacle from my leg.

"Stay still." Her voice had changed, sounding much deeper and more commanding. When she released my arm, I instinctively cradled it due to the pain. Cold sweat was pouring off of me, and I blamed it on going into shock. I needed the girl to find my way out... if we survived the next few seconds.

The fog retreated as warming red and amber lights flared into brilliance. An ethereal being spun in place, and several translucent faces spun by on the body as if it were a small tornado. The fog cleared enough for me to see that a dozen basketball-sized orbs hung and bobbed, breaking the darkness in a variety of colors. I was shocked by my arm. Instead of a flopping, bloody mess, it was intact except for a couple of fading red streaks.

The opening in the fog had grown to a twenty-foot diameter around us and continued to expand.

A stretch of mottled gray-and-brown tentacle about a foot in width whipped out of the fog and snapped within feet of... her... it... whoever or whatever my savior was. A greenish bolt flowed from her arm, and the limb disappeared back into the fog just as quickly.

"Move," commanded the voice from the shifting, indistinct form.

Not knowing where to go, I ducked behind her. A mass the size of a barrel crashed down where I'd been standing seconds before and snapped it back into the darkness, pulling the mist with it.

"There you are," she muttered to herself. Fiery orbs arced into the fog to be met with another of the piercing cries. As darkness settled back in with the fog, the girl's small hand grabbed mine and yanked me to my feet.

"What is that?" I stumbled as we ran at full speed for what seemed like an hour. I got no answer other than my own ragged breathing. I only knew she was still in front of me because of her unyielding grip, but I couldn't even see the end of my own nose. We finally slowed as the fog lightened. The unseen distance in front of us became brighter until we walked into an open field, and the fog disappeared.

"Now will you tell me what just happened? And what are you?" What I wouldn't give for one simple human being.

The small girl smiled up at me and transformed into a tall, lithe woman. She only seemed solid when she was perfectly, eerily still. Her brown hair was tightly woven into a braid that wrapped around her shoulder. When she moved, she became translucent, and she seemed to be looking in any and all directions at once.

"Dear Greyson, I am Varian." We walked and talked until we stopped in the middle of a dirt crossroad, whose paths stretched into the points of a compass.

"How did I wind up here?"

"You were lost." She stroked the side of my face. "Do you remember?"

Everything was fuzzy, indistinct. I had been in the middle of something. What was it?

Varian whistled, and a couple of etheric hounds appeared at her feet. The furball appeared from behind her, trotted to me, and pawed at my leg.

"You're familiar. He seems to approve of you most days." Her laugh was gentle but came from all around me. "Even if you have been teaching him bad habits."

"You sent him?" I reached down and scratched his head. He trotted back to Varian and sat at her feet.

"Yes." She bent down and scratched his head. "He was the runt of one of my temple guardians. It seemed a good fit."

"Why?"

"This little one here was destined for a great place in my temple, but others took shortsighted actions. Things changed. I thought you two might find some commonality in that."

I felt dizzy and nauseated. An old oak on the edge of the road provided a shaded respite.

49

The woman handed me a large cup. "This should help."

Soothing water flowed down my throat as I drank, and my mind slowly cleared. I still couldn't remember how I'd gotten there. Fifteen pounds of fury curled up in a ball by my side and nudged my hand. A swath of white left a jagged streak in his midnight fur. "I think I have somewhere to be."

"Possibly. That is up to you."

"Why can't I remember?"

A furrowed brow formed across several of the faces that looked back at me from one head. "Trust it will return in time. Timelines, prophesies, destinies. They are all in flux. This is hard on someone such as yourself."

I leaned back against the rough bark of the tree. "What if I don't want to play anymore? I'm tired of... I don't remember what. I'm so tired."

"I understand." She waved to the road. "Come with me, just for a moment."

I pulled myself up and followed. As I stood there, everything swirled around. It was hard to focus.

She supported my arm and pointed to all four roads at once. "I offer you new paths, new futures."

"They all look the same."

"Until you crest the hill and get a look at the landscape."

"Let me guess. I only get to pick one?"

"Yes." She nodded. "But this way, you get a glimpse of that future and the power to influence it."

"As I said, I think I'm going to rest for a while. Thanks for the offer, though." I looked back to the old oak. It faded out of existence.

"If you do not choose, others will do it for you." She waved her hands around. "Would you not at least desire some knowledge?"

I shrugged. "So far, prophecy hasn't worked out so well for me. I'd screw it up anyway."

She nodded, and a thin smirk of understanding spread across her lips. "Very well." She placed her hand on my heart. "A different gift for you, then."

My body seized up as every muscle and tendon threatened to tear loose from bone, but the pain was just as quickly gone. "What the hell was that?"

"A different way to prepare you for what is to come."

More crap from pseudo Divine beings. I looked at the furball. "Are you coming?"

Snort.

Varian spoke as I walked away. "I understand we must all make our choices. May you find good fortune."

"Thanks."

"I was talking to the dog. He shall need it for as long as he is with you." She knelt down and rubbed the scar on his side. "He still waits to be given a name. See to that, will you?"

Varian disappeared in a twist of the wind. I'd be damned if I was playing her game. I lay down in the field where the tree had been. I had no idea where I was, and I didn't care. It was quiet. I closed my eyes.

51

And I couldn't breathe.

Smoke and incense burned my lungs. Ragged screaming pierced my ears. I pitied the poor bastard doing the shrieking, until I realized the cries came from me.

MY EARS RANG. I felt fuzzy. I felt as if someone had used a wet goat to paint my tongue and then used my head as a base drum.

I vaguely remembered being in a room. There was something going on outside. A fight maybe? The snake thing wrapped around Drea's arm. What was it called? Something exploded.

Then a monster appeared in the dark. And a woman. And my mutt.

Was I having some sort of weird dream?

Was I in another of Ladon's twisted tests? It wouldn't be the first time he'd concocted some dream world in my head, or wherever he and my not-quite-a-guardian angel resided.

Everything was a jumble. Something was wrong with Brighid. Didn't she stab me? And Drea. When was the last time I saw her? Either of them?

Oh, hell no. The trial. I'd failed. And this was my punishment. This was Hell. It was the only thing that made sense. But I'd survived, hadn't I? Had everything in the last few months just been an illusion?

Something hissed and sputtered. Silverware clanked against ceramic.

My mouth watered as sizzling bacon wafted into my nostrils. I opened my eyes and stared at a greasy, cheap, faux wood tabletop.

A nasally voice woke me up. "Greyson?" A doughy, middle-aged man with gray skin and a scraggly brown goatee wore a dark trench coat and hat that dripped rain onto the table.

I smacked my lips and sat up. "Who are you?"

He removed his hat, uncovering a thick mane of unkempt frosted hair. "May I sit?"

"If you're picking up the check, sure."

He squeaked across the plastic seat as he slid into place. "My apologies. I'm a little late meeting you." He stuck out a meaty hand. "You may call me Rahm."

Time instantly froze. The clock on the wall had stopped. The air was deathly still and quiet.

"I should have gotten a cup of coffee first." Rahm looked at the withered waitress, bent over in a precarious position as she reached for something on a high shelf.

"You have my attention," I said.

Rahm pulled a wrinkled file folder out of his briefcase and laid it on the table. "You ever heard of the Vogt Wunderkammer?"

"No."

He opened the file and spread out a stack of pictures. "Johan Vogt was a German explorer. In the late 1800s, he opened his collection from his travels to some friends. For a short time, it became a famous cabinet of curiosities, a kind of small museum. After his death, the collection was locked away and stored in his old house by some of his friends. The last caretaker of the estate has passed, and the executor has temporarily reopened the collection. It's on display in Seattle."

I sniffed. "And you're from the tourism board?"

He returned my bored look and sighed. "It's going to be burgled tonight."

"I'm really sorry, but isn't this more of a police matter? I've got my own troubles right now. I think."

He slid a photograph across the tabletop. The blurry picture showed a black tube with a sphere in the middle. I couldn't really make out the engravings that covered the device, but it looked as though it could be from the Armory of Abaddon. *Why do I know that?* Memories swirled around. I knew it was important, but I didn't know why. "What is it?"

"Something that shouldn't get out in the public." A knowing smile crossed the man's face as he leaned back in the bench. "And something that might help you out with that certain problem you have with the ladies."

Drea and Brighid. Why was the device in the photo important? Was it, really? Why were they? I didn't even know. Why did I need it? Did I? "Why are you telling me this? What do you get out of it?"

"You have a mark." He crossed his arms. "I'd like to see it."

My mark. An area the size of a paperback warmed on my left side. I could feel its shifting shape. "Why?"

He shook his head. "There's no quid pro quo here. I'm just curious." He shrugged. "There are items in the collection that are sought by people who wish to use them for nefarious intentions. Bad things happen when children play with toys they don't understand. I don't wish to see any of the items fall into the wrong hands. Isn't this something that you do?"

"I'm not sure I want that job anymore."

"Too bad."

I rubbed the sleep from my eyes. "How did you know I was here?"

"Oh, that." A chuckle rose from deep in his chest. "We have some mutual acquaintances. They were a bit tied up right now, so I came as quickly as I could. Shall we call it fortuitous timing?"

I flipped through the folder. "You're going to have to give me more than that. What has everybody tied up?"

"Your little war." He tented his pudgy fingers and leaned on the table. "A lot of different players are making the best of the chaos going on. That's what the break-in tonight is about. Taking advantage of the shifting energies to get to something that's been protected."

"Why don't you protect it, then?"

With some effort, Rahm pried himself out of the booth. "Long time since I've been in that business, kid. Are you in?"

"I'll think it over."

"Think quickly. If not, I'm certain some of your friends will be able to pick you up in a few days."

"And if I decide to check this out, how am I supposed to get there?"

"I managed to acquire an old truck on short notice." He tossed a set of keys on the counter. "If you walk around the block, it's an old red beater, but it runs. The Vogt place is a couple of miles from here."

"Where am I, anyway?"

"That must've been quite a bender you've been on. Welcome to Seattle."

A thick business card appeared in his meaty hand, and he slid it across the table. "Let me know. And if you decide to intercede in the robbery, there're other items in that collection that probably shouldn't be allowed to remain in the public either. Afterwards, I think I should be able to help you with your other problem."

He walked to the door, snapped his fingers, and time began to move again. "You don't mind picking up my tab, do you?" He grabbed a doughnut from under the glass case on the counter and waddled out the door.

I looked down at his card. It was emblazoned with a symbol in Enochian script—the language of the angels.

Maybe I would be better off dead.

HOT TEA STEAMED in the ceramic cup while I waited on breakfast. My skinsuit was tattered. I Pushed it into something a little more respectable than shredded battle fatigues, but not by much.

I searched my pockets and found a little cash, my ID cards, and one of the Calypso credit cards. But no weapons. Not even a piece of chalk to raise a portal.

How in all of creation had I gotten there? I couldn't grab onto a clear memory of anything more than waking up on the table.

The waitress hadn't been any help. She said I'd shown up in the booth a few minutes earlier.

"Got a phone?" I asked her.

She took my order and pointed to a closet in the back. The pay phone would have been brand new when Eisenhower was president.

I tried Priscilla's private number. It routed me to the Calypso line, and I got her voice mail. A coded message at the end of the greeting meant no one would be checking it any time soon. I left a message anyway.

I called the private number I had for the very special Agent Wynn, but it was disconnected.

Raines's voicemail was full. What was going on?

The clink of a plate hitting the table got my attention. I dug into limp bacon and runny eggs as if they were the first things I'd eaten in weeks.

I got desperate and scribbled a sigil in the thin film on the table. "Melvin? You out there?"

And I waited. I stared into my empty cup. The tealeaves weren't telling me anything either.

THE TRUCK ROARED to life with a turn of the key, making me long for Ktesippe, my possessed classic Indian Chief. She would've driven. On the plus side, she wasn't complaining in my ear.

My credit card had been rejected, and the tab in the diner had made a dent in my available funds. I had a little money stashed in my lab, but after being brought into the Calypso fold, I'd never gone back to make sure it was fully stocked until we were on the run. Then it had been too late.

I'd flipped through the file Rahm had left with me, and even though I hadn't figured out his game, I decided I needed to investigate for myself. There was some risk that it was just a ploy to flush me out into the public, but it seemed doubtful. And I didn't have much else to do. His little stunt of freezing time, along with his business card, lined him up on the angelic side of the Divine, but I couldn't really trust angels, based on my experience with Melvin.

He'd been right about one thing. The drive to the bungalow that held the collection was short. One side of the small museum had peeling paint, but the rest had been restored to its original glory from a century earlier when it had been new. The area looked as if it was undergoing a revival, and a lot of the houses were empty and on the market. A small hand-painted sign in the yard read, "See the Oddities before they're gone." I parked and made my way to the house.

Dust flew as I opened the door. A gentle wash of old and stale energy flowed over me then fled out the door. A teenage girl wearing all black sat at an old desk, studying. She didn't look up as she waved a pamphlet at me. "Twenty bucks."

"Can you—"

She shook the pamphlet. "I'm not a tour guide. Anything you want to know is in here. Just don't touch the junk."

She pocketed my last bills as I grabbed a bad photocopy of the "museum" guide. I used the term generously.

The front room was full of dusty taxidermy. A crudely painted sign that read, "Don't touch the exhibits. This means you!" hung from the arms of a standing porcupine missing half its quills, wearing a cowboy hat, and holding plastic six shooters in alligator claws. Red and gray squirrels were posed as though they were reenacting the shootout at the O.K. Corral. A chipmunk in a small trench coat and carrying a wooden shotgun played the role of Doc Holiday. More squirrels were enmeshed in a reenactment of the Alamo along the back wall. Santa Ana was a prairie dog dressed in doll-sized finery, wielding an antique dagger as a sword.

The next room was full of bizarre medical instruments and specimens floating in formaldehyde. One entire wall was lined with antique devices that had been originally designed to take advantage of the new miracle of electricity. The tools looked more like torture implements than devices to restore humors and vigor as they advertised. The collection even contained a couple of sketches in frames, signed by Nikola Tesla.

Reading the notes framed by each of the exhibits, I could tell the collector of these hadn't been an Edison fan. A stool in the corner of the room had been made from the foot and leg of an elephant electrocuted in one of his stunts.

The back room was the largest and was the focus of the collection—implements of war, torture, and death. The energy in the room felt as though I were swimming in tar. Who was this guy, and how had he collected all of this? A worm-eaten chair with restraints called to me to have a seat. The placard read *Witches Dunking Chair. New England, ca. 1760.*

My newly unbound Senses had a severe case of sugar-dipped *oooh shiny*. With only a few exceptions, everything glistened in an aura of power that made me feel a little intoxicated.

A dozen spears from as many cultures hung in a case. Next to it, a rack of swords in various states of decay were laid out on cracking leather. A few other soul-sucking objects called out with hunger, but I found the case that held the object of my attention. It sat in a disintegrating red-velvet enclosure inside a glass display, on the bottom shelf. A pair of tubes stretched away from a central spherical basket of woven black metal.

Even without the Sight, I could easily see this was made from the same material as the Anima Arca. The black metal had the same glassy shine and resisted the dust that coated almost everything else. The basket seemed designed to hold a pair of the crystals. It was clear that old Johan had no idea what he had possessed in this item. The hand-written placard read *Decorative Hilt for Two-headed Axe with Spike. N. Ireland, ca. 550.*

I didn't remember reading any descriptions of an object like this in any of the texts, so I couldn't be entirely sure what its designed use was. But I seriously doubted it had been made as the hilt for an axe. Rahm had alluded to the idea that it might help with my problem. Staring at the object helped bring back some of my memory. I'd been trying to help Drea and Brighid switch back to their rightful bodies. This thing could be the solution to restoring Drea and Brighid. I couldn't tell for sure, but it looked as though the blade from an Anima Arca might fit into each of the ends.

The thought of doing a smash-and-grab came to mind, but I didn't need that kind of attention. Besides, I was here to stop a robbery. I didn't have much in the way of resources these days, but if I could negotiate a deal, I was certain Priscilla would back it... if I could find her in time.

Another display caught my attention on the way out of the room.

A scorched ash bow with a broken string hung in the back of the box with a crossbow. Several short swords and daggers lay in the bottom of the display with a few other objects and pouches, all of which lay on top of a closed wooden case. The placard rested in the corner of a sketch that showed a party of five and an eviscerated beast. *Weapons from Werewolf Hunting Party. Kingdome of Bohemia, ca 1704.* My focus was on the shield-shaped broach. The emblem of the Longbow Initiative was next to one of a short sword and a quill. The remains of a deformed sigil were in the center, but they were unrecognizable because of what looked to be a bullet hole.

COLD RAIN DRIZZLED on my hiding spot behind an empty house across the street from the Vogt collection. The uncomfortable bench was sheltered in a small gazebo that provided good cover. I hadn't called Rahm to let him know I was looking into the situation. I wasn't sure what was wrong, but something bothered me. After not being able to reach anyone I knew, a lot of things didn't feel right.

I'd tried to find out who the buyer was for the collection, but the girl manning the museum had used her superpowers of indifference and boredom to ignore me. Her attitude most likely guaranteed her a long career in customer service management. She had finally broken down and given me the card to an attorney, who was equally useless but was willing to steal some of the taxidermy and give it to me. For a price.

At the moment, I couldn't afford the dry-rotted iguana in a tablecloth or the letter opener labeled, "William Wallace."

If there was going to be a burglary, I wanted to see what the thief was after that had Rahm so concerned. And if certain objects of interest happened to fall out, they could wind up being borrowed for a while. Maybe they would wind up in the Longbow vaults.

A little after dark, Miss Customer Service locked the door and left for the night. Fewer houses than I expected were occupied. Only a handful remained lit up as the evening drug on, giving the empty and abandoned feel of a Romero flick.

A little after midnight, I decided Rahm probably had spun a lie about the break-in but had wanted me to see the objects for some reason. Maybe it was just his subtle hint that I was supposed to be the master criminal.

I couldn't afford a hotel for the night in any case.

Barely audible whispering pulled me out of my sleepy boredom. Nothing looked out of place, but I could Sense someone or something skulking nearby. I Willed myself to open my Sight to the world around me. The more I used the talent, the wider my range was becoming, and the unbinding had made the effect almost overwhelming. The darkness gave way to deep blue and violet colors around us. I stared at the Vogt house. Nothing was out of order except... there. Nothing was readily visible, but waves had been left in the ether around the house. Something was moving.

A swirl formed under a low window, which popped open. An invisibility glamour.

A little late, it occurred to me I was unarmed. My hands warmed as energy I hoped I wouldn't need flowed into them. I made my way to the side of the house and peeked through the open window.

It opened into the room of terrifying taxidermy. A few of the small figures were moving, but it didn't seem to be of their own accord. The last thing I needed was a cursed capybara wanting to get friendly.

I tripped over a jackalope in chaps while I was stealthily sneaking into the house. A flurry of chirps deafened me, but I still didn't see anyone. Defensively, I unleashed the fireball equivalent of a flash-bang. Instantly, my senses reeled from the discharge. Of course, that had been the idea. I just should have been smart enough to do it before I entered the room.

My senses recovered a little faster than the other beings in the room, mostly because I knew what was coming with the blast. From the dim lights in the room, three short creatures glared in my general direction. The blast must have been enough to shatter whatever they had been using to mask themselves.

They chattered in low clicks and grunts as they drew daggers and looked around. They still seemed blinded.

"No need for those. Can you understand me?" I didn't think hurling around magic in there would be a good idea.

Three heads snapped in my direction. A thick row of short spikes rose up their backs, poking out of their robes and onto the top of their heads like a quill Mohawk. Another burst of chatter among the three of them was followed by the one in the middle speaking in heavily accented English. "We taking him home with us. You no keep Adalric Wedel any more."

"What's that?" I assumed their loud gasps followed by a flurry of excited chatter meant they thought I was an imbecile.

"Our leader, long frozen in his duty." He pointed to the unfortunate cowboy porcupine. "We will save him."

I raised my hands and backed away. This was the major robbery? Some fae creatures taking back their stuffed leader? "How'd he get here?"

"Betrayed by the Vogt. He promised new world for all of us. Brought the Adalric here, and we no hear from him anymore. No message to join him here as promised."

I tried to keep a straight face as the short leader of the group waved his small blade at me in an attempt to be threatening. "Are you of Vogt?"

"No." I grinned as I shook my head. If the owner didn't care about the taxidermy, I sure didn't. "I'm not. My name is Grey. I won't stop you from taking… him."

"I am Schmutzigen Schwamm." The little creature stood straight up and lowered his knife. "You are Hexe? Can lift die Verwünschung?"

"The what?"

The creature looked pained as it struggled for the right words. "The spell. You can reverse it?"

"I'm sorry, but I can't undo death."

"Not dead." The three shook their heads simultaneously. The leader smiled as he found the word he had been seeking. "Torpor."

SUBTLE ENERGIES FLOWED like lazy rivers through the house. I couldn't believe I hadn't felt them earlier, but I'd been too focused on my own concerns. I opened myself as much as I dared and mapped out the house.

No wonder the house was brimming with old and powerful energy. What I hadn't noticed were the fading energies of magical existence. It must have been what Rahm had referenced was protecting the place. Musty air masked the hint of ozone that hung around powerful magical energy.

The history of the bungalow indicated the house had been untouched since sometime in the 1920s until a sleazy attorney sold the estate and opened the house to tourists. Now it was rapidly decaying, as whatever had held it in a state of perpetuity had been broken.

I followed my Sight until the stream of energy led to an old wooden spinning wheel. The motion was barely perceptible, but the wheel was being turned backward by the circulation like a water wheel. It was sustaining the protections in place.

"I think I can help him. Them." Most of the animals in the room looked as if they were still alive, but barely. Some had no life force left and had begun to slowly decay.

The spokesman of the three creatures in front of me, whom I mentally nicknamed Shmutzy, chattered away, and the other two snapped to attention. "Please, you will?" he asked me.

"But first." I dared to turn on a small lamp in the corner. By its dim light, I studied the trio. They were gray with long pointy ears and were a few inches shy of three feet. Their quills had relaxed but still poked through the threadbare robes they wore. Their knives were kitchen utensils. They were a bigger threat to themselves than to me. "What are you?"

Shmutzy looked at me expectantly. "Kobolds in the service of the house of Vogt." He sighed. "But their clan is no more."

House fae. Homeless ones from the looks of it. "Yeah, I'll try."

The inscription on the wheel was easy enough, and I Pushed a burst of energy into the wheel, sending it turning forward again. Slowly at first, it fought to reverse the stream of energy that flowed through the house. Nothing happened until the wheel picked up to a perceptible pace.

One of the red squirrels of the Dalton gang sneezed, sending a cloud of mites flying.

The wheel gradually gathered speed.

Doc Holiday tossed his tiny wooden shotgun down and coughed out clouds of dust. Slowly, all but a few of the creatures in the room began to stir. A small raccoon nudged at what must have been its partner and mourned as it crumbled.

Excited chatter erupted as Adalric Wedel coughed and shook off a century-thick layer of grime. He dropped the sign with an upturned snout and stripped off the cowboy outfit except for the vest. He shined up the small tin sheriff's badge and joined in the high-pitched babbling before facing me.

Shmutzy translated for the rekindled kobold. "He wishes to know why the guardians have been awakened."

I coughed. "You asked me to. All of this stuff, including them, had been sold off." I wondered how smart they really were.

"He wishes to know if the protections are still working."

"What protections?" Without knowing what had been put into place, I couldn't know for sure, but I assumed if there had been wards, opening the collection up to the public had likely destroyed any safeguards that had been left.

A trumpet blared loudly, and Wedel let out a shriek, bringing all of the reanimated creatures to rapt attention.

"Shmutzy." I grabbed my translator. "What's happening?"

"You will help us?" His face plead more than any word could. "We must protect the collection."

"From what?"

A loud screeching howl came from outside. Seconds later, my borrowed truck crashed sideways through the front of the house. A chunk of brick shrapnel sent my world dark.

RAHM ROUSED ME. The hard way. I was no more than a rag doll as he held me two feet off the floor and shook me. One corner of the house had collapsed where the front and side wall had been turned into a crater.

"Well done, sorcerer." His voice boomed off the walls. He uttered a guttural phrase, and a straitjacket of energy wrapped around my body.

"I could have paid the twenty bucks if you wanted a tour," I said.

"If it were only so simple." His laugh rattled my head. "I couldn't enter until the wards were lifted, and I couldn't wait for all of the rats to die." He hung me from a hook on the one remaining solid wall.

"This is how you knew there would be a robbery?" I asked.

Rahm slowly moved from case to case before stopping in front of the wall of spears. "Yes. I needed someone to lift the remaining wards."

"Me." A twinge of guilt grabbed my heart. "Why me?"

Shmutzy tried a flying tackle around Rahm's leg and was met with a fluid kick that sent him hurtling through a display case of South American tribal fetishes. Rahm leaned over and grabbed the small house fae from the case and slung him through the glass case protecting the spears.

68

"You're no angel," I screamed. "Who are you?"

He reached in and grabbed one of the spears that had a long, cold iron blade. As his hand enveloped the shaft, the aging wood and rusting blade burst into flame. He shook the ash away, and a pair of fiery serpents wrapped the shaft in a caduceus around the renewed weapon.

I struggled to free myself, even to breathe through my shock as muscles and bulk filled out Rahm's flowing shirt. Years of age melted away with his flabby bulk, and he looked like a bodybuilder in his twenties. He continued to transform and grew several feet until he had to crouch so he wouldn't hit the ceiling. Bristling fur sprouted until he had a full, thick black pelt. His features sharpened significantly. A pair of long saber-like canines and a snout stretched from his face. If he had power enough for that entrance, what could he do now?

He posed in front of me, icy green eyes mocking me. "At one time, I would have killed you where you moped in that sorry dive. I too had been stripped of much of my power, and a certain queen gave me an opportunity to be restored." He reached into another case and put a few more items into a bag.

I couldn't hold back my shock. "Abhile?"

The grim smile of an apex predator answered. "My patron is quite displeased with you from what she had to say when I was summoned. In exchange for her assistance to regain my stolen life, I agreed to pass on a message and not end yours."

"Don't strain yourself. Feel free to shove the message up your furry hole."

"I would kill you where you hang if not for the fact I'd have to take on your debt." A thick claw clenched around my throat.

69

"Listen carefully. I shall not repeat myself. My patron says that your time runs short, and you need to not end your life. Not yet. All in Heaven and Hell is breaking loose. And you are reminded of your oath, your debt." He tapped the spear on the floor, unleashing a bright flash.

"Tell her…"

"I shall tell her nothing." He surgically swiped a sharply clawed finger, slicing my shirt open without leaving a mark on my skin then ripping the shredded remnants open. He let out a snarl as he placed his hand over the mark then jerked back as if he had been burned. He clenched his fist and punched me. His jab was rewarded with the loud cracks of several ribs breaking. Again.

"You got what you wanted," I groaned. "Now let me go." The pain and shock dissipated the small amount of power I'd pulled into my hands.

"Yes. We too had an arrangement, didn't we?" The now fully formed wolf's head bared its fangs and snarled. "I shall fulfill it now." He threw me to the ground and whipped the spear around, shattering the glass case. He thrust the tip of the spear through the woven cage of the device and flicked it in my direction, slicing it cleanly in half as it left the blade and landed at my feet.

"You moth—"

The butt of his spear cracked into the side of my head.

ACRID SMOKE BURNED my lungs as I forced myself to roll over. A glowing green haze hung over a small case that had been hanging in the other room. Flying sparks were igniting the wall and floor nearby, threatening to engulf the house.

Sirens wailed in the distance. It was a good bet they were on the way here. I grabbed the two pieces of the device from the floor and staggered to the truck, which was still half-embedded in the wall. By some miracle, the truck roared to life. The lone working headlight shone on the case that held the antique Longbow items. Something pulled me to climb out of the truck, break the case, and take the items from the display. I threw the collection on the front seat and climbed behind the wheel. I was thankful for rear-wheel drive as the truck yanked free from the house with a crash.

Neither the truck nor I was in good enough shape to go far, and the sirens were closing in. I'd traveled a block when I found a dark house that had an empty garage with the door open. Police and fire vehicles raced by as the door closed behind me.

I lay down on the worn seats with a thin blanket covering me and listened to the commotion nearby as I contemplated my situation. My head throbbed, my vision blurred, my body ached, and I wanted to sleep. I was pretty sure I had a concussion. I didn't have a phone or any other way to call for help, not that I knew whom to call. I could go to the emergency personnel, but they would raise too many questions I wasn't ready to answer.

I finally decided that if I survived the night, I would find help in the morning. I struggled to keep my eyes open, and lost.

Tsauriel impatiently tapped her foot as she stood in the doorway. I lay in my bed in the tower. "This is what it takes now?

71

Must you be rendered nearly senseless for us to talk? Where have you been?"

"Hello, Tsauriel. I'm not sure I'm the one that's kept you locked away. Can we do this later? I'm a little busy."

"I can help you heal if you will let me. I can feel your pain even with the blocks in place."

A sudden warmth spread through me. It felt good to be able to move without the pain of healing broken bones and torn muscle. Even after months of potions, rituals, medical treatment, and time, the wounds Drake had given me still ached. Rahm's efforts to add to them wouldn't help either. "Thanks. Any idea what's happening?"

Tsauriel shook her head. "Whatever has been done has blocked our awareness of the outside. I sense a great power now, though. And something is wrong. It will take time to figure out what is transpiring."

"I need a little help. I'm getting my ass kicked right now."

Ladon leaned in the door. Heavy bags hung under his eyes. "You haven't been training. We had feared you were somehow lost."

"I regret you are on your own for now, but should you survive, we must resume your training in earnest," Tsauriel said.

Fantastic. Critiques while dying.

She gave a rare compassionate smile. "This will hurt, but our visit must be short. Return soon, but you must wake up. Now."

"FORRESTER, YOU ALIVE?" Delicate fingers raised my eyelids against my will.

Tsauriel hadn't lied. Everything hurt, making me want to hurl. "Don't get your hopes up. The jury is still out."

"We need to get you out of here." Not for the first time, Beth Raines pulled me up and half-dragged me out to a waiting car.

"Wait. I need the stuff in the truck." I struggled to get back out of the car as my head cleared.

"Stay here." It took three trips for her to move it all. She climbed back into the car, holding the two pieces of the Anima device. She knew well what to look for after all of our missions recovering artifacts for Longbow. "I'm assuming this is what you really wanted. Not sure if it will do you much good."

"What about the rest of them? Did you see the little people?"

"The house is empty. I did a quick check before I tracked you here. We have to go."

She forced a seat belt around me. I slid down in the seat as emergency vehicles passed us, leaving the neighborhood.

My head hurt like hell but had cleared somewhat by the time we reached the main road. "What were you doing there?"

She gave me an icy look. "Following a lead. The better question is what were you doing there?"

"Following a lead on a way to reverse the effects of the Anima Arca. And stop a break-in."

She snorted. "How'd that work out for you?"

I slipped in and out of consciousness until we stopped at a nondescript hotel a few blocks away. She had reserved a couple of adjoined rooms. One was full of surveillance intelligence, including a picture of me from earlier in the afternoon. She helped me onto a bed and inspected my obvious injuries.

"Your turn." I pointed to the pictures. "Why didn't you make contact?"

She sighed. "You've been dead for six weeks."

"What?"

She leaned over me and flashed a penlight in my eyes. "Yeah. Six weeks. Until a couple of hours ago, as far as any of us knew, you were dead. After Canada, we lost contact with Priscilla and the others. I didn't believe it was really you until you got your ass kicked."

"Are they okay? Drea? Brighid?"

She shrugged. "Good question. Those of us that made it out barely escaped the fortress. The shaman was just gone. Priscilla, Drea, and Brighid were trapped and couldn't make it to the portal. The Dagda went to help them."

"You left them?"

Angry tears welled in her eyes. "We didn't have a choice. You were... the place was falling apart, and we had casualties to get out. There was nothing we could do. We took everyone we could to the portal and waited on the other side. We carried your body through, but it never came out the other side. Priscilla, Drea, Brighid, and Dube never came through. And we haven't heard any more about Onyx. Wynn took a strike team as soon as he could get to the base, but when he got back to the fortress, the place had been

74

razed to the ground. No sign of anyone. Haven't heard anything since."

I lay down on the worn comforter and closed my eyes. I hoped I wouldn't wake up.

Raines shook me. "Stay with me."

I fought to keep my eyes open. A few minutes of sleep would help my throbbing body. Why wouldn't she just let me rest my eyes? "Why were you there tonight?"

The cold steel of a needle bit into my arm. Whatever she hit me with jolted me awake.

"Stakeout." She flipped through surveillance pictures on her tablet. "I've been staking out the museum, trying to find out who was acquiring the stuff. There are a number of powerful items in there we need to stop from falling into the wrong hands. We've been looking for some of those items for a while. A week or so ago, a couple of things showed up on the black market, and we tracked them here. I've been trying to figure out who the buyer is. Imagine my surprise to see you walk in the front door."

"Who else knows? That I'm here?"

"Wynn and myself. I talked to him a couple of hours ago. He was very specific about not letting anyone else find out until we knew what was going on." She coughed and looked down. "Things have changed a lot since you've been gone. The storm. You going missing again."

"How bad has it gotten?"

"The entire southwest is a disaster. The body count was a couple of thousand, but a lot more have been displaced. Regent Kelso is on the edge of being retired. In a couple of days, I go to

75

HQ to assist him in getting ready for the transition of his power. LeGasse is in charge of the Americas and keeping Wynn on a tight leash. Only thing keeping him sane is he's been looking for you up north and staying out of the office." She sighed and handed me a tablet displaying my profile. "She has you flagged as missing, presumed dead. But should you ever show up again, you're to be detained indefinitely."

"What's the good news?"

RAINES LEFT ME in the hotel room, alone and juiced up, before she returned to the smoldering ruins of the crime scene. After she left, I found a secluded spot and opened a portal to my only truly safe place. My lab.

I told Raines I would call her when I was back, but I didn't want to leave a trace of how or where I went in her hotel room. Before she left, she filled me in on a few more details of the situation.

Wynn was in charge of all operations for Longbow, but not by LeGasse's choice. Their working relationship was contentious at best, and the Bureau was threatening to recall all of their resources. From what Raines knew, the partnerships between Longbow and governments in general were getting shaky. In response, Longbow was rounding up as many high-value Veiled people as they could.

Since Priscilla was missing, all but a few of her people had either gone into hiding or were protecting various sanctuaries out of the reach of mortals.

Their top targets were still Abhile, Sonja, Drake, Betty, and a few other leaders of the Erebites. My file questioned which side I had fallen on and lay a lot of responsibility on me. Calypso assets were untouched so far but were now on everyone's watch lists. It was only a matter of time before anyone who wasn't a mundane human was on their list.

I knew I couldn't trust LeGasse or her people. I couldn't be sure how far I could trust Raines. But she hadn't taken me into custody. She'd given me a safe number for Wynn and a new one for herself, but I needed some time to think before I made another move.

On a more personal note, she also told me that she saw my attacker rip open my shirt and inspect the sigil after he knocked me unconscious. I didn't fill her in on my short history with Rahm. The skin around the sigil on my side was still warm over my shattered ribs, causing me to wonder what he may have done to it. After he knocked me out, she saw him take the spear and a few other items before vanishing into the night.

I placed the broken device from the collection on the table and tossed the other items from the museum unceremoniously in the corner.

My old leather chair welcomed me as I landed with a healing concoction in one hand and an ice pack in the other. My ribs felt as though Rahm might have cracked them where they had still been trying to knit together after my last bout with Drake. I still got the better end of that deal.

I choked down the healing mix that tasted like a cross between a freshly mowed cow pasture and hot ash, but the pain subsided within a few minutes. I tried to ignore the grinding sounds of my shattered bones knitting themselves back together. I closed my eyes with a good idea of what would come next.

"WELL DONE, PADAWAN." Ladon stood over me, dressed in layered golden robes. A hood was pulled over his head, and he was wielding a flaming sword.

I sat up in the grassy field outside of the keep that housed my inner self. My problem was the perpetual houseguests. "What's this?"

"I dug into your memories." The sword shed sparks, and the fire died as he plunged the blade into the ground and folded himself into a lotus position across from me. "I believe it's time we adjust your training, and I searched for something that might give you a more comfortable point of reference. I believe this is something called a Jedi."

"That's enough Obi Wannabe Kenobi."

"As you wish." His clothes shimmered and re-formed into a golden herringbone-weave Battle Dress Uniform. "We may as well work in some more modern skills and tactics—though they lack style, they make up for it in efficiency."

I lay back down in the grass and stared at wispy clouds in a blue sky. "Why bother?"

I hadn't seen him move, and the words had barely left my lips when I found myself dangling upside down off the ground in Ladon's powerful grip. "The war is heating up. You no longer have the luxury of quitting."

"So what? Die now, die later. You heard just as much as I did. Priscilla, Brighid, Drea—they're all dead and gone."

Ladon tightened his grip as he snarled. "A few comrades fall, and you give up? Many more will fall before it's over. And yes, you may be among that number. But would you not be sure? Would you not avenge them?"

"Why not go ahead and end me now?" An angry burst of energy erupted from my hand into Ladon's face, knocking him back and forcing him to drop me. I tucked and landed in a less-than-graceful roll, sprang up, and leaned over him. "Oh yeah, because you can't. You can't hurt me. You can't do a damn thing."

Tsauriel's singsong voice came from behind me and nearly made me jump out of my skin. "You really believe they are gone?"

I spun around to find the angel with her wings held high behind her back. "I don't sense them. And they didn't leave me any messages. What else am I to think?"

She placed a gentle hand on my shoulder, and all my fury faded. "Maybe they have fallen. But Ladon is right. If you act, you may be able to save many others. End the war before it really even starts."

"And how am I supposed to do that?" I shoved her hand from my shoulder. I wanted to be angry. I needed to feel the heat. "Everything I touch turns into a flaming pile. Everything and almost everyone I know or care about is gone or has turned against me."

"Maybe." She took my hand into hers. *"Or maybe you want to lose everything so you're free. Free to fail without disappointing them. Free to brood and watch the world burn. Free to be angry about everything you've been through."*

I tried to pull away, but her grip held firm.

"The truth is you have survived. Even thrived at times." She pulled me closer. *"It's time you pull yourself together. Save your friends if you can. Avenge them if you can't. No matter what, you cannot quit. Take that lesson from the Alpha. He's been trying to recover his implements for a very long time."*

"Who?"

Ladon brushed the grass from his otherwise impeccable suit. *"The one you call Rahm."*

Tsauriel made a motion to Ladon before speaking. *"The Alpha. The first Werewolf. He was cursed through his own selfish actions a long time ago. You allowed him to recover the spear and shield that had bound his power for many generations, and now he will try to reclaim his full power and his throne. He must be stopped before that can happen."*

Her tone carried the implicit message that she expected me to be the one to fix this. What did she expect?

"You can't keep dancing with death," she whispered. The angel placed her hands on the sides of my head. She sang a few words in her angelic tongue, and my head throbbed. Ideas, pictures, even fragments of memories floated by. *"That will help get you started with your recovery. Now it's time to train."*

Ladon shifted his appearance again. He now had a silver breastplate and manifested a set of wings even larger than Tsauriel's. *"Excellent. Now there's something I can get into. Full-*

on champion combat." He drew the sword from the ground, and flames erupted along its razor-sharp edge. "Shall we?"

I remembered enough to know I wasn't fond of this exercise.

MY MEMORIES COALESCED through several hours of meditation. There were a lot of gaps, and I sensed a lot of what I could remember was out of order.

Had I left the lab this much of a mess? I wasn't a neat freak by any means, but the place was a disaster even by my standards. I looked at the books that lay open on the lab table. Notes in my handwriting about arcane weapons and old magicks.

I didn't exactly remember doing all of this, but it wasn't exactly unfamiliar either. I knew I needed something to clear my head and pull myself together. I fought back a wave of nausea from the pain and all of the crap I'd taken to heal. My old leather chair caught me on the way down as I risked blacking out.

I closed my eyes, and the formula for a potion took form in my mind. I wasn't sure what it really meant, and at the end, it had a note. *It will make you feel better.*

Feel better? I'm all for that.

I sipped down a bottle of lukewarm water from the shelf next to me and popped a couple of aspirin. It stayed down, so I risked getting up and pushed myself out of the chair to get to work.

I was a little woozy, but I'd live. For now.

Did I have any willow bark? Where was the volcanic earth? The recipe was incredibly simple, thankfully. I even had all of the ingredients that were needed. I set them on a low simmer and leaned against the lab table, waiting to see the color change.

To kill some time, I flipped through an old book that sat to the side. I didn't remember really looking through it yet, even though it was full of notes in my hand next to various sketches and descriptions. Most of it was seemingly copied from some of the other books lying around about nasty weapons from the... Armory? I dug through my notes. Armory of Abaddon. That didn't sound good.

I found a listing of Anima Arca blades toward the back of the book. I already had that information in the notes on the table and walls. Two pages listed some other devices with crystals. The more I read, the more it all came back to me.

There it was. The device from the museum that now lay in two pieces. It was called the Anima Tactus. "Soul Touch?"

The details were sparse. Translating the text was hard, but it read like a description of a device that allowed for direct interface between two souls. It was more than I could process at the moment.

The swirling lake of mud on the burner let off an odorous wave that smelled like a rabid skunk swimming in a sewer. I made a note on the recipe card so I would remember never to make this concoction in a closed space again. Slowly, the mixture cleared until it was a light-green color. Something told me it was ready.

After it cooled for a few minutes, I pulled a chipped *Queen Mary* shot glass off the rack and filled it.

82

I downed it in one gulp, and it burned on the way down like a mint julep made of poison ivy and pepper spray with a napalm chaser.

And then the pain really started.

How is this feeling any better?

COLD. WET. GROGGY. Must have been one hell of a party. The haze cleared, and I was staring at the furball's water bowl. Where was my mutt?

My throat felt like used sandpaper coated in dried pluff mud, flavored with manure. I hoped the swamp I was floating in was sweat, but it was that and more. And my head... was clear. Nothing hurt. I couldn't remember the last time I could move a finger without discomfort. I was able to breathe without agony. *Am I dead?* Nope, I was starving.

The scattered pieces of my memory were coming back together. Drake stabbing Drea. Brighid being stuck into Drea's body. Drea being pulled into the body of my childhood love.

Abhile.

The Trial.

The underworld.

Trying to return Drea and Brighid to their own bodies.

Had I been killed when the ritual went wrong? *I was here, wasn't I?*

At the moment, it was enough for me to remember what had happened. Maybe I could make it work to undo what I'd caused. Then I remembered it didn't matter. The broken implement lay on the lab table in pieces.

And I had no idea where Drea and Brighid were, or even if they were still alive.

If they weren't, then I didn't give a damn at all. I would have one mission—kill as many of them as I could until they got me. Screw the rest of the world. They were on their own.

I pushed myself up and stripped. My clothes would have to be burned, but they may as well sop up some of the mess.

I pressed on my chest and readied for the agony from broken ribs. They felt solid. A little tender, but healed. Several bottles of water, protein bars, and some mouthwash stripped down the aftertaste and left me feeling more human.

I looked at the cooled pot of Day-Glo-green miracle juice. Next time, I wouldn't put so much in a dose. A quarter of a shot maybe? It took a few minutes to seal the rest of the batch into single-dose ampules.

The soggy mess on the floor was more than I wanted to deal with. A fireball dried it out and took care of most of it. The remaining residue was easy to clean up. Now if I just had a shower. A box of hand wipes had to do.

My supplies were low. How had I let that happen? I'd gotten lazy. Secure. In the short time I'd been surrounded by friends—no, family—I'd gotten complacent. I'd had access to anything I would have ever needed but didn't restock my cache when I had the keys to the cabinet.

Two skinsuits were in sealed packs on the shelf. They went into my old pack with the Sig, a stack of magazines, and boxes of ammunition. I slipped into an old pair of jeans and a black *Firefly* T-shirt. A dozen blades clinked unceremoniously in the bag. Two more blades slid into sheaths on my leg, and the 1911 went into the shoulder holster. The pouch now contained a few basics I might need for any magic. It felt good as I cinched it tight. Just like old times. On my own and in deep.

I may not have had everything straight in my head, but I remembered enough to know what I needed to do next.

The old safe held my most-valuable possessions, which included hair and other samples from both Drea and Brighid. Every sample I'd ever surreptitiously collected from Priscilla had disappeared. The door hung open. Since no one else had access to the lab, I had never bothered locking it.

Mixing up the base for the tracking spells took another hour. It went into the side pouch along with my maps.

Time to go hunting.

THE HOTEL ROOMS Raines had used were empty. My new concoction had knocked me cold for nearly five days while I was healing. Unfortunately, that meant all trails had gone cold. The museum was a gutted hole. Nothing was left inside, and no sign remained of any of the revived taxidermy either.

I still needed a few things, then I could go north and start my search. I just hoped my portal would work and that my source was still around.

An afternoon storm was brewing. It would wash away any of the minor traces from the portal on this end.

The soft earth made for an easy canvas. I drew a circle and some old familiar sigils. I stepped inside, and a small Push of Will connected the circle. It felt intact.

"Casa de playa." Home on the beach.

I emerged in the closet of the suite I'd called home for a while and immediately rolled through the doors and crashed into the bed and the rest of the debris that was held in the room by what was left of the wall. My penthouse suite had become an open-air terrace hanging at a bad angle. The floor had broken, and most of my bedroom formed a ramp to the floor below.

Using rebar and cracks in the floor as a ladder, I climbed over the debris to where the bedroom door had been and rolled over onto relatively level floor. I wouldn't be moving back in any time soon.

The living room still had furniture, electronics, and materials from its time as a war room, but they were all rotting in place. The door hung open, and a large X had been spray-painted on it, showing it had been cleared.

I watched the sun setting on the ocean as I had done so many times before, but the skies were a hazy red. A lot of dust must have still remained in the air from the Barstow explosion. The other half of the resort had been reduced to piles of rubble, with girders and

86

the occasional wall reaching for the skies. Using a dark space in a collapsed room below, I shadow-walked to the ground. The tower I'd lived in wasn't in much better shape even though it was still standing.

One of Kizzy's fleet of Harleys was hidden in a corner of the resort that still stood. I hoped Ktesippe wasn't in one of the vehicles buried somewhere in the rubble that made up most of the garage. I couldn't imagine what would be worse for her, a final death or being broken and trapped.

After a few minutes of tinkering, the bike roared to life. A small Push of energy blew open the gate in the construction fence that secured the complex. Condemned signs hung every fifty feet.

The drive to the Gin Sluice was slow and eerily quiet for Los Angeles. The major roads were clear, but once I got back into the neighborhood, the streets were littered with the discarded husks of burned cars and debris. A soaking rain settled in and pelted me further, adding to the rising waters of clogged drains that weren't designed for such downpours. Based on the high-water marks on some of the buildings, the area had seen some torrential rain recently.

If I passed a dozen people or other living beings hiding in the dark, they were deeply hidden in the lightless neighborhoods.

I hid the bike behind the building next to Obi's place and stepped under the small shed in the back, trying to feel out what was going on. Thank goodness the pad was raised a few inches for the emergency generators, or this one wouldn't have worked either. The back door of the Gin Sluice was barricaded from the outside. I relaxed and opened my Sense to the world around me. Seven—no, eight beings were inside the building. I couldn't see any more than that. It was half the crowd that should have been there at opening time.

With my hand firmly wrapped around the 1911 in its holster, I swung around the side of the building to the front door. The sign hung loosely at a sideways angle. The door was cracked open, and music floated into the empty street.

The outer door was warped to the point it wouldn't ever close again. The inner door was gone. The debris of broken furniture was piled in the corner. The rest had been made serviceable with duct tape. Alvin's bandaged head glowed from behind the bar, where he slowly wiped unused glasses.

Where's Ichabod?

I stepped inside and took a quick peek by both doors. "Hey, Alvin, can you grab—"

The Puckwudgie looked up, his eyes saucers. "You didn't get the message?"

"What—"

Large hands shoved me from behind.

I rolled and dropped the pack off my shoulder, trying to draw my weapon. It was kicked from my hand by a steel-toed leather boot before it cleared the holster.

One of the large dark shadows let out a howl. The other dropped to all fours and changed.

I didn't need my weapon, and I had some frustrations to let out. My hands turned translucent as power surged into them with a warm glow.

"CALM DOWN, EVERYONE." The deep voice came from a wall of muscle in an expensive suit standing just inside the door. A stick figure in his midtwenties with a scraggly hipster beard leaned against the wall behind him, his taut arms crossed over a black T-shirt with a company logo.

"Excellent." The stick figure pushed wire-framed glasses up on his face and stepped forward. "No need for the glow sticks," he said in a deep Texas drawl. "We're just talking here."

I lost myself for a moment in the pattern on the floor, semi-visible through my hands. That was new.

"Ahem."

I took a deep breath and decided I was outnumbered. May as well hear what he had to say. My hands solidified as the glow faded.

"Great." A skinny hand stretched my way. "Paul Tinka, CEO of the Tinka Think Tank Group."

His grip was stronger than his spindly fingers would have suggested. He tried to hide a strong musk underneath expensive cologne. *A lycan.*

"Grey Forrester."

The suit placed a table upright and straightened a couple of the least-damaged chairs from nearby. A tall brunette with cropped hair, a tailored suit, and six-inch heels took the position to his left.

"Please, sit." Tinka sat in the chair on his side of the table and waved to the wall of muscle in a suit. "My usual, and whatever our new friend wants to drink."

I smiled as Alvin poured me a stout. "I'll stand. And whether or not we leave as friends or you need a new pack depends on the next few minutes."

Alvin cut me a look to remind me that without the friendly neighborhood Kraken around, the odds weren't in my favor.

The skinny Werewolf leaned back in his seat. "No need for that. Hired security, nothing more. I'm here for a business deal. Nice and clean. I can get you something you want in exchange for something I want."

"What do you have that I'd want?"

A half chuckle, half growl escaped his wolf-like grin. "There's a couple of ladies I think you're interested in." He slid across pictures of Brighid and Drea.

The room lit up, and I realized I was glowing. "Hand them over. *Now*." Memories of the failed ritual and the lycan assault flooded back.

He shook his head and chuckled. "I didn't say I've got 'em. I said I can get them. More specifically, help you to get them."

"In exchange for what?"

"This bastard." The next picture was my new friend, Rahm.

The next growl was mine.

"So you two have met. He has that effect on people."

The suit placed Tinka's bourbon on the table, then my stout.

90

Tinka grinned and sipped the drink. "You ready to have a seat now?"

I glanced at the chair and stared at the pictures. I took a deep breath and slowly slid the chair away from the table, positioning myself so it would be harder to pin me in. "How does your friend fit in?"

"Friends?" He drove a pointed claw through the picture. "Friends we ain't."

"I thought your kind all ran around in the woods, sniffing each other's behinds."

"Now, look." A thin snarl curled his lips, and his canines tripled in length. His loose shirt grew taut under flaring muscle. "I heard you could be a pretty fair player. It don't have to go down like this."

"Cut to the chase, then."

"All right, here's the deal. About a year ago, he came into my office outside of San Fran. Told me he needed to have some scenario modeling done for some projects he had going on. My company evaluates resources and organizations and helps to project how different scenarios will go down. Most of what we do is mergers and acquisitions, blending leadership from different companies and groups or helping governments plan negotiations. I first thought what he brought me was a joke. Then I saw some of the people and groups listed in the evaluation."

I took a deep breath. "What did he want?"

"Don't know exactly. Said he was representing a larger interest, and it looked like they were planning an all-out global war. Not countries, though. High-powered individuals and very exclusive service providers. Like your friends Priscilla and Calypso."

I rubbed my hand. Now that I was calming down, a mild burning sensation coursed up my fingers and into my arm. It bothered me less than the amount of information this guy had on me. "And then?"

His nostrils flared as he breathed heavily. "Told him we wouldn't do the deal, and I tossed him out. He burst back in, turned loose this big beast thing, and turned all of my people. Said we'd do it one way or another."

Lycans have a notoriously bad temper, but what he said rang of the truth. "So you ran the assault on the castle a while back."

He growled as he nodded. "Didn't have a choice. We physically couldn't refuse. He had us run a number of large operations over ten months. Your name kept showing up. Couple of times, it seemed you were dead, then you weren't. Week or so ago, he came in and cut us loose. Said he had what he needed and didn't give a damn what we did, but his employers would be in touch. I'd rather reach out and touch them first."

I leaned back in the chair and sipped my drink. "What do you want from me?"

"I want that son of a bitch hog-tied, bound, and brought to me so I can find out what kind of hell he brought down on my people and what's coming next. And I want to reverse this curse if it can be. I want to just be me again, not this monster."

"Where are my people?"

"Well." Humanity fully retook Tinka's form. "That's the hard part, but I think we can help each other. A partnership."

TINKA'S PACK RETREATED from the Gin Sluice. In another time, I might have liked the guy. But I wasn't real fond of being threatened the first time I met someone. Especially when they made sure to bring enough reinforcements.

Even so, it was admirable that he cared about his fourteen staff. An intern and a pizza guy with bad timing had been turned into Werewolves. The suit was his attorney and chief of security. The tall brunette ran his logistics and operations. And she was also the only one to have taken a life. It was a long shot, but maybe the rest could have the curse lifted. Once the beast was inside and had a taste for blood, the curse would be complete.

I doubted the lawyer had noticed the change, but the brunette certainly had. As far as cursed beings went, by far they weren't the worst.

Alvin trotted over with another stout and a glass tumbler of reddish-brown liquid on ice that he nipped into before sitting down.

"Where's Obi?" I asked. "Ichabod?"

The small gray Puckwudgie folded long ears back against his head. "Out of town. I was closing up the bar when the mutts rolled in."

"How long have they been here?"

"Two days." He rubbed his small, beady, bloodshot eyes. "I told them you were dead. Had been for more than a month. They said you'd come back from the dead. I managed to slip out a message to tell you it wasn't safe just in case they were telling the truth."

93

"Didn't get it. Would have come anyway."

He downed the last of the contents of his glass. "You been dead or what?"

"Or what as best I can tell."

"Lot of that going around. I'm supposed to close the bar and meet the boss at the new place in Napa. He wants to do wine for a while."

I nodded. "What do you know?"

The stubby spines on his head vibrated. "LA has gone to hell, not that it had far to tip over. Most anything living or undead has left town with whatever they had on their backs. Something bad is coming. Real bad. You need to run too. Far and fast. The pack weren't the first ones to come looking for you."

"Who else?"

"I'd let it go if I was you."

"Good thing you're you and not me. Who?"

He shuffled from the chair and disappeared behind the bar before returning with a sheet of paper and the bottle of reddish liquid. "Here. Maybe that'll convince you. You gotta be running out of your nine lives."

What am I, a cat? "Thanks, Alvin. There're a few things I need, if you can help."

"Give it to me. I'll see what I can do. Then I'm gone."

Most of the names on the list weren't a big surprise. Couple of people from Longbow. Kizzy. Couple of regulars. Tinka's friendlies. A couple of others I didn't know.

94

While Alvin rounded up my list, I thought about the conversation with the nerdy lycan. According to him, once the barrier fell, the Weres easily took the fortress and handed it over to the mages who had brought them in. The different packs were returned to their home territories, the survivors at least. He didn't know any real details since none of his people were there on the ground but instead were entirely out of the loop.

I still didn't know what to think. Maybe they were setting up an elaborate trap, but they'd brought enough muscle to have a good shot at bringing me down. It was more disturbing to wonder if they were telling the truth and needed my help.

I decided to sleep on it while Alvin went shopping.

"WELCOME BACK, GREYSON." Tsauriel closed the book she was reading without looking up at me standing in the doorway. She motioned at the other side of the crystal chessboard. "Sit." Tsauriel had already made the first move. Her knight was parked in f3. With that opening, she was in an aggressive mood.

I mirrored her move, which always aggravated her. I wasn't in the mood to play. "I need help."

"You're just figuring that out?" She moved her pawn to d4.

I countered with my pawn. "Something happened. My mind... my memories. It's all a mess."

95

She brought her queen out to play. "You were foolish. If you dance with death often enough, she will trip you on the dance floor."

"What happened to me?"

"This time, she helped you back up, but her touch always has a price." The angel blocked my escape. "Move."

I slid a pawn into the battlefield.

Her queen picked it off. Within a few moves, I'd traded two more pawns and a rook for only one of her pawns.

"You aren't focused. Match within twelve moves."

"I just said that." One of my bishops left the game in response to my disgraceful move.

"You aren't learning from your past, so it's time to move forward to the future. Some things cannot be undone. Others carry a high price for fixing errors in judgment."

"What are you trying to say?" I captured another pawn.

It cost me a knight. "Very simple. Treat your injuries and fallen friends as collateral damage. Cut your losses now, or risk everything on a losing bet."

"If you're saying what I think you are, then no. I created this mess." I took her knight.

My remaining rook fell. "And what have you done that helped the situation?"

I moved my king out of danger and sighed.

"In that case, what makes you believe anything you do will achieve your desired result?" she asked.

I moved my bishop to block her next move.

It fell. "And what makes you believe that your desired path is the best outcome for all involved?"

I fumed as I moved to protect the king.

"Check," she said calmly.

"What is it you expect me to do? Sacrifice everyone?"

"If need be." My queen retreated to the sidelines after having been taken in a careless move. "With things as they are, hard choices will need to be made."

"I don't know if I can do that." I shook my head. "And if I do, what's the point been to all this?"

The angel rolled her eyes. "Checkmate."

COLD FOG SETTLED over the woods. Alvin had acquired the rest of what I'd requested, and now I needed to see for myself. Tinka had provided enough information that I was able to open a portal nearby to the fortress, using their own gateways. It was time to pick up the trail where I had last seen so many of the people I loved and cared about.

With barely a conscious thought from me, the skinsuit thickened to protect me from the damp wind that sliced through the woods.

Musty, stale smoke hung low as I pushed through the woods. A wide trail wove and ended in a field of debris, which was all that was left of the fortress. From the looks of it, the fortress had surrendered in a massive explosion, throwing stone and brick hundreds of feet into the woods. The tallest piece was a corner of the stone wall that stood head high.

I dug through the debris, down to the staircase that led to the basement. Scorch marks marred the remaining stone walls. The roof to the portal room had collapsed and knocked the heavy oak door into the hall. The door to the ceremonial room hung from one hinge and leaned against the frame. I knocked it to the ground with a touch.

A few holes in the ceiling opened to outside air. A scorch mark shadowed where the shaman had been vaporized. Dried blood stained the floor.

I cleared out the worst of the rubble in the circle embedded in the floor and tried to ignore the large brown spot where I'd... almost died. A touch powered the circle and dammed out the flood of residual energy around me.

My spread of implements included the tracking potions I'd prepared earlier, maps, and scrying crystals. Before I began searching, I needed to know if Drea and Brighid were still alive. At some point, I had to know.

My heart surged when my sample of Brighid's flaming hair sparked as it touched the pale-green elixir. At least she was alive. Drea's black lock glimmered and writhed in the second vial. What in Hermes's hell? What did that mean?

98

With maps spread all around me, I picked up a glowing scrying crystal swinging from the end of a delicate silver chain and dipped the tip of it into Brighid's solution. Slowly, it swung in a low circle until it pointed at the California map. It swung in low, lazy circles as if confused until it jumped in violent tremors and shattered into a gentle gemstone snowfall.

Damn.

With a little conjuring, I was able to identify a dried pool of Brighid's blood. It was old and carried little of her life energy in it, but I was running low on options.

Seven drops from the vial seeped into the dried patch, and I added a drop of my own fresh blood with a tap of my finger. I watched in sick fascination as the entire patch liquefied into a pool and slowly reshaped into an outline with hundreds of lines, squares, and circles. A pentagram that looked like a wheel formed in the center. The streets looked like spokes running in all directions. I should have known. It was a map of Los Diablos, Los Angeles's even more evil twin.

A small spot on Ba'al Halland Drive bubbled with a tiny spark. That had to be where she was.

Wait.

A second spot formed near the Griffin Park Psychomanteum.

Even there, she couldn't be in two places at once.

Bile climbed the back of my throat as horrific thoughts formed in my mind.

I repeated the process for Drea on a separate patch of blood.

The quivering pool looked as if it would repeat the process of making a map, but then it slowly snaked its way to the outline made in Brighid's lifeblood. The infusion flowed and joined with the map, and the two location beacons formed small red intertwined towers with tiny embers on top.

Good thing there was a particular djinn on that side of the realm that owed me a favor.

ICY WIND SLICED through me no matter how much I tried to insulate the skinsuit. The temperature had dropped so quickly that the fog had condensed into thin sheets of ice on every surface. Dry snow drifted from gray skies. The cold had an intensity to it. I Sensed…

Winter.

Damn.

My gloved hand found the cold iron blade at my hip as a voice stole all warmth from my bones.

"Hello, Greyson."

Where was that Ice Queen? "Mairsaile. Is that you?"

Her cold laughter echoed, shattering icicles as it danced through the forest. Queen Mairsile of the House of Edur. Queen for the Winter Lands. Supreme Queen of the Winter fae.

A wall of ice formed and cut off my path. I had no choice but to work my way back to the remains of the fortress.

Another ice wall took form. Where was she steering me? "Mairsile?"

Spears of glistening ice shot up in the path behind me. The path before me was trimmed with icy spikes and blades. *Subtle.*

I formed a small fireball in my hand and bowled it through the ice, clearing a narrow path that closed before I could take the first step. "Can we play this game later? Maybe somewhere like Tahiti?"

If she wanted me dead, she could have done it before I knew she was there. Either she wanted to talk, or she wanted to toy with her prey.

An ice tunnel formed, leading into the woods and clearing a way through the forest. It was as good of an invitation as I was going to get. Three steps inside, the exit behind me froze over. Only one way to go.

The floor crunched beneath my feet with every step. A hundred feet later, it sharply angled downward in a staircase. The first step cracked but held under my weight, then the second, then the third.

The tenth step collapsed under my full weight, sending me careening through a chain of paper-thin steps until the tunnel became a long, smooth slalom. I grabbed my cold iron blade from its holster as I bounced uncontrollably from wall-to-wall, but I lost the iron knife while trying to drive it into the floor to slow my descent.

The slide ended in a small dip, launching me into a dimly lit igloo dome.

Fae sigils were carved into the floor, and walls sprang to life with a stark glow.

Even if I could've climbed back up, the channel behind me had iced over.

My hands trembled from the cold as I picked up the knife and sheathed it then brushed myself off. With a deep breath, I stepped across the center threshold. The door melded into the rest of the dome behind me. "I'm here."

A dense mist streamed through the wall. A tall figure materialized in the fog, and tapered fingers on a long, thin blue hand reached out. Cobalt eyes studied me for a moment before Mairsile's melodious voice chilled the air and dissipated the last wisps of the cloud. "Thank you for accepting my invitation."

"Ever heard of a phone? A call would have been a lot easier on both of us."

Her blue lips drew back to reveal a mouth full of white teeth. "I believe in the personal touch. Please, sit." The stump of a tree broke through the ice, splitting a pair of grapevines that twisted their way into a chair.

"I'll stand," I said.

"I really must insist." She made a minor gesture, nudging me into the nest of vines.

The chair gripped me in an instant and pulled me into the seat. "Who does your decorating? Very nuclear winter. So 1980s."

Mist rose from the floor and froze into a throne as she moved to sit. She tented her hands and stared at me. "How are you?"

"You're my therapist now?"

"Excellent. We can dispense with the pleasantries." Icicles formed where she grasped the arms of the throne. "You have broken our agreement."

Agreement? "Could you be more specific?"

"You have forgotten our pact so quickly?" A chilled claw grabbed my heart. "Curious. It makes me wonder how seriously you take what others know to be binding."

I struggled to pull energy into my hands. The best I could do was take off the worst of the chill. I wouldn't be doing any major incantations while she was there.

She rose and floated to me. Her finger traced my jawline as she seated herself on my lap. "You may remember bringing that cursed box into my kingdom and opening a forbidden portal to Hell?"

Oh, damn.

"I pardoned you and allowed you to go free under two provisions. One, you would deliver the traitor, Drake, to me. And secondly, you would protect my daughter."

"Are you and Abhile still estranged?"

She unlatched the front of the Leviskin suit and exposed bare skin to the frigid air. "My understanding is that the mage you were to return to me is deceased."

"She wasn't hurt, and the one who betrayed you has been eliminated." My memory rushed forward. Drake had been flung into the Void by the fae princess of winter possessing the body of Brighid. Ironically enough, she had done it to save me. "And technically, it was your daughter that took him out of my control."

"No matter how or why. You were to return him to me for my reward. I have been deprived of that pleasure." Her raw breath left a trail of frost across my bluing chest. "And now, my daughter is at risk and without protection. At least Drake was there for her."

"What about her army? Didn't they wreck the fortress and take my people?"

She teased her finger around my throat. My heart throbbed, sending blood flooding from my brain to somewhere I didn't need it at that moment.

"There has been some splintering of the factions, as it were. And no, she did not attack your little castle."

Was that a hint of castle envy? "Then who did?"

"Forces who were in my employ."

"Grrraaahhhhhhhh!" Flames leapt from my fingers and set the chair on fire.

"COOLED OFF ANY?" The fae queen clucked at her own joke. She had extinguished the fire I created by encasing the chair and most of my body in ice.

"Where are they?" I growled.

She folded her hands in her lap. "Who?"

"My people. The ones you took from the fortress."

She clucked. "I do not know."

"You said they were your damn people. Where are they?"

"You misunderstand." The Queen of Winter formed a small ball of energy that danced just above her fingers. "They were in my employ. Their orders were to bring you to me. Instead, they found a new allegiance and followed a new command."

"Who?"

"I was betrayed by one of my senior vassals. I expect he has them for his own purposes."

"Who, damn you?"

"The Prince Alpha of the Werewolves."

"Rahm." He was making friends everywhere. "You sent him after me?"

"You broke your oath. I was having you brought to me to begin your service."

"I don't serve anyone, especially not you."

"Tsk. If I had a pebble for every time I've heard that, I would have a mountain reaching into the clouds." She flowed from her seat to crouch behind me. "I am amused you feel you serve no one. You lap at the bowl of the mortals that wish to control and destroy us. You bow at the feet of the Amazons and their ilk. You take the scraps from the pathetic people of your village that ostracized you. Tell me again how you serve no master."

I shivered under the ice but not from the cold.

"Through your failure, you are now mine to do with as I wish." She knelt in front of me until we were eye to eye. "I now give you the opportunity to make your place in my house. Serve well, and you may even earn your freedom. But serve me well enough, and you will never wish to leave me." Her icy kiss left lip-shaped frostbite on my forehead.

Come on, blood flow, back to the brain.

"What do you want from me?" I asked.

"I'm not asking. I give you a choice. Return with me, and we shall see what makes your mind and body work. It's been a long time since I've dissected a sorcerer. Or take a mutually beneficial path and bring me the pelt of my former servant."

"Any suggestions as to where I should begin?"

She stroked the side of my head. "I think you already have a good starting point. This should help you as well." She placed a small wooden box covered in runes on the table.

"I seem to be a little tied up. What is it?"

"A little something belonging to my daughter that will be quite useful when the time comes. Now, go find my daughter. Rahm has his own plans for her. Fail to live up to that part of your oath, and you will find out how long you can survive as a subject to my whims… ones I doubt will be as pleasurable to you." Without looking back, Mairsile formed a fog around her and disappeared into the wall of ice.

I looked around the empty room. "How am I supposed to get out of here?"

Warmth flooded into my hands. I tried to focus enough to melt my way through the ice, but a slow drip landed on my head from above.

Drip.

Drip.

Drip.

The dome vaporized in an instant and poured down in a single wave. The chair beneath me unwound into a tangle and dropped me into the newly created lake.

I stared at the box on the stump and shivered.

There's something to be said for always having a towel.

THE PORTAL RING snapped, and I stepped out into my private lab. My safe place. It was just as I'd left it. The water in the furball's bowl had evaporated. The place was a mess. After clearing a spot, I dropped the unopened gift from Mairsile on my worktable. One of the great things about the skinsuits is they can be snapped dry with a thought. Unfortunately, because I was cold and wet, that didn't do much to dry me off and warm me up.

The wood stove in the corner sprang to life with a touch, and the room was sweltering in no time. It was still barely enough to warm me from the Winter Queen's touch after some time.

I grabbed one of the remaining clean skinsuits and hung the muddy one to dry.

The box Mairsile had given me was covered in an arcane script, but some of the sigils were strangely familiar. Rough carvings in the wood made it clear that someone had tried unsuccessfully to crack the combination that held it secure. If the box was really bound to the rebelling heir to the Winter throne, it might be beneficial for me to find her. Unfortunately, the case's protections stopped any of my usual tricks from working.

I walked along the corridor, browsing the racks of artifacts, pretending I didn't know where I would end up. Without finding a better alternative, I stopped in front of a mirror covered with a white cloth. *The mirror of lost desires.*

I'd never used it. I'd watched my mother use it only once with great apprehension. I swallowed and yanked away the covering then stared at my own pale and shrunken reflection. Did I really look that old? That beaten?

No. I shook my head. The image served as part of the reminder of the cost to use the device. The box landed with a crackle as it melded with the magical energies in the alcove.

"Mirror, mirror, on the wall…" My reflection winked and shook his head with a grin. "Nice try," he mouthed.

I braced both hands against the wall and clipped myself into the harness. I closed my eyes and leaned into the opening, hovering just above the glass. When I couldn't hold it in any longer, I unleashed my hot breath, fogging the mirror over. At first, I had to push, and then it became a vacuum, taking as much of me as it could, warming me. I felt as if I were swimming in a bottle of champagne lifting me to the top of the looking glass.

My lips hovered just above the surface. The words *"Wake up, jackass"* reverberated through my head. I pushed away, my reflection looking much haler, but I was drained. The cost was the breath of life. The mirror had taken a year from me, maybe two. It had also taken most of the energy I had built up in my system, but with enough time, I would recover that.

My reflection crossed his arms with a sneer. Ladon appeared in the background. His voice had stopped me from going all in.

My voice echoed in my head as my reflection spoke. "What is it that you seek?"

My eyes fluttered in a battle to keep focus. "The owner of this box and its contents."

"That's all?" I peered back over the frame. "You can call up the owner of that box anytime you want. As to what's inside, I can't help you. It's hidden from me."

"That's it?"

"It's what you asked."

"Where can I find Abhile, Princess of Winter?"

"Hey friend, I've answered your question. A second one will cost you."

"Screw this." I used all of my Will and summoned a fireball. It lasted a half-second before I was drained. The harness was the only thing that stopped me from hitting the floor or falling into the mirror, holding me inches from my reflection.

"There isn't much left on your bones, but hey, you've kept me locked away, and I'm hungry. Come forward a little more, and you'll know everything you ever needed—"

Through the haze that covered my eyes, Ladon lifted my reflection off the floor by the throat. My other self was getting along with him even less than I did.

My gold-suit-clad friend's coat lay on the floor in the background. He looked at me from the other side of the enchanted looking glass. "You still in there? Wake up."

I couldn't be sure how long I'd been out, but my reflection had a fresh black eye. "Yeah, I'm here."

My reflection glared back at me. "I'm not sure how you pulled that off, but your friend convinced me you might not have gotten your money's worth. The one you seek is with the ones for whom you yearn."

"What are you rambling about?"

"Put the cover back on me. I'm tired of this ugly mug."

I wobbled while struggling to put the cloth back in place.

"And don't wait so long between visits. It's been a long time since I was fed. It gets lonely in…"

The cloth covered the last corner, and I was thankful to not have to listen to my own voice any longer. Reaching behind me, the D-ring sprang loose, and I fell to the floor. The cool stone was a nice place for a nap.

"ARE YOU INSANE?" Tsauriel knelt over me on the floor of the keep. "You used the looking glass without preparation? You had no idea what you were doing. You could have not only killed yourself, but sucked the two of us in with you."

My head was swimming. The floor beneath me hummed like a choir with a hammering, rhythmic drumbeat. "Where is the golden boy, anyway?"

"Checking on... things." She glanced at the door. "Your little stunt may have exposed us to great risk. You're too weak to hold off the continual assault by..." She stomped into the stairwell.

I rolled over and climbed into a chair. "By? By who?"

She stood in the doorway as if she was waiting for someone. "You are under continual assault by forces that want to influence you, control you, and ultimately own you. When you drain yourself like this, you are much more vulnerable."

"Do any of them have aspirin? I could sell out for some about now."

"You still don't get it. Your actions have consequences, and not just for you."

"I get it." I wobbled as I climbed out of the chair. "Everything I've touched has gone to hell. As soon as I make things right, I'm gone. Either I'll be dead, or I'll be in hiding where the trouble that finds me can't harm anyone else."

"I see. And how do you think you'll set things right? What is done cannot be undone."

"I'm not going to let them suffer for me. Priscilla, Brighid, Drea, even the damn ice princess."

"A little late for that, don't you think? Maybe it's time for you to cut your losses. Collateral damage in the war. It's time you accept your role in things and prepare for what must come next."

Power trickled into my limbs. "And what is that role exactly?"

She motioned for me to sit and folded her wings behind her. "You are the agent of change. You have been marked as the instrument that will bring about the new world. What that looks like depends in part on you. You are very correct. If you run from trouble, it shall find you. This is why you are so sought after. The belief is that whoever controls you will control the direction of the change."

"More psychobabble."

"No. You have the ability to lift the Veil, reunite all of the peoples, and reopen the world to all that is Divine, or close that window forever."

"No pressure, then." I leaned against the wall to rest. "And how am I supposed to do this? How am I supposed to be the savior or the final damnation?"

"You aren't either. You're the guardian, the weapon, the lock."

"In that case, who has the key?"

MY BODY ACHED when I awoke on the cold floor. I'd been out long enough for the fire to spend its fuel. The hangover abated slightly after a cup of herbal tea and over-the-counter painkillers. A hamburger, a stout, and a month of rest on a beach, and I would be back at full strength.

Only, I didn't have a month. Or a week.

The strongest concoction I had in the cabinet juiced me up enough to load my pack with essentials and strap my weapons into place. If I needed them before I was ready, I was in real trouble.

And where I was going, trouble wouldn't take long to find.

I tried to open any of the few portals I knew in Hellywood, but I couldn't connect with the other end. I did have one other option, but it was risky.

One of Priscilla's fae healers owned the Aether Apothecary, not far from an emergency portal I kept in Calypso's now-abandoned offices. After porting through and walking the couple of blocks, she buzzed me through the door and into the real shop upstairs. The lower level was a basic pharmacy and made for a handy front.

Coleana was tall and lithe, and her gray webbed hands were amazingly dexterous. She was a water sprite, built for swimming in the open ocean, but humidifiers and misters casting a fine curtain kept her comfortable during working hours. She locked her large dark eyes onto mine. "You look like hell, Greyson. What did you do this time?"

"I asked the wrong question from the wrong source."

She nodded as if the answer made sense and handed me a vial. "Take this. It'll help. You have almost no aura at all. What fed on you?"

"Alice, through the looking glass."

"Lovely." She pushed a second vial of green goo to me. "What else can I do for you?"

"I need to borrow the back door."

"To where?"

"The flip side of this town."

She drew in a deep breath. "It's not really meant for that kind of travel. You shouldn't even know it's there."

"Please? All other paths are closed."

She crossed her arms. "You're in no shape for this. You need a week, maybe two."

"I don't have that long."

"You never do. It takes a lot of power to control the rings. *Old* power. I don't know if you're ready—"

"It's Drea. And Brighid. And maybe even Priscilla. They're all missing. And my leads go there."

Coleana had been the one to acquire most of the implements for the rituals to help my two loves and knew well what was at stake for me and them. And she knew I wouldn't stop for anything. Her fast hands loaded a bag and shoved it at me. "Be careful. Things have changed underneath, and not for the better. And you'll have to find another way back if you make it there at all."

114

I nodded.

She reached under the counter and tripped a switch. Part of the wall swung open to reveal a reinforced door. She touched a series of sigils etched into the dull metal, and a heavy clank revealed a dark passageway.

"Thanks," I said. "For everything."

She frowned and kissed my cheek. "Don't thank me for sending you into the abyss." She thrust a note covered in symbols at me.

"Thanks for the care package, then." With instructions in hand, I ducked into the musty hallway before she could change her mind. The door slammed behind me. She was probably thinking this would be the last time she saw me. I was wondering as well.

Thin torches cast dancing shadows for a few feet in front of me before taking a downward turn. The cantilevered staircase wound a tight spiral four stories underground. The narrow stairs only gave room for only one at a time to pass. I recognized it as a defensive measure in the event that something unwanted came through. Sigils could be triggered every few steps to collapse the staircase and seal the room below. I'd tried to get Longbow to design something similar in the portal room I'd helped build, but it wasn't their way. If it had been, things might have gone very differently.

Or maybe not.

The portal room was protected by a closed circular aperture. The door could only be rolled open from outside the room. Rumor was it had been built by the Titans for the old gods and could contain almost any magic thrown at it. The room even had the ability to defend itself if attacked. It also contained one of the few gates that could reach almost any realm, or so the legend went.

Once, I would have thought them just stories.

Once.

I'd seen too much to believe otherwise. Done too much.

Priscilla had brought me through the portal a while back to reach The Elysian Fields so I could harvest some herbs for one of the failed rituals. Once I crossed the threshold, I would be committed. *No time like the present.*

Carved directly into serpentine granite, the walls formed a tall cylinder. The portal in the floor was old, consisting of three concentric rings. I pulled a piece of chalk out of the bag, filled in the missing sigils, and stepped in the center.

Unlike any other ring I'd ever used, this one felt... almost alive, as if I was being judged to determine whether I was fit for my requested destination. The rings took on an etheric glow, filling the chamber. Some of my scribbles on the floor began to fade. I concentrated to keep them whole. As soon as I locked onto one, another would begin to disappear. If they faded before I crossed over, who knew where I would wind up... if anywhere at all.

The symbols had me dancing in circles. A giant game of Simon Says. Faster and faster.

"Damn you, either send me where I want to go, or send me to oblivion."

I swore it cackled at me as the portal flashed open.

I FLEW OUT of the second O in the Hellywoodland sign and landed in charred scrub. The portal winked out, and I emptied my stomach. "I definitely will not be going back that way."

It was still early afternoon, based on the eerie dusk. I didn't want to be out in the open when night fell and the sign changed to Hellywood. Behind me, a large palisade made of great trees stretched in both directions. It hadn't been there in the past, and despite some large scars, it still appeared new. Great thorny bushes formed outer fence lines that slowed any assault.

From the surprised looks on the faces of a large group of heavily armed demon warriors and the lone woodland dryad they had surrounded, no one was sure what to do about the party crasher—me.

There wasn't much of a decision involved on my part. I tended to root for the underdog. And either way, I wasn't about to side with the thick beasts. Running didn't seem like an option either.

Seven Hell-marked warriors already lay dead, scattered around the hillside. I would do what I could to trim their numbers some more. Power surged into my hands, and I hurled a pair of fireballs at the two nearest warriors, catching one in the face and dropping him instantly. The other set the warrior's armor on fire, and he did a jig trying to peel it off.

With the spell broken, the dryad nodded at me in acknowledgment. His obsidian Kopis flashed by, sending the lower part of an arm flying from the nearest soldier.

My trusted Colt 1911 was in my hand before I could give it a second thought. I lined up my sights on the fire dancer and turned him into an immobile bonfire on the ground. My weapon barked five more times, dropping two more to the ground.

A scaly red fist swung a mace in a wide arc, aiming for my head. I ducked under the swinging arm to meet the warrior's other heavy fist with my right shoulder. The Colt fell from my numb and useless hand. The mace whipped back at me, and I jumped backward, rolling down the hill and sliding to a stop.

Pins and needles stabbed at my arm as the nerves woke up.

Mace smiled at me. His four large tusks clicked as he stomped down the hill, jeering as he prepared to strike. From the looks of it, he commanded these troops. Two more of his men broke off from the dryad and stood behind their leader, eagerly anticipating the show.

I flicked a ceramic blade at his head, more as a distraction than expecting it would do any real damage to his thick hide.

I rolled out of the way, trying to push myself upright. The mace left a divot as it dug into the ground where I'd just lain.

As Mace tried to free his weapon, I pulled all of the power I could into my one good hand. I unleashed a messy blast, soaking him and splashing his two friends with magical napalm. It gave me an opening to stumble past them back up the hill and grab the Colt. I emptied the magazine into the air around the nearest warrior, but one lucky round struck home.

With a sideways glance, I saw that the dryad had managed to drop three more of the warriors, but a lot of the blood on him was the wrong color. It was his, but he kept fighting.

With my hand shaking as the feeling fought to return, it took me three tries to ram a fresh magazine home.

Mace had mostly extinguished the flames, except for the ones still dripping from the end of his weapon. It looked as though fire

118

was little more than a nuisance for the demonic soldier. His grin displayed a desire to return some of my juice.

Blessed rounds were more effective if I could aim properly with the tremors in my hand. Of my next seven shots, only one drew blood. But it caused Mace to howl loudly enough that when he backed off, the soldiers that he sent in looked a little less certain.

A loud cry drew my attention. The dryad fell to the ground underneath the blade of a soldier. The last two were coming in as reinforcements. Five of them, and one of me.

They spread into a wide circle and waited for me to take aim. My arm throbbed, but feeling had returned, and I wasn't shaking anymore. At least, not as much.

I took a chance. If nothing else, Mace was going with me. He'd circled around and was uphill, the farthest away. If I was lucky, I could shake up the others long enough for me to have a chance. I drew the silver blade into my left hand and prepared to block an attack. Then I fired the last two rounds into Mace. The first one caught his shoulder, and the second blew away a tusk and part of his face. I dropped the 1911 and pulled out a second blade as I spun on my heels and lunged at the soldier trying to come at me from behind. Flying downhill, I drove the blade deep into his throat, sending him staggering back. I kept running until the handle from Mace's flying weapon caught my leg and sent me spinning.

I rolled over as the wounded leader staggered downhill after his weapon to finish the job. The last three soldiers closed in around me, cutting off any escape.

I hadn't been prepared for a firefight. I'd already been drained before I had to control the portal. Warmth flooded into my hand, but nothing else. I doubted I had enough power left to light a candle, much less one of these creatures.

119

I pushed myself to my feet. If I was going to die, it wasn't going to be on my knees.

Mace grunted and yanked the heavy weapon from the ground. He swung it in a wide circle over his head in what I took to be a victory lap.

I held my remaining ceramic blade in front of me and slashed a small sigil in the air. I seemed to be the only one who felt it start to hum.

With a derisive grunt, Mace drew back for the killing blow, and I threw the blade. I didn't have any juice left, but that didn't mean there wasn't any in the explosive knife. The blade caught Mace in the chest and exploded into his breastplate, throwing him backward. Blessed silver dust formed a cloud. Shrapnel blew back and traced bloody lines across my arm and face. I'd have to let Mel know her latest toy needed some work in the shaped charge.

I ran the only way I had left. Muscles burning, I cut uphill past the wounded leader. He stretched out a large paw and wrapped it around my ankle, yanking me to the ground.

Mace stood up. A deep dent cut into the armor, and the shrapnel had done its job, leaving him bloodied but alive. He kicked me in the chest, knocking all the wind out of me, and leaned over to stare into my face. A snort of heavy brimstone breath washed over me.

He reached around and opened clasps, dropping his breastplate to the ground. More blood trickled from his chest where the blast had cracked his large scales. He grabbed me by the throat and dangled me off the ground.

In the back of my mind, Ladon's voice chided me. *You're making this position too much of a habit.*

I struggled in Mace's firm grasp and tried to pry his steely talons open. My vision tunneled as I began to black out. Something large and green appeared behind Mace. *I must be hallucinating.*

Mace's arm loosened slightly, and I slammed into the ground. *He's going to beat me to death, and there's nothing I can do about it.*

Mace fell to the ground several feet away from me. *That's odd. He's over there, but his hand is still around my throat.*

A large green face appeared inches away as I blacked out.

I WAS BREATHING. I wondered which realm of the dead I had wound up in. Did the dead breathe? And why did the place smell like a dog dipped in chamomile tea and had rolled around in manure?

"He's waking up."

I opened my eyes and found myself surrounded by dryads armored in woven fibers with obsidian plates. They faced me with a collection of obsidian knives, swords, and axes. One shaded like bark held a water skin. "Drink."

Cool water ran down my throat. A half-dozen more dryads from green to brown were looting the dead, as was one large green walking plant.

Both of its legs were a weave of thick brown vines ending in a tangle of roots. The torso and limbs were thick bundles of rich green covered in splatters of garnet demon blood. The head sported a bed of lush sod covering soulful brown eyes. "Come with us."

"Thanks for the rescue and all, but I've got a thing... with a guy." I wandered up the hill and recovered the Colt and my blades.

A dryad held my pack over his shoulder. "We must treat your wounds."

The Leviskin armor had saved my life, but I was bleeding from several places. I flopped down and had to put my head between my knees to keep from passing out. "If you insist, maybe I can stay for one drink." I popped open an ampule of my healing potion.

It gave me enough strength to walk the rest of the way up the hill. Mace's glassy eyes stared at the sky as I passed him. The hand that had grabbed me lay with most of the arm a couple of feet away. His torso was ripped almost in half. I wondered how he would do as plant food. The rest of his soldiers lay dead across the field, twenty-seven in all.

The palisade pulled back to create a gate as we marched into the woods. They carried the body of the fallen dryad on a litter between them. He was still alive, barely.

The forest opened into a circular clearing. Six wooden roundhouses surrounded a bonfire. One of the dryads motioned for me to follow the walking ficus into the largest of the huts.

His words were hollow, as if they came from the bottom of a barrel. "It's been a long time, Grey. I regretted that I never expected to see you again."

"I'm sorry, have we met?"

Some of the leaves covering his head drew back into a thin almond-shaped face. Vines tightened and merged into a solidified lithe amber body.

"Anraoi," I said. "Good to see you. Why the disguise?"

Anraoi was the former Chief of the Woodlands, ejected Lord of the Summer Lands, consort to the deposed Queen of Summer Dáiríne, and a dozen other titles. I was happy enough to call him friend even though I hadn't seen him since before my trip to the underworld.

My mother had worked with Priscilla to hide his daughter Claire with their most trusted aides in the mortal world. Their true identities had been hidden, even from themselves. The plan all fell apart when Ailbhe, daughter to the Queen of Winter, who was also in the care of the House of Summer, discovered her true nature and decided she was ready to take her birthright.

"I'm manifesting the Green Man identity for its power." He breathed heavily as he fell into a wooden chair. The sheen of sweat from the transformation was wicking away on his skin. "Most of the people here don't know who I truly am. If I fall, it will be easy enough for one of my inner circle to take on the role and continue the battle. Hiding my identity protects them more than it does me."

"Yeah, but why here?"

A woodland elf with lemon-streaked light-green skin ducked under the small door and knelt next to Anraoi. She handed him a gourd, which he downed in one gulp. "I'm stranded like everyone else here. Los Diablos is in a fae realm and backs up to the Summer Lands. I was here evaluating the defenses of the woods when everything changed. Almost all of the gateways and portals stopped working, and the few that did work weren't available to us. Days became weeks, and those stranded in LD no longer saw it

123

as a vacation spot but took it as a chance to expand their holdings. We lined up and fortified our defenses in kind and have fought back. For the most part, the daemon and others that were trapped devolved into even bloodier battles for resources and territory until a few factions solidified control."

"Is that who I ran into outside?"

"Negal's men. He's taken control of everything along our border to halfway to the sea. Ba'al and a couple of the other factions that controlled this section fell, and their remaining troops fell in line with him."

I barely knew the name. He'd been a low-level general. "How'd that happen?"

"Simple. He was here with his troops. No others had real leadership here. With a little ruthlessness, daemon troops fell in line."

"What about the rest of the city?"

"I don't know much. We've had enough to deal with here. Rumor is there are two other factions, and the three are fighting for control. I want to take advantage to secure the fae border. Do you know what happened to cut us off from the rest of the realms?"

I was pretty sure I did. Working with my aunt and Anraoi's son, I had enabled Ailbhe and unleashed a power that echoed through all of the realms. At the very least, it echoed through the ones directly connected to the Longbow facility, which had been destroyed using the portal system I'd built. Then we had destroyed the device the Erebites had been using to merge the realms. I didn't know what had really happened or how long it would last, or even if it was permanent.

"It's complicated." I tried to describe the battle with the Erebites and how we had then tried to bring their dark god back from the dead.

"And Drake?" he asked.

His son. In the time-aged practice of hostagery, while Dáiríne held the throne, they had exchanged their son Drake for Queen Mairsile of Winter's daughter, Ailbhe. They'd been trying to reach an agreement to restore peace and order between the two houses when Mave had stormed the Summer Court and taken control. "Gone."

His simple nod was one of acceptance. He'd seen the madness that had taken control of his progeny.

"Before you ask, I haven't seen any more of your Queen. I've looked for her."

"I understand." He swallowed and took a deep breath. "So if the powers that control transit between realms have been so disrupted, how did you get here? And why come?"

"There are still a few rarely used portals active. I managed to get a one-way trip. As to why, it's for Drea." He'd been there when Drake took her soul. I didn't tell him everything, but enough.

"You shouldn't have come."

"You'd have done the same."

"Yes, which proves it's a bad idea." He laughed. "I would do anything to help you, and her, if I could. I owe you everything. But my people, they need me more."

I shook my head. "I'd never ask it of you. You've given me plenty, saving me back there."

"You got into trouble saving one of my own."

"I sort of fell into it. How is he, anyway?"

"Thanks to you, he should survive. Speaking of, please go with Swyn." The healer nodded. "You look like you need some tender attention, and it is the least I can do."

"Anraoi, I appreciate it, but I need to get to the Gin Hole. I need some supplies stored there to continue the search."

The diminutive elf shook his head. "You really have been out of touch. We should be able to get any materials you need, but Buziba's club has become the nexus of the action. It's at the center point of the three factions. If you go there, it's unlikely you'll leave. At least not as a free man."

"YOU ARE CURSED." Swyn looked through a crystal prism as she turned it at odd angles. "Bindings from several sources. Etheric wounds. What has happened to you? It is no wonder you don't heal."

I stood in the middle of a circle of sea salt, my arms and legs spread wide. "Wrong place at the wrong time. Or right time. Depends on who you ask."

"I can help you some. But the bindings—I cannot affect them. You appear oathed to multiple masters. That cannot end well. It is a wonder you are cohesive at all."

"You're not the first one to think that. Anything you can do…"

She broke the circle and handed me a robe. "Follow me." She had me immerse myself in a nearby stream while performing a cleansing rite. Once we were back in the hut, she mixed herbs into a tea and poured it into me. Then she examined me through the crystal again. Another tea. A salve. A ritual. More examinations. Rinse and repeat with a little less lather.

It was nearly dusk again when she laid the crystal on the table and placed her hand on mine. Her eyes were deep pools of doubt. "I have done what I can. I do not know how long it will last."

I felt better than I had in, well, years. Nothing ached. Power welled within me, ready at the least of a thought. Working incantations and potions flooded through my mind even more than when my power had first been unbound. "What is it, Swyn?"

"Your body is failing. Power has been bottled up in you for too long without release. The bindings, the blood oaths. They are pulling you apart. Unless you can free yourself of these—"

"How long?"

She tilted her head. "I cannot say. The more you use your power, it will release some of the pressure, but it can also cut you apart. Your oaths are in conflict. When you serve one master, you go against another. That is what is draining you. The wrong act could kill you instantly."

"Can you tell me who holds these oaths? These bindings?"

Her eyes widened. "You don't know? How can you not know to whom you have fealty? The power of the bindings, these are all old power."

"Thanks for everything you've done for me, Swyn."

"I fear I may have only extended your pain."

"LEAVING SO SOON?" Anraoi had retaken his potted-plant form. "Swyn tells me you insist on leaving at daybreak."

I'd created a small portal ring in a cave not far from the camp. If it worked at all, it wouldn't get me far, but it gave me a quick escape route from where I was going. I was in the process of cleaning up the remains of the seeker rituals I'd used when Anraoi approached. It was getting harder to separate the signals for Drea from Brighid, and they both seemed to be in two places at once.

"The traces I have for them are getting weaker," I said. "One of them is still at a location on Ba'al Halland Drive. I've got a strong indication they're both there, but I'm also getting a weak signal that both of them are in central LD. It's getting weaker quickly, and the map keeps shifting."

Anraoi balled up next to me. A branch stretched out and pointed at the weaker marker. "This realm is changing on the whims of the powers that control it. Do you know this place?"

"I'm not sure." Some of the nearby landmarks seemed familiar, but others weren't. "A lot of places aren't where they used to be."

128

"That is the Gin Hole, Buziba's establishment. As it has been used as a neutral meeting point, it shifts as the borders do. A nexus."

What had the younger djinn done? "Any idea why he'd be holding prisoners? Last time I got a hit on this one, they were near the Psychomanteum."

"That is Hadurian territory, but I'm unsure who their lead is. They absorbed many of the smaller tribes and war parties."

I pointed at the third location. "And here?"

"Reshephian. But that fortress is independent. We believe it holds mercenary forces either waiting for everyone to thin the ranks or for the right offer to be made. There are several such groups that have formed—ones who wished not to swear allegiance until there was a final leader."

"That's probably not good if they stop fighting each other."

"Agreed. That is why we undertake efforts to ensure they continue to battle each other. I doubt we could hold out long against a united force."

"I'll try to stir up a little trouble along the way."

His laugh sounded like someone drumming on a log. "You don't need a plan for that. You seem to do that naturally. Here, trouble seeks out anyone willing to have it, and it hunts the unwilling."

"I hope to see you again soon," I said. "Thanks for everything."

"I owe you more than can ever be repaid." The weave of branches spread to clasp me in an embrace. "Before you go, I have heard something that may interest you."

"Shoot."

"Mave. She has not sat on her throne for some time now, and has her proxy in her stead. We may have an opportunity to retake the seat if we can have a proper queen."

"No one knows where she is?"

"She was often away from the capital. It's possible she wasn't in the realm when…"

I nodded. "When I blew up the transits. What's the effect if she's away for too long?"

"Winter." His leaves fluttered in a shudder. "We could lapse into a very long period of cold across all of the realms."

THE GATEWAY CLOSED behind me and disappeared, replaced by the solid palisade. A hidden trail ran down the cliffside and emerged in the scrub behind a burned-out no-tell motel.

LD was formed at the conjunction point of multiple infernal dimensional realms and specialized in entertainment that made ancient Rome's depravity look like kindergarten. Where else besides Los Angeles would someone model the latest incarnation of a vacation spot for the damned or celebrities?

I was betting that if Anraoi was correct, most of the troops would be gathered around the borders. No one worried much about invaders from the woodlands. The new palisade probably worked as security both ways in their minds.

A few roving bands dashed from building to building in an effort to avoid patrols. None of them had the old gleeful look I'd seen in the past when they would have been looking for a recreational skirmish. Now, they were out for survival.

Progress was slow, but I made my way into the city before the eerie twilight took hold. Coleana and Anraoi had been right. Things had gotten much worse. I needed to close in on Buziba's before the nighttime denizens came out looking for entertainment.

Obi's nephew was known to hold a grudge. Since I'd thrown a fireball into my room at the Gin Hole on my last visit, I didn't expect the reception to be warm unless it was from the business end of a flamethrower. And the little incident where his uncle Obi had torched his whole staff in retaliation for having set me up might still have been a little raw. Without the elder around to exert his influence on his impetuous nephew, I needed to know what I was walking into, especially since I was alone and needing a favor. Possibly one in which I would be taking prisoners and hostages from him if my indications were correct.

My hands warmed with power at the thought of action.

I managed to avoid the small roving bands of thugs, predators, and demons until I was within sight of the Gin Hole. The cries of battle and crashes of weapons and armor had led the way.

A battalion of well-armed creatures underneath a ruby battle standard of Negal fought Reshephian warrior monks in dingy robes. So far, Resheph was losing followers at a rapid pace. I ducked into the burned-out shell of a three-story building that had served as Ba'al's barracks for troops on leave. They'd been popular customers and regulars for Buziba. They'd also owned this whole sector and kept it more or less orderly. I couldn't imagine who'd been able to take them on, much less drive them out.

The Negalians closed the loop, surrounding the remaining monks, who then surrendered, dropping their weapons and falling on their knees. Blades flashed, and the war party marched north without prisoners, leaving a lot more litter in the streets.

It may have taken me extra time, but I refused to walk through the massacre. The front of the Gin Hole had been renovated and fortified. Converted to a keep, it covered several square blocks and had one entrance over a moat.

Most of all, it looked as though business was better than ever.

The line stretched across the bridge and around the corner of the block. The crowd was energized after being spectators to the bloodbath nearby. I wasn't inclined to wait in the line.

I hoped I still knew the basic layout of the building inside the walls. I climbed up the least rickety set of stairs to the third floor and made use of the ramp that had been part of the roof over the husk of the barracks building. From here, I had a good line of sight to the walkway on the stone outer wall. A pair of guards marched by, and I shadow-walked into the wall and out of the shade of a smoking chimney. I still didn't fully have control, but as long as I could see where I was going, I could create the portal between the two pools of darkness and make the short hop.

What had once been a back entrance to the Gin Hole had become a large walled-in courtyard. It was a farther fall than I would have liked, but I dropped over the wall onto soft, grassy earth. The décor led me to believe this courtyard was reserved for only the most exclusive of guests.

132

The back door hadn't changed, but it was now located in an armored garage. Surprisingly enough, my code still worked, and the bay door rolled open long enough for me to step inside.

I guess I should've been expecting the large welcoming committee. The fire furies made sure it was a warm welcome.

Energy flowed freely into my hands as I raised them in a sign of non-aggression. Even at full strength, I wasn't able to sense how many people it would take to restrain me, but they'd brought enough, especially considering I would be lucky to get off more than one shot.

My welcoming committee was made up of six fire furies, a dozen well-armored soldiers from as many underworld denizens that had changed allegiances, and what looked like a D-list comic book villain with purple wings and red talons.

The garage had also undergone reinforcement. Scorch marks on the floor and walls marked the zones in which the metal spikes above could fry the lower platform.

"No need to have a surprise party on my account," I said.

"Forrester." My name rolled off of a familiar tongue. Buziba Ramla. His voice echoed in the chamber through tinny speakers. "Greyson Forrester. What land of the dead expelled you?"

"Reports of my passing are greatly exaggerated." To prove the point, I Pushed a small ball of energy from one hand to the other. Only living practitioners were able to cast that kind of magic. "I need a favor."

"A favor?" The deep laugh crackled in time with sparks dancing between the steel leads. "I knew you thought well of yourself, but a god complex? I didn't know your stones were that big."

"You owe me a debt of honor."

"I? I owe you?" Low barks I took to be laughter filled the chamber. "Even if I were to agree with you—and I fervently disagree on who owes whom—that is a debt I can quickly erase by dumping your body outside with the rest. No one would ever be able to trace it back to me. Assuming there was anyone left to care about your hide."

"Obi—"

"Isn't here. And he abandoned me here. For old times' sake, and for that of my family, I make you this offer. You may leave un-accosted through the front door, and I will grant you safe passage back to the woods."

I had to get inside. If there was even a chance… and there it was. The sigil was still on the wall. "I invoke the right of sanctuary." The mark flared with the binding oath on me, and on Buziba. It would restrict what I could do, but it forced him to house me safely under his roof for a day and a night. Violation from either of us brought Dire consequences. Refusal would break the treaty that protected him, and that which safeguarded the Gin Hole as neutral ground.

"Very well." His tone was cold and calm.

I'd forced him into a corner. Either way, there would be consequences. But it got me inside. And it gave me time to find out what was going on.

"Sanctuary is granted for one night and a day. Your quarters are just as you left them. Freshen up, and we can rekindle our relationship."

HE HADN'T LIED. The room was *exactly* as I'd left it. It wasn't quite as charred as I'd feared, and most of my wards were still in place. The furniture was mostly a loss, though.

I'd firebombed it the last time I'd been there, partially for spite, but mainly to prevent any of the stuff I was leaving behind from falling into someone else's control. Most importantly, the portal ring I'd built looked fundamentally serviceable and could be rebuilt with the right materials. The fact that it was in such good condition both relieved and bothered me. The possibility existed that someone else had figured out how it worked.

My escorts had allowed me to lower the wards I'd left in place before they shoved me through the door. I Sensed I had a half-dozen guards outside. I wasn't sure for whose protection.

I spent a few minutes fixing the damaged wards to the room so that I would be able to secure it again. My luck continued to hold out. Of the three trunks I'd stored, one was burned to the frame. It looked like the result of the fireball I'd used rather than someone trying to break into the box. The other two were blackened but secure.

The wards lifted from the lockers easily. The first one held most of my remaining stash of clothes along with a pack of my common magical elements. The other was stocked with my basic ammunition and blades along with some explosives. Magically infused grenades could be especially effective. Not that long ago, I would have considered all of this disposable, especially since I'd

135

had Priscilla's resources at hand for the last few years. Before that time, this would have been a treasure. It felt as though it was again.

I fixed the portal ring and was happily surprised when it worked. I opened the gate, moved the two trunks to the cave in the woods, then rushed back. I had enough time left to erase the sigils and other evidence of my activity, when someone knocked on the door.

One of my guards let out a grunt that was either "Come with me" or "Prepare to die." I Pushed my skinsuit to be padded jeans and a leather jacket. I was ready to push my luck a little further and hoped that the old accords of sanctuary were upheld.

For whatever else he'd done outside, Buziba had overdone inside. The glimpse of the club was an energetic combination of pop dance club and ritual sacrificial altar with a dash of secret-society sauce on the side. Unnatural illumination glowed from sigils covering the floor, walls, and ceiling. And the place was wall-to-wall... beings. Human, fae, Divine. All were represented.

The office in the back had kept the same layout, a large sunken circle in the floor with thick couches surrounding a platform table. Buziba had upgraded the furniture to a thick leather from a beast I didn't want to think about. The master of the house was seated at an elaborately carved desk that dominated one corner. Two other beings of a questionable nature sat across from him, bickering about something. The good news was they were in suits, not armor. Nine guards ringed the room, including a sergeant at arms.

My escort held me at the door until the other guests dispersed. One wore the uniform of an officer of the ranks of Ba'al but had the insignia of Resheph. The other was Negali and was still covered in blood. I guessed he'd been involved in the slaughter outside.

Buziba remained seated and waved his hand at one of the chairs. "I'm surprised to see you, Greyson. I'd have thought if you had been trapped here, I would have heard something of you by now. How long have you been hiding in the woodlands? I guess it makes sense with the defenses they were able to raise so quickly that they would have a sorcerer with them."

"I had nothing to do with it. I was only there a day. A little less."

He looked up from a scroll he was reading. "Then where have you been hiding since the portals stopped working?"

"I came in from LA a couple of days ago."

"Impossible." He pushed his chair back and walked to the bar against the wall. "No one has come or gone since the collapse."

"We probably should have this talk in private."

He looked around the room at his guards.

"If I wanted to kill you, there's nothing they could do about it anyway," I said. "I could take them all-out and then do what I wanted at my leisure. I'm the one who asked for sanctuary. You're safe in your own house."

The nearest of the soldiers flinched and tightened his grip on the handle of his blade.

Buziba motioned for me to sit and called over his sergeant. A moment later, the demon soldier snapped out a command, and all of the troops marched out the far door except one—the jumpy one. The sergeant whipped his blade, taking off the soldier's head from behind. The poor guy never even saw it coming. Two of the soldiers returned to the room and dragged out the body before closing the doors.

Buziba was short and a little thicker around the middle since I'd last seen him, but he was well built and in good shape. He'd traded in his traditional black suit for one of ruby red. A thick drink sweated in his hand. "A wise recommendation to clear the room if what you say is true. I am not aware of any outside travel or communication in months. I tried to contact uncle. He told me something was about to happen and then abandoned me here. How *did* you come through?"

"It's not just here. Almost all travel between realms has been disrupted. All except for a few rarely traveled paths. My way here was one-way. I've got to find another way out. I'd hoped…" I wanted to make it look as though I'd expected his gateway to the Gin Sluice still worked. It probably did, but Obi had disabled it not long after the incident in the desert. Other beings kept trying to break through.

"No." His hand shook as he drank from the glass. "My gateway is blocked as well. What happened?"

"An Erebite ritual gone wrong." It was mostly true. No need to tell him that when I'd directed Longbow to destroy the focal point of the ritual, it had disrupted everything.

Buziba poured another glass from a brown bottle and placed it in front of me. "Tell me, my old friend, how do you plan to get back out?"

The drink was sweet and strong with a hint of brimstone. Hell's bourbon. "Since yours is out, I'll have to find another way."

"There are no other ways. All of the gates have failed."

"I'll have to try."

"Why would you take this risk? Come here? Now? Are you running? Hiding?"

"Nothing like that." I had to gauge my words carefully. I didn't trust him even when I held the threat of Obi over his head. "I'm looking for someone. Several, in fact."

The small man slid behind the desk and clasped his hands behind his head. "Who? Maybe I can be of service."

I dug into my breast pocket and pulled out pictures. "Brighid and Drea."

"I do not know the first one, but you seek Priscilla's daughter? These must be dangerous times for you."

"Priscilla herself is missing."

He rubbed his thin beard. "Dangerous times, indeed. And desperate as well. What makes you believe any of them could be in Los Diablos?"

"Because"—I placed my glass on the desk—"I traced them here, directly to your little establishment."

He swallowed, almost undetectably, but I knew the little man. And I knew his tells. "Buziba?"

He pointed to Brighid's picture. "She is here, but I do not know her name. I saw her taken to the Hadurian section. I've not seen Priscilla or her daughter. On my honor."

For what that's worth. But I did believe him. "Get me in to see her."

"I cannot."

Power surged into my hands as I fought back the desire to prove that the djinn really could die. "You will."

139

"You do not understand. I am as much a prisoner here as any in chains. I just have better accommodations. This may be my establishment, but I cannot leave. I'm trapped here unless I'm given another way out. I can only break the bonds from another realm. The central keep is mine, but I'm surrounded by the outer walls. I've been unable to secure my independence of the powers. Each of the three factions holds a sector surrounding me, even inside the keep. They each have their own prisons and dungeons. I have no power there beyond my inner walls."

"There has to be a way to get me in to see her."

He took a deep breath. "Possibly. There is a gathering of the three remaining powers here tonight. They have been negotiating a cessation of hostilities, each solidifying their claim to the territory they hold."

"What does that have to do with her?"

Buziba sipped his drink. "If the accord is signed, then there will be a large celebration. She may have been brought in as a courtesan or a sacrifice. If that is the case, you will have little time."

"Why?"

"If I help you, you must take me with you."

"I'm not sure—"

"Forrester. You don't have to tell me how you plan to escape if you so desire. But unless you give me your oath that I may go with you, I will just serve you up to the factions to curry more favor."

"Fine. If you can keep up, I'll take you with me. You just had better be ready. What happens tonight?"

"Just remember, these are demon horde and fae factions. By the time the party is over, any humans, fae, or other creature on the receiving end will welcome death as quickly as it can come."

I MADE PREPARATIONS as best I could. The portal ring was hidden in my room but ready for a one-time trip to the woods. No one would be following me after I triggered it. The main hall consisted of two flights of stairs and one block of floor directly below me. I'd hated it before when I took refuge here, trying to ignore noise from downstairs around the clock. Now, if I needed this exit, I would need some luck to make it. At least it was nearby. If that failed, I had a backup plan. It sucked, but it was a plan. I rubbed the small spot on my hand that warmed as I touched the sigil incorporating the incantation.

One of Buziba's servants delivered a package with my invitation. It took a great deal of work. Buziba provided the ingredients for me to be able to use the skinsuit and a glamour so I would pass as a guest. I would look like an unimportant daemon, someone who wouldn't get a second look. But not so far down in the ranks that I would be an easy target. Middle management in Hell's backwater.

A roar echoed through the room from below. Whatever negotiations were going on had gone to plan, and the celebration was in full swing. I checked myself one more time and counted as I walked down the staircase to the main hall. Once I had Brighid and we made the door, it was forty-two steps to safety.

Buziba stopped me inside the door. I wore a patch so he would know whom to follow when the time came. "The preparations are as you requested."

Several corners were completely darkened. My plan was that all three of us would gather in a dark corner and shadow-walk directly into my room upstairs, with no one else the wiser. I had a piece from my bed upstairs in my pocket and another in the center of the ring creating the sympathetic link. I just had to be touching them both when we were fully in the darkness for all three of us to be whisked away.

The representatives from the three factions gathered at a nearby table and rambled on with some speeches. The crowd didn't seem to care as long as the drinks flowed and no one let out a war call.

Brighid, or at least her body, was with a group of human and fae, about evenly split between male and female. Guilt chilled me. I would never be able to get all of them out alive. All of the innocents. I reminded myself this was LD. Innocents didn't come there, not by choice. And what I had planned was probably much more merciful than what would happen otherwise.

Guards pushed the consorts out a few at a time. Most looked as if they'd done this before and knew what to expect. From what Buziba had said, it was going to wind up being a totally different ending tonight for most of them.

Brighid had her arms wrapped around her and looked a little dirty but otherwise unhurt. From her body movements, it looked as if Brighid really was the one behind the wheel. After being pushed out to the floor, she worked her way to the nearest wall and worked

142

to make herself as small as possible. I could Sense the gap from the Veil she was Pushing over herself.

The burning in my hand reminded me that time was still counting down for my backup plan. Buziba stood near the conclave in the middle of the room under amber lights. We locked eyes for a moment before he returned to his duties with the ceremony. The Reshephian finished his speech and was bent over the parchment, signing the treaty.

In the packed room, it was hard to keep my concentration and the glamour in place. I stopped working my way through the room to center myself. A waif of a fae touched my arm. I stared into her vacant eyes. She was wandering around like a broken toy, stopping when she bumped into someone in the event she could be of service. For her, it would definitely be a mercy.

I nudged her back into the flow and navigated to Brighid. A pair of low-level officers had cornered her and were negotiating between themselves for her. They scattered on my approach. The rank I wore must have been enough to scare them off.

She stared at the floor, mumbling something. At first, I worried she too had been broken. Then I felt the Push from her, trying to send me back into the masses.

"It's me." I tried to touch her arm, but she recoiled. "Stay calm. It's Grey."

She intensified the incantation, but it must have sunk into her consciousness. She looked into my eyes. "Forrester? Is that you?"

"Yeah. We've got to go."

"Why are you here? How did—"

"Wasn't easy, but I managed to trace you here. What about Drea?"

"Drea." She shook her head. "I… I don't know."

"Let's get out of here first."

She tentatively wrapped her arm in mine, much like the other unwilling guests.

I nodded to Buziba. He returned the signal. The Hadurian representative was fae. It was hard to tell what kind underneath the glamour, powered by the runes in their robes. A tapered pale-blue hand returned the blood quill to its host.

The djinn stepped into the light with the signatories and the parchment. "Thank you for letting me be your host for this momentous event. The treaty has been signed, and Los Diablos is united for the first time. Your assembled Triumvirate is now ready for the final step to seal the agreement. The sacrifice."

An officer from each of the factions approached the group with a consort in tow.

If Buziba didn't hurry up, we would have to leave without him. The heat in my hand told me we only had a few minutes. I tugged Brighid with me toward the door, hoping Buziba wasn't too caught up in the moment.

"And now for the main event."

A dozen heavy soldiers flooded into the hall, trying to look through the doorway, blocking the exit.

"Our surprise guest," Buziba said.

Bright lights locked onto us, flooding every angle, every corner. There wasn't enough of a shadow to send a mouse through.

144

"None other than the Sorcerer, Greyson Forrester."

Lying bastard.

WE WERE BLINDED, backed up against the wall by the glaring lights. Brighid squeezed my hand.

I dropped the glamour and shifted the Leviskin into body armor with barely a thought. Forces from the three factions kept a safe distance but ensured we couldn't make it to the stairs. We wouldn't be taking the portal out as planned.

Without the glamour, the sigil glowed dimly on my arm, counting down until plan B kicked in. I pushed my doubts aside. I couldn't stop it now. The plan had been for it to go off after we were safely away, helping create the disruption I'd promised Anraoi. Just a few more moments, and either we would be away, or it wouldn't matter. I slid my hand down and unlatched the Colt in my holster but left it in place. I rubbed the handle of a sheathed ceramic blade in the other. I Sensed Brighid readying herself as well.

"What are you doing, Buziba?"

"High Marshall Ramla is my new title. Well, it will be once Lord Erebus arrives. Master of the Central Keep of the Los Diablos Dominance. And it is all thanks to you."

"You give me too much credit." I should've paid more attention to the crowd. I took my first good look at the three representatives.

"Come now." The djinn wrapped his arms around the three senior leaders. An ancient dark magus from the Winter Court led the Hadurian contingent, High Abbot something or other for the Reshephians, and none other than General Negal himself. "These three would never have united without you."

"One little wizard is worth all this?" I asked.

"Takish mentored many of the Dark Mages and oversaw the acolytes you executed, including some of his best students, in fact. Abbot Cessare holds fealty over the Fomorians and the other lost peoples who wish to return to their world. General Negal lost thousands of Reivers who catered to the fields of Purgatory, reclaiming the lost. You massacred hundreds of his elite troops operating the great machine in the underworld that was building the channels between the realms. Your interference drove them all here as a final escape, trapping them. Of course they're interested in you."

Negal motioned, and a pair of soldiers stepped forward. I whipped my hands forward, releasing a pair of energy balls, blowing the pair into the crowd.

"What's the next move?" I asked.

Buziba motioned for everyone to remain still. "That, my old friend, depends on you. Tell us your plan for escaping Los Diablos, and maybe even take your place leading them into the darkness so they can resume their mission. Or they take you and find out in a much less pleasant way. For you and your companion."

The sigil on my hand faded. "I'm going to have to take door number three, old friend."

"What would that be? The portal in your room? Where does it go? A Longbow facility? My uncle's home?"

"None of the above." I shielded my Senses as best I could.

The detonation cord I'd taken from a Longbow explosives locker outlining the floor of my room upstairs exploded with a magically fortified flash and thundering crash that vaporized a rectangular outline of anyone directly beneath the floor. The slab of wood and stone groaned then dropped onto the floor beneath like a giant shoe, smashing Buziba, the Triumvirate, the treaty, and about twenty others like roaches. The rest of the surviving crowd rolled around, stunned from the flash and the blast.

I grabbed Brighid and threw her over my shoulder, running for my relocated room floor. A jump from the back of a fallen and half-crushed soldier boosted me onto the platform. The circle looked intact on a half-second inspection. I kicked away a piece of debris crossing the circle then jumped onto it with Brighid in my arms.

With the circle already charged, it took next to no Will to trigger the portal.

THE KEEP SMOLDERED, flames still flickering within the grounds. The outer walls and much of the building that had been the Gin Hole had been blasted for blocks in every direction.

Anraoi, still impersonating the lumbering log, and I stood on the palisade walk looking over the city. It was mostly quiet, but shadows were moving all over the place.

"You said you wanted a disruption," I said.

"Overachiever."

"I might have put a little more power in it than I thought." I'd charged up several smaller portals around the room that had nowhere to go. The feedback loop plus some magically enhanced plastic explosives had leveled a couple of blocks in every direction.

"Yeah. The agreement has been destroyed, and their leaders decimated." Anraoi took a deep breath, his foliage fluttering in his own breeze. "It will take them time to recover if they don't decide to just pick up where they left off and kill each other."

"There may still be some innocents among the hostages in the dungeons."

The elf lifted a spyglass in dexterous vines to his eye. "Yes, I see much movement, even within the walls. There may have been many survivors."

"Ahem." We turned as Brighid approached with her hands clasped in front of her.

Anraoi fluttered leaves, which I took as acceptance. "This is your consort? Brighid?"

The moment came that I'd dreaded. I'd had my suspicions, but they were confirmed. "No. It's her body, but it's not her. Drea either. Who are you?"

She stared at her feet. "How did you know?"

"Hard to explain. Inside the castle, I thought it might just be the shock. But it wasn't you… her. And the magic you worked to hide, that's never been her strongest point. But I wasn't positive until you were standing there."

"Who are you, child?" Anraoi asked.

A lone tear welled in her eye. "It's me. Tellia."

"One of Priscilla's shamans?" I thought back to that night. "You were vaporized."

She nodded.

The large tree shuffled down the ramp. "Let's go where we have a little more privacy."

The elf and the shaman disappeared on the path back to the camp. I stared at the burning ruin a few miles away. This meant either Drea or Brighid was gone. Maybe both.

When I caught up to them in Anraoi's hut, he had shifted back to his diminutive self. Brighid sat folded on the ground near him.

He waved me in. "She is Tellia. I know her too well for this one to deceive me."

I couldn't stop the fire that burned in me. "Where's Brighid? Drea? Their essence. Their souls."

She stared at the patterns she drew in the dirt. "I don't know."

149

"How'd this happen?"

"The ritual." She traced invisible lines in the floor. "When the circle broke, I ran. I knew the power could not be contained. There was a brief surge of pain, and then nothing. I just… was. With the power of the ritual going on, I was drawn, and then thrust into this body. I awoke in a transport wagon some time later. Then a cell. Another transport. Interrogation by Winter. Lycans. Others. They thought I was some sort of assassin. I tried to explain what happened, and they eventually gave up. Whether they believed me or not, I do not know. I was shipped to the castle a few days ago. Told I was to be sacrificed."

"Have you seen anyone else? Priscilla?"

"No. I heard her voice once outside my cell. That was a long time ago. Maybe Drea too. Not long after we were taken from the castle. We were being held somewhere. I do not believe I've left this realm since we came through."

My Sense told me there was something else. I felt the energy from her. She was holding something back. I knelt in front of her and forced her to look into my eyes. "What else? Who was in charge? Who else did you see? Hear? Anything?"

She pulled away and closed her eyes. "I don't know. It's all foggy. I've been drugged. Subjected to powerful magics. I can't even be sure what's real."

Anraoi laid his hand on my shoulder. "Leave her with me for a little while. Maybe things will become clearer once the shock has worn off. I've known Tellia a long time. She served in our court."

"Okay. I'll check back."

"Where are you going?"

"I still have a trace on Drea. I need to find out what I can."

The deposed Lord of the Summer Lands pursed his lips and handed me a scroll. "I suspected as much. I sent spies to the location you marked. Here is everything the survivor was able to bring back."

"Survivor?"

"I sent six of my best. One returned with this."

"Can I speak with him?"

He shook his head. "She did not survive her wounds. Will alone allowed her to return with this information."

"I am grateful."

"I only hope you change your mind after you read this. If any of them live, they are likely lost to you. No one leaves the Coldstone Estate. No one."

I WASN'T OPTIMISTIC. If anything, I thought I had a better chance of surviving the trials a second time. It wasn't going to stop me from going in. I just needed to have a better plan than usual, which meant I actually needed some sort of plan other than something pulled out of my nether regions.

I repeated the ritual to find Drea and compared it against what Anraoi's people had found. She was in the rear tower. It didn't make sense to me that Brighid was still showing up in the same place. It was a physical link. Maybe that meant Brighid still controlled Drea's body. I didn't want to consider what that meant, even though I knew. It didn't matter. I had to know for sure.

I unloaded my pack and was doing a quick inventory before reloading. The box Mairsile had given me was glowing softly. I thought back to what the mirror had said. "The one you seek is with the ones for whom you yearn."

Maybe Abhile was here too. My attempts to track her had failed. She was Veiling herself very well.

Swyn did some of her magic and supercharged me. I didn't know how else to describe it. She helped me work up a few potions and made a final, futile plea for me to change my mind. Then she helped me build a last-ditch plan.

She wrapped around me and whispered in my ear, "Not every problem can be solved with explosions and death."

Showed how much she knew.

DARK TOWERS CLIMBED seven tiers, piercing the low clouds. Everything along Ba'al Halland Drive was rubble from the edge of the city into the hills. Not even scrub rose more than a foot off the ground.

I came in from a steep cliffside to within a mile of the Coldstone Keep to get my first close look at it.

The shining eyes of gazers stared out at the night from along the inner wall and the corner towers. Guards marched in slow patrols.

Between the rows of short outer walls and trenches, a hundred feet of gravel and glass formed a solid border, more of a speed bump than a real defense. A wide ember trench outlined the inner wall. The gate doors were closed, and the bridge was raised. An energy barrier prevented porting in and likely would dump anyone who tried into the raging ocean behind me. I wasn't really in the mood to experience that again.

I reached deeper with my Senses. The energy barrier meshed into the natural stone slab that was the foundation for the region.

I wouldn't be sneaking in. I didn't think I could summon enough energy to blast my way in. I decided on a new approach. I'd knock on the front door. If only I had a box of Girl Scout cookies.

It was unsettling to see the dozens of pairs of shining eyes that watched from the walls as I hiked up the curved road. It was designed so nobody could take a straight run at the front gate with a vehicle or a ram. I could've hopped over the barriers, but who knew what surprises waited there. Besides, I had to be fair and let them prepare their defenses. It was *me* coming, after all.

I'd gotten within a thousand yards before I decided this was a really bad idea, but thoughts of Drea pushed me on. I didn't even get to knock. The drawbridge clanked as it started its downward trek. Archers and snipers looked over the wall at me and the surrounding space, searching for the rest of my army. I stopped at the edge as the walkway touched the ground with a puff of dust and crunch of gravel.

The Leviskin was doing a good job of wicking away my sweat as I readied myself for whatever reception was readied for me on the other side. An army? Another demon horde? The heavy gates squealed in protest as they swung open. Three people walked out to greet me. A bulbous woman in brown robes stopped in the roadway and drove a staff sizzling with power into the ground.

Sonja, my aunt, followed her, dressed formally as a War Witch in a rich lavender uniform. Her smile was warm and familial, but I knew she would kill me if ordered. Or she would at least try.

The third person floated out in deep-blue robes and drew the hood back from her head. A crystal tiara was woven into her raven hair. Her eyes glinted with satisfaction. "My consort has come to his senses. I knew you would. Welcome to your new home."

I drew in a deep breath and nodded. "Hi, Abbie."

"YOU'RE LOOKING WELL." Abhile sat on a throne in an oval chamber. Sonja stood just behind her, and we were otherwise alone.

Abhile rose and stood within inches of me. "You look tired, my love."

"I've been busy."

Sonja laughed and fought to stifle it when her queen cut her a withering look.

154

"I had a feeling you might have arrived when the treaty signing was disrupted and several blocks downtown were leveled." Her finger traced a thin scrape on my face. "You are unhurt, though, I trust."

"I'll live. You should see the other guy."

She smiled and gazed into my eyes. "I've seen many of them."

I backed away. "Nice place. When did you move in?"

She took me by the hand and sat close to me on a bench. "The prior owners didn't need it anymore after the collapse. They were kind enough to cede not only the property, but the staff as well. The survivors, at least."

"What happened to Ba'al?"

"No idea."

I Sensed she was trying to probe me.

"When we had to escape the underworld, this was one of the few working addresses during the collapse. One of Ba'al's generals who was working with us escorted us through. We'd used this as a base of operations off and on, and it looked like a good place to resume consolidation of my power."

"How's that going for you?"

"Better now that you're here. But I sense you've not come to join me."

"Not exactly. Your mother wanted me to come check on you, for one. She's decided to make me her new pet since I can't bring Drake to her. Seemed to think you were in danger. You know how she worries."

155

"I see her binding on you." Abhile placed her hand over my heart. "I can lift it."

"For a price, right?" I asked.

"I hope you don't see wedding me that way."

"Less than I used to." *And only as a last resort. One problem at a time.*

"I knew you'd come around." She looked at Sonja. "I told you."

"There's another matter," I said.

"The Amazon."

I nodded.

"I know she's important to you. She is here as our guest. I was able to rescue her but not the others."

"Rescued her from whom?"

"One of mother's *other* pets who got off his leash. A lycan. His name is Rahm. And now he pursues me."

"We've met."

She swallowed and edged toward Sonja. "You can't be with him." I Sensed the power as she readied her defenses.

"Not even close." I took a few steps but left a safe distance. "Last time I saw him, he'd just acquired some old objects and choked me until I blacked out."

"You were unable to defeat him." She visibly relaxed but stayed where she was. "I'm not surprised."

"He wasn't exactly what I expected, and he got a drop on me. It had been a rough day."

"You may get a rematch soon enough. He wishes to make me his."

"You wanted a strong general."

She snorted and turned away. "I will die first. He has thrown his lot to Erebus."

"Jealous he's horning in on your action? You don't want to share the credit when you summon the great dark god?"

A sharp, cold blast fired across the table, knocking me across the room. "I don't want it here. We're trying to protect all the realms from its return."

I pushed myself to my feet and braced for another attack. I manifested a pair of fireballs and held them in front of me, ready to release them. "Did all of your little acolytes know that? What about the big ceremony in the desert? Attacking the Longbow facility?"

"Collateral damage." A swirling mist formed in front of her. "We had to let it partially manifest to banish it indefinitely."

Sonja walked between us, her arms outstretched. "Cease fire before something happens we can't take back."

Abhile lowered her hands, and the mist disappeared.

I extinguished the fireballs. "I think you need to tell me a little more." I kept the energy close at hand as my aunt mediated the truce.

Abhile fidgeted with a knife as she sat in her throne. "When Mab, or Mave, or whatever name she chooses these days, moved to take over the Summer Court, she needed outside power to shift from the Winter Court to Summer. I've long believed this was a conspiracy between my mother and her sister to take control of both courts, but I don't know. Seventy or more years ago, she seduced some humans to perform a working in the desert. A spell to bring her this power. Over time, those mortals paid for their foolishness with their lives as the working took hold. But they succeeded in opening a rift to the old powers."

"Mystics and scientists should never mix," Sonja quipped.

"In any case, she finally tapped enough power for the shift and to compel the forces she needed for the coup. You know the story of how I was with the Summer Court, and we were shipped off to the mortal world, forced to live as children. As the fae go, I am but a youth. In human terms…"

Sonja gently touched Abhile's arm. My Senses felt the Soothing energy.

"When your mother helped us create new identities, your aunt remained and took a new identity of her own to watch over us. Several years ago, before I remembered who I was, I was driven to study old texts. I came across some medieval stories that unlocked some of my memories. I showed them to Claire. We were as sisters. Closer, even. The enchantments blocking our memories— our real memories—began to fade. We even found ways to cross over into the courts. Claire's blocks came and went. Sometimes, she had perfect clarity. Most of the time, she only remembered the fake life. I found my way home, and one day, I accidentally ran into Drake."

I stretched my Senses. It all rang true as best I could tell.

Abhile rose and began to pace. "He'd been there so long that the essence of Winter had taken hold. My mother had taken him as her son, to be mine when it was my time to ascend as heir. He began to cross the Veil and come to the mortal world. He brought stories of what was happening in the courts. He brought me the story of the working from the courts. Power was still flowing through the rift, but it was no longer a trickle. It was a flood. It was pouring into all the realms, but most of it pooled in the mortal realm."

I found myself rubbing the sweat from my hands onto my legs. "Why not just close it?"

"It had been tried many times. Once, Sonja led us into the desert to try a ritual ourselves. It had become too strong. And the old cult of Erebus had been revived. It was a siren's song to some people, descendants of the old followers. Each of the individual followings that formed sprang up around a divinely inspired leader. A little piece of the old one himself. Sects merged. One leader would sacrifice himself to another, leaving one more powerful leader for a larger united sect. Too much of him had come through." Abhile stared at the floor.

Sonja knelt next to me. "We had to close the portal. I met with anyone who might have knowledge. I consulted the Library."

"Josiah knew all this?" I couldn't believe my grandfather would have gone along.

"Not exactly." She chewed her lip. "I spent many years in Phoenix Grove, studying. One night, deep in the bowels of the restricted texts, I got a calling. Everything led to one solution. Bringing enough of the old one's power to one place and performing a sacrificial ritual to send it back across. And then closing the gate. Forever."

"You used the acolytes—"

"Pawns." My aunt rose and placed an arm around Abhile. "They were to bring us their pieces of the old one. They believed it was to merge him, resurrect him."

"And the device on the mountain?"

"It was built to close the portal off and secure all of our realms from the other side. It was based on designs from a much older device, something I found in the Library."

"Other side?"

Abhile spoke just above a whisper. "The Void. It's where all the oldest gods come from. It's where everything comes from. All of creation."

"I DON'T KNOW." I finally broke the uneasy silence. "I don't know whether to believe any of this."

Cold seeped in through the stone walls. The stone hearth had logs in it, but it was dark. I took some of my frustration and lit the fireplace with a larger fireball than necessary. From across the room.

Abhile glared at me. Sonja silently extinguished embers that had splashed out.

"Why rescue Drake?" I asked. "And turn him into something Victor Frankenstein could have only come up with in Hitler's wet dream?"

"The Erebites saw him as the fulfillment of some prophecy. I needed a sword. He was the broken weapon I had. We fixed him as best we could and armed him for what was coming." Abhile flushed. "I just didn't know how mad he'd gone. Marsaile had made him unstable. Raised him to be her weapon. Then what you did…"

"What I did? I defended myself. He attacked innocents. People I love."

"Like I said. He'd gone mad. If you had taken your place then, none of this would have happened. If you'd let the change in the tent be completed. If—"

"If you had tried talking to me. Or anyone, for that matter. The whole Fomorian army. Kidnappings."

"I was doing what I could to prepare. To fight. I was—"

"In over your head." I fought exhaustion and pulled myself out of the seat. "I'd like to see Brighid now."

Abhile nodded. "Of course."

"Please follow me." Sonja led the three of us up two levels inside the central tower, stopping in an alcove holding a pair of guards.

"We've kept her close," Abhile said. "Sonja's floor is just above, and I have the two top levels." She gently took my hand. Her eyes glistened. "There's something you should know."

My heart sank. I wasn't entirely sure why they were taking such care with her, someone who not so long ago had been an adversary.

"She's insane. Completely gone over. We've tried to speak with her, but she either attacks us or hides any time we've entered the room."

Something inside me believed it. How could someone handle having their soul stripped out, imprisoned, stuck into another body, and subjected to the rituals I'd performed to get her back into her own body? Was Brighid still trapped in the body that wasn't hers? Or maybe it was just Drea, really pissed off. "Let me in."

Abhile nodded at the guards. They stepped aside, lifting the pair of bars that held the door closed.

I pushed through, and it took several seconds for my eyes to adjust. The suite was regal. The bed was large enough to use for a volleyball court. Half-read texts lay on every table. Thick rugs, couches, and oversized pillows covered most of the stone floor. It was incredibly immaculate for someone who'd lost it.

"Drea?" I Sensed the shadow moving just in time to brace myself. Arms and legs wrapped around me like a bolo. We were nose-to-nose in the entryway.

"Grey. Is that really you?"

"Yeah, it's me."

She shook her head. "I can't believe it. How'd they catch you?"

"They didn't catch me. I've been... searching for you."

She narrowed her eyes. "What took you so damn long? And who let you in here?" Her elbow connected with my temple. I wasn't aware when she softened my landing on the floor.

DREA GENTLY STROKED my hair with my head in her lap. My temple throbbed where she'd hit me.

She leaned over and kissed me. "You're awake."

"Yeah." I rolled over onto my hands and knees to center myself. "What was that for?"

"I missed you."

"I meant knocking me out."

"You're working with them." She knelt next to me, rubbing my back. "She was a little mad."

"She?"

"Drea."

"And you're?"

"Brighid. Who else?"

I sat back and leaned against the wall. "What?"

She became rigid, and the softness left her face. "Both of us are in here, and it's a little crowded." She leaned over and kissed the side of my head. "Sorry about that. Sort of."

"It's okay. I understand. I think."

"What's the situation?"

"We're guests of Abhile in Los Diablos."

163

"Damn." I could tell from her motion that Drea was still driving. "What's the plan to escape?"

"It's not that easy."

She leaned forward. "What's not that easy? We break out and head for the border. There're plenty of ways out. We just need out of this tower."

"Things have changed."

She stood up. I couldn't tell who. "Have you—"

"No, nothing like that… exactly." I stood to face her. "The portals between the realms aren't working. And there're bigger problems."

"Really. I haven't been out that long."

"This fortress is probably about to be attacked."

"Good. We can get out in the chaos."

"That's part of the plan, yes." I braced for another attack. "I think we have an opportunity."

She clenched her fists. "Explain."

THE DOOR OPENED on my signal. Some small part of me thought it wouldn't when I knocked. Drea sat cross-legged on the couch meditating as I left. She wasn't happy but reluctantly agreed to my plan after attacking me with anything not nailed down. She had enough power to hurl a pillow like a ballista. Now I had to convince Abhile and my aunt of what I'd come up with. Or hope they had a better idea.

A guard led me on an ascent to the top floor. He opened the door and marched back down to his post. Abhile's suite was much like Drea's but maybe a little more elaborate. More books, scrolls, pictures, and faded tapestries.

A large table bearing a model of the fortress and surrounding countryside dominated the near end. Abhile and Sonja argued about where to station their meager troops, pushing small figures between areas within the outer wall.

I leaned over the table and studied the diorama of destruction. Tiny buildings stood where rubble was all that was left in town. "Neither of you knows how to defend this place, do you?"

"No," Abhile snapped. "Do you?"

I laughed. "Not a clue. Any idea what's coming this way?"

Sonja moved a block of figurines representing the enemy forces to the end of the map on Ba'al Halland Drive. "Our intelligence is that General Negal took control of all the regions at the ceremony tonight. They have burned the central keep, which will force them to come here, to take the most secure fortress in the realm for their new base in service of Erebus. Or die trying."

"That might be a little dated. I'm the one who blew up Buziba's place." I shrugged. "I also squashed the Triumvirate in the process."

Sonja crossed her arms and stepped back. Abhile leaned on the table, slack-jawed.

165

"Problem?" I asked.

"I don't know where to begin with that." Abhile slumped into a nearby chair. "Why? How?"

"I was there to get Brighid out. Buziba double-crossed me. Again."

"Are you sure they're all dead?" Sonja looked out of a window overlooking the front of the fortress.

"I didn't have a chance to look the bodies over, but I saw a good chunk of the ceiling drop on all three of them. And I jumped out just before it blew to hell. Well, blew to pieces in Hell."

"Someone has taken command." She motioned to the window. "They're setting up camp on the lawn."

"Can you hold the fortress?"

"Not against a full assault. Most of what're out there are duplicates, images, and glamours. We're relying on history and fear. All told, we have a hundred soldiers."

"They're setting up for a siege."

Sonja nodded. "We have plenty of supplies. The fortress was stocked to support over a thousand troops and another few thousand support staff."

"They'll set up camp until they figure out what's really going on," I said. "We should have a few days at least."

Abhile reached for me with a shaking hand. "Does that mean you'll help?"

"I have a few more questions first. Then maybe."

"Ask anything."

"Why attack me in the underworld?"

"I needed to see how much the Void had reclaimed. We found you among the Reivers largely by accident. You do leave a pretty big trail wherever you go. Drake never knew it was me in Brighid's body. He hoped you'd come for her and leave me for him."

"And the hotel? You blew up a hotel full of fae refugees. Why Edana?"

"Drake. He'd gone quite mad with power. I think he had even gone over to the Dark Lord by then. The Fire Elemental gave the ring an etheric boost. He wanted to eliminate you, Priscilla, and as many of the ones who he saw as interfering. I came to rescue you. Save you." Her whole body was shaking. "You turned me away."

"And the attack on the Longbow facility? Destroying all of the portals?"

"You did that. We needed to get Richard Gibson. He was the only one prepared for the ritual. It wasn't like your friends were going to just hand him over." She flushed. "You need to know. Longbow is part of a bigger order. A much older one. One dedicated to eliminating all that is not mortal or Divine. And most of the Divine are on their hit list too."

"I…" The tightness in my chest stopped me. "It's not like that."

Sonja nodded. "You should ask Josiah. The Librarium Occultus was created because of this group. They tried to destroy all knowledge and keep it for a very few. Alexandria, Nalanda, Timbuktu, Constantinople, just to name a few of the great libraries they pillaged and destroyed."

I slumped into a chair.

Sonja leaned over the table, pressing. "What else do you wish to ask?" she snipped. "Are you sure you're ready for the answers?"

I shook my head.

Abhile came around the table and knelt next to the chair. "Does this mean you're ready to help our cause?"

"How many do you have on your side?"

"The three of us in this room are the only ones who know what's really happening," Sonja said.

I shook my head. "I don't understand. Not really."

Abhile swallowed and stared at me, drawing me into the pools of her eyes. "Erebus is both day and night, life and death, creator and destroyer. Now that he's here, he will consolidate his power. And when the time comes, we will be judged. All of the realms. Together. He is the instrument of infinity. The creator. The God."

"And when we're judged?"

"It's not called the cycle of destruction for nothing," Sonja said.

Melvin will be excited.

"HAVE YOU DECIDED?" Abhile placed her hand on my shoulder as I stared out at the encampment. More fires came to life every few moments as troops set up camp.

"I really don't want to believe this," I said.

"Who does? The prophecies say you'll be there at the end."

"Prophecies? Did they name me personally? Or did they just foresee my charming personality? I've not seen those things have a good track record. Usually, if there's anything in them at all, there's a generic description that some poor sucker can fulfill by being in the wrong place at the wrong time."

"Not all of them can come true." She sighed. "But when the circumstances foreseen arise, the ones that are more likely to happen come to the surface. Seers are subject to many possible futures. They just don't know which ones are most likely until the time draws closer. For those beings who have free will, it has a great influence."

"And what do these prophecies say?"

"There are dozens of which I'm aware. Sometimes you live. Usually you die. Sometimes you defeat the forces that oppose you. Sometimes you join them. A few of them have you saving everything. Most of them still end with the final judgment. No one can see past that."

"And if I decide not to play?"

"Someone will take on the mantle. You've seen how that worked so far. The prophecies tell us it must be the son of the Amazons."

I sighed and pushed away from the window. "Any word about Priscilla?"

"No. Early on, she was being held by Rahm. I haven't heard anything since. But I've only been able to keep limited communication with the other realms for obvious reasons."

"Who else did they capture at the fortress?"

She walked away and stared at the map. "As best I know, they only took Priscilla, Brighid, and Drea. I don't know about other captives or casualties. Nor did I ask."

"If I help you, you'll help me get them back from Rahm, and help get me out of this deal with your mother?" I gently stroked her face. "No strings attached. We'll be even."

She swept my hand down and took it in hers. "You have my word, but there are no easy ways out of a binding agreement."

It would have to do for now. "FaeMail still works?"

"Yes."

"How?" I was astounded at the resilience of the underground communication system. I'd been on the receiving end of a very personal message when I'd been summoned for the trial. It was the only time I, or anyone I knew, had ever seen one of the insipid delivery agents.

"I'm not privy to their inner workings. They just do."

"Nor rain, nor brimstone, nor depth of eternal night." I needed to get a message out, and quickly. And I needed to get to the woodlands once the sun was up. I had a few hours for some much-needed sleep. "I'm in. But you may not like my plan."

"CHECK. YOUR MOVE." Tsauriel left me an uncharacteristically easy escape.

I took her rook and dodged the attack. "Something bothering you?"

"You. You're taking ridiculous risks. Your good fortune cannot hold forever."

"It's not luck this time." I pressed the attack even though I knew she had me within a few moves. "I have a plan."

She backed off her piece. It was a move that would extend the game a few moves but not enough to give me an opening. "Do tell."

I took a pawn. "I thought you knew every little thought that my neurons produced."

"No, and thankfully so. I can't imagine having to process every bit of your drama that takes up so much productive time."

"I need whatever may be in here about the history of Longbow, but more importantly, I need whatever may be in here about siege warfare." I followed her movement and realized too late she'd drawn my queen into a trap.

"Check." She nodded at Ladon, who sharpened a sword next to the fire. "He would be the one to educate you on the finer aspects of fortifications and castle warfare. Both sides of the siege. And breaking them. Mate in two."

"What about Longbow?"

"Are you certain you wish to know?" My rook, the final useful piece, fell. "You have become quite enmeshed with the organization. Check."

I moved my king behind a pawn. "I need to know. And one more thing."

"Check. Yes, what else do you wish to know?"

I made the only move I could. "Prognostication. Prophecy. The future. Fortune telling. Can we really know? Or get a reasonable facsimile?"

She pushed away from the table. Any one of three moves would put me into mate, and she made none of them. "Go bother Ladon. I have research to do."

VIOLET TWILIGHT ROLLED over the hillside. I'd slept on the top of the tower, waiting for this moment. Organized camps ringed the fortress, well outside of the range of their archers, and at the edge of small-arms. Heavier weapons could be effective, but we didn't need to expend ammunition and possibly incite them to attack sooner than we were ready.

Most of the troops lined the lone road that led to the entrance, but enough were scattered along the hillside to completely surround the fortress. There was no sign of a senior commander, and for the most part, the troops looked to be doing their usual routines. Maybe Abhile had been right. When the troops saw the

172

downtown fortress burned and leveled, they must have followed standing orders to come here, and retake their only way home.

We held a meeting with the unit commanders. Abhile had underestimated her forces and had about three hundred men in total, counting the forty Fomorian mercenaries and a dozen practitioners. A rough count still put us at a ten-to-one deficit. And more troops were setting up camp by the hour outside. Ladon estimated that they wouldn't consider an attack until they had at least twenty-to-one odds at a minimum. If gaps existed in the command structure, the soldiers would continue to muster until they were at the breaking point and the demon-driven leadership ordered them to attack just to relieve the stress.

Abhile stared vacantly through a window on her top floor at the assembling horde. She jumped as I touched her arm. She hadn't heard me call her name twice.

"You're leaving?" She looked at the pack slung over my shoulder.

"I won't be gone long."

"How do you plan to get past them and then back in?"

"A lone person has an easier time getting by than a thousand. They won't see me."

She wrapped her arms around herself and shivered. "How long do you expect to be gone?"

"A few hours. By nightfall at the latest." I dropped an envelope on the table. It had some hurried notes from what I'd been able to remember from Ladon's flood of information. "Meet with the commanders again. Give them these instructions."

"Where are you going?"

"For help. I know someone who may have some reinforcements."

"Don't go. This is a fool's pursuit." She grabbed my arm. "Who would provide us assistance?"

"Look." I pulled her to the window and pointed to the soldiers on the wall. "I'm not convinced what they'll do in an assault. Most of our defenses depend on daemon troops that were left over when you took control of the fortress. If the Negalian forces capture the tower, I wouldn't bet against them changing sides. We can't hold the fortress."

"We must. It's the last resort we have while we're stuck in this realm." She pointed at the troops camped outside. "If we cede to them, they'll be unstoppable."

"That's why I'm going. I'm going to ask the Summer fae in the woodlands for help. Many Winter have taken refuge there as well as others. They have an army. It's not large, but it's organized and effective."

"You intend to hand us over to them." Her face went slack as she closed her eyes. "You want us to surrender to the lesser of our evils."

"No." I lifted her chin and forced her to look at me. "I want to give us a chance against them. The woodlands can hold out longer, but eventually they'll fall as well. And they know it. If we join forces, we may have a shot."

"They may trust you, but they'll never trust us."

I laid my pack on the table. "You have a better idea? Another option?"

She turned a chunk of stone emblazoned with sigils around in her fingers. It looked like a key of some sort. "No."

I pulled the wooden box Marsaile had given me out of my pack and held it up. "What's this? Your mother said it would be helpful."

"Give that to me."

"Will it help us?"

"No." Her voice was sharp. "It belongs to me and has nothing to do with this. Please, give it to me."

"I think I'll hold onto it." I tucked it back into the side pocket.

"Then you had best come back safely." She chewed her lip and stared at my pack. "Go."

"If I'm successful, I'm coming back with their leader."

"You really believe he'll come?"

"Yes. He trusts me, and he owes me." I took her clammy hand in mine. "Be welcoming. He's going to be as suspicious of you as you are of him. This only works if we put history aside."

"It will be Sonja and I only. And you of course."

"And one more. Brighid. Well, physically. Drea's not insane. I think. Both of them are trapped in one body, fighting for control. Brighid's body is being maintained by a shaman. I wish to bring her through. There still may be a chance."

She released my hand. "As you wish. Go. And may fortune be with you." Her voice was chilled.

THE DOOR SEALED with a heavy thud as the heavy cross braces fell into place. I couldn't risk someone accidentally or intentionally disturbing the portal, so the room I found was isolated and could be sealed off. It would be a lot harder to get back in through the front door with all the guests on the lawn.

I drew a wide circle on the floor, taking up most of the room. The damp stone wanted to soak up the chalk mixture, so I judiciously added salt and crystal powder, using most of my supply. It took most of an hour to complete the sigils to connect to the portal in the woodlands and incorporate every protection I could think of. Depending on how well the plan went, this gate might be needed to move a lot of people both in and out of the fortress.

Finally satisfied, I closed the circle with a dab of powder. I Pushed energy into the crystals at the cardinal points and locked my focus on the woodlands. The energies from the main gate to the underworld realms trickled up, making it hard to concentrate, but the circle did most of the work with the preparations I'd made on the other end. Hell's main gateway may not have been open for business, but it wasn't sealed either.

Transits were usually instantaneous. This time, it felt like being poured into a blender with cheap mescal, the worm, and the chip off an iceberg then poured into a fine sieve.

When the world stopped spinning, I locked onto the pair of uncertain Drow who halfheartedly aimed short swords in my direction as they peered over the wall.

Anraoi had taken my suggestion to heart. I'd told him to isolate the circle, much like what I'd done in the fortress, to make sure it was secure. I'd wanted to make sure there were no accidents on this end, or that if someone unwanted came through, there was a fighting chance of handling the problem. Anraoi had responded by ringing the entire portal with heavy hardwoods in another tall palisade. Traps were built high above, ready to drop spiked logs and rocks just shy of boulders.

I waved with a smile. "Take me to your leader." It sounded a lot funnier in my head.

THE WOODLAND GENERAL in his treelike guise chewed on a stem as he listened to my proposal. A Drow, a brown tree sprite, and a matching set of elven archers held their breath and waited for something to bellow from deep within their leader's trunk.

From the amount of time I waited for a response, I knew he was giving it real consideration, but the odds weren't in my favor. I was asking him to gamble all of the gains he'd made and more.

The fluttering of a leaf under his nose was the first sign he was ready to speak. "Let me make sure I understand. You want me to take most of these defenders—and you know we barely have enough as observers on the wall, let alone enough to defend it— and have them defend the daemon castle?"

"I've already put a dent into them. We have a chance. An opportunity. With combined forces, we can send what they have left in tatters and have the fae hold the woodlands and the ancient fortress. You'd retake all of Los Diablos and secure the border. We might even be able to reopen the portals to the Summer and Winter lands."

"And if we fail, we gift wrap the back door when the portals reopen, and Hell's soldiers flood through."

"It's a risk. But even just to hold the fortress, your men could make it near impervious to attack and give more safety back to your people. And you get to secure the rift opening to the realms of the damned. Or just wait and continue to let them pick off your men one at a time in skirmishes until they get reinforcements."

"You believe the gateways through the Veil will be repaired?"

"I think they're already strengthening. It's just a matter of time before the disruption fades. Who knows which gateway will open first, and who's waiting, ready to come through?"

I knew that was a shot at Anraoi. He was in just as much danger by any fae that came through from Summer or Winter as he was if the doorway to Tartarus opened wide.

Anraoi's sprite tapped his foot for a few seconds before opening pursed lips and spending his ire. "Why trust this one? It smells of a trap. Throw him over the wall, and let's see what his horned friends do with him."

"I know him, and I trust him." Anraoi's voice drummed. "If you doubt him, you challenge me."

He swallowed. "Sire, I simply caution—"

"Caution?" Anraoi raised his full frame. "I value your advice, Jyli, but your nature is to wait. Sometimes that is prudent. This time, I believe it is worth the risk to investigate."

"I really must object."

"Noted." The sculpted bulb of foliage serving as his head swiveled my way. "Greyson, when do you wish to depart?"

I nodded. "As soon as you and Tellia are ready. And anyone else you wish to join."

"Tellia as well?"

"I'll fill you in on the way."

He swung back to his attendants. "TalShynt, you will be in command in my absence. Jyli is your second. Can you ask ShriWod and Phaer to join us at the portal in one hour?"

"JUST ONE MOMENT." Anraoi shifted to his natural form once the palisade closed, leaving the five of us alone. "Tellia, I trust you can keep my secret?"

She answered with a gentle nod. "It is part of my calling. Your truth is bound to me in a way that cannot be separated, even by death."

The pair of Drow kept a vigilant eye to their surroundings, even though we were still within their camp.

"We will cross over into a secured room. You'll be able to change form again then. No one there knows any details. Just that the leader of the Woodlands defense is coming to negotiate." I turned and whispered into his ear. "You trust them this much?"

A gentle smile crossed his lips. "I trust ShriWod and Phaer here, and their brother TalShynt like few others. Despite their appearance, they are not Dark Drow like many of their kin in the camp."

"Why am I along?" Tellia asked.

"I need for you to talk to someone. Drea. They claim to have rescued her after you were all brought here."

She stared at the thatched ceiling. "What do you need from me?"

"Just…" I debated telling her the whole truth. But I needed more for her to be objective. It was hard for me to see Brighid, knowing how many had occupied her body recently. It might be dangerous for her to see someone else in her body, but Tellia was the most knowledgeable one here about the situation. "Just please check her out."

"As you wish."

Anraoi stretched a final time, snapping his arm into place. "Any time you're ready."

I'd reinforced the circle to strengthen the connection to the fortress, and the trip was instantaneous. Waves of nausea hit as soon as we appeared in the chamber. My Senses knew it to be the Hellgate below powering up.

I looked around and realized I was the only one who'd been affected. No one else noticed me on my knees.

Anraoi looked intent on making an impression. His torso was a gnarled tree trunk, larger than a barrel. He'd dressed himself with flared red-and-yellow vines and leaves. He looked like a living fire of color, richer than fall in Maine.

180

The Drow strapped on decorative armor, but I had little doubt it was fully functional.

Tellia waited next to the door with her pack slung over her shoulder. Her expression was flat, and I wondered how she would feel about interviewing the owner of the body she inhabited.

I placed my hand on the floor and stretched my Senses. I felt into the Hellgate below. It was still blocked, but I couldn't guess how long it would stay that way. I Pushed outward. Everything felt as it should. Beings wandered the halls or stood at their posts. Understandable anxiety seeped into the stones. The good news was that there were no signs of a breach or that the siege had become an active assault. "It's clear."

Anraoi made easy work of sliding the heavy beams aside and unlocking the door. I knocked and called out the all clear. Deep thuds on the other side of the door signaled the sentries had removed the outer barricade.

The guards were backed up by the sorceress who'd been with Sonja and Abhile when they had opened the outer gate. Her scowl made me think she'd been sipping on spoiled sour mash. I stretched my Sense to pass over her. She was bound to the fortress, the house act, as it were. She was doing her job, but she clearly wasn't happy with her new masters. Seeing Anraoi, Man of the Wood, dip beneath the archway of the door caused her to take a half step back. She recovered quickly and was curt as she spoke. "Follow me." She was halfway to the inner throne room before we caught up to her.

OUR ESCORT POSITIONED herself at the threshold of the door where she could eavesdrop and allowed only Anraoi and myself through. I wasn't of a mind to trust her, and I had no idea how Abhile felt about it, but I was about to find out.

Sonja crossed her arms and leaned against the wall with a mirthful smirk as we entered the throne room. Abhile cocked her head as if she was processing the sight in front of her.

Anraoi had piled it on a little thick and had to stoop under the low ceilings, making him look as if he were a weeping willow. The ceilings had been designed to hamper larger daemon from being able to use their size if they attacked the resident of the throne.

Abhile rose with a nod. "Welcome."

I raised my hand, motioning for silence, and dropped a small box on the floor. A pale-blue light filled the room. Our silence was absolute. Looking at the entranceway we'd come through was like looking at the surface from deep under the water. Outside the room looking in would be an absolute blur.

"Now we are in absolute privacy," I said.

Abhile extended her delicate hand to Anraoi. "You seem... familiar."

"He should." Sonja gave an exuberant curtsy. "It's good to see you again, Anraoi."

The long branches shook as the woodland leader pulled back into his fae body. "You as well."

Sonja had once been a guest of his queen's court and had served them both. She then had taken the role of keeping watch over their daughter Abhile in the mortal world beyond the Veil.

Abhile sat back into her throne without completing the pleasantries. "You are safe here. We have extended safe harbor for the extent of your visit."

He popped his neck and shook off the last of the bark from his skin. "I think we have much to discuss for both of our benefit."

Sonja raised her hands. "Anraoi, I think we should start with a clean slate here. What's been done is done."

His lemon-peel skin flushed red. "I forgive you for trying to kill me, enslave my family, and betraying our accords in exchange for what?"

Abhile clenched her fists. "Forgiveness for allowing the accord between Summer and Winter to be broken, your regime to fall, stripping away my identity and memories, feeding lies to me and your own family, placing us all at mortal risk because none of us knew about anything outside of a fantasy." I Sensed the power building in her. I'd seen what could happen when she didn't, or couldn't, control it.

"Oh, that." Anraoi swallowed and stared at the floor. "I did what little I could to protect you. All of you."

Sonja and I locked eyes. Suddenly, I was feeling a lot better about my dysfunctional family. I broke the tense silence. "As much fun as this reunion is, we have bigger problems."

Abhile nodded, and the flare of magic faded.

"The most immediate of which isn't the army outside." I glanced out the window slit. The camps were getting packed, and it

183

looked as if they were settling in for a long siege rather than an immediate assault. Flames from a bonfire flickered out of the top vent hole of the large red tent recently erected in the middle of the central camp. It screamed "this is where the head demons party." And it was where whoever was leading this rabble would be. "We have problems inside these walls."

Sonja pushed away from the wall and walked to the middle of the room. "I've spoken with the guards bound to the fortress. They'll do anything necessary to protect it. If their own kind gets inside the walls, though, I don't think it'll take much for them to change allegiances."

"That's not the only thing." I placed my hand on the floor and stretched my Senses. "Can't you feel that?"

All three of them looked back at me with blank stares.

"The Hellgate. It's in the bottom of this tower. I can feel it. And it's powering up."

Sonja shook her head. "There's a portal room in the basement. It's dead. Just as much as every other gate between the realms seems to be."

"I came through one. It was difficult, but I used one that had mostly been shielded. If the disruption is fading, all the gates could be powering up. I'd think a direct line to the less-pleasant parts of the underworld, especially one that powers this place, might be one of the first ones to show signs of life. If it opens up, there could be a whole lot of pent-up daemon ready to flow through. Hellbeasts or who knows what might pour out."

Sonja paled. "I think we need to take a look."

I nodded. "Abhile, Anraoi, can you two hug it out and behave for a few minutes without us?"

184

BLACKENED AND CHARRED by the power of the Hellgate, the portcullis guarding the room stood tall enough to let a Macy's parade balloon through with room to spare. Hammered black cold iron bands reinforced and locked the opening.

Sonja winced at the feel of the room. I'd turned my Senses down as much as I could. I couldn't remember the last time I'd been without them, reaching out, touching everything around me. The power flooding out of the underworld portal was thick, draining, and wrong.

I pointed at the opening. "What do you think they built to let through there?"

"I try not to think about it." Sonja headed into an adjoining tunnel. "We can get in through here."

The walls were tacky and felt like a coat of old tar that had never quite dried. The air was heavy and tasted of copper. It didn't take much to guess what had been used for paint.

The two of us wound in a wide spiral walkway, passing doors pocketed into the walls every few feet or so. "Are these meant to keep something in or out?" I asked.

She grabbed the next one we passed and pulled it out about a foot. Spikes sprung out on both sides and dripped a thick syrup. "What do you think?"

"Both." I nodded. "If this is the vacation spot, home sweet home must be a lot of fun."

The last door at the end of the passageway stood open. The spikes were firmly affixed to both sides. Sonja used the end of her blade to push the door open. "Be careful as you walk past. The slightest nick from any of these would… well, let's just say if you scratched your arm, I'd cut it off for you."

"Thanks. I think." My head throbbed from the energy in the room.

Sonja was slowing down and wore the effects like a cloak as well. She translated the engraving over the door to an antechamber that could have held a hundred uncomfortably crowded Clydesdales. "They call it a well of descent. This translates roughly into 'Abandon all hope ye who enter here.' I think it's an inside joke."

"Dante would be proud." I gasped as I crossed the threshold. Heavy blackened stone blocks rose hundreds of feet into the air, forming a silo that surrounded us. Tree trunks cantilevered out of the walls high above us like perches for pterosaurs. Sulphur, ozone, and brimstone hung heavy, crowding out the oxygen in the room.

The portal ring in the floor was big enough to hold two Olympic pools. It looked like a lake of smoky glass with small waves rolling in chaotic patterns on the surface. Occasional cracks showed a sea of lava underneath.

"This is what you consider inactive?" I asked.

Sonja covered her mouth with her hand, but I couldn't tell whether it was from shock or the fumes.

"Sonja?"

She danced around the narrow path outlining the lake of energy and disappeared into a nearby hidden doorway. I bumped into her as I chased her through the door.

Behind three glowing panels embedded into stone blocks sat a daemon unlike any I'd seen before. I guessed he was a little shorter than me, but his feet were kicked up on top of a nearby panel next to the bench he lounged on, so I couldn't be sure. He could just has easily have had some shapeshifting abilities. I'd have thought it comical if it wasn't so surreal. The daemon almost looked human, with short-cropped hair, a small goatee, and a skull earring. If only his flesh weren't a sickly green.

I pushed Sonja aside. "Um, hello?"

Black eyes spun up to meet mine. "Where'd you come from?"

"Upstairs. What are you doing?"

He stared at the glowing sigils floating around. "I'm Nate. I'm here to fix the Hellgate. Downstairs is real backed up."

I caught a glimpse of the glowing panels but couldn't figure out any of what I was seeing. "Hey, can we talk for a minute?"

"Sure. You got any snacks up there?"

NATE THE DAEMON was emptying out another basket of dried fruit as Sonja, Anraoi, and I studied him. He seemed oblivious to us and read through scrolls as fast as he could finish off any nearby food.

"So, Nate." I lost the bet as to who would talk to him. "How'd you get through?"

"It wasn't easy." The limb of something roasted disappeared into his mouth. "I had to possess one of the guardians and shove myself in through his body. It took almost a dozen tries before I made it through."

"Why did you come?" I asked.

A pair of buck-toothed tusks hung down. "What do you mean? Ba'al summoned me."

"When?"

"I don't know. Two hours ago. A thousand years. Kinda hard to tell." He shook an empty bag, staring into it for another crumb. "Don't you guys work for him too?"

"Not exactly." I pulled a bag of pretzels out of my pack and tossed it on the table. "Do you know what's going on up here?"

He shrugged and opened the pretzels. "There's a whole lot of really pissed hordes below that were promised their trip up here. I used to be an alchemist and an IT guy in engineering. I got pulled from the pits and tossed up here to fix the gateway. It's my shot at a promotion."

Sonja inched closer to the daemon. "All inter-realm travel is down." She gave me a sideways glance. "Almost all."

"Yeah." Nate licked the salt out of the bag. "Any idea what caused it?"

"It's a long story." I grabbed the last protein bar out of my bag and set it on the table. "How long before the gate is active again?"

He picked up the bar, looking at it as if he were debating the merits of something healthy. "I'm not having to do anything. It's fixing itself." He devoured the bar in two bites. "I'll still take the credit, though. Couple days, and it should be powered up again."

"Can you stop it?" I asked.

"No." He snorted. "Slow it down, maybe. I'm trying to stretch my visit up top out as long as I can. I'm hoping to get a week out of it."

"Maybe we can work something out."

"HOW'D THEY WORK?" I sat across from Abhile. Sonja flanked me on the right, Anraoi at my left. "The ring devices? How'd they function?"

"I don't know exactly." Abhile stared emptily at the diorama table.

We'd run out of the figures for the map, intended to show the location of enemy forces, and had begun to use spice containers and small scrolls to fill in their places on the map at every major camp. It didn't begin to tell the story of how bad things had gotten over the last two days. The sieging forces now encircled the fortress in a solid flaming ring of bonfires and torches, which glowed through tents and makeshift walls. The focal gem sat at the top of the road—an octagonal tent that had to be a hundred feet or more on each side. The only good news was that Nate had been true to his word. It had been two days, and nothing was storming through the Hellgate. Yet.

"We're not going to be able to hold the fortress, are we?" Abhile asked.

"It's going to be hard, I think." Someone had put small figures onto the map where different camps were staged. "Doesn't mean we can't do something useful while we have it."

Abhile's face sagged as she nodded. "The devices were a pairing. The small rings open a portal to a matching gate, pulling energy through. They can either reinforce or supersize a gateway. Or shrink it to nothing and jet the power back into them, creating an energetic implosion. The small rings fed power to the larger central ring, and it created the disruption field by taking all of the different active portals and pouring them into the target. Or that was the plan until someone showed up."

I ignored the comment. "So it stepped up the power from all of the sources until it got to the top. Do you have any more of the small portals you were using as sources?"

"A few. We've set them up in strategic places and have been using them to get around." Sonja sat stone-faced. "What are you thinking?"

"We set this place up. I think we can use the energy from the Hellgate to power our trip back to the other side of the Veil. At the

190

same time, we blow this place, shut the Hellgate, and let it suck as many of those creatures outside as possible back to where they belong."

Sonja nodded. "It might work. We'll need to make some modifications, which I don't know how to do. We tried modifying one as a gateway out but couldn't get anyone through who could help once we escaped here."

"You didn't have enough power," I said. "I'm hoping our new friend can help us out."

"You want to trust a newly minted daemon with this?" Abhile ran her hands through her hair, leaving fine trails of frost in their wake.

I smiled. "Better than one that's fully indoctrinated. Besides, he wants to stay out of the underworld as long as he can. We can make him a deal."

Abhile put her face in her hands. "This is worse than Necromancy."

"We didn't summon him. We're just giving a poor soul another chance."

"There's still one more problem." Sonja made a swirling motion with her hand at the pale-blue light surrounding us, keeping our conversations private. "At some point, the fortress's defenders will figure out we're up to something not in their best interests. They may open the gates to the invaders. Or they might just decide to attack us outright."

I nodded. "That thought occurred to me too. Any ideas?"

NATE GRINNED SLYLY, drool dripping from one tusk. An elephantine foot slammed into the desk as he kicked his feet onto the table. Lacing his fingers behind his head, he leaned back, despite the protests from the chair. "What's in it for me?"

"What do you want?" I'd expected more protests before he started to negotiate. Instead, he looked like he'd expected it.

Beady black eyes glimmered with a response. "Let's start with you helping get this thing off me."

A spiky device that looked like an anemone from a lava pit was strapped around his leg.

"Satan's ankle bracelet?" I asked.

"Something like that." He glanced over at Abhile. "And how about some time with tall, blue, and lovely over there?"

Sonja took several wide strides, landing her last one in the middle of Nate's chest, tipping him and the rest of the chair to the floor with a crash. She leapt along for the ride, plunging her heel into his throat upon landing. "Try again."

He struggled against her foot strangling him. After a few seconds of him thrashing on the ground and beating on her leg, she took two wide steps and landed in a chair.

"I want to go home. Out of Hell." He rubbed his throat. "What do you think I want? I'm not stupid. I know it's temporary, but I'll take what I can get."

192

"Then we have a deal." I leaned over and offered him a hand to help him up. "But if you don't stay out of trouble once we're home, I'll package you up with a note to make sure you're the tail end of a daemon centipede."

He grabbed my hand. "Deal."

I shoved him out of the blue field toward the door. "Get to work."

He glared back before stalking out the door.

Sonja took a deep breath. "Can we trust him?"

"No." I laughed. "I won't take off the ankle bracelet without another failsafe."

"Can you get it off?"

I grabbed a half-dozen tomes from a nearby shelf and dropped them onto the table. "Let's find out."

TELLIA MEDITATED QUIETLY inside of Abhile's chamber. I'd sat on one of the oversized pillows and watched her for nearly an hour when I felt her returning to Brighid's body. I'd stretched my Senses around her, feeling the conflict inside of her.

It was hard for me to see her this way. I could only imagine how hard it had been on Tellia to go into the room unprepared. She'd been asked to help guide Brighid back to her own body. Now the shaman had lost her own and was trapped in the shell of the person she'd come to help.

She unfolded herself and stretched catlike, finishing the exercise with a wide yawn. "Have you been waiting long?"

"No," I lied. "How are you feeling?"

She sipped from a bottle of water. "Don't you mean, what's my appraisal of Drea?"

"That too."

"You already know."

I nodded. "I think so. I want to know what you think."

"I don't think." She took a deep breath. "I joined with them. Both of them are in there. Still separate mostly, but they are starting to meld."

"What can we do?"

Her graceful movements made it look as though she were floating across the room. She knelt in front of me. "We finish what we started. Get her back into her body."

"And what about you?"

She shook her head. "My physical body is dust, but I have an opportunity to finish my work. My time draws near."

I swallowed. "You'd give it up so easily?"

Her laugh was sad but gentle. It was hard for me to forget it wasn't Brighid. "Easy? No, not easy. But I've never been one that was tied to my physical incarnation. You have been to the next life, have you not? There and back? That is the tale told about you."

I couldn't explain the great weight that fell on me as I was hit with the binding that kept my trip to Purgatory to myself. It was hard to breathe. My hands turned cold and shook. It was hard to keep my eyes open. Then, just as quickly, it passed. "That's part of it. Yeah. I've been to other realms. I've been with some of the dead." I thought about having seen my father. Him looking like a child. Having shed so much of himself. And the part of him that was left being so ready to race into danger. Another death. And no sign of my mother. Or any of the others from that night.

"Yes." She ran a gentle hand through my hair. "Now I see it in you."

"See what?"

She patted my face and rose. "They want to see you."

"What is it you saw?"

She folded herself again onto the mat and closed her eyes. "What they see in you."

"What?" My shout echoed in the chamber. "What!"

"I must work on your other problem for a while." She released a breath and was gone to whatever mindscape shamans roam.

MY HAND POUNDED on the door before I could stop myself. I hadn't decided what to say. What could I say? We were running out of time. I had to get Drea and Brighid ready to travel.

The door opened slowly. Drea looked as though I'd woken them up. Her hair hung loose past her shoulders. Hard eyes softened immediately as they locked onto me, and she stepped aside, closing the door behind me.

"I hear you wanted me," I said.

"Always." She sat on the edge of the narrow bed, repeatedly smoothing the thin tunic against her legs with trembling hands. "How are the preparations going?"

"You know about that?"

"I know you." She pointed to the window. "And I can see what's outside. Unless you're a fool, you're working on a plan to attack or escape."

I nodded. "I'm hoping we can get the portal ready in time. If not, I've got a backup plan. If it looks like it's not going to work, I'll get you to safety."

"Is there such a thing anymore?"

I placed my arm around her, bringing her close to me. "I don't know. I don't know if we ever had a chance for it, but I'll do everything I can."

She took my free hand in hers.

"Which one of you is driving right now?" I asked.

Her answer told me what I expected. "We're sharing right now, but it's mostly me, Brighid."

"How are you? How'd it go with Tellia?"

She choked out her answer. "It's hard. I feel myself slipping away. We both do. Tellia showed us both some ways of keeping

196

ourselves separate for now. She said she'll give me back my body when we find a way. If we can hold out that long."

I opened my Senses, wrapping them around her. I felt both entities, each familiar in their own way. Even though I distinctly felt them separately, I could almost feel where they were melding. It wasn't much, but enough. I also Sensed Drea fighting her nature to conquer Brighid and drive her out. If I could sense it, so could Brighid. She was giving up, losing herself. I guess I couldn't blame her, considering everything she'd been through.

I didn't want to give her false hope, but she needed it. They both did. "A few more days. I acquired a device. If we can get back to the world, I think it will work." If I can find a way to repair it or copy it. But they didn't need to know Rahm had split it in half.

"We'll hold on." I knew that response had come from Drea.

"I've got to go."

Brighid pulled my hand. "Not yet. There's one more thing we want to… propose."

My heart thumped as she whispered into my ear. "Are you sure? Both of you? About this?"

Drea responded. "We've agreed that we will have to share you. And we may never have another opportunity."

"Don't I get a say in this?"

Brighid pulled my lips to hers. "Always, our love."

THE PORTAL BUBBLED an angry red. Wisps of etheric energy formed a thin fog around the ring, holding one of the portal boosters afloat. Its partner was on the far side of the portcullis that now stood open. I waved at Sonja, our signal that the rings looked to be in sync and ready to use.

Now we just needed Nate to hold up his end.

Anraoi had sent messages back to his camp to prepare their assault. They'd feigned an attack against the light troops at the back of the fortress, near the woods. As soon as they were able to draw more troops tighter around the lava moat and away from the farther camps, they would let the woodland fae retreat and trigger the device. If everything worked as planned, the portal would implode the Hellgate, drawing in everything nearby and pulling it back to where it belonged. At least, that was the plan.

I was less sure about the second part. I would know in a minute if it was going to work.

With a brown cap advertising FaeMail, a one-foot-tall golden pixie in a small brown uniform crossed his arms and tapped a small foot.

Tuck flashed a mouth full of razor-sharp needles for teeth. "Hey, mac. I don't often get repeat business, especially for where you got sent."

"A small misunderstanding," I said.

"That's what they all say." He held up a small envelope. "You needs to sign for it. You knows the drill."

I stuck my thumb out. In a blur, the creature nicked me and stamped the receipt in blood.

198

I held up the envelope. "Wait one minute."

The ping-pong-sized orbs Tuck used for eyes rolled dramatically. "Yeah, I know. You gots a response."

Josiah's note was simple:

The reception is prepared.

Two sigils sizzled with energy. One would open the gateway to the assembly chamber underneath Phoenix Grove. The other would pull anyone in the circle through.

"Thanks, Tuck." I handed him a similar envelope. "Nice seeing you again."

The creature sneered. "You've really made my job harder, but then again, business is up. I'll call it a wash. I'll be seeing you, bub." He stepped into a sliver of light and vanished.

I wasn't sure about going home, but it was the only safe way I had to get out of there. Maybe not safe for me, but people there could help Brighid and Drea even if I couldn't. The message I sent Josiah had all of my notes and instructions. I hoped he'd been able to keep them a secret from Brighid's family. I wasn't ready to see Sinclair so soon.

But I wasn't sure what to do about Sonja and Abhile. They were fugitives within the fae community. And Longbow. And the Erebites. Somehow, I doubted the list of beings hunting them stopped there.

"ARE YOU INSANE?" Sonja slammed her hand onto the table, sending pieces flying that had represented the enemies outside. "You're just going to hand us over?"

I held my hands out. "No." Magical energy was building in the room. I didn't want things to break down, killing us all before the enemy outside could. One slip, and the fragile truce in the room would shatter like crystal. "Just listen for a moment. I haven't found another way out. The portals here won't lock to others outside this realm."

Anraoi spoke softly. "We can hide you with the woodland people if you wish. I'll guarantee your safety with my people for as long as I can, but I will be returning to the Grove with Greyson and the rest of them."

"You're abandoning your people?" Sonja's power flared. "We might as well die fighting these creatures. Or try for a truce."

Abhile shook her head. "If we are to have any chance to set things right and finish what we've started, we will need the support of our people, all fae. We have a better chance there than here. We'll run until we're caught."

"I will do everything in my power to guarantee your safety and a chance to plead your case." Anraoi held out a softball-sized globe of energy. He was offering a binding bond. "I go not to abandon the few here for my own sake, but to find a way to restore the peace for all."

"As will I." I held up a pale-yellow globe, offering my own bond. "But my word may carry less weight with the Winter Fae than yours, Abhile."

Sonja and Abhile shared a wordless conversation with just their eyes. Abhile nodded, holding up a ball of pale blue.

Sonja scowled. "You're all mad." The power in her hands congealed into a yellow sphere.

The energy dissipated. A warmth spread up my arm and into my chest, signifying the oath.

Anraoi took a deep breath. "ShriWod and Phaer will come with us. Their word will carry weight. And their muscle will back it up."

"Drea, Tellia, and Nate make nine." I made some quick calculations. "It'll be tight, but I think it will work."

"You're really going to bring it along? The daemon?" Sonja snapped.

"I gave my word."

THE RING GLOWED with a near full charge as it hung barely over the portal. The Hellgate glowed a deep red. The etheric mist formed clouds, with cracks of blue static discharging between them.

I made my way along the narrow ledge surrounding the ring to the control room. Nate leaned back in the stone seat behind the control panel, his feet resting on the corner of the console.

"Is everything ready?" I asked him.

"That depends on you, chief. Your toy out there will be charged up in about four hours. I can hold the gate closed a little longer than that." He pointed to the spiked device around his ankle. "Are you ready to hold up your end of the deal?"

"Everything is set for us to get out of here and for you to go along for the ride."

"That doesn't do me much good as long as I have this babysitter." He patted the device on his leg.

"I've got a way to cut you loose if you're ready."

He jumped to his feet, rubbing his hands and bouncing on the floor. "Let's go."

We edged along the pathway to where Tellia waited in the flat staging area. "This isn't going to be easy."

"Let's just get this over with so we can all get back to regular programming."

I grabbed him by the side of his worn vest and tried not to think about what the leather was made from. "Remember our other deal. You stay out of trouble, and I don't have to come find you."

"Look, man." He locked his beady coal eyes onto me. "I'm only looking to make amends, starting with your little merry band."

"As long as we're clear."

Tellia stood at the edge of the portal with her hands clasped behind her back. One of the bound fortress defenders waited at her side. She'd found a ritual to free Nate from his personal prison, but it wasn't going to be pretty. She'd rifled through the fortress's medical supplies and found what we needed.

Since then, she'd had a couple of hours of meditation to prepare. She held out Brighid's hand to the daemon. "I'm going to do another transfer like the one you used to get here, but this will free you of the device and transfer it to our friend here."

He contorted his face and crossed his arms. "Is this really going to work? I mean, it's attached to me. *My soul.* Not this body I swiped."

"It's your best chance," I said.

"Don't forget." He sneered, and a row of spines I hadn't seen before stood straight up on his back. "If I don't go, no one does."

Tellia kept a stone face. "I am aware. May we begin?"

His spines lay down.

She positioned the defender with his legs spread and his hands in the air. "Face him and mirror the position."

The daemon complied, and Tellia made slight adjustments in his stance before placing one hand on Nate's forehead and the other on the defender. She closed her eyes, and a moment later, the daemon and the surrogate followed suit.

I focused my Sight onto her. She tied a thin trail from Nate to the defender, which was the sign she'd told me to watch for.

Nate was relaxed, barely standing. I Pushed the Leviskin to reveal the blessed blade on my thigh. In a single move, I drew the blade and spun low, slashing the blade through Nate's calf just below his double-jointed knee.

Tellia's eyes flashed open, and she shoved him backward onto the ground. As his eyes opened, an unearthly howl echoed through the chamber.

I grabbed the detached leg and jammed it into the defender's face, thrusting him and the leg into the portal, vaporizing them both.

Nate thrashed on the ground, swearing, as blackish blood gushed from his leg.

Tellia pointed at a blanket on the ground. "There. Quickly."

I unrolled the blanket, dumping a metal tube on the ground. Tellia knelt on Nate's thigh, trying to hold him still until I slammed the black cylinder onto his stump. We both moved back, not entirely knowing what to expect. Nate's screams rose three octaves as the cylinder glowed red hot, forming and reshaping on his leg. A minute later, it was over. Nate was passed out with a brand-new shiny black foot and lower leg.

"TIME TO GO," Sonja shouted through the open doorway. She flushed, and through my Sight I saw that she was slowly pulling energy from the environment around us and storing the power within her herself at the ready should she need it. Weapons were slung around her body, ready for use. "I've been searching for you everywhere."

"We still have a little over an hour before it's fully charged." I slipped the scroll into my breast pocket. "What's happened?"

"They're marching on the gates, and the fortress guards are acting strange. And you probably need to see what's happening at the portal."

"Get everyone together. Go get Anraoi and Abhile. I'll bring Drea and Tellia." I pushed away from the table and grabbed my pack. Weapons were already in place, and my Leviskin suit configured for medium armor.

"They've been summoned and will be there shortly," she said. "I've asked them to gather in the throne room until we're ready."

I hadn't spent that much time around my aunt, but I'd seen her face in combat several times, usually with me on the other side. I'd never seen her nervous, almost shaken. For a moment, I wondered if she was feeling anticipation, but her eyes said otherwise. If what she'd seen was enough to scare her, I didn't want to think about it.

I looked out the window. Thousands of troops were marching up the roadway and had already reached the outer gate. They stood at rest but with weapons at the ready. Farther down the road, soldiers were still marching and gathering into the line. From the arc I could see, troops were staged at the edge of the lava moat, surrounding the entire fortress. Smoke rose in places where traps had been set off, but I doubted they had thinned the troops enough for anyone other than the dead to notice.

We ran at full speed down the staircase that looped the inner circle of the tower. I slowed briefly to see everyone gathered in the queen's chamber except Nate and Tellia.

We found them in the Hellgate. The stone walls glowed garnet from the energy pouring from the portal. A skin of pure energy stretched over the gateway, threatening to burst forth. It poured over onto the walkway, and barely a footpath was left to get to the control room.

Nate glared at me from the console. His skin had paled from a deep red to a sunburned pink. "You could have warned me."

"No, I couldn't." I wanted to feel bad for the daemon, but I didn't have it in me. He'd been freed from his punishment, even if it was temporary. "If I'd told you, it wouldn't have worked. The curse on the device would have snatched you away immediately."

"I get that part," he snapped. "But when you threw the body in, especially with the anklet, it really tested the hold I had on the gateway."

I hadn't thought about that. We just had to destroy the body before it and the cursed device figured out what happened and reattached to him.

"And I lost most of my memories about a great road trip in '89 and a party in '94." He shook his head. "Your witch told me how it attached to certain sins, and those are the ones they used, but damn. To have those torn away." He ran his hand over the bumps running along the top of his skull.

"Tellia is not a witch. Not exactly, anyway." I shrugged at the daemon's whining. "I kept up my end of the deal. Is everything ready to go?"

"Ready?" He snorted out a blast of muck. "I can't hold it together much longer. Your little stunt supercharged your exploding Frisbee. You can set it off anytime with this remote. Let's get on outta here." He handed a small ring to Sonja.

"Okay, do what you can and meet us in the staging area outside the portcullis," I said.

Tellia touched my arm. "I'll have to help him around."

I nodded. "Don't take long, and leave him if you have to."

Sonja spoke quietly but urgently into my ear. "We have company."

206

THE FORMATION STOPPED on the pad where we'd done Nate's impromptu surgery. Twelve of the fortress guards were led by the headmistress of the fortress. The woman was large and round, but nothing about her was soft. She'd traded her brown robes for the black armor of the guard.

As if they wanted to make sure I saw the whole display, they waited in a semicircle around the sorceress until Sonja and I reached the edge of the platform.

"What's the situation?" Sonja shouted. "Have they started the attack?"

Silently, the headmistress spun to face the troops and motioned to them. Five lay down on the ground and intertwined themselves into a star. The rest lay down around them, encircling the pentagram. The twelve on the ground closed their eyes and opened their mouths, bellowing a chant.

"What are they doing?" I asked.

Sonja stepped back into me, pushing me back onto the path. "Get back."

"What is it?"

She pushed against my chest. "Get back to the chamber."

"I'm not moving."

She grabbed the front of my armor. Her eyes darted to the portal. I wasn't sure if it was a signal or if she was debating whether to throw me out of her way. I threw my arms between hers, breaking her grip, and grabbed onto her breastplate. "What?"

She shook her head and mumbled. I could barely hear her over the chanting. "I think it's a summoning. I've never seen it, but I did see something like this in one of the texts upstairs. This much blood has got to be something… huge."

"Blood?"

The guards forming the circle fell silent. The sorceress filled the void with a warbling, mournful song. The guards let out one great cry and burst, as if they were balloons of red paint that had been pricked with a pin, leaving the pentagram and summoning circle in a grisly pool of red.

The sorceress gingerly stepped over the circle and into the center, careful not to smear the lines. Her hard square face turned to us with a blank look. Her eyes turned to coal, igniting with a low flame. Her skin stretched taut, and with a final grin that would chill a furnace, she screamed.

Her skin fell away as the creature grew in size, doubling, tripling, quadrupling her size, and growing. Leathery wings thrust out behind the thing as it towered forty feet over us. Despite the great bonfire burning behind her eyes, the stare was cold, predatory.

I'd never felt more insignificant in my life as I wiped sweat from my palms and wrapped my hand around the handle of the 1911. Although Sonja's eyes were locked forward, she seemed to sense what I was doing and reached behind her, placing her hand over mine. I released the weapon, and she stepped away.

Wind whipped as the beast cracked its neck and gave the wings a couple of flaps before folding them behind it, as if she was trying to adjust to her new form.

I took a few steps, edging backward on the narrowing path. Sonja followed. I feared one of us would fall over into the portal. Not only would that kill us, but it would likely tip the delicate balance holding it all together.

STOP!

The command wasn't verbal but nearly brought me to my knees. Sonja wasn't in much better shape.

Come forth.

It wasn't a compulsion this time but felt more like a request. I couldn't be sure whether the beast was concerned one of us might fall in or if it just wanted us within easy reach. I nudged Sonja forward. As she took the first tentative step, a thought crossed my mind. *At least she'll be eaten first.*

I let out a small laugh and got a nasty look from her in reply. All I could do was shrug. We only had one choice. Find out what Big Red wanted.

He stood patiently, professor-like, as we made our way to the pad. Careful to not break the circle, we moved around to the ramp, up to the palisade. The creature made no move to stop us.

I could tell Sonja was thinking the same thing I was, that we could try to sprint for cover when we got to the open space, but the beast spoke first.

Its breath was as dry and hot as a Santa Ana wind, but its voice held mirth instead of malevolence. We were no threat to him. "Who enters my house uninvited?"

I figured I would ask the obvious question. "And you are?"

The beast's voice echoed off the stone walls. "Ba'al."

The way he said it scared me more than anything. Usually, these full-born demon types—Satan's spawn, the fallen, or whatever they were—liked to pontificate. They would tell their prey how great they were before the attack. Big and bad. Hell's general expected those before him to know exactly who he was. In one word.

Sometimes, I wished I could keep my mouth shut. This was one of those times. "The place was unoccupied at the time. Well, except for the hired help." I looked at Sonja. "It was, right?"

Her glare told me she wished I knew how to keep my mouth closed as well.

"I see you have managed to keep the gate closed so far," Ba'al said. "But not much longer."

I fought to sound as though I wasn't ready to run screaming like my inner child, which had already fled. "There has been a bit of a problem with all travel between the realms."

Ba'al twitched ever so slightly, as if I confirmed something he wanted to know. "The only question I have is are you going to open the gates and return my home to me, or must I take it?"

I spread my hands wide. "Welcome home?"

"LEAVING SO SOON?" Ba'al stood inside of the summoning circle. He hadn't tried to leave or break out. He just stood, waiting and watching as I prepared the circle for our own departure.

I'd hesitated to engage him further. I needed to focus because I didn't want to leave anything to chance. Sonja was bringing everyone else down from the throne room. Tellia was helping Nate as he limped his way around the Hellgate. A crack had formed along one side. Shrieks and howls bubbled up from below.

Ba'al's voice dug into me. *You are the one who freed me?*

I looked around to see if anyone was directly behind me to take the blame, but no such luck. I scrambled to figure out what was he talking about, but either I looked puzzled enough, or the beast was rattling around in my head. Maybe he'd get lost in there. My inner juvenile delinquent wondered who'd be more scared having one more being running around in there, and how long it would take Ba'al to pack up and leave after listening to Tsauriel for a while. *I see. You did not mean to do so when you destroyed Negal's little plan? The Triumvirate.*

He was reading at least some of my thoughts. I was starting to Sense him at the edges of my mind. At the same time, I was reading some of his thoughts, and it was enough to make me feel like I was drowning in molasses. Even so, I only lowered Tsauriel's odds to 50:50 in a fair fight. I did see through his mind where and how he'd been held under Buziba's pleasure palace in the dungeons. What else had I turned loose when I blew open Buziba's house of sin?

Even so, it is worthy of reward. What is it you desire?

I ignored him, pouring the ring of salt.

Free me, and your wish is my command. But do not wait too long. I cannot control the Hellgate or those who come through as long as I remain in here.

"So that's your game?" I turned to face the beast. "If you're stuck inside the ring, why come through now? Why not just attack? It's obvious you knew there were only a handful of us in here, and we have no control over the defenders."

His lips thinned, a small curl at the edge of his mouth. *I will be released as soon as the gate opens. And why spend troops when all I needed to do was come in and talk?* Bony nubs along his back and arms shot out into long spikes.

A bony crocodilian head on a long undulating neck broke through the crack in the Hellgate, wearing the sheen of the portal like a collar.

Tick. Tock. This thing isn't going to hold much longer.

Tellia stared up at the beast as she edged by with Nate in tow.

"Hurry up." I pointed to the circle, barely holding the beast in check. "Whatever you do, don't break it."

You are beginning to fall out of my favor, mortal.

Tellia shouted. Ba'al held a watchful eye on Nate. I couldn't be sure if the daemon really tripped, was influenced by the dark god, or was just looking for a better deal. His foot slipped into the blood, but Tellia grabbed him and threw him into the clear with more strength than I knew she had.

"Tellia?"

She looked up at the beast then at me. "It's fine."

I wasn't so sure things were fine as I watched the way Nate bent down in the circle to study the breach. It wasn't enough to break it, but I could see the field weakening. The portal ring bobbed on the energy waves coming from the Hellgate. If the charged portal ring made contact with the Hellgate, we wouldn't have time to know before the fortress and everything for a mile around was vaporized. "Get up here."

A great claw reached through the gap, snagging the wall of the Hellgate and tearing back more of the skin of the portal. Then another appeared on the other side of the reptilian head and its snapping jaws.

Ba'al chuckled. "How I have missed my pets."

Sonja arrived with the rest of the party. Abhile stood agape.

I waved them back. "You didn't tell them?"

Sonja shouted back, "Tell them what? Hell was opening up shop in the basement, and the proprietor of the establishment was behind the bar?"

Bars. "Sonja, get the portcullis closed while I make the final preparations, then get to the circle." I got everyone inside as she unleashed a ball of fire against the chains.

Sonja drew a short blade. "It's not working."

The creature pulled itself through the hole and unfurled a long set of wings. If it wasn't a damn dragon, I didn't know what it was.

Sonja pointed up to the top of the wall where the chains ended in a pair of great spindles. "Blast the winch."

I unleashed everything in a chain of fireballs, dousing everything in a spreading blazing pool. "I've done what I can." I glanced over. Both heavy wooden spools were burning. One had cracked and left the gate sagging but open. Sonja threw her hands in the air but didn't unleash another blast. "Forget it. We're out of here."

She crossed into the circle, and I filled in the last gap. I touched it with power to charge it, and at the same time Ba'al rammed against the field that held him. I unrolled the scroll and touched the first sigil. The field around us shimmered, and it seemed as though we were looking through a waterfall.

The dragon hissed but took flight, rising into the rafters.

"Are you ready with the ring?" I asked.

Sonja held it between her fingers. "Now?"

"Not yet." The second sigil was dull. Josiah's note said it shouldn't take but a couple of seconds.

A loud crack signaled that one of the tree trunks holding up the gate had given up its hold. The gate sagged further but gave us no protection.

"What are you waiting for?" Abhile shouted.

The scroll crumpled in my hand as I clenched my teeth. "Another moment."

Abhile stared at me. She looked so small as she hunched over. But it was the look in her eyes that did me in. I'd failed her.

Another of the winged creatures drug itself through the Hellgate. The opening was widening.

Free me, and live another day. I heard Ba'al's voice clearly in my head.

I focused on the sigil. A faint glow formed around the upper edge. "Almost there."

Ba'al slammed his mighty shoulder against his cell. If I could see it cracking, I was sure he could too. "Sonja, if he gets free, punch it and blow the Hellgate. No matter what."

She licked her pursed lips and nodded.

A dull roar raced through the fortress, followed by a shock wave.

The blast sent the gate crashing down between the forces racing our way. I hoped the wood and iron could hold the tide back long enough for us to escape.

A third dragon, this one larger than the last two, landed on the edge of the gate. Its tail flicked into the ring floating just above the Hellgate. The trigger in Sonja's hands dulled but stayed lit.

The big boy didn't have wings big enough to fly. Like a Komodo with a body the size of a truck, it waddled in our direction.

The sigil glowed dully. "Punch it, Sonja."

She dropped the ring, shattering it. The charged ring over the portal screamed like a banshee.

Ba'al stared at the object he'd been ignoring. With some realization, he slammed against his cell. Again and again. The dragon slammed his head against my delicate ring.

"Why are we still here?" Abhile asked with a tremble in her voice.

I hit the second sigil for a third time. "It's not—"

The bottom fell out from under us. I tumbled. The air was burning, singeing my skin. If not for the intense heat, it felt just like my last trip to the underworld, just not as wet.

"…working." My voice echoed around the inky blackness of the chamber. Compared to Los Diablos, the room was cold. The stones. The cold, damp stones felt good on my singed skin. "We made it."

"Yes." The voice of Reginald Sinclair echoed in the darkness. "Yes, you did."

"THIS IS INCONVENIENT." Sinclair fired up a lone torch in the darkness. "I'd hoped we would be able to meet in private."

Reginald Maxwell Sinclair the Fourth, mayor and governor of Phoenix Grove. The high counselor and wizard who put the ass in assembly. He was also Brighid's grandfather, who believed I'd been responsible for her death and a lot of others.

"Some things have changed," I said. "We don't need this feud."

"The trial may have been resolved but not to my satisfaction. I still have a right to challenge by duel."

I couldn't be sure what he'd done, but the barrier around us held fast. Through it, I could Sense something else. I assumed it was a trap. "Yes, and if you want to take that path, I'm ready. But at least make sure you—"

He huffed. "I know everything I need to."

"Not even close."

The elder Sinclair stepped to the other side of the barrier. He was hunched over, and everything about the once-proud man drooped. It was as if he'd aged a thousand years for every day I'd been gone. "It'll have been an unfortunate accident. So many people being summoned here. The incantation just couldn't take it in these difficult times."

"Sinclair, just listen for one minute."

"I've listened enough." He leaned in, almost touching the barrier. If it hadn't been there, he would have struck out. Instead, he let his tongue do the work. "Josiah will be here any minute. Let's just get this wrapped up, shall we?"

"Grandfather." Drea's voice strained to the edge of breaking. "It's me. I'm here. Your little *Bandia*."

The old man's hand shook, dripping flaming oil to the floor. "Brighid? It's not possible."

Drea walked forward, her hands splayed out as she'd done when we were kids. "It is."

"No. A trick. Another of his lies." Sinclair violently shook his head. "You're *her* daughter."

"Yes." She grabbed Tellia's arm, thrusting her to the front. "And no."

He dropped the torch and fell to the floor. He half-covered his mouth and eye with one hand while crawling backward, pulling himself with the other. "You're a Púca. Get away."

217

I grabbed and held them both. "It's true. Her body and spirit, just not joined. We can—"

Sinclair uttered a garbled cry and ran for the darkness. I barely Sensed when he left.

"That went better than expected," Anraoi quipped.

"No. No, it didn't," I said. The room was getting warmer, and a mist was seeping up from the floor, lit only by the torch lying nearby. "We need to get out of here, or we'll be really crispy."

We all began using every bit of magic at our disposal. Between eight practitioners of different arts and one geeky daemon, the mist was winning.

It had reached our waists when I Sensed another presence in the room. "Sinclair, are you back to let us out or just watch us die?"

The voice was gravelly. "Damn."

"Josiah?"

"I ain't your fairy godmother." The burly figure of Josiah MacGregor, my grandfather, snapped out one of the old words, bringing the braziers around the room to life. "Tutu's at the cleaners."

"Can you get us out of here?"

He stared at the rising mists. "What did that crazy old bastard do?" He reached into his pocket and pulled out a mason jar. Opening the lid, he threw it at the edge of the circle. A bright flash and crack of thunder stunned us.

I shook my head and found my six-foot frame snatched off the ground in a great bear hug. "Good to see you, boy."

218

I returned the hug.

"Bad news, though." He set me down. "The punch'll have to be straight. That was the good stuff for your party I had to waste."

"I DON'T KNOW." My Kodiak bear of a grandfather pulled out a towel to clean up the residue in the chamber. My cousin Mari came in with a soft whoosh and took the rest of our merry band to the Grove. "That message was secure. Only a few people knew you were coming. But I'm going to get to the bottom of this."

"He knew about the incantation and messed with the scroll. How'd he do that?"

My grandfather stuck out his paw of a hand. "Let me see it." He took the scroll and shook his head. The edges were charred, and a few spots were blackened. "This isn't what I sent. Very close. But it's not even the same parchment."

"So he managed to tamper with FaeMail?" I tasted a handful of the crystals from the floor. Sea salt, but very bitter and smoky. A heavy negative charge. Serious dark hoodoo. "Is that even possible?"

"Little bastard." He touched the innermost ring of the circles that made up the chamber floor. The place I'd been held captive before the trial. The place I'd almost died. The place where I'd been made an offer to join the Divine. And refused.

The stone embedded in the floor glowed a pale green. Josiah chanted in a blend of languages, mostly an extinct form of elvish.

The pale-green stone rose from the floor and gradually turned into a sphere. Once it took form, it spit out a pixie wearing a small brown uniform and cursing a blue streak.

"Tuck." Josiah's bark froze him in place. He waved the scroll just outside of the circle. "What's the meaning of this?"

"I was in da' middle of a delivery." The pixie chewed on the corner of one of his six fingers. "That's a scroll. I suppose dis is a rush? Where you want I should takes it?"

Josiah knelt next to the fae, still towering over him. His eyes narrowed as he spoke in a harsh whisper that echoed through the chamber. "Haven't you already delivered this one?"

He leaned over, pretending to study it. "I deliver lots. If dat's the last one you gave me, I'm sorry. I guess the parcel didn't make it through."

The pixie leapt as I spoke from behind. "Disappointed?"

"Oh, ah, good to see youse again." Rows of needles flashed in his mouth. "Good to see you made it through."

Josiah slammed a wave of energy into the circle. "Unless you want your next route to be delivering pay stubs in Tartarus and love notes to Xibalba, start talking. Where's the one I gave you?"

"Isn't that—"

Another wave of energy pounded the cell. "Try again."

The pixie knelt, his hands in the air. "Governor Sinclair. He summoned me. Made me switch with him."

"How did he know you were carrying it?"

"I... I... I don't know. He summoned me here. Took the one you gave me and brought that one back a few hours later. I swears." He bowed over. "I didn't haves no choice."

"Betray me again, pixie, or violate the oath, and you'll have thought this was heaven." Josiah chanted again in the old language.

"Now wait, I tolds you—"

"Be gone." The pixie was sucked into a green ball of energy that shot through the floor.

I stared at the spot where I'd stood not that long ago. "Where'd you send him?"

Josiah chuckled. "Gehenna. He'll be delivering fresh parchment to the scribes for a few weeks and then delivering the notes from the inquisitors."

"That doesn't sound so bad."

"Besides that being one of the starter jobs for FaeMail delivery folk, it's a nasty demotion." The old man wiped his hands on his jeans to disperse the last of the energy. "What's bothering me is how Sinclair found out. Only one person could have told him."

"Who?"

"Mari."

JOSIAH'S HOMESTEAD BUSTLED with energy. The rest of my party had cleaned up, except for Nate. He looked as good as he was going to get.

I didn't know what to do, and I sensed Josiah was shaken. Mari was his protégé. She had taken over the daily operations for the *Librarium Occultus*, the repository of lost and hidden knowledge. She'd even put in a small cafe, although I didn't think Josiah was thrilled about that part.

Was it possible she'd betrayed Josiah? Me? She'd been the one to prepare the summoning incantations and embed them in the scroll. Who else could have made subtle changes so quickly or would have known what they were for?

If she had, I didn't really want to know. But more than just my life was on the line. If she would betray her own family, she was a threat to the whole town, one of the last few refuges for the Veiled peoples.

Mari turned the corner. She carried her strength under a deceptively soft exterior. She was shorter than me, curvy, but solidly built. Her daily sparring seemed to have given her build more definition and more confidence in the way she carried herself.

Her eyes beamed as they locked with mine. We'd been closer than siblings once. Nothing in her gaze led me to believe that had changed. She threw her powerful arms around me with a squeal.

"We need to talk, cuz," I said.

She grinned. "This sounds serious."

Josiah grimaced. "It is."

She rubbed my arm. "One minute. Let me finish—"

We both bristled at our grandfather's command. "Now."

She shrugged and cut me the same look she'd given me any time we'd been caught as kids playing in the restricted stacks. We all packed into the large closet that served as a safe room. Nothing could have penetrated those walls while we talked.

She crossed her arms. "What's up?"

Josiah held the scroll in his hands. "Did you prepare this?"

She took the crumbling parchment in her hands. She bit her lip as she ran her fingers over the embedded incantations. "No. Where'd this come from?"

"It's what was delivered to me," I said. "It barely worked to pull us all through."

"How?"

In the small space, Josiah's whisper was deafening. "I was hoping you knew."

"The parchment, it isn't ours. I'd never use this. You're lucky. I'd have to experiment a little, but I think this wasn't meant to work." Tears welled in her eyes. "You could've been burned alive."

"We nearly were." I rubbed my singed skin.

Josiah let out a deep sigh. "Did anyone else know what you were making? Anyone know about the summoning?"

"No. Never." She paled. "Oh."

I took her clammy hand. "What?"

"This is a copy of the first one." She slid down against the wall.

I knelt next to her. "First one?"

"I know why you survived." She scrambled to get up. "There were too many of you. I had to rework the incantation after I found out it was more than just the three of you."

Josiah blocked the door. "Where do you think you're going?"

"The office. It's the only possibility. Someone got hold of the first attempt."

MARI SEARCHED FRANTICALLY through the small office in the Librarium. "It was here. Right here." She pounded on a pile of notes and papers that looked like works in progress. "I hadn't destroyed it yet."

I flipped through the nearby stack of books. "Has anyone been here? Visited?"

She sorted through the same box for the tenth time. "No. Who would've cared or known to look?"

"Did you leave at any time?"

She shrugged. "Only long enough to run to the greenhouse. I was out of bindweed. I needed to make more ink for the sigil."

"Who else was there?"

"At Kukka's?" She sat in the worn rolling chair and ran her fingers through her cropped hair. "A dozen people. All the regulars."

"Any of Sinclair's people?"

"How would I know? This is a small town. He's lost a lot of his support, but he's still managed to hold onto his power." She closed her eyes. "I don't remember. I was so focused on getting this done. I wasn't paying attention. I could've run into the old man himself and not known."

"Maybe it's time I have a talk with the governor. He found out from somewhere."

She sat in silence. I couldn't believe she would have intentionally endangered me or anyone else. I could believe she'd been sloppy. I couldn't blame her, though. Much of what she did for the library was preparing these types of devices, magical contracts, and capturing histories. On her desk at that very moment were a half-dozen semi-completed projects. How could anyone have guessed what they were?

It only made sense someone had been watching them very closely for any sign I might return. With the travel between the realms so difficult, what had they been expecting?

"Mari? How much have people been traveling from the Grove?" I asked.

She shook her head. "Virtually none. A few private passageways to the near realms and private estates are rumored to still be traversable some of the time, but none of the major gates."

"And the summoning circle in the assembly chamber. Has anyone else come through?"

She sniffed. "Not that I know of. Josiah'd know better than me. But it does sit on the edge of several of the major realms."

"And the bindweed. Could someone have been watching for that?"

"No. It's used for almost any number of common bases for workings." She mindlessly shuffled papers on her desk. "But I did get a couple of Wych leaves."

She moved to a cupboard on the wall and pulled out one of the hundreds of jars. "I used one of the sprigs. Two are missing."

JOSIAH LISTENED PATIENTLY as we explained what we'd found. Mari did a quick test on the scroll that had brought us through. Someone had worked enough fennel into the ink to have incinerated one or two people but not explode in the assembly chamber. Nine of us had shared the dosage, and Nate had doubtlessly absorbed more than his fair dose, with his daemon nature and all. It looked as though it had actually sped up his healing process with the new leg.

A couple of healers had come and given us all a dose of something blue that tasted like honeyed vinegar to speed the healing from the mild burns. We sat around the kitchen table, discussing what to do next.

Anraoi wanted to go to the Summer fae village outside of the Grove to see his daughter Claire and friends. He invited Abhile along, but everyone agreed that she and Sonja should remain in the shadows for now and would stay at Josiah's.

Aindrias, Anraoi's former Sergeant at Arms in the Summer Court and caretaker for his daughter, was trapped in Los Angeles, where he'd been living under his mortal identity of Evan Underhill. The rest of the family was in the Grove.

We didn't mention the breach to anyone else even though Abhile remembered triggering a snowstorm during transit. I didn't want to tell her it wasn't a dream. She may have saved us by keeping Sinclair's trap to a low sunburn.

Mari led everyone to guest rooms for rest.

I felt for Nate. He was out from under Hell's thumb, but for how long?

It wasn't my problem. I'd fulfilled my vow. As long as the daemon stayed out of trouble, I didn't care. If he managed to do that, I would deal with him when I could.

I'd gone out to the barn. Josiah led out Drea and Tellia. Brighid lay in wait, but we all knew the problem. We had five personalities and four bodies. Someone had to go.

If Tellia were to be believed, she'd already made the tough decision. She would return Brighid's body to her. But it wasn't fair. It wasn't right. It wasn't my choice.

I just knew what I felt was right. What I wanted. What I needed.

I couldn't be the one to make the choice.

Tellia did.

If I could have the device repaired or find another way, she would surrender the body to Brighid, no matter the consequences.

227

No matter what, I would be an executioner.

THE SIGIL GLOWED in midair. I'd done the rite, and I held out faith he could find me.

Melvin, you demented angel, you're my only hope.

I was so screwed.

Minutes ticked by, and I stared into the box holding the broken device. I still only had a guess, even if it was an educated one, about the nature of its true purpose. I couldn't be sure it would work even if it was intact. I hated to admit it, but with Tellia in the mix, I was afraid I couldn't do anything but make things worse.

Melvin had never taken this long to respond to my summoning. Even if he wasn't going to come, he would send some sort of message. Maybe he couldn't traverse from wherever he was. Or maybe I'd crossed some sort of line and was on my own.

I gave up after more than a half hour. I only had so many ways to try to keep my mind off of everything that was going on.

It was a hundred yards from the barn to the back door of Josiah's house. I had made it less than ten feet out the door of the barn when a loud whooshing sound came from behind me. I spun, grabbing the blessed blade I'd spent fifteen minutes of my solitude sharpening.

Melvin finished folding his wings behind him. "I was beginning to wonder how long you were going to keep me waiting."

The angel's platinum hair was long and pointing in as many directions as there were strands on his head. And he'd grown a beard. He wore patterned pajama pants and a brown cardigan over a stained T-shirt. And bowling shoes.

"What gives?" I asked.

"I was at The Dude in the Desert fest when you called." He crossed his arms and mustered a scowl. "You know I can't go in the barn without, you know. Permission."

"Oh, damn." I'd forgotten Josiah had warded it against Melvin after an incident involving a carton of imp eggs, a portal to Times Square, an automatic pitching machine, and a gremlin in a Gremlin on New Year's Eve. "He hasn't forgiven you yet?"

"Let's just say he still won't let me use his lathe." He shook his head, the thick mane swaying in the wind like shimmering sea grass. "It's good to see you, little nihilist. So what's been going on?"

I handed him the box and updated him on the latest situation with Drea, Brighid, and Tellia, and told him what I was trying to do. "Look in the box."

He sat rapt as I recounted getting the device and encountering Rahm. "Man, you keep making soup sandwiches." He held the two parts in his hands. "And you got this where?"

"A really strange museum in Seattle. I doubt there's much left now."

"I hate missing the magic carpet ride tonight." He ran his hands through his hair and snapped his fingers. The beard was gone, his

229

sharp jaw was clean shaven, and he wore a cream suit. "There's only one person I know and trust that might be able to help you with this. He's been wanting to meet you anyway."

"Who?"

He flashed his pearly smile. "You'll see."

THE ANGEL SNICKERED as he folded his wings around us. "Hold on tight."

His arms were vises as they crushed me. He smelled like five-day-old chicken wings, pizza, sweat, and a hundred other things I didn't want to think about. "Melvin, you really need a shower."

"A what?" His feathers fluttered in an invisible wind. "Oh yeah, well, you're the one that called me. I was busy. Came anyway."

For the few seconds it lasted, we were in the eye of a tornado. The world grew dark, and shrill winds howled in protest as we crossed the realms. The scent of ozone mixed with cotton candy, a hint of dill, and beads of sweat built under my nose. Melvin's wings stretched wide, letting in a blast of frigid air that turned pools of sweat into a sheen of frost.

When he put me down, I sank two feet into a snowbank. My reflexes kicked in, and the Leviskin shifted to arctic gear. "Where are we?"

Melvin flexed his shoulders, retracting the wings into his back. A gust of wind almost knocked me over onto the sidewalk. The snow was falling so heavily, it was hard to see the wall a few feet away. Somehow, Melvin didn't seem all that out of place in a summer suit in the midst of a whiteout. "Toronto. The office is over here."

I got madder with every step. I was frozen, wet, and couldn't get Melvin's barnyard scent out of my head. He floated, stepping lightly as he jumped from snowbank to snowbank then through a wide archway into a Gothic building.

The doorman, in an improbably clean black coat, grimaced as I kicked snow off onto the marble floor of the lobby. I sneered back and caught up with Melvin where he leaned across the redwood reception desk, his gleaming pearls not working their charms as well as he'd hoped. The wall behind the pair of twin receptionists read H-Forge Technologies.

"Hit the button," he said.

A tall blonde rose from behind the desk, pushing Melvin back. "Mr. H is currently unavailable. Try making an appointment."

"C'mon." He flicked his own golden hair over his ear. "He'll answer for me."

She pursed her flaming lips. "I am trying to be courteous, but the last time I did this for you, I wound up in the lab for a month. On the wrong end of testing."

"I promise." He stuck his thumb over his shoulder in my direction. "He wants to meet him."

"And the last time I heard that line—"

His voice was singsong as he pulled a dozen tulips out of the air and stuck them in a water glass on the counter. "He's on the list. It's a surprise for your boss."

"Name." Her voice was cold enough that I almost walked back outside. "And if he's not on the list, I'll be plucking feathers in a way you *won't* like."

"Trust—"

"Name."

He drew a deep breath. "Forrester, Greyson."

For the barest moment, her skin flushed. "Well then. It seems he may be on the list."

Melvin relaxed and leaned against the edge of the desk. "That wasn't so hard, was it?"

"Keep your damnable self-righteous grin to yourself, angel." A whip-like tail wrapped around his throat and pulled him over the desk toward her. He braced himself against her desk and spread his wings for balance. "And you still owe me a weekend in New York. None of the off-Broadway stuff, either." She locked her lips onto him so tightly, I feared she might swallow him whole.

I drew power into my hands to help him, but he folded his wings and grabbed onto her. If an angel couldn't hold her off, what was I supposed to do?

The receptionist's twin shook her head at me as Melvin knocked over a potted plant and the camera used for temporary IDs.

The tail unwound, releasing him. He and the blonde shared that smile that only the well-acquainted have and whispered something between them. He stood up and straightened his tie. "Check my calendar. And let me know what shows you want in advance. You know how hard it is to get the seats on short notice."

"I'm fickle. You should know that by now." She gave him a shy smile. "And if there's anything left of the wizard, I'm open to appetizers."

Hidden doors opened to reveal an elevator.

He ran his hands through his hair. "Come on."

The doors closed behind us, and the box jolted as we started a rapid ascent.

"What was that about?"

Melvin shrugged. "She's a succubus. It's a little game we play."

Melvin shook as I shoved him against the wall. "I thought those were demonic type beings?"

"We're all still Divines. And yeah. Things can get a little messed up at the office Christmas party."

THE ELEVATOR SHUDDERED to a stop. Melvin hummed and tapped out of step along with an instrumental version of an a capella harmony, which was insidiously playing just at the edge of human hearing.

His out-of-tune harmony got louder as I Sensed an energy field sweep over us. As it faded away, the doors peeled back to reveal a blinding light. Melvin stepped through with the tune still on his lips. I hoped he would work it out of his system quickly. Angelic obsessions could last for months or longer.

The brightness died down on the other side of the door as I stepped into an open space surrounded by windows. It was an office, taking up the entire floor. The skyline was clear, and the CN Tower gleamed in the daylight.

"Where'd the snow go?" I asked.

Melvin sang out to the tune in his head. "Heph, you have visitors."

"One can't be too careful these days." A tall and tawny man stepped through a pocket door hidden in the column housing the elevator. His charcoal three-piece suit moved with him as if it were skin. Gray tufts of hair strategically framed his olive face. "How are you doing, my fine, feathered friend?"

"I've brought a guest." Melvin strutted like a peacock with his feathers spread.

"I see." A wry smile crossed his face, and he maintained a measured pace as he approached me. "Mr. Forrester?"

I nodded, drawn in by his infectious grin. "And you are?"

"I go by many names." His hand, tortured by the ages, extended toward me. "I expect you are used to that. I am Hephaestus, but you may call me Heph if you like."

I shouldn't have been surprised by the strength and power from his grip, but I was. My Senses told me he was evaluating me through the short but draining contact between us. I briefly

234

wondered why all old gods spoke in a clipped British accent. "Blacksmith of the gods," I said.

"You flatter me. Yes, I've made a few gadgets over the years."

"I'm hoping you can help me with this." I drew the box holding the pieces of the device from my pack.

"One moment." He motioned toward the door he'd appeared through. "Shall we go to somewhere more suitable?"

I didn't know what difference it made, but I followed Melvin through the door with our host on my heels. As bright and orderly as his office may have been, the workshop we entered had been touched by a maelstrom. Even so, it seemed as if there was some pattern in the great disorder of workbenches, kilns, ovens, crucibles, anvils, and tools. And that was just near the door. Though the air was heavy and hot with sulphur and wood smoke, the lazy river of creative energy that flowed around us was intoxicating.

Our host shimmered and changed into a pair of worn leather pants and a flowing shirt. He wrapped his now significantly longer hair into a ponytail. "Much better."

"I've got—"

"Before we do that, let's fix your wardrobe." He fired off a few words, and the power in them felt like a simple incantation. My Leviskin shifted, turning into the basic skinsuit. "That's an older version. Try this one."

One of a half-dozen metal beings lumbered over, gears clicking with every movement. It carried a wrapped parcel, which Heph took and tossed to me.

Underneath the paper was a pale tan bodysuit that weighed half of my current skinsuit. I switched into the bodysuit, and as I pulled it on, it made tiny changes to perfectly fit to my body. I'd thought the old ones were comfortable, but this was like wearing a cloud. After arranging all of the items I carried with me, I shifted into my normal jeans and shirt with just a thought. "What is this stuff?"

Heph took a gentle bow. "My latest incarnation of the suits. They're made from cultured Leviathan skin, woven with some faerie fibers, and a few other trade secrets."

"Leviathan?"

"Don't tell anyone." He winked. "They're quite difficult to find these days. They have the ability to morph at will, and I had a small sample of skin. It's taken a few hundred years, but it's finally working out."

I shook my head. "Amazing."

He reached out toward me. "Shall we see what you've brought?"

I took the pieces from the box and placed them on a nearby workbench.

He lifted a piece for study. "Do you know what you have here?"

"I hope so."

"Why would you need such a damned implement?" He gently laid the piece next to the other half.

I described the situation with Drea and Brighid, and now Tellia, and how I'd acquired the device. He listened with the patience of ages until I described Rahm slicing it in half.

236

"Wait, this Rahm. Can you describe the weapon? Few should be able to do any damage to anything forged for Abaddon."

"A spear." I held my hands about two feet apart. "The tip was about this long, four inches wide, and diamond-shaped. Reflective, almost like mirrored sunglasses. The staff was unstained wood, light in color. I didn't get that good a look at it while he attacked me."

"And your assailant? What did he look like?"

I cut through the fog of everything that had happened back to that night. "Once he had the spear in hand, he grew a few feet. Musculature doubled in size. The soft exterior he wore melted away. A lycan I think, but not like any I've seen before."

"Fur? Did he grow fur?"

I shuddered. "Yeah. Thick, bristly stuff. Just before he knocked me out."

"Well then." He rose and looked around. He deliberated and loped to the far end of the room. Seemingly haphazardly, he glanced into and discarded a dozen boxes or more from shelves. He returned with a long wooden box. "Deliver this to Priscilla. She will know what to do."

"I'd be happy to, but she's missing."

"That is impossible. Unless…"

"We were attacked and overrun by a pack of—"

Heph nodded. "Let me guess. Werewolves. You must tell me everything."

"THERE'S A POSSIBILITY." Heph opened the wooden box and withdrew the bladed stave it held. The shaft was made of pristine white wood. The wide blade on the end shone like polished silver and hummed a deep melody. "You may be able to subdue him with this."

I took it in my hand. The shaft stretched to eight feet and snapped back to a little over a foot. The blade popped into a mace, an axe head, then back to the blade. All in under two seconds. "What the hell was that?" The blade sank into the floor where I dropped it.

"That is the dhia marbhthóir. One of the finest weapons I ever created." It sang to me as he drew it from the granite. "She likes you."

"She? She likes me?" I backed away even though I Sensed a pull from it. "How do you know?"

He spun the staff in his hands. "She was showing off for you. A taste of her capabilities."

"And if she hadn't?"

"You might have lost a hand." He laid the weapon back in the box. "Or she might have put an eye out."

The feeling changed to an odd melancholy that eased as I approached it. Her.

"The shaft is Yew. The blade is crafted from airgidon, a form of living silver steel. The straps and grips are Leviskin. If you can command her, she'll take most any form you might need." He pointed to the box. "Pick it up."

"I don't know if this is such a good idea." Even then, I knew I would wield this weapon. Without touching it, I could feel it calling to me, wanting to slice through air and bone, shatter wood and stone. We were connected.

Melvin wrapped his arm around my shoulders. I expected him to say something calming or reinforcing… or at least helpful. But no. He shook my shoulder. "We're on a clock. Tell the pocketknife you two are going to have a happy life, and learn to use it later."

I elbowed the angel and paused just above the blade's gleaming surface. It leapt from the case the final inch into my hands. A husky voice tickled the back of my mind as I turned the stave over in my hands and twirled the staff. The shimmering Chaldean bands wound around me and flowed back to the staff. A wave of euphoria passed over me, and I knew it was time to put it back in the box.

"The weapon finally has a master." Heph grinned. "Now that the bonding is over, I think we need to meet the devil in the details."

The intoxication evaporated to be replaced by a garrote around my throat. "What do you mean?"

"It's an enchanted weapon. A very powerful one. Its first master is the most important, like a parent to a child. It will define all it is and will ever be. Anyone who wields it in the future will feel your influence. Its power will come from you." His eyes clouded over. "And so will the cost of its use."

"Cost? What kind?"

He had the look of a proud parent as he stared at the stave. "Nothing is free, lad. The more you ask of her, the more she will ask of you. As to what she wants? I suggest you two get acquainted and dance a bit while I delve into the device from the armory."

I tucked the box under my arm. "Does my new prom date like flowers?"

"Ask her."

MY BODY ACHED. It felt like only minutes, but I'd spent two hours with the stave. As long as I held it, I was energized, almost supercharged. Heph had proved right, though. At first, she—and I really had begun to think of her that way—would change hesitantly. The shaft lengthened, shortened, thickened, and thinned. The blade stretched, blunted, and curved. We fumbled with each other, stepped on each other's toes, and bumped our heads. Like trying line dancing unprotected in a mosh pit. I bore the wounds to prove it.

Then we clicked.

We moved as one. She anticipated me, my moves, my thoughts. We sambaed. We tangoed. We salsa danced. We were tribal. She led me through a Kathak.

We danced until we were spent. She went back in the box, and I went looking for somewhere to pass out.

Melvin snored quietly in the corner, and I found myself envying him. His leg twitched like a dog dreaming about chasing a car.

Hephaestus was bent over a long streamer of woven parchment. He waved me over and made me recount and relive most of the last ten years as he wove multicolored threads through the blank slate into a fractal river, occasionally making short notes along the timeline.

"This makes no sense, lad." Heph tried to connect two threads woven through the chart. "You're missing something. Mairsile would slit her own child's throat to make a point, let alone someone who failed her. Second chances aren't exactly her modus operandi."

I slumped into a corner. The sparring had taken more out of me than I'd realized. Or maybe it was the weapon. Either way, I looked around for anything that would keep my eyes open or give me any sense of focus. "Are you saying I'm special?"

He left the budding tapestry of my life to kneel next to me. He opened a small medical kit and dabbed at the blood splattered on my face. "I can only come up with a few reasons she would do this. Either something is keeping her from unleashing her murderous temper, or you are being the good little puppet and doing exactly what she wants."

The illusion of the nursemaid vanished as he plucked a hair from my head and walked away. "The question is not who's beating your drum, but who is leading the orchestra."

I stretched my jellied muscles to see what the old craftsman was doing as he dabbed my blood onto the stretch of parchment. He strung the hair through a needle and wove it with the thread like a snake undulating through the grass.

He ran his thick fingers along a mostly blank stretch. "You have gaps in your memory, I take it."

"An understatement." I couldn't understand anything happening in the designs formed in the cloth. The look on the old god's face proved that he did. "What do you see?"

"It's incomplete," he stammered as he fumbled with one of the spools feeding thread. "I think we should let the process take its course. You should rest."

My exhaustion fled. "You're stalling. What is it? What is it you see?"

The blacksmith's fire reflected in his gaze. "It's what I do not see. Your past is more than just unclear. It's uncertain. As if it could be rewoven. And there is something fixed in your future."

"Is that possible? Like time travel?"

He scoffed. "No. What is spun is woven. That which is on the spool is yet to be incorporated into the pattern."

"You're not making any sense."

"Exactly." He waved and paced back and forth along the length of the cloth. "You are here. This time has not yet happened, but there it is." He pointed along one end. "And here, there are huge gaps. It's like there is something hidden, buried inside you, your past, your future. But I cannot see what it is."

I Pushed the new Leviskin to open up and reveal my ever-changing mark. "Something like this?"

He gasped. "A Fato Sigillum. This explains much."

Just his mention of the words caused the mark to flare and warm me. "A what?"

242

He trembled as he held his hand barely an inch over the sigil. "It's an indelible mark. You bear the burdens of the incomplete task of another. You carry not only your own destiny, but theirs as well."

"Whose? What is it?"

I WAS SPENT. The artisan to the gods had no more answers, at least for the moment. Or if he did, he wasn't saying.

He tried to distract me with some of his other toys. His explosive devices infused with silver would have made Melanippe drool to have them as a prototype for her own armory. He had ampules of pheromones and said, "One drop would draw in every Werewolf, dog, hound, and canine lover for miles." I had to be sure not to get any of it on me, or I'd find out a new meaning for dog pile and animal love.

Fascinated by my ceramic blades, Heph took one and in return gave me a box filled with "improvements." He even included some new formulas to try in the injector-tipped ones.

I lost myself in the flurry of devices he presented, but I finally pared them down to a list of implements and items I thought I could use. If I'd been willing to open a portal back to my lab, I could only imagine the stuff I could've taken with me, but I was keeping the secret of my hideaway to myself. Who knew what a devious old god like Hephaestus could do if he even had a hint such a place existed, much less knew what the sigils to call it looked like.

He refused to answer any more questions and started tinkering with the cloth that detailed my life again. Something about my mark had inspired him, and he set to work with more threads and sentient needles. I decided to rest while I had the opportunity, and before I fell over and passed out.

One of Heph's automaton assistants appeared with a blanket. I wasn't sure whether he had commanded for it to be done, or if I just looked that tired. I accepted it and found a quiet corner. I'd never known Melvin to sleep. I didn't even think about angels doing so, but he was still passed out, drooling on a couch that was way too small for him.

I closed my eyes, and the streaks of color wove patterns before me. They danced around the stave and intertwined with the Anima Arca blade. Crystals grew and fell from it. They unraveled and ended at a wall. I Sensed something behind it, but I had no idea what, beyond the power.

Finally, there was blissful silence. Darkness. Peace.

The bed beneath me was soft, comfortable, and warm. I didn't have to open my eyes to know. And I Sensed her there. "Hi, Tsauriel."

Her deep sigh was confirmation enough.

I pulled the covers away and visualized my clothes. The stone floor was cold beneath my feet. A cool breeze sneaked through the cracked window. The fireplace held smoldering embers.

The angel swayed in a rocking chair, her eyes closed and hands folded in her lap. "We must speak. You have been avoiding us."

The good news was that my body didn't ache. I hoped it would be the same when I woke up. "I wouldn't go that far, but I have been a little busy."

"Humph."

"If this is another speech about how I'm endangering you and the golden boy, save it."

Her face was grim as her eyes snapped open. "I think we both know there is no point in again having that conversation."

I didn't need any magical abilities to detect the scorn in her voice. "What, then?"

"The weapon. The stave. You must learn to master it." She wrapped her fingers around my throat. "Or you will be its servant."

Her grip was closing to the point I couldn't speak. I tried to pry her hands apart, but my gurgling and head nodding was enough to prove she had my attention.

She pushed me away. "Ladon awaits you."

"WE'VE GOT SOMETHING." Melvin shook me awake. The cold from the stone floor had soaked through me and left me stiff, but soothed the aches and pains of the beating I'd gotten from my golden trainer.

Ladon had taken the essence of my experience of the weapon and its magical signature to manifest a version of it. As impossible as it was to believe, he'd been holding back on me in our sparring sessions. This time, I had gotten some pleasure from drawing blood more than once, even if he'd refused to acknowledge my small victories.

If the experience of sparring with Ladon validated anything, it was that the blade was powered by life energy. For lack of anything else, it would feed on me. Ladon's idea was that much of the draining was an imprinting on the weapon more than being a power source, but I couldn't be sure. He had much more experience than I did in such things. Or so he had said.

My body screamed in protest, and I unlocked my body and pulled myself up. "What is it?"

The angel bounced around. "We figured out what your museum piece is." He grabbed me by the arm and babbled incoherently about the mind's eye and manifesting visions as he dragged me to a far corner of the workshop. Heph had the two pieces of the black basket held in clamps.

The engineer in him had taken over, and he had recreated the basket on paper. Notes in an alien shorthand outlined each spire, and arrows had been drawn that were running in every direction. "The Anima Congero." He spoke without looking up.

I looked over his shoulder in the hopes of understanding more.

He touched the end of a wire of the basket with the probe from an oblong contraption. Not getting the response he'd expected, he glanced over the top of his violet-hued glasses. "Loosely translated, it's a life-source consolidator. Two come in, one comes out."

My stomach was in knots. "What would that be used for? Can it help us separate Drea and Brighid's spirits?"

I could see why Melvin got along so well with the old god. They were both mad scientists at heart. There was a certain malevolent glee in his tone as he got lost in his mind. "All of this is before my time, you see, but I have studied them well. In those early days, it was all about power. Imagine if you had someone weaker than you, but who had a power you wanted. Or needed. You would draw them in, and whoever's spirit survived emerged with the life force, the power of the other. This device did that. It took the earliest beings and made them gods, monsters. Both. Divines feared and envied them."

I grabbed and shook the old god. "Can it do what I ask?"

"Possibly. More likely, it could merge them permanently or destroy them both." He stared at me blankly until a smoky haze cleared from his eyes. "Or it may not work at all. I can repair the damage, but you're asking me to change its purpose. Its nature. Its reason for being."

I leaned against the table and buried my head in my hands. I was empty. How could I ask them to trust me again when I couldn't guess what would happen? Could I really try to use a broken piece of mystic technology from a time before history? One that ultimately created myths and monsters?

Part of me wanted to throw the pieces of gnarled black metal into the furnace, or take a hammer to them, or shred them.

But it wasn't the device I was mad at. It was me. I hadn't been the one to create the problem, but I'd surely made it much worse. "No. I won't do it. Too risky. There has to be another way."

Melvin broke into a gaping smile. "Tell him about the other part."

For the angel to be so proud of himself, I expected that he knew of some new weapon. A way I could vacuum up the lives of my enemies with the device. "Let me guess. It also slices and dices? Combines my frequent flyer miles? What?"

Heph placed the two pieces into a box, out of sight. "What do you know of Zeus and the creation of man?"

"Not a damn thing."

He sketched out a series of pictures. "There is a tale that man once had two heads, four arms, and four legs. And came in three sexes. In a fit, Zeus split man into halves, never to be whole again."

I rested my head against the bench. "More myths."

"Almost." He continued talking as he walked to a nearby shelf. "The reality of the story is a little different. One of Zeus's daughters was seduced by a man, one who turned out to have some abilities. The man tried to take her power, but instead, he was slain, and his spirit drawn into her. It took some work and a ritual, but they were able to remove and banish his spirit."

"So an exorcism." I pounded on the table. "You want me to have Brighid exorcised like a common demon and sent wherever to free Drea."

Melvin nodded. "In essence, yes."

"And what about Brighid? I'm supposed to banish her off to some Hell?"

Heph returned with a wooden box under his arm. "That is where Zeus's story comes in. He was displeased at what the sorcerer had done to his daughter for the time they were joined. This little treasure can capture the spirit before it flees for the afterlife. You should be able to transfer it into the Anima Arca blade to move back into her body."

He opened the container and unrolled an object wrapped in leather. A golden hawk was perched on a multicolored cluster of crystals. "Here is the ritual and the instructions." He rolled up the paper he'd been sketching on and placed it in the box next to the vessel.

IT SEEMED SIMPLE. Simple enough, at least. Which meant it was horribly complicated, risky, and likely to blow up in my face. Then they hit me with the part that made me want to back away quickly.

I wouldn't be comfortable with the prescribed ritual unless I could test it first. And I couldn't figure out a way to test the soul catcher.

We also needed a particular curate to perform the ritual. If Priscilla had been around, she might have had another idea. Josiah's response to my message was reluctant, but he didn't have another option either.

Heph was tight lipped on the actual performance of the ritual. I was frustrated because I couldn't interpret many of the sigils or instructions. As a final clue, he drew a symbol I knew on the parchment. A golden quill.

Melvin looked uncomfortable as I asked questions, and the antiquarian inventor made some snide comment about only spoon-feeding me so much.

I'd have to call someone who was better versed in the wielders of the quill than I was. And I was still really pissed at him. I didn't know if I could trust him any more.

Maybe he didn't believe in me either.

But damned if I wasn't going to try to get his help.

Melvin dropped me off in Las Vegas with my freshly loaded pack of toys from Heph. I daydreamed about my garnet 1955 Indian Warrior that was possessed by the spirit of Ktesippe. Priscilla had never told me outright, but I'd begun to suspect the intelligence had been one of her Amazons who'd fallen in battle.

Ever since Priscilla had taken us on the run to find a way to reverse the effects on Drea and Brighid, and with the realms in chaos, most of the Amazons were in hiding. So were almost all other Veiled peoples. Wherever she was, I hoped Special K was being well cared for.

I had to settle for an abandoned Gremlin that Melvin assured me was safe. He worked a little of his magic, and it started right up. He laid his own version of a glamour over the car so no one would notice it, especially anyone who might be interested in a car whose plates hadn't been legal since the 1980s.

The streets were lightly populated with tourists as I cruised the strip on the way to the Mission of St. Cayetano. The little Erebite party in the desert had powered storms for hundreds of miles, and Vegas had taken the brunt of them. The major hotels and attractions were open, but a lot of glass in the buildings was still replaced with plywood.

The mission was a small chapel, but the only lights came from the back of an adjacent ranch-style house. Few of the other buildings in the neighborhood showed signs of life other than spray paint and broken windows.

I sat in the car and stared at the front door, knowing what I needed to do. I didn't worry about locking the car. Anything that could pierce the Veil could open my car like a can.

The porch step creaked as I put the least of my weight on it. My Senses felt something shuffling on the far side of the door. I froze in place and reached for my Colt.

The yellow bulb next to the door flickered to life, casting a golden pall onto the porch.

The door opened, and a figure filled the frame. The man's white T-shirt stood out starkly against his wrinkled black dress shirt that hung open. "Welcome to the mission..." he began. Then recognition lit his eyes, and his mouth hung open.

"Hi, Jake." I pulled my hand away from the weapon. "Did I wake you up?"

The giant man closed the distance between us, uttered an oath, and wrapped me in his crushing grip as he lifted me off the ground. It had been decades since his last bout in the ring, but it felt as though he could step back in it tomorrow.

Brother Jake had been Father Mike's assistant for as long as I'd known him. The pair were like two halves of a person. Mike was the brains, and Jake was the brawn. Not that Jake wasn't intelligent, but few people were as knowledgeable as the Padre.

I let out a little croak, hoping it sounded like, "It's good to see you too."

251

"Is Father Mike with you?" His voice cracked with the plea.

I swore. "No. I'd hoped he was here."

"I thought with your return…" He swallowed and nodded. "He went looking for you."

"When? How long has he been gone?"

"A little over a month." He pulled out his phone and began flipping through the screens. "A cop type showed up. The two of them talked for a long while, and then Mike told me they had a report about you. Over the border, I think. Things have gotten really strange, and I haven't been able to reach him since."

He flashed me a picture of Wynn on his cell phone. It looked like it had been taken through the window.

"Was there anyone else with him?" I asked.

He shook his head. "Do you know him?"

"He's a good friend. A good man." I didn't know how, or more importantly, why he would have come to Mike. "Did he say what he needed?"

"No." He placed his paw on my arm. "If you haven't found each other, I think it's best if you get moving before—"

"Before what, brother?" The deep voice from inside the house could have cut glass.

I hadn't Sensed anyone until he spoke. I looked around Jake and spotted a swarthy priest, not much older than I was. I couldn't place the accent entirely. Italian maybe?

"Greyson, this is Father Lupochetti." He grimaced. "He's come to *assist* in Mike's absence," he whispered.

252

Subtlety had never been Jake's strong suit, and I couldn't help but feel the warning in his voice.

"PLEASE COME IN." The sinewy priest held the door open. "Brother Jake, would you be so kind as to check on the people inside the chapel?"

I patted Jake on the arm in an attempt to reassure him and myself.

"Father Giraldo Lupochetti." A tapered hand stretched out as I passed by the priest. "Have a seat, Mr. Forrester."

I was getting very tired of everyone knowing who I was before I knew they existed. I plastered a grin on my face and took my usual spot on the couch. "No drink offer?"

Lupochetti closed and locked the door behind him before standing in front of me with his hands clasped behind his back. "We have much to discuss."

"Nothing as far as I'm aware."

His chortle was cold and flat.

"Something I said?" I Sensed the crackle of energy in the room. It was unlike any magic I'd ever felt before. Subtle but powerful.

"Yes, Mr. Forrester." He drew a sigil on the doorway that led to the kitchen. "Your acknowledgment that you lack awareness."

253

I jumped up and moved for the front door, but I was stopped less than a foot away by a ward. I pulled power into my hands and drew my 1911. It had just cleared the holster when I found myself frozen.

Lupochetti pulled the door open.

A high-pitched voice greeted me from where the kitchen should have been. It rang with powerful reserve even as it scratched like fingernails on a chalkboard. "You shall not need the weapon, but you may keep it if it makes you more comfortable."

I'd never had a conversation start out that way that ended well. The field holding me faded away, and I decided I may as well go for the ride for now. It wasn't as if I had a choice. All I could do was muster my most menacing look with my eyes as the warmth of power built in my hands.

A girlish giggle was followed with a command. "Please show our guest in."

Lupochetti motioned for me to come. "After you."

A bloated figure in a simple brown robe sat behind a mahogany desk with a singular stack of papers. Ornately carved walls bore a few painted icons. I stepped through what I believed was a portal. As far as I knew, Mike hadn't installed a mahogany suite into the kitchen or quadrupled the size of the house.

"Who are you, and where is Mike?"

Another shrill giggle came from the deathly pale, stubbly jowls that sagged from under the hood. "That is one question of the day, an important one, I assure you. And one that if we knew the answer, this would be a very different conversation, in the unlikely event we were having one at all."

254

Something in Jabba the Monk's attitude told me the 1911 wouldn't do me much good if I decided to use it. I tapped into more of my inner power and kept it in reserve then returned the Colt to its home. "I'm tired. I've had a couple of long weeks, and I've had enough of the transcendental crap. Cut to the point. Who are you, and what do you want?"

He drew the cowl back. Ancient blotchy flesh that hadn't been exposed to the sun in a long time hung from a bulbous skull. Small tufts of hair rolled along the tundra of his head. Thick glasses were perched precariously on the tip of his nose. The chair protested as he shifted his mass in the chair. "I'm Brother Cyril."

"And where is this place?"

"Not important." He pushed his glasses up. "We are where we need to be."

Time for a different approach. "What is it you want?"

His neck skin flapped in waves as he spoke. "You have something that belongs to us."

"I still don't know who you are. How can I have something of yours?"

He let out another creepy giggle. It sounded more like a pre-teen girl rather than something that should come from Jabba's cousin. "You may recognize us by this." The emblem of a golden quill was emblazoned on the card he slid across the desk.

"Is that supposed to mean something to me?" Inside, I was fighting the urge to grab the card so I would have something tangible.

His grin was insipid. "Oh now, Mr. Forrester. No need to be coy."

I gave into the urge and quickly pocketed the card. "I've seen the symbol. It still really doesn't mean anything to me. So, who the hell are you?"

His chair protested loudly as he leaned forward. "Our order, we are historians, archivists, curators, and chroniclers. I myself am a historian of the future."

"How does that work?" I leaned over the desk, causing Brother Cyril to involuntarily recoil. "Are you some kind of seer? Or just another bloated blowhard that believes too much of his own BS."

Cyril removed his glasses and wiped at the lenses with a dirty handkerchief. "In a way, Mr. Forrester. I see everything going on, and I can extrapolate the most-likely outcomes."

"What is it you see for me?"

"A missed opportunity." He pushed the glasses back up his nose. "I had higher hopes, but now I see you are still a petulant child with power. Pity. It shall be your undoing."

"You're going to have to do better than that. You brought me here."

"Have to? There are few things I must do. You have a parchment, given to you recently. It contains information which is not meant for you. Only one of our order would be able to interpret it."

I had no idea how they could know about the information Heph had given me, but I had come looking for help to use it. I pulled it from my pack and threw it on the desk. It didn't look the same. The symbols were jumbled and flowing as if the ink were alive. "Tell me what it says. How can I use it?"

He pushed the thick glasses higher on the bridge of his nose and grinned. "I do not believe this is what you think it to be." He rolled it up and tried to place it in a drawer. "Our business is concluded."

"I don't think so." I reached across the desk, grabbed the parchment, and shook it at him. "I was told it would help my friends. People I care about."

"We capture history. We do not interfere in how it plays out."

"You're interfering now." I pounded the desk, releasing a burst of energy.

He sighed loudly and rubbed his sweaty neck. "You aren't going to let this go, are you?"

"No."

"Well then, beware that for which you ask." He pushed all of his impressive bulk out of the chair with a grunt and retrieved a scroll that he pretended to stare at intently. "I am aware of the actions that harmed those around you. The message in that scroll confirms our intelligence. Someone interceded and changed the flow of events long ago, changing time and destiny. If you had undertaken the trial to which you were intended, the damage may have been undone, and this world and timeline would never have been."

"Who?" I swallowed. "What was supposed to have happened? What was I supposed to have done?"

"I can't tell you." The giggle was more nervous this time. "We don't—"

"Interfere. Yeah, I've heard that line before." I ran my hands through my hair. "Can you at least give me a hint?"

"Sorry, no. Is it not enough that you are not a scorch mark on the floor?" He let out that damnable giggle again.

"Can things be set right? Tell me that much."

"Those things that are done, are done." He removed his glasses. "As to the things you care about most, fate usually finds a way if it is meant to be." He placed the scroll on the desk. "But try this if you must."

I couldn't understand anything on the page, but I rolled it up and stuffed it in my pack just in case. "I can't read a damn thing here."

"Then maybe you should consider you are not the one to use it."

I swore and threw a fireball at the wall for show then stormed out the door.

LUPOCHETTI RUSHED ME out the front door with a scowl. Jake was nowhere to be seen.

How had I let them push me out? I'd lost my temper and left with nothing but another piece of magic paper. One more useless trinket to send me on a fruitless chase. Maybe it would grow a library if I planted it in the ground.

I was tired of being a pawn, so I took it out on an inanimate object and kicked the old car.

"I thought Gremlins were more of a threat when you were inside them, Mr. Forrester." Agent Aurelie Dube stepped from the shadows.

I swore and placed my hand on the 1911. "Where in hell did you come from?"

She took a deep breath. "I have come a long way to ask for your help."

"Get in line. I've got enough—"

The short woman lunged, landing a heel strike in my chest and launching me onto the hood. Before I could recover, she grabbed my throat and held me on the hood. "This is unpleasant for me, but if you value those who have risked everything for you, it's time you repaid that debt." She shoved me down before releasing me.

I rubbed my throat and rolled to my feet. "Where's Wynn?"

"Missing. He disappeared after talking to the priest. He left me a message saying they had a sighting of you." She wrapped her arms around herself as if she'd had a chill. "That was the last I heard. I've had the house under surveillance ever since, hoping for his return."

I swore and kicked the car again. "Let's talk."

"I suggest we go somewhere public. I could use a cup of coffee."

I couldn't remember the last time I'd eaten. "I know the place." I opened my door to climb in.

"Get your gear, Mr. Forrester. I will not ride in that death trap."

259

THE GREASY SPOON was the well-named diner in which I'd spent many hours with Father Mike, watching people as they walked the strip.

The ride in Dube's SUV was a lot more comfortable than the Gremlin. I wasn't sure the smooth ride made up for the awkward silence that didn't break until we sat in the old booth at the diner. I felt for Dube as she slowly stirred cream into her cup. "You must be desperate," I said.

"As long as we understand each other, Mr. Forrester." She locked her eyes with mine. "I would not be here if I had any other choice."

"In that case, call me Grey."

She grunted. "I believe Longbow has been infiltrated. Corrupted. Wynn is one of the few I've ever been able to trust. Now he's gone."

"Do you know where?"

She nodded. "In the general area we first met at the Amazon's fortress."

Who would've known I'd been back? Who could've seen me in the woods? The only one I knew of was the Winter Queen. Had Marsaile laid some sort of trap?

260

"Mr. Forrester... Grey?"

I must have been lost in thought longer than I realized. "Yeah. I was there for a few hours, trying to track them down. I wound up in Los Diablos and found Drea and Brighid. No sign of Priscilla. But that was over a month ago. And I don't know who would've known I was there."

"There are more eyes out there than you know."

I laughed. "Aren't you concerned about being seen with me, then?"

"I've taken precautions. I assume you have as well?"

I had my usual protections in place, but I had little doubt that most of the entities I dealt with could cut through them with a little focus. "What is it you want?"

"Do you not care that your friends are missing? That they search for you?"

"I do." It was my turn to look for meaning from the leaves that escaped in my tea. "Very much so. I don't know that I can help. I'll just make it worse. It seems to be what I do these days."

She crossed her arms and leaned back in the booth. "I care deeply for Girard, and I'm going to go in search of him. I need your skills and your support. I cannot trust anyone at Longbow. I have no one else. And the way I see it, you owe it to him. And your friend, the priest. And let's not pretend that my coming to you is anything other than what it is. A *last, desperate* resort."

The silence that sat between us while I contemplated an answer was no less disconcerting than when she was speaking. Her look was that of a caged predator. I wasn't sure how she would react if I declined. "What are you proposing?"

She unrolled a map of the Canadian wilderness. "Here is where the Amazon's fortress was. I have good intelligence that they and others are being held here, about eighty kilometers away." She pointed at a mountainous area.

"Any idea by who? How many?"

"Lycans. At least two tribes. It means they're still acting as mercenaries for someone else."

"What about Priscilla?" The close-up image of the base revealed a couple of hidden sentry stations, which meant there were probably other hidden defenses as well. "Is she there too?"

Dube sipped at her coffee. "Possibly."

I had to concentrate on stopping the power flowing through me from an involuntary explosive response. "Possibly? Who else do they have? Why are they holding them?"

She rubbed the scar on her arm. "You must prepare yourself. It's possible none of them are still alive. Every two weeks, whoever is in control of them rotates the two lycan clans out. They are notoriously bad tempered, and not good about sharing territory. The last rotation was ten days ago. A number of bodies were removed at that time, and a few prisoners transferred."

"How do you know this?"

"I was there." She was nearly shouting as she pounded the table.

I smiled at the few other patrons in the diner to show everything was all right. "Okay, then. Who else do you have for this little plan?"

"Just the two of us."

I shook my head. "What do you think two of us can do?"

262

She sighed. "It shouldn't take much to start a clan war between the two sides. While they slay each other, we free whoever is inside and sneak out using one of your portal tricks."

"Great plan." My hands were shaking. "Two of us against two packs of frenzied Werewolves? And then trusting me to create a portal to escape when those aren't working real well in any of the realms right now? I've done this before when things were a lot better and with a lot more support, and the people with me barely escaped. I had to find another way out even then. It won't work."

Her eyes narrowed. "You have a better idea?"

We both knew that we would have to try something. "I don't know about better, but maybe something that gives us a chance."

DUBE RELUCTANTLY AGREED to let me return to Phoenix Grove. I gave her a sigil to use, and hopefully I would be bringing help with me when we met at an abandoned logging camp a few snow-covered miles from the Werewolves' hideout. She said she would be able to reach the site by sunrise in two days. We planned to meet up a few hours later as soon as the portal was ready on her end.

I didn't tell her I wanted some verification of intelligence data she'd provided. It was time for me to live up to my half of another deal. I pulled Paul Tinka's card out and made the call.

A thick Texan accent greeted me on the second ring. "'Bout time you called, wizard."

"How'd you know who it was?"

He laughed. "Burner phone. You're the only one with this number."

"I've got a lead. I need you to verify some information."

"Whatcha got?"

I rattled off the coordinates. "I think it's a lycan fortress. I think they're holding some people that I want back. And it sounds like our mutual friend may be pulling the strings."

Soft clicks floated through the phone. "Yeah, I know the place. Surprised they're still using it. How recent is your intel?"

"A couple of days."

"Source?"

I wasn't about to reveal Dube, just in case Tinka and his people couldn't be trusted. Then again, I didn't really trust her. But if Wynn had faith in her, I would give her the benefit of the doubt. "Trusted interested party."

"Alrighty, then." He huffed. "You planning on crashing the party?"

"I hear they're using two different clans to stand guard."

"Makes sense." Someone was speaking to him in the background but not close enough for me to make out what they were saying. "Yeah, it looks like they've got a couple dozen around. Using two clans keeps them as honest as bloodthirsty thieving animals can be."

The conversation continued in the background.

"Look, if you're going in, why don't I bring a few of my people to help out?"

I stared at the phone. The offer seemed to have come too easily. "You remember that none of your people can kill if they ever have a hope of reverting. Even being close by might trigger a frenzy."

"I ain't forgotten." His voice was heavy and throaty. Even through the phone, I could Sense him fighting the change into the beast. "I do want to see the light go out of that bastard's eyes, though."

Part of me feared turning more of the beasts loose in the woods, even for the best of reasons. But I wasn't in a position to refuse the support. He'd come through on his end for Drea and Brighid. I would live up to my end as well. "Keep it small. The fewer, the better. We're assembling at—"

"The old logging camp? I know the place. We used it as a staging area for the attack on the fortress."

I shuddered, remembering Onyx falling. "Is there somewhere close by you can stay out of sight? I think it's better if your team stays hidden."

"Well, damn." He sighed heavily. "I guess that makes operational sense. There's a mine shaft about a half mile from the camp. Still has power and supplies. I'll send you the coordinates."

"How soon can you be there?"

More muffled conversation. "Ten hours. Base camp set up in twelve. Monitoring of the cave entrance in fifteen, sixteen tops."

"My lead should be there in about twenty-four hours, and I'll be a little behind. If there's anything you can tell me about the cave system or the people inside, I'll get it then."

TRUTH BE TOLD, I was ready for it all to end. The Gremlin was still safely parked across from the mission. The jog back to the car gave me time to clear my head and get myself straightened out. Even knowing there would be no response, I tried activating the emergency protocols one last time for Priscilla, Wynn, and Raines. I even considered calling LeGasse for help. I don't know what stopped me from dialing the number, but I just couldn't do it.

Dorian and Nicomedes were nowhere to be found. Anyone whom I'd grown to trust in the earthly realm was missing.

I left a nebulous coded message on the Calypso line, but I was pretty sure no one was around to get it. If any of them were around, they wouldn't stop until Priscilla was safe, and anyone responsible for her abduction razed to the ground. If somehow none of the Amazons were left, that mission would fall to me. And I would start with a cave in the Canadian badlands.

That left me with one option. I had to go home if I could. I would go to the Grove.

The house behind me was vacant, with a mostly obscured garage. I doubted anyone would see what I was doing this time of night anyway, but I still wanted to be safe.

266

It took three trips to carry all of my gear from the car to the garage. Hephaestus had given me a lot of supplies to go with the skinsuits and the staff weapon. I had no idea what some of the things he'd given me were. Most everything would need to be stashed safely away.

I drew a wide circle around the duffel bags and packs then filled in the sigils for my lab. The ride was rough, but getting easier. The Veils between the realms were weakening again, and portals everywhere would begin to open.

With a freshly loaded pack and my gear in place, I unrolled the parchment that would invoke a different portal. The mate was safely hidden inside Josiah's barn. As soon as I crossed over, it would disintegrate. No one else would be able to use it to get into the lab.

Standing on the circle, I looked at the furball's water bowl. I really missed that mutt. "At least you aren't going with me this time. Wherever you are has to be better than where I'm going."

I Pushed the power into the parchment and snapped the command to take me home.

LIGHT SNOW COATED the ground. I didn't remember it ever having snowed when I was growing up in the Grove, short of invocations for festivals. It crunched as I made my way into the house.

Josiah peeked over the top of the book he held in his grizzled hands at the kitchen table. "Did you find what you went looking for?"

"No, but I didn't come back empty handed." I dropped my pack onto the floor. "How is… everyone?"

He closed the tome and slowly laid it on the table. "Drea and Brighid are still separate identities, but we've kept 'em away from everyone. Only a couple of people know they're here. Same with Tellia. Can't risk you-know-who finding out."

I was relieved to know Sinclair was still in the dark.

"Abhile and her friend are in hiding in the fae village with your friends down there. Underhill Productions has another movie in production, and so they blended in down there as extras."

"No word from… outside?"

He shook his head. "What did you find?"

I dug through the pack and pulled out the parchment Brother Cecil had given me. "I can't figure out anything about it. Supposedly, it can help reverse Brighid and Drea's condition."

He unrolled it, anchoring the corners with nearby objects. He made sure to put the salt across the room, where it couldn't spill and affect any enchantments in the scroll. "Where did you get this?"

"Let's just say I got it through Melvin's connections." In a way, that was true. It may have even been his and Heph's intent. "Can you decipher it?"

"No." He ran his finger along a line of the changing ink. "But it can be translated. I'll just need time."

"You know what this is?"

"I believe so." He chewed on his lip. "We will need to be very cautious if I'm right."

"I'll be gone for a few days. A week at most."

"So soon? You just got here."

I nodded. "I need to help some people. I may have found a lead on Priscilla. I needed to bring this to you and do a few things before I headed out."

"Where are we going, then?"

"I need you to figure this out." My hand was trembling as I touched the parchment. "Help them. I need to know this is happening."

He stroked his graying beard. "You're not sure you're coming back."

I nodded. "I can only push my luck so far before it runs out."

"You can't think like that." He reached out and took my hand. "People here need you too."

"I have to do this."

He let go of me and leaned back. "Take your few days. Do what you need to. Then get back here. I think our little town is about to get really busy."

"The snow?"

"And other omens. Scattered words have come in about raids and skirmishes as the Veil is lifting again. We could see another war between realms like no one has seen since the last great fall."

He rolled up the parchment. "Phoenix Grove is one of the last few sanctuaries. We've already taken in a few refugees. There'll be a lot more coming."

THE FAE VILLAGE sat nestled in a low valley outside of the main town. Winter and Summer fae had claimed opposite sides of the valley, more for creating their preferred environment than taking sides. Anyone who took refuge in the Grove was blood-bound to defend the Grove.

Today, a huge battle between fae and frost giants was being fought on the winter side. The fae were being led by one giant Werehamster wielding a large morning star with gleaming plastic armor plated over his fur.

Aindrias, aka Evan Underhill, watched the battle rage on, a scowl on his face as he shouted directions to the actors on both sides. A momentary flash of anger turned to a smile when he realized it was me who'd tapped him on the shoulder. "They'll let anyone into my sets here, won't they?"

It had been a long time. In fact, the last time I'd seen Aindrias, he had been sitting in my beach condo in Priscilla's resort before he moved his family here. And before my place was destroyed. "My skills at sneaking around have gotten pretty good."

"So I hear." His grin widened as he clasped my arm in the Summer sign of friendship. "Looking to get a part in Robbie's first feature film? His TV show has exploded."

"Thanks for the offer. I'm looking for The Dagda."

"He's up on the hill, playing adviser for battle tactics." He pointed to a peak on the far end of the valley. "We'll be wrapping for the day in a few minutes. I'll be back shortly."

My mind was free to watch Underhill enjoy the creative process and see Robbie play the hero. It wasn't too long ago that he would have curled into a ball at the thought of the mildest threat. Sesha Aislinn had her wings spread wide as she flew over the heads of some sort of ice beasts, swinging at them with a sword.

"The rumors are true." Brianna Coterie, another fae and one of the hottest properties in Hollywood, leaned over and kissed my cheek. "My feelings were getting bruised. It's been so long since you came to see me."

Even her mildest flirtations were enough to fire up a dead man. It had been hard enough to resist her when I'd been her bodyguard for a few hours. So I returned the affection. "Life of an endangered wizard."

"Well then." She looped her arm through mine, leaving a lot of the nearby crew to wonder who I was. Let them. "Let's go to the reading room and get a few minutes alone before the rest of the kids come in from the playground."

BRIANNA'S CHARMS LINGERED as the others came in an hour later. Aindrias had apparently given orders to most of the

271

crew to knock off for the day and had invited a select few to the log roundhouse that served as Underhill Production's offices.

The first through the door was Anraoi, Chief of the Woodlands, former Lord of the Summer Lands, and consort to the missing former Queen of Summer, Dáiríne. Carlyn, Aindrias's wife and guardian to the House of Summer, rushed in.

After a few minutes, Sesha sauntered in, giving Brianna the same competitive smirk the pair always shared. Robbie and The Dag were followed by Aindrias, who locked the door.

Aindrias stood guard at the door. "You have good news, I hope?"

"I really only came down to get counsel from The Dagda."

Carlyn shook her head. "That means no, and he's off to do something foolish."

The Dagda hummed as he sipped from his horn. "Spit it out. We've all been here before. Where's the war?"

"Canada. I think I've got a lead on Priscilla. And it looks like Wynn and others are being held there too."

He downed the contents of the horn, and it was magically refilled before he set it down. "Well then, let's get moving."

"Hold on." I walked to the middle of the room. "That's not why I'm here. I need to know more about this." I plucked the folded enchanted staff from my pack on a nearby table. It sprang to life, tripling its length.

"Huh." The old god took another sip. "Maybe we should talk in private for a moment."

I followed him into a side office and closed the door.

272

"Where did you get such a thing?"

"Hephaestus." I offered him the weapon for a closer look.

He drew back. "Don't touch me with that." He held his hands apart but leaned in for a closer look. "What did that crazed old tinkerer tell you?"

"Nothing. It's why I hoped you could tell me more about these enchanted types of weapons." I laid it on the table.

He guffawed as the blade swung and sliced a hole in the conference table. "It's imprinted on you. That's certain. It won't fully bond with you until you go into combat with it. Then it'll show you its full power. And this one has a personality on it. Been locked away for a long time. Unused. Undeveloped. Untempered."

"How do I use it?"

"I wouldn't." He shook his head. "Not unless I had to. But you can't leave it here. Not anywhere someone might accidentally pick that thing up."

I knew it had been given to me for a reason. I wasn't about to leave it behind.

"Did he tell you why he was giving this to you? Has anything… more unusual than normal happened?"

I shook the handle of the stave, and it snapped back to its shortened length. "Define normal. The Inquisitor unbound more of my power. I've been trying to deal with that. The least bit of an aggravation, and I'm flooded with angry energy, ready to strike."

"Yeah, we'll need to work on that. If you don't control it, it will definitely control you."

"You mean like going to the dark side," I quipped.

"I mean, that's how Loki got his start on crazy." He hooked the horn onto his belt. "Let's get ready to move. You have a plan? How many troops on the other side?"

"I didn't come to ask for you to join me. I've got a couple of questionable support people doing surveillance, and Agent Dube."

"Gods, boy, have you learned nothing?" He picked up the slice of the table. "I know I couldn't stop you and wouldn't try even if I could. If there's a chance of finding Priscilla, I'm going."

"Do you know where the other Amazons are?"

He nodded. "At least some of them are trapped in another sanctuary village. They went there to get it ready. Mel managed to get to them, but they're out of play for now."

THE ARGUMENT LASTED for more than an hour before the rest of them capitulated. Aindrias finally, albeit reluctantly, agreed to keep the rest in the Grove and come in the second wave if we needed help. The portal I'd been able to construct and send with Agent Dube would barely carry The Dagda and me.

I drew a large portal ring on the floor and charged it. Aindrias and the rest of the small gathered cadre of fae agreed to be ready at dusk the next day and would wait for my signal. I hated lying to them, but it was the only way.

I refused to endanger the rest of them, even though I'd stood beside all of them at some time or another in the last few years.

274

With the exception of Robbie, all of them were far more experienced than me in combat. I didn't understand why they followed me then, or why they would do it now. Or even why they had all risked so much for me in the first place.

The portal ring I left wasn't entirely a ruse. It was another one-way trip, but hopefully from the other side. Besides, none of them had the power to break through as long as the Veil was still so thick and indeterminate. Not surprisingly, Abhile and Sonja had all but disappeared in the days after they had first arrived. I still wasn't convinced they weren't somehow involved, even if indirectly. Even if they'd been around, I wouldn't have brought them in on the plan, and all of our little group agreed.

Josiah raised an eyebrow as The Dagda followed me into the kitchen of his house. The parchment I'd left was again pinned down on the table. Tellia, in Brighid's body, leaned over the fluid inks and gently touched some of the fluctuating lines, whispering and blowing on others to create eddies on the paper.

The gleam in her eye made me twitchy. My hands were charging before it registered that I was about to attack, and probably destroy, Josiah's kitchen. "What's she doing?"

I didn't resist as Josiah released a blast of Soothing energy, something I couldn't do. He hadn't needed to do that to me since I was a hotheaded child. "Seshat gave her the amulet. Its enchantment, plus Brighid's power and Tellia's knowledge, have allowed her to understand it."

She cocked her head with a cold smirk. "It's the language of Abaddon before its corruption. We can restore the order of the Amazon and the sorceress."

"What do I need to perform the ritual?"

275

She shook her head slowly. "You cannot be the one. You will play your part, and then you must leave before the final ritual can be done."

I froze. "I'm not leaving while this is in process."

Her back arched as she stood straight. "Then all three of us will die."

"Who is to perform the ritual, then?"

"Rhea," Josiah said. "Rhea Sinclair."

Brighid's mother? "I thought we weren't involving them until it was done?"

"We will keep Reginald out of it. " My grandfather moved to look into my eyes. "But Rhea, she's a shaman with the proper skills in her own rights, as well as a sorceress. And she has the interest and drive to make it happen."

Tellia laughed softly. "It's you trying to force your stubborn will on them that caused the other rituals to fail."

Josiah caught my arm and lowered it as I slumped into the chair. Was it true? I'd been blaming myself, but was it really, truly my fault? My responsibility?

Tellia nudged my grandfather aside. "We need to discuss your role in this. In private."

I pulled myself to my feet and nodded at Josiah and The Dagda. "It's fine."

Josiah pulled The Dagda along with him and went in search of Rhea.

I sat back in the chair. Tellia pulled another up and sat where she could face me.

My stomach was churning. "What is it you want me to do?"

"How long before you plan to return to the mortal plane?"

I checked my watch, which was synchronized with Agent Dube's on the other side. "About ten hours."

"That's a little tight, but we can make it. It will be critical that as soon as you have done your part, you leave. You go as far away as you can, as quickly as you can. The mortal plane is not ideal, but it will have to do. And you will have to take me with you."

I pulled back. "What do you mean?"

"We both know I must be removed from this mortal coil. Once removed, my essence must be as far away as possible. It's the only way to restore the order of things." I jumped as her hand touched mine.

"The blade. The Anima Arca."

"Yes." She nodded. "You must draw out my essence and take both of our influences away."

"What do I do with you then?"

She shrugged. "My body is gone. I do not wish to inhabit one that belongs to another. I must trust myself to you."

HER EYES FLUTTERED as I stroked their face. Her face. "Drea? Brighid?"

Her eyes softened. "We're both here."

"Has Tellia talked to you?"

She pushed herself up in the bed. "Not really. She said she had found something but hadn't talked to you yet about it."

"She and Josiah figured something out from what I was able to find. It sounds like an option. But I won't be the one doing the ritual. I'll have to be gone to not… interfere."

Their hand was warm as it took mine. "What do you think?"

I shook my head. "I don't know what to think. But I'm long out of ideas. I don't have anything else to try."

"And we're dying in our own way." She leaned her head on my shoulder. "Let's do it."

"Okay. I'll let them know."

"Where will you go? How long will you be gone this time?"

I didn't want them to worry, but Drea had a right to know about her mother. "I'm following up on a lead about Priscilla."

She lifted up to look at me. Her eyes hardened. "What do you know of Mother? My sisters?"

"I think she's being held by a clan of Werewolves. Recon is being done now." I decided to let her believe it was a Longbow operation. "From what I've heard, the rest of Calypso went to another sanctuary to open it up and get ready for what's coming."

A thin smile formed. "I know you'll do what you can."

278

"I need to start the preparations."

"How long"—she held onto my hand—"until we need to be there?"

"A few hours."

She stroked my arm and lay back on the bed. "Go let them ready the procedure. Then come back to us. Spend your time here."

DREA'S HEAD RESTED on my arm. She was asleep, releasing slow deep breaths. I wrapped my other arm around her, around them. I wanted to watch her sleep, listen to her breathe, but exhaustion was taking over, and the hardest part of the next few days hadn't started yet.

"I knew it was too good to be true." I opened my eyes and found myself leaning on a chessboard. "A couple of hours of quiet."

Ladon leaned his elbow on the table, a scowl slicing across his face. His coat was folded over the back of the chair. I never remembered his clothing being the least bit wrinkled, even after sparring. I certainly wasn't familiar with the disheveled and unshaven being sitting in front of me. "You were to return to continue your training." It felt like an accusation.

"It's been a busy few days." The crystal pieces tinkled as I backed away. "Where's our fine, feathered friend?"

279

"You're walking a dangerous path. We've been preparing you for what is to come. Your avoidance of us isn't making it any easier."

"I'm not avoiding—"

His fist transformed into a taloned claw as it swept the table aside, sending the chessboard and pieces flying. "There is so much more going on here than you know. You are haphazardly tripping over destiny like a drunk in a minefield."

I jumped out of the chair and pulled power into my hands and through my body. I visualized the armor on my chest and shield on my arm, which I brought around between us. "Why don't you tell me, then? What are you holding back?"

"I'm not holding back any longer." I ducked down as he hit me with a wave of fire, splashing over and around me. My shield was still smoldering as I peeked over the top. Ladon had turned and faced the window. I rushed and rammed him, shoving him through the opening. He let out a deafening screech.

I thought he was going to slam into the ground, but halfway down, he turned his body and landed on the ground in a tight roll then exploded to his feet. Fire burned in his eyes, and a malevolent grin crossed his face, a split of pride and rage as he motioned for me to come down and face him.

The new stave materialized in my hand as I landed on the last step. I snapped it into a two-bladed axe as my foot touched the drawbridge.

I batted away the first volley of fireballs into the hillside and ducked the second round as they splashed into the keep's walls. The third round was deflected off my shield. Between blasts, I was able to charge and close the distance. Ladon had chosen a hilltop *and wanted to know if I could knock him off. We'd played this game before, but this time was real.*

As the blast hammered my shield, I pulled together a chain of lightning rings. I didn't close the distance as he'd expected, but instead the chain surrounded him and closed the electroshock net.

He bellowed out a roar as he seized up, and I was able to get within a few feet of him before the effect wore off.

I swung the shield at him to knock him down, but four talons sliced through it. He closed his grip and ripped it away, throwing me off balance.

I turned into the fall and used the momentum of the axe to pull myself up.

Ladon ducked, and the blade missed his head by less than I'd intended and drew blood from the scaly arm that reached up to deflect it.

He pulled back, unleashing a jet of fire. The axe head glowed, spreading a shield between us, protecting me and blowing part of the flames back onto him. He didn't seem to care that his golden suit was burning as he charged, talons flaming as they sliced at me, bouncing off the field the axe projected.

"You've made your point," I yelled. I drew the axe back and readied the attack.

"No," he grunted. "There have been caretakers before. Maybe there will be another after you. Maybe not. But I'm done with you." Taloned feet broke through his shoes as leathery wings broke from his back.

I retreated slowly, holding the axe between me and the growing golden beast before me. A shimmering light surrounded him as his body grew and sprouted thick scales. My trainer and mentor shifted into a golden dragon the size of a two-story house. He breathed out a great blast of greasy flame that sliced across the sky.

I hit him with one of the incantations I remembered since having my power returned. A concussive blast of power released a formidable shock wave that knocked him off his feet.

He flapped his great wings to right himself then drew back, taking in a solid breath to power his assault. The shield from the axe deflected most of the fire hose of flame but singed my unarmored flesh and warmed the armor.

The fire died down, and Ladon bellowed another great roar. He blew a smoke ring that surrounded me. "Until next time."

As he reared back for a final blast, I spiraled once, twice, and a third time. I released the axe, letting it fly. It did a slow tumble and struck him high in the chest, disappearing deep inside his body.

His eyes grew wide as flames dribbled down his lips and out of the gaping wound. Staggering, I had to roll as he took a final swipe at me before falling over. One great eye burned as he lay rasping on the ground. Even then, I could still sense a small bit of pride as he lay dying.

I knelt next to his head where he could see me. "Why? What is it you wouldn't tell me?"

The eye closed, and the beast let out a last gasp.

I collapsed next to him. I couldn't really say I'd liked him, but I had felt a real affection for him. I'd wanted to earn his respect. Had killing him been the only way to do that? "Why?"

"Why indeed?" Tsauriel stood on the drawbridge.

"And you said he didn't have it in him." Ladon walked out from inside the keep to stand next to the angel. His suit was as pristine as ever.

"You do have that effect on people." She shrugged. "Frequently, I think of slaying you when you're drawing in a breath to unleash one of your pathetic profundities."

He walked across the lawn and touched the dead beast's head, said a few words, and watched as it floated away in a mass of embers.

"What was that all about?" My staff lay safely on the ground. I thought about burying it into Ladon.

"An illusion." He offered his hand to pull me up. "We needed to know how far you'd come."

Tsauriel stood beside him. "And how far you'd be willing to go."

BRIGHID KISSED ME and roused me out of slumber. My time with Ladon and Tsauriel hadn't improved after their little test. Something more was going on, but they spent their time telling me how unprepared I was and berating me for avoiding my training.

I did get bonus points for having slain the dragon, but even then, Ladon was unforgiving. I should have never let the thing get to full size, and I should have attacked during its transformation. "Sentimentality be damned," he'd said.

I assured him I wouldn't hesitate again and debated taking a swing right then.

I didn't know if either of them could be killed, or what it would mean if they were. I still wasn't entirely sure they were real, at least not once I'd woken up and shaken off the dream.

I hesitated leaving but finally gave a halfhearted good-bye to Drea and Brighid, not knowing if it would be the last time for some, or all, of us.

I staggered downstairs. Josiah sat at the table with Tellia and Rhea. Brighid's mother had a few more streaks of gray in her hair since the last time I'd seen her, but there was life in her eyes. She had more hope than I'd seen the last time I saw her.

She moved slowly as she greeted me, afraid to take her eyes off Tellia in Brighid's body, as if it might disappear. She finally wrapped her arms around me and buried her head in my chest. "You lived up to your word. You brought her home."

"You do know—"

"Yes." Josiah cut off my question. "And she knows what we're asking her to do."

Tears welled in her eyes. "I need more time to prepare... I'm not ready for this kind of ritual. A few days and—"

Tellia spoke. "We need to move quickly. Every moment that passes will make it harder to keep them apart, and make it harder to get her back where she belongs."

Rhea pushed away and faced Tellia. "Why are you so willing to give up her body? Are you really ready?"

Tellia placed her hands in her lap. "I do what I must. My body is already dust. I am ready for my spirit to find its next journey."

She spun back to me. "And you? You're going to... make the vessel ready?"

"Yeah, I am."

"Josie." She turned to my grandfather. "Are you going along with this?"

He nodded.

"I must speak with my daughter."

Josiah looked at me. "Library. One hour."

THE CEREMONIAL CENTER underneath the library was mostly used for consulting unpleasant spirits or entities about restricted knowledge in a safe environment or purifying items that carried too much bad energy. And it had been used to host the occasional clandestine party when Mari and I were kids.

It was designed much like the inner chambers of the Coetum Atrium beneath the Phoenix Grove City Hall. Thirteen concentric circles radiated out from the center. Each ring admitted or prohibited specific energies and entities.

Instead of podiums for the council, various altars, furniture, and implements were staged along the walls. The Dagda helped me pull two low tables to the middle of the room, one for Drea's body and the other for Brighid's.

In a corner alcove, I set up the portal ring and placed our gear in the circle. The portal just waited for The Dagda and me to port to Werewolf country. I laughed to myself at the thought. The ring hadn't yet started to glow, which meant Agent Dube was not ready for us on the other side. It was just now getting near the time I'd expect her signal.

Rhea entered, placed a case on a nearby table, and began removing implements. I'd already placed the owl-headed vessel as instructed.

I walked over to where Rhea stared into the now-empty case. "Is there anything you need?"

She refused to look at me. "No. I just don't know if I can do this."

"I wish you didn't have to." I gently rubbed her hand. "But you're the only one."

"So you say. What if it doesn't work? What if I mess up?" She barely looked my way. "I can't lose her again. She's my baby."

"You'll do what I haven't been able to do."

She nodded. "I have to. I'm almost ready. Tellia will be here in a few minutes." She turned to leave the room.

"Wait," I said. She stopped but still faced away. "I'm sorry for how this has happened. I did what I could."

"I know. I don't blame you. Not really." She disappeared around the corner.

The Dagda cleared his throat with an echo in the chamber. "No signal yet. What do we do if it doesn't come?"

"She'll deliver." If she'd been caught and it had been taken from her, or if the portal had been destroyed, it would have combusted. "It's not time to worry yet."

I dug out the oilcloth bundle from my pack before handing the rest to him. "Put this with the rest."

As he disappeared with the rest of my gear, I made a few small shifts in the Leviskin and readied the combat rig. I wouldn't have time to make more adjustments between the time I extracted Tellia from Brighid's body and when we had to make the jump. Even though I wanted to trust Dube, there was no telling what could be on the other side. It was always possible she'd ready the portal and call us in for support. We wouldn't know until we were in the middle of it.

Whatever "it" may be.

We were going in unsupported. No backup. No net. No Longbow to call on. No Amazons to come to the rescue.

I held out hope the ritual would work. At least Drea and Brighid would be themselves again. If not, I didn't want to know.

Unrolling the oilcloth, I watched as the night-black Anima Arca blade glistened in the torchlight. I opened one of the containers holding unused crystals and dumped its contents into my hand. I'd inspected them all repeatedly but still looked for any flaw that might cause a problem.

After staring into several of the clear crystals, I found the one I would use. I Pushed a little energy into it and said a little prayer before sliding it into its place.

TELLIA SLOWLY MARCHED into the chamber with Rhea at her side. Both wore ceremonial gowns that hid little and freely allowed the flow of power and energy.

Rhea's stare was vacant. She teetered on the edge of the trance she would need. "Whenever you're ready, Greyson."

Tellia took Rhea in a gentle embrace and whispered in her ear. A small nod was the response.

"Rhea, we'll need a few more minutes. Then we'll be ready to start."

In her role as priestess rather than a mother, she gave a slight nod and left.

Tellia held her arms to her sides as she approached.

"How are you feeling?" I asked. "Are you ready for this?"

"You mean, am I ready to die?" Her lip curled slightly. "No, but it is time I take that next step in my journey."

"Almost."

"May I see the implement?"

I drew the blade from the sheath on my hip. "Don't touch it. I've prepared it and myself as best I could."

She ran her fingers around the weapon without touching it, feeling its power. "Will it hurt?"

I remembered when Abhile, in Brighid's body, had shoved this very blade into my chest. "It's not exactly pain, but I won't lie and say it's fun. Relax, and it should go easier than it did for me."

She brushed my hand. "You may put it away."

I gently slid it back into the sheath, both of us knowing what would happen the next time I drew it. "Is there anything I can do for you? Anyone to tell? Any messages to pass on?"

She shook her head. "No."

"Grey, it's golden," The Dagda bellowed from the alcove. "We have a connection. Let's get this show on the road."

Josiah stood in the far corner. Rhea and Drea stood just out of sight. I waved. "Two minutes."

"Good luck," my grandfather mouthed. He vanished around the corner.

I took Tellia by the hand and led her to the center of the room, next to one of the makeshift beds. "It's time."

She closed her eyes and began a slow chant. "May you, the Norns, wash me with your waters into my next life."

The blade was in my hand. It seemed to know what to do and was ready to guide me. It became a beehive in my hand as the business end turned etheric.

I hugged her in a close embrace. Her breath brushed against my skin. "I'm sorry," I whispered.

Her fingers laced with mine around the hilt. She let out a thin gasp as the blade passed through her flesh and began siphoning off her essence.

"No. It's not your fault." Her voice was barely a whisper. "I *am* the one responsible."

"What? Responsible for what?" It was too late. Her head tilted back as she slumped against me. The Anima Arca took solid form as soon as I withdrew it from her body.

The crystal glowed a brilliant cobalt. I slipped the blade into the sheath and lowered the body to the table, giving her forehead a quick kiss.

The Dagda watched from the alcove. "We've got to go."

I shouted the signal and ran for the portal.

Rhea came into sight just as I gave the word that brought the portal to life.

ICY WINDS HOWLED outside as sleet plinked off the cracked window. Aurelie Dube leaned over a rusted cast-iron woodstove that radiated welcome heat.

Seeing everything was quiet, The Dagda relaxed his stance and leaned against his staff. I holstered the Colt and shook off the energy I'd pulled into myself. The adrenaline surge slowly subsided.

"I had expected you would be alone." Dube pried herself away from the small aura of warmth.

The Dagda's voice shook the small wooden shack. "Well, Aurelie, being an adviser for movie production was getting to be a little tedious. I couldn't let the boy go by himself with this wonderful little distraction."

Standing a little over half his height, she had to crane her neck to look at him. "Your company is most welcome, Dagda of the Tuatha de Danann."

"How's it looking, Agent Dube?"

She made a space next to her at the stove. "You may as well call me Aurelie, Greyson. Shall we see how that goes?"

"Sure thing." I stepped into the tight spot to take advantage of the warmth. "How's it looking, Aurelie?"

"The weather has turned. An unexpected storm moved in a few hours ago while I was still making my way here. With the delay, I've not been any further."

The thought that heavy winter weather had come in from nowhere didn't fill me with confidence. Maybe it was just weird weather. Or it could have been a sign of Winter fae. Maybe it was someone invoking weather magic.

Not knowing could make a big difference in the next few hours. "I'll be back. I just want a feel for the storm."

Her nod told me she knew what I was looking for, at least in part. It also gave me an excuse to find Tinka and his crew and see what they had for me.

The new and improved Leviskin lived up to its promise. The insulated dragon-scale armor kept me warm against the piercing winds and slush falling from the skies. I opened my Senses to the weather. Plenty of magical energy filled the air, but not enough to tell if the storm was natural or not. The energy also let me follow a direct track to the mine shaft where Paul Tinka and crew had set up camp.

Tinka's lawyer had traded his suit for heavy winter Battle Dress Uniform and a camouflaged AK-47 rifle. He stalked from his position in a protected blind, keyed a code into a hidden panel opening the entrance, and walked me inside. One of his contract security tucked himself down into the blind.

After being let in through a second door, I saw Paul Tinka making notes on a whiteboard and discussing a map with the tall brunette from Obi's. Three hired guns made a show of checking the weapons slung around themselves. They all wore similar winter gear.

"Howdy, Grey." He gave me barely a glance. "You remember Leslie."

"We weren't really introduced."

"Logistics," she stated flatly. "And combat operations."

"Before you ask, yeah she's always that friendly." He slapped me on the back. "And yeah, her bite is worse than her bark, even before we were all cursed."

I leaned in close. "And none of your people have drawn blood except for her?"

The lanky CEO shook his head grimly. "I remember. And no. Davis understands, though, if he needs to. That's part of the reason he was on point outside. He was a ranger. And he'll do his duty."

"Good." I turned to the operations boards. "I don't have much time."

"Leslie, you're up." Tinka dropped into a rolling office chair.

She shifted catlike from an at-ease stance into a whirlwind, flashing past images with barely enough time to glance at them, much less keep up with the flood of information. Then she caught my attention. "This is where you all die."

"Whoa." I shook my head. "Can you back up a step?"

She uttered a sound between clearing her throat and a growl. "Were you not paying attention?"

Tinka slid from his chair to take a position between us and pointed at the map. "Four of the feral lycans are tethered by enchantment near the entrance. Once you're inside, it's one long chamber. Outer bulkhead, inner door. There'll be the other three or four ferals waiting in there. The Blazing Claws are on point right now. We've counted nine individuals but haven't seen any of the pack leaders. Means a minimum of ten of their guys. The pack leader of the ferals will probably be deeper in with his two lieutenants. So, two dozen lycans total. A couple of other casters that look like fae. A couple other unknowns, so call it thirty in total."

"Any sign of Rahm?"

"Nah." He zoomed out to a larger map. "We think his real base of operations is here, deeper in the mountains. One hundred and five kilometers farther North, a further one hundred and five kilometers into nowhere. One of the last Saguenayan outposts. The little we know says it was abandoned about three hundred years ago. Was never breached."

The angle on the satellite picture looked somewhat like a fortress carved into the mountain. The entrance looked like a dome-shaped crop of rocks, like a Sphinx. Or Dr. Evil's mountain retreat. Or just the trick of light on a pile of rocks. "What are they protecting here, then? Is this where they're holding our people?"

"Your people," Leslie snapped. "We are here as intelligence support, nothing more."

Tinka glared at his lieutenant then turned back to the display. "It ain't good. We have a bet. She thinks they're just splitting up the packs to keep down trouble. Maybe keep few prisoners down here as an excuse. I think they're converting soldiers here. Keep 'em away from the rest in case something goes badly. But yeah, they've got about a half-dozen down there, but no identities."

"Where are they being held?"

"Assuming nothing's changed"—he flipped back to the facility layout—"there's a dozen cells back here on this side, and storage on the other. You've got to go right through here to get to them."

He pointed to a long, narrow hall lined with notes about security measures.

Leslie pointed at the display. "This is where anyone who goes in will die or be captured," she snapped. "If they've made it that far."

FIRMLY TUCKED AWAY in a Leviskin sling, the intelligence package did little to convince me we would make it all the way to the hall of doom. Tinka had some footage of the inside of the outpost from when Rahm had been spending hundreds of this troops to capture the entire facility, even though it had been abandoned for hundreds of years.

A telluric node was parked at the back of the base, undoubtedly part of the reason for choosing that location. The hall was lined with natural quartz growth and held an enchantment powered by the ley line as an almost inexhaustible defense. Rahm had tested exactly how many beings had to be thrown at it before it needed to be recharged, and we were a battalion short on my side. Whoever controlled the far end of the hall controlled the switch that would safely allow passage for a short period of time.

Three of us against thirty. The numbers weren't in our favor.

But if any of the people taken were in there, I owed all of them my life. I would give it in the attempt to pay them back for all the times they'd pulled me out of the fire. My best chance was to go in on my own. It wasn't as if I would easily be able to explain the boon of information I had anyway.

Where the meager path diverted back to the mining camp, I went straight until I was within sight of the entrance. I was shivering, and not just from the cold. I needed to improve my ability to move, and beads of sweat were forming against my skin. The Leviskin shifted and made sure the armor was heaviest on the vitals.

With a blessed silver-infused blade in each hand, I stretched my Senses against the worsening storm. Six other beings were out in the storm with me. None of them felt as if they were faring well.

The first of the feral lycans I came across was naked. He'd run out of strength and turned back into his human form. Hypothermia had almost done its job, and I did the pitied creature a favor and slid my blade between its ribs. The second and third were already frozen solid.

The fourth was larger and heavier. He was fighting the change back to human. He even got in a weak swipe with a claw that took the last of his energy. My blade flashed, and his head rolled.

The ice was taking the last of the warmth from the fifth sentry. The last creature gave a sad whimper and closed its eyes.

I hoped the fact that things were starting this easily was a good omen.

Then an icy wind howled around me.

THE WIND DIED as the dome formed around me in an instant. I looked around for the trap I'd triggered, but there was only a minimum of magical energy.

Power flooded into my hands as I readied to make a doorway in the ice.

Not yet. I grabbed my throbbing head as the message pierced my mind.

The walls somewhat muffled the shrieks and howls from outside. Mist rose from the floor until it filled nearly half the small chamber. I backed away, still on my hands and knees, until I was trapped against the wall.

A tapered hand tinged with blue reached from the mist. "Please rise."

I paused before accepting her help. Even the smallest gesture could carry a price. Then again, her yelling in my head was what knocked me down here, so I guessed we were even. Unless she had come to collect her debt.

I braced myself against the wall as my senses returned. "Marsaile, this isn't the best time."

"I so disagree." She reached out and gently stroked the side of my face, taking away all of the pain from her shoving herself into my head. "And no appreciation for having thinned the pack for you."

"And why would you do that?"

"It was much more than I should have done. Mock me at your peril." She slowly bent over, locking her eyes, which burned with cold rage, onto mine. Her long, frigid fingers slowly wrapped around my face and throat. "If you fail me this day, I have something so delightfully special for you. Hel herself would shrink away, and back to her lair of the dead."

I began shivering uncontrollably as my blood became a glacier. The Leviskin was nothing against her power. "What is it you want?"

She waved her hand against a section of the ice wall, causing it to become transparent. The outer doors of the lycan base had been ripped open. A dozen ice statues stood between me and the inner door. "My daughter is in there. Bring her to me."

"Abhile is safely hidden away. I took her—"

"To your sanctuary." Her breath left ice crystals on my skin. "I am aware. And she left of her own accord weeks ago to be captured by these animals."

"Go get her yourself."

Her grip tightened. "If only I could. There are places I cannot go, by the accords. This is one. Seeing as how they have violated them by taking the princess and successor, I can give you some assistance."

I fought to shake her grip. If I lit her up with a little fire, she'd pop my head off like a flower from the stem. "I was going to the store anyway. I can pick up your junior miss ice queen."

Iced lycans shattered with the flick of the Winter Queen's finger. My skin burned when she released her grip, taking some of my dermis with her. She stared at the bits of skin and smiled as she licked them off.

"You owe me, wizard, and I am short on patience. Bring me my daughter, and the pelt of these beasts' master, and I may take out the rest of my fury on you lightly."

"Marsaile"—I reached up and rubbed my raw skin—"I will do everything I can to protect Abhile and bring you a piece of Rahm, just like I put your old lap mage out of his misery. What else do you want from me?"

"You forget. You were to bring Drake to me alive, his body, if not. I have neither. Your protection of my daughter has certainly not met my expectations. And here you stand, ready to destroy yourself. This act will not let you escape me or your debt."

"I've gotten out of tighter spots."

"Do tell, wizard." My chest tightened as she ran her finger across my lips. "Did you bring another gateway to unleash the fury of the underworld? Shatter the Veils that separate the realms?"

"Nope." I set my pack on the ground and dug until I found a small ampule, one of Heph's modified blades, and a bundle of gauze. "I've got a chew toy for the puppies."

MARSAILE FADED AWAY into a cloud of mist. Her last words hung in the still air. *May Fortuna give you her blessing. You'll need it.*

A small Push of energy blasted open the shelter of ice she'd constructed around me. I shivered as the wind howled and churned in the shattered space. The Leviskin thickened around me but did little to stop my tremors.

A dozen or more lycans had been flash frozen and shattered inside and just outside of what remained of the exterior gate. As I held my makeshift grenade in hand, I hoped Tinka had kept his attorney indoors and heeded my warning about sealing themselves in.

I charged up the blade with the ampule strapped to it by the roll of gauze. As soon as it hit anything, the blade would release a blast of power, shattering the ampule and soaking anything nearby in Heph's Werewolf love potion.

The walls and doors had been well reinforced but were built to protect against magic and the earliest days of gunpowder. I was about to find out how well they would do against a shaped charge of plastic explosives as they went off in a jarring blast.

I hid behind the rubble of the outer wall as the shock wave caused rubble to fall loose and more frozen objects to shatter. A black cloud billowed out of the newly formed gaping hole as I sprinted with the blade in hand. I released a blast of energy followed by a fireball to light my way as I came through.

What looked like a magical hallway of death was at the far end of the room. I'd made it halfway to the hall when the first of the lycans, half-transformed and wearing a Blazing Claw leather vest, loped out of the haze. I sent him backward, on fire.

More of the pack were in mid-transformation, giving me time to get close to the hall. One of Leather Vest's bigger friends swiped at me. The dragon-scale took the hit, but the force was enough to throw me off balance. If I dropped the blade inside, I was done. It had to reach my target for me to have a chance.

As I fell to the floor, I gave the blade a sideways toss into the hall and sealed myself in the Leviskin armor. I couldn't see, and the suit took most of the impact, but my stomach couldn't do enough flips to keep up, and I became a magical vomit comet. Bile burned in my throat, wanting to be free. I didn't think puking my guts up in a closed suit was the best of ideas, and I opened a slit in time to shower the growing frenzy of fur-laden soldiers in a long-forgotten breakfast.

The Leviskin shifted and healed itself as quickly as it was damaged, but it couldn't last forever. Had the ampule not broken? Had whatever magic that defended the hallway destroyed it? Had the demented god given me the wrong stuff? Was it so old that it didn't work anymore? Was I about to become the amorous interest of a room full of excited wolf men?

Being the main entertainment for the bacchanal party the lycans were having seemed worse than anything Marsaile could do to me.

I gambled and shifted the suit to have a slit creating a visor. The blade had landed about ten feet into the hallway, and the only guess I had was the gauze had dampened the impact. It hadn't gone off.

The hall vanished from sight as I was yanked upright. Pale-amber eyes glared at me through the slit. I closed it as a sharp claw tried to pry me out of my shell. He changed tactics, and my vertigo was cured by a sudden, jarring stop. Cold air seeped in underneath my armpit. The armor was reaching its limits.

I took another peek. I was on my side and propped up against the wall. Lycans were lined up to play pin the tail on the wizard. The first player charged with a leap. He slammed me with his claw and slam-dunked me into the floor. Unseen hands lifted me back into place.

The second slammed into me with the full force of his charge. More frigid air crept in around my torso. Warm dampness spread around me, to the howling delights of the competitors.

A fight broke out as to who was next. I pieced enough of the argument together to figure out that whoever got to me first got my juicy insides.

The hallway was fifteen feet to my right, but at this angle, I couldn't see the blade any longer.

The argument at the far end of the room had been settled. The loser was bleeding on the floor. The winner howled and loped on all fours in a frenzied charge.

When he was only feet away, I lightened the armor and dropped to the floor. The Were flew over my dropping body and chipped the wall with his head instead of my ribs. I let loose with a fireball from each hand and raced for the exit.

Most of the pack moved away to block me, giving me a clear shot to the blade. I loosed a blast of energy into the hall and curled into a corner, hardening the armor again.

I was rewarded with a sharp crack to my ribs as a one of the gang members bowled me across the floor. Had I missed? Was the damn thing useless?

The howling changed tone. The shrillness cut through me more than being naked in the icy tundra outside. I dared to look when no one had used me as a plaything for more than a few seconds.

Some of the gang members fought and clawed their way into the hall, trying to be first. None were anywhere near me, so I unfroze the armor and crawled across the floor, backing away.

One danced with the head of one of his former brethren in his hands as he leapt over the frenzy. His touchdown dive ended in a blaze of lightning and the stench of burned fur. It was enough to shake loose the mass of meat and growling as they poured into the fiery grinder. More dove in from the far end.

One had chained another of the pack to the wall, and a hind foot got caught in the lines from the generator powering their lights and heat. He didn't drag it all the way in with him, but one string of

302

construction lights trailed him into death and carried the charge back to the generator. The fireball from its detonation carried over my head and into the storm outside.

A chunk of ceiling big enough to be called a boulder broke loose and fell to the floor.

The only sound left was the mournful whimpering of the chained lycan. I shifted the armor back into a medium configuration and studied the pitiful creature. He clawed at the steel collar around his throat and glanced at me before looking at the hallway that had destroyed the rest of the pack. At first, I thought he was whimpering because of his wounds from the blast, but then realized he didn't care about that. He wanted to follow the rest of his gang into the pheromone-laden hall of death.

Who was I to deny him?

I slashed through the lock holding the collar closed. The beast growled at me. For a moment, I wondered if turning him loose had been a mistake. But in the end, he got to roll around in the ashes of his clan for a few seconds before joining them.

"HELLO, DOWN THERE." Whatever enchantment created the lightning field did a pretty good job of cleaning up the mess. After a few moments, most of the stench of overcooked Werewolf had faded.

I still had no idea how I was going to get to the far end of the hall, or if there was anyone alive and free at the controls.

I destroyed the generator on my end, making the cold stark glow at the far end of the hall almost welcoming. I looked for any way to get around the deadly obstacle course in front of me.

"Can anyone hear me?" I shouted at the top of my lungs. If there was no one to respond, was it worth getting to the other side?

I tossed an energy ball into the wall and triggered a blinding flash. I opened my Senses and focused on the hall. The power coursing through the walls ran deep and was powered by a telluric node, as I suspected. None of my power was going to put a dent in it, much less get me to the far end. How could the lycans have powered it?

I directed my Senses down the hall and stretched to see if I could feel anything or anyone. The power in the hall dampened what I was able to Sense, but there were at least a few living beings at the other end.

I pulled together a small fireball and flung it down the length of the hall to splash on the far end. The enchantment tested my power but let it through. Something at the far end stirred.

I poured more power into the second blast. Again, the hall probed it and let it through. The scream from the other end told me I'd reached out and touched someone.

A volley of ice spears flew back at me as my reward.

"Hey," I yelled at the shadow that quickly vanished. "It doesn't have to happen this way."

The response was syrupy. "How, then? Will you trust me to let you all the way through? Should I violate my duty in the idea that you will allow me safe passage?"

He had a point. "Do you have prisoners down there?"

"Maybe."

"Are you alone? Do you have other guards with you?"

"I had many." Another halfhearted icicle flew past me. "Maybe there are a few left."

"What do you propose?" I asked. "I just want the prisoners."

"Any in particular?" A hooded being glanced around the corner. "Or will just any do to make you leave?"

I hid halfway behind a stack of crates with an energy ball glowing between my hands at the ready. "All of them."

He chuckled softly. "Why would I do that?"

"If you make me come down there the hard way, there're worse things than death."

"By the time you find a way to reach me, I can have done anything I wish with anyone I have here. And reinforcements are on their way." He unleashed a blast of icy stilettos that shattered on the top of the crate. "Why don't you run along before my master arrives?"

I'd never taken well to threats. I had only half an idea how to get to the far end of the hall, and no idea if it would work.

I pulled together all the energy I could hold and flung a concussive wave straight and true down the hall. The blast triggered a shower of sparks and crashing objects before part of the wave rebounded down the hall and sent me flying.

I looked up from my landing spot. Only a few spots of light were left. More importantly, a large area within my sight was in deep shadow.

I shifted the Leviskin so all of my weapons were in easy reach. I drew the 1911 in one hand and a blade in the other and selected a shadow on the wall where I could enter.

Suck it, ancient trap. And if I was wrong, then hopefully I would go out quickly in a blaze of glory.

STATIC CHARGES PROBED as I flew through the hall. I stepped out of the shadow with every hair standing on end, but I was unsinged. Pins jabbed at every inch of my body until I was numb.

A young dark elf mage lay unconscious on the floor, his skin a rich, deep blue. After making sure he wasn't faking, I rolled him over and used riot restraints to hold him in place, with an extra few loops of woven cold steel and silver wire to bind his power.

By some miracle of physics, a single light bulb had survived the blast. A bluestone panel in the wall had sigils engraved deep into the rock. It had to be the switch for the hall.

Another of the thick-plated doors was closed and barred in the alcove. I drew in a deep breath and held my 1911 at the ready. Then I pushed the bar upward.

Are you sure you want to do that?

I spun and drew the Colt to find the source of the voice. It had sounded as if it were just behind me. "Come out."

If only I could.

"Tsauriel? Is that you?" The voice was thready but deep and feminine.

Who?

"Who is this? Where are you?"

Tellia. It's Tellia.

"Impossible."

This is where you draw the line? You can't believe I'm communicating with you from inside this crystal? I've now seen much stranger things inside your head than this.

"How?"

We were connected somehow during my transition. I couldn't reach you before now. I could feel you, but it was shrouded.

I took the hilt of the Anima Arca in hand. The connection strengthened, and her voice came in clear and strong. I could even Sense her presence. Maybe having the blade wrapped in Leviskin blocked her connection.

"I'd love to catch up, but right now's not the time."

You don't sense it, do you?

I was still numb from the shadow-walk through the charged hall. I cleared my mind and tried to stretch my Senses. I felt something but couldn't be sure what it was. "What is it?"

The door is charged.

I ran my fingers around the frame and received a shock. "Thanks for the warning. Any idea how to disable it?"

No, I just Sensed the energy through you.

I shuddered. Just what I needed. Someone else riding along in my head. Even if she had just saved me, there wasn't a lot of room left for someone else's voice in my head. "We'll have to talk this situation out later."

As you wish.

I rolled my new blue friend over and leaned him against the wall. "Wake up." I slapped his face lightly.

He blinked and returned a glassy cerulean stare.

"Are you in there?"

He nodded. "You spared me?"

"So far." I pointed at the door. "If you want to stay that way, tell me how to open the door."

"You removed the crossbeam. Open the door."

"And blow us all to the next world?"

"We would be fine," he stated flatly. "The prisoners would be, as you say, sent to their just rewards."

"I'd prefer that not happen."

"I will not turn them over to you to be tortured."

"Look, kid." My Senses were returning. It felt as if I had a mild sunburn and had been rolled in salt. "I don't want that either."

308

"The First should be able to read and understand the script."

"The what?"

"The First Lycan. Are you not him? No other was able to transverse the hall."

"You mean Rahm? Roman? Whatever he calls himself?" I knelt and leaned in, nose-to-nose with the blue creature. "Do I look like a Werewolf?"

The uncoordinated inchworm squirmed away until he was trapped in a corner. "Who are you?"

"A tired sorcerer who's running out of patience and wants to see if his friends are on the other side of door number three."

"Who do you seek?"

"A cop, a priest, and an Amazonian queen."

He snickered. "It sounds like the start of a bad joke."

I shoved his head into the wall behind him. "Do I look like I'm laughing?"

"Why should I help you? Either you deceive me and intend to slay the ones behind the door, or you free them. Either way, you have sworn to kill me."

I shook my head. "If I wanted to kill them, you said all I need to do is open the door."

"And maybe I lied."

The mage was young. Very young. He was still growing into his full elven form. Why would anyone trust him with this kind of duty? He also must have thought himself immortal, a common sin for us both. "You're stalling."

He beamed a grin at me. "My mistress will be here shortly. She left me here as the only one who could use the controls and keep the ones inside safe until she arrived."

"Marsaile?" I paced and looked down the hall. "She's outside somewhere. Helped me clear a path coming in. And she didn't say anything about you."

He snorted. "My mistress surpasses the Queen of Winter, but I hold allegiance to her as well. She would have no use for one not of Winter."

I touched his forehead and tapped into the blood oath she held over me. His eyes went wide.

"Do you want to try that again?" I asked.

"You do serve her." Whatever he'd seen in me turned him several shades lighter. "Release me, and I will open the door. You have my oath."

THE BLOODBOND COURSED between us. The rush left me lightheaded. I'd never been on this side of the deal. If he betrayed me, I had not only his life, but his power and the knowledge to collect on his bloodline.

310

His bonds snapped from the light touch of my knife. Freed, he rose, stretched, and rubbed where the restraints had been. After straightening his mist-colored robe, he tugged the hood forward, covering most of his face.

"Your turn," I said.

He nodded and touched three sigils on the panel. "You may enter now."

I stood beside the entrance in case something or someone was ready to burst forth from the other side, but all remained quiet. I felt nothing as I touched the door this time.

"It's not that I don't trust you." I backed away from the door and held the Colt at my side. "But you first."

Raising his closed hands with his palms clutched to his chest, he edged along the wall, his eyes darting between me and the door. He stopped beside the door and grabbed the lever. "On your word."

"What's your name?"

"What?" He curled tighter against the door. "Why?"

"What do I call you in case I need to tell you to look out or get out of the way?"

"Oh." A small nod came from under the hood. "Dyli. Call me Dyli."

I took a deep breath and released it, Pushing power through myself. I trained the Colt on the door. "Now."

The dark elf jerked on the handle, and the door fired open like a cannon, expelling a bloody and mostly human creature. It flopped to the floor and jerkily undulated like an eel on land.

With the Colt trained on the wretched creature, I stepped back, not wanting to fire unless I had no choice. It snarled and flung out a three-fingered hand, and its long claws dug into the floor. In a twisted swimming motion, it worked its way upstream into the hall. In a blinding flash, its misery and ours in watching it ended in another blinding flash.

Three more lycan bodies lay inside the room. The inside of the door was ripped apart where they'd tried to escape. The table where they'd been playing cards was upturned. Two of the six cell doors were open. Dirty, sagging faces gaped from the small windows in the four locked cells.

"Dyli, stop."

The elf froze, his hands hovering above the lock on the first door.

Dark, sunken eyes moved into the small porthole of the cell, attracted to the glow from my small flashlight. I knew the face even if there was no acknowledgment from that side other than a blink. It was Irika. The second chamber held Sonja. Father Mike was in the third, and Wynn in the last.

I motioned for Dyli to back away and opened Wynn's door first. The cell exhaled stale air tinged with bergamot and mace, as well as a static cloud that turned my muscles to gelatin.

I waved my hand and whispered an incantation to disperse the muddling field that held Wynn in a stupor.

He sat on the edge of the shelf he'd had for a bed, his head in his hands.

I grabbed a bottle of water from the meager supplies in the room. "Gerry?"

He took the bottle and sipped down the contents. "What's the trick this time?"

"Trick?" I tilted his head back so I could look into his eyes. The clouds behind them were fading slowly. "It's me, Grey."

"Does that mean I'm finally dead? Or are you a ghost?"

"Neither." I took him by the arm and walked him into the guard room, placing him in a chair. "How long have you been here? Are you hurt?" I began a quick scan, looking for any signs of bites or scratches, but I had to believe if he'd been marked, he would have already been drawn to the remaining pheromones in the hall. I didn't know what I would do if I thought I had lost him.

"I'm okay." Vinegary sweat poured out and soaked the meager clothes he wore. "I'm okay," he muttered to himself over and over.

ALL FOUR RECOVERED quickly once they were free of the muddling force in their cells and sweated out the potion that had kept them docile. None seemed hurt other than still being tired and confused, and it wasn't the time or place for an extended debriefing.

I found a locker of winter gear that fit them well enough to keep them protected.

I pulled Dyli to the control panel. We needed to be gone before reinforcements showed up. "How does it work?"

313

The dark elf traced three sigils with thin fingers. "Someone must stay behind. Press these two, and then hold the third sigil for as long as people are traversing the hall."

"Let me get them together."

"I understand." He clasped his hands in front of him and bowed. "I will live up to my vow and remain behind. I will see you through the gate safely."

"Um, no."

He shuffled back into the corner, mostly hidden by the door. "I've... I've done as you asked. Please—"

"No." I raised my hands and turned them inward like he'd done earlier as a sign of peace. "You misunderstand. You're going with us."

His body trembled. "Someone must stay behind."

"Let me worry about that."

He drew his cowl back to reveal he was barely the elven equivalent of a teenager. "What will you do with me, then?"

"Once we're out of here, you can go wherever you want. Come with us or not." He flinched as I patted his shoulder. "But I'm not leaving you behind."

He looked around the room. "You mean I'll no longer be a bondservant?"

"Whatever that is. I guess not. Unless it's something you want to be."

"Gather your people. Let's be gone from this place."

THE HALLWAY HUMMED as I held the gateway open. Dyli checked my hold on the sigil and closed his eyes before taking a tentative step into the hall. After he wasn't vaporized, he motioned for the others to follow.

Every step they shuffled down the hall sent a surge of pain through my hand, tempting me to pull it away. The elf had prepared me for this, but words did little to describe the jolting sensation I felt. I had to brace my hold on the sigil with my other hand and my back against the wall of the alcove, lest I be knocked loose.

Dyli had explained the hallway had to dispel the charge somehow. It couldn't actually be disabled. The logic of the trap plus the forceful nearby Earth energy adding power made me doubt there was any kind of real switch that could be put into place. The sigil was the equivalent of holding back a pack of starving mastiffs from a steak and using barbed wire as a leash.

Fire poured through me, and I was barely able to understand when they gave me the all clear from the other end. I slumped to the floor and stared at my blackened fingers. My pack with all of my healing elixirs was just outside, and a hall of death away.

I had to settle for the bottle of water Dyli had left.

The sounds of the rushing flood cleared from my head and were replaced by frantic shouting. Someone was calling me.

I rolled over and crawled around the corner, where I could see down the hall. Everyone was on their side. No, I was sideways, lying on the soothing floor.

I rolled over and lay on my back and let the cold soak through me until I was shivering.

My head cleared, and I was able to sit up. I centered myself, and concentrated, filling my body with warmth and power. The dark corner along the back wall was big enough for my intended purpose. I focused on it until a tunnel formed, and all I could see was the darkness.

The darkness called me and pulled me through. A bright flash tugged at me, but the darkness wouldn't let it have me. So I screamed.

"GET MY PACK." I pointed vaguely outside the half-collapsed entrance as I stared at the faintly rosy skies overhead. The sun was coming up to give its few hours of light.

"Drink this." Wynn knew what to grab and handed me an ampule.

The top snapped off between my fingers, and the icy liquid was bitter as it flowed down my throat. "Another," I managed to groan out.

Numbing warmth spread though my body. I dreamed I lay next to a stone hearth with a pot of tea brewing over its flames. When the potion reached my charred hand, I saw and felt it steep in the boiling pot.

The vision faded, and I sat up, shaking. Steam was still rising off my body from the trip through the telluric lightning.

Wynn held out another vial. "How do you feel?"

I waved him off. Blackened skin crackled on my hand as I flexed it. "Like we need to get moving." I doubted how long the elixir could keep me going without some food and sleep.

Wynn picked up my pack, pulled the Sig out of the side pouch, and pocketed the spare magazines before throwing the pack over his shoulder. "How far do we need to go?"

I looked around. Father Mike was pale and shaking. Sonja and Irika were silently staring into the light snow drifting from the skies. "Not far, but it's going to be a hike in this weather." I handed him a map with Tinka's hideout and our current location with a snaking path to the mining camp. "Follow this trail, and we'll do an extraction from here."

"Let's get going."

"Get them started." I stretched as I got to my feet. "I've got a little cleanup here. Won't be more than a minute or two behind."

Wynn tied a rope around his waist and looped it around everyone in the party, with Dyli taking up the tail. Once they were all together, Wynn led them off into the woods.

After moving the five-gallon cans of fuel that had been intended for the generators into the hallway, I dumped the first few so they poured into the deathtrap. I piled the rest up at the edge. Standing outside in the snow, I didn't have a direct shot, but I didn't need one.

It wasn't so much that I cared about the remaining pheromones attracting more Werewolves to their destruction, but rather I was more concerned about what other canids might be drawn in by accident. The blast wouldn't damage the hall carved into the stone, but it should incinerate the remaining attractant and collapse the structure built in front.

I tried to summon a fireball and quickly discovered that my burned hand couldn't control it. I wound up burning myself in the process and shoved my throbbing hand into the snow, releasing a burst of fire with the other.

I ran in pursuit of Wynn as the fortress behind me belched out a flaming ball.

"YOU'VE BEEN BUSY." The Dagda snipped at me as he and Agent Dube found us about halfway between the fortress and the mining camp. "Or did you get lost on the way to meet up with us?"

"I went to grab some takeout and ran into a few people."

"You're injured." His beard did little to hide his grimace. "Let me take a look."

I sat on a fallen tree and pulled away the glove I'd wrapped around it. "How'd you know?"

"You were protecting it." He knelt in the snow, where he could whisper. "We were being watched in the camp and are being stalked now."

"Lycans?"

"I haven't seen them, but it's the most likely answer."

My hand itched and tingled as he waved the end of his staff over it. Dead blackness sloughed off my hand, leaving tender pink skin underneath. "Thanks."

"It was foolish of you to do this alone." He shook his head. "It will take a few days for it to fully heal. No magic until then."

With a Push, the Leviskin wrapped my hand in a protective glove. "We're being stalked, and I still need to juice up the portal home."

He huffed. "Keep it to a minimum, especially with the fire."

"I'll try."

He sniffed as he shifted in place. "Any sign of Priscilla?"

I shook my head. "Abhile either. Any idea how or when she and Sonja left the Grove?"

"No. I wasn't going out of my way to spend time with them either."

I understood the old god's desire to avoid them and sensed him questioning my judgment about having given them sanctuary in the first place.

He pushed himself to his feet with the assistance of his staff. "We'd best check on Aurelie. She became quite agitated when you didn't return. I had to chase after her, and that's when we ran into you."

"I did pretty much just come in and out." I pulled on his coat, and he leaned down so only he could hear. "Marsaile came to me. It seemed to be a better choice for you to stay clear."

He grunted out a laugh. "Shall we make an exit before any more uninvited guests show up?"

AURELIE DUBE PACED around the shack as I outlined the portal ring in the floor. Her pacing was making my skin crawl and my concentration wander. "Why don't you get everyone else ready to travel while I finish the preparations?"

"How much longer will this take?" She grabbed a chair that nudged her path and threw it into the corner. "You've got the thing set in the floor, and a circle around it. You said that would do it."

"I'm having to charge it up slowly as I go." I pushed her attitude aside while I traced the delicate features of a sigil. "And there's a little more than that. The parchment sigil is a key, but I've got to finish building the door. And I'm a little drained."

Her tone was sharp. "You should not have gone without me. Us. You brought The Dagda with you. Or was he meant to distract me?"

"I had an opportunity to go in. I took it. It wasn't my plan to go in alone." She didn't need to know the Winter Queen had helped clear the way.

"So you say." She pounded against the table that held my implements, knocking several objects to the floor. "What else was inside their base?"

320

I pushed her away and picked up the fallen objects. "Nothing good."

Though I was more than a foot taller than her, she stood toe to toe with me. "Tell me. How did you get past all of their defenses? What if they follow us here?"

I leaned over to make sure she understood me. "There's no one there. Not alive, at least."

She swallowed and stepped back. "You slaughtered them all?"

"More like I let them destroy themselves. The plan, remember?"

She closed her gaping mouth. "What intelligence did you leave behind that might have told us where to find the others?"

"There wasn't much there. I doubt they even knew where they were, exactly. They're transported in every couple of weeks."

She cocked her head. "How do you know that?"

I couldn't tell her about Tinka and his group. I didn't think someone who hunted lycans for a living would be sympathetic. "Something I heard one say while I was in hiding."

She pointed a stubby finger at me. "This discussion is not over, but I don't want to be here any longer than need be. Hurry up."

The wooden shack threatened to collapse as she slammed the door.

AFTER COMPLETING THE circle, I hoped I had enough power left to transport us all to the other end hidden in the Grove. I knew I would have to return to get to Rahm's new fortress, so I found a hidden spot in a root cellar under a storehouse and left a small portal ring under the loose soil.

My Senses had been so shocked and stretched, I couldn't detect anything in the woods. Even so, I still couldn't shake the feeling I was being watched. If there was nothing else I could agree with Dube about, it was that I was ready to get out of these frozen woods.

Father Mike was the first to greet me as I came through the doorway. His body was slow and stiff as he moved, but his mirthful grin was reassuring.

Sonja was the only one not gathered around the potbellied stove in the corner of the room. She rubbed on a gold ring as she stared out the window, barely glancing at me when I pulled up a chair next to her. "I can't feel her."

"What?"

"I can't Sense Abhile." She held up the ring. "It's bound to her. I feel nothing from her."

"Why did you leave the safety of the Grove?"

Dark bags sagged under her eyes. "A message gave us directions to your old family domain. We believed it had come from you."

"I don't even know how to get there," I stammered. "It's been sealed off since…"

She nodded. "We stepped into a portal trap and emerged in a stone room. Priscilla was being held in one of the cells. The others were empty. They shoved Abhile into one and me into another. That's the last I remember until you arrived."

"You saw Priscilla?"

"Yes." I worried the hollowness of her voice meant she was lost. "She was shackled and jacketed. Barely glanced at us as we were brought in."

"Same enchantment they used on you, I expect."

She turned her gaze out the window. "What will we do?"

I placed my hand on my aunt's knee. "I think I know where they're being held."

"You think they're alive?" She held up her hand. "Why can't I sense her, then?"

I couldn't explain why she couldn't feel the connection, but something deep down in me did. Maybe it was just hope. Maybe it was the fact that Marsaile hadn't reappeared to haul me away to whatever torments she could cook up. "You've been under a powerful muddling. That, and there's a lot of telluric interference. She's out there."

"Let's go get her."

"We need to regroup first."

She pointed out the window. "We'd better hurry."

A group of shadows moved in the brush.

TINKA SMILED BROADLY as I met him outside in the darkness, The Dagda following on my heels. Leslie and Davis flanked their boss. Everyone else stayed in the shack, keeping a close eye on the proceedings.

I offered my hand to Paul. "I thought you were staying out of sight and getting out as soon as the job was done."

"Job ain't done yet." He firmly took my grip. "But you've made a good start."

"Where's the rest of your team?"

"Sent 'em ahead to get set up, like what we did here."

The Dagda stepped to my side. "Would someone like to finish the introductions?"

"I'm sorry. It feels like I already know ya." Tinka smiled and offered his hand. "Paul Tinka. My little company is doing some advance work in trade for your friend here, helping to lift the curse put on us by the big bad wolf."

The Dag stiffened his grip on his staff. "You're lycan."

Davis and Leslie moved their hands to their weapons.

I held my hands out. "Not by their choice. And yeah, it's a mutual arrangement."

I Sensed the easing in my old friend, but he was still on guard. "In that case, I am The Dagda." He shook Tinka's hand in greeting, dwarfing it with his own.

I lowered my hands as the tension lessened. "Let me get them out of here, and we can move on. Do you have any new intel?"

He handed me a folder. The top picture was Priscilla and Abhile, shackled and strapped into cages barely large enough to hold their upright forms as they were being offloaded from a truck.

I sighed. "They do have them."

The Dagda snarled. "Where?"

Tinka flinched. "Couple hours north. We've got a half-track ready to go."

I handed The Dagda the folder. "Let me get the rest of them out of here, and we can be moving within the hour. I've got the portal ready."

WYNN STOPPED ME at the door. "Who's that outside?"

"Local support, after a fashion." I knew there would be questions on both ends. First, my team was going to wonder why I wasn't going through the portal with them. The reception committee on the other end also might be a little surprised. On the plus side, Mike always had wanted to visit the Grove. I'd let Josiah figure that part out. "Let's get moving. It's ready to port you out of here."

Wynn followed me outside while the others extinguished the stove and braced themselves for the short walk through the cold. "I know that look," he said. "You aren't coming back, are you?"

"Not yet." I leaned in. "I've got to go get Priscilla and Abhile."

325

"I understand Priscilla, but the Winter princess?" He shook his head. "And no backup? I've seen roadkill in better shape."

I shrugged. "The Amazons are all stuck. It's a long story. And it's not like I can call Longbow for support."

"What about Raines?" he pleaded. "She couldn't make something happen?"

"I don't know. I haven't received any communication from her since..."

He nodded. "Any word about Drea? Brighid?"

I tried to explain what I knew, that last I'd seen them, they were alive. The thought of how I'd left made me weak.

"I'm going with you," he said.

"That's a bad idea." I pulled one of my oldest mortal friends and mentors into a tight hug. "You know you're nowhere near in shape for field work. If you can bring help, do it. I'll fire off a transponder."

"Damn it, kid, you shouldn't be going in alone." We both knew he would never be able to raise any kind of support in time. And he didn't know where I was about to deposit him. He looked at the ground. "I'm southern. I never liked the snow anyway."

As they shuffled out of the shack, I pointed them to the building where the circle was prepared.

"What the hell is she doing here?" Tinka shouted.

The hair on my neck stood on end as I heard the deep growl of a response.

AURELIE DUBE SLAMMED an iron fist into my side and leapt over me. Her legs stretched, and fur sprouted over her collar. She stripped her bursting clothes as she loped around the corner.

I held my side and slumped against the wall, frozen while I tried to process what had just happened. How'd she hidden her nature?

Tinka sprinted past me with The Dagda in pursuit, shouting at me to get moving as he raced by. Leslie unslung her rifle and aimed where I hoped was past me. Still focused on the weapon aimed in my general direction, I was distracted as Davis drew his sidearm. Instead of giving pursuit, he fired twice into Leslie's side, knocking her to the ground, then took aim at us.

Wynn snapped out of his shock, reflexively drew my Sig, and returned fire. Three rounds found their mark, dropping Davis to the ground.

I hopped the first few steps then broke into a sprint, following the trail of footsteps in the snow. A volley of shots popped between two of the dilapidated buildings. A muzzle flash caught my attention, but I couldn't tell who'd fired.

I took cover behind a rusted trough and inched my way forward. My Colt in my hands was loaded with blessed silver rounds. I was ready to fire back at anyone who shot first.

My Senses screamed for me to move, so I jumped from my cover. I spun around as a shorter lycan with a graying stripe landed where I'd just been crouching.

I leveled the 1911 on her center mass. "Stop there."

Dube shifted back to her human form and rose from all fours, naked except for her satchel bag and shoulder rig.

"Did you forget to mention something, Aurelie?"

"Forget? No." She flashed her canines. "Turning you would have been a big step for me."

"You look a little cold. Want to go in and talk about it?"

Her laugh was hoarse. She sprang into the air, shifting into her lycan form before she landed. Her second leap crashed into me, sending me spinning. I pulled the trigger, but my shot went wide. She pushed off the trough and landed on the shack's tin roof.

I ran along, trying to keep pace, but got slowed by debris from abandoned equipment and collapsing structures. More shots rang out to my left, and The Dagda cried out in a string of Gaelic obscenities.

He crouched at the edge of the woods, leaning against a collapsed workshop, holding his staff to his thigh. "She shot me. Damn cursed rounds burn."

Tinka was panting as he staggered out of the woods, bleeding from several gashes. "She got away."

"How far can she get in this mess by herself?" I looked back at the main part of the abandoned town and saw yellow-and-orange flames licking the sky.

"THAT WENT WELL." Tinka sat shirtless while Sonja inspected his rapidly healing wounds.

Leslie lay semiconscious on a table. She would live, but she couldn't do much until the silver bullets were removed.

Davis was cuffed and snarling. His wounds were healing around the standard rounds.

The Dagda was healing himself with his staff. It had been fun to watch Sonja remove pieces of cursed metal from him as they'd glared at each other. She finished with a smirk, and they retreated to different corners.

I looked out the window at the smoldering remains of the shack. "She destroyed the portal."

"Make another one," Sonja quipped. "It'll just take some time."

"I can't." I rubbed my face and fought the desire to find my own spot to rest. "She destroyed the key. With all of the residual disturbances, portal travel is messy at best. With this many people trying to cross a Veil... I don't have another safe destination."

Sonja's frown told me she didn't either.

Tinka wrapped the bloody remains of his shirt around him. "Then we stick with the plan, and everyone goes with us. Anyone not up for the hunting trip can stay at the base camp. I'll make sure we have medical resources ready by the time we get there."

I pointed at Davis. "What about him?"

"Good question." Tinka winced as he started to pace. "Why? Why betray us after all these years? Why me? You and Leslie go back even further."

Davis flashed a slow grin, revealing his long canines. "Why would you give up this power? You may want to. I don't. The Alpha wants to show me so much more."

Tinka shoved a bag over Davis's head. "He goes, but somebody better make sure I don't sack up this pup and drop him in a river."

THE HALF-TRACK GROUND its way through the lone trail that cut through the snowy back country. The modified surplus Soviet vehicle was meant for arctic use.

I wasn't the only one stretching my Senses into the countryside as we closed the distance to Rahm's mountain citadel. Sonja's probing touched my mind every few minutes.

Tinka and I rode in the front cab with the driver and watched the road ahead. We had to assume Dube was running straight back to Rahm. In her lycan form, she would beat us by hours. If she had a satellite phone or radio stashed, they would be preparing for us even sooner.

It had been bothering me for hours, but I had to wait for Tinka to calm down. The attorney's betrayal had cut him deeply, and he bled his ire out as he babbled about the countryside. He talked for ten minutes about why he'd pick one spot to set up an ambush along the piece of road we were on, versus Davis, who'd have used another, just to argue.

I cut into a brief moment of silence. "How'd you know Dube?"

His pupils were dilated, a tinge of yellow around the irises. "I should ask the same thing."

"She is, or at least was, a Longbow agent. Their expert on lycans."

He snorted. "Expert. Sure. First-hand."

"You next."

"Do you remember how I told you about how Rahm came to my office?" The veins in his neck throbbed. "She was with him. She's the one who turned most of my people. Everyone but Leslie, Davis, and me. He did that himself."

I rolled down the window to get a few breaths of sub-zero fresh air and bleed off the heat building in me.

He growled as he rubbed his face. "I guess we're both going to have some trust issues with our people."

Was that true? Was it possible that some of the people I trusted most in the world were ready to betray me? And might they do it of their own will? How deeply had Longbow been infiltrated? Did it even exist anymore? It wasn't as if I'd heard anything from them in months.

I had to push my doubts aside even as they grew deeper roots. If I doubted them, what were they thinking of me? The two women I loved were possibly dead. Priscilla was captured, her once-powerful organization in hiding. The Longbow Initiative was seemingly in disarray, possibly taken over by the beings they were meant to watch over. I'd even been responsible for disrupting and hardening the Veil and trapping people in disparate worlds.

Would any of it have happened if I hadn't been involved? Was I about to make matters even worse?

Something slammed into my shoulder, and I reached for the Colt strapped to my hip.

"Grey, wake up." Tinka had a wide grin on his face.

I took a final deep breath of frigid air and rolled up the window.

"How did you clear out two full packs back there?" he asked.

"Wolf bait." I was happy to have something to talk about. "I was able to use pheromones to draw them into their own trap."

He took a deep breath and sniffed at me. "Whoa. That makes me feel better. I was feeling a lot of attraction to your leg."

"YOU'RE DAMN CRAZY." Tinka had listened to my plan.

"I should've realized how they were tracking us." I'd been too lost in my own misery to listen to what my Senses had told me. "I've still got some of the lycan juice on me. Not enough to drive you over the edge, but plenty for them to follow us."

"And you think hyping up the rest is a good idea?"

"I saw what happened when they got a full dose. You don't want to be anywhere near if I open one of these vials. I can pull them off, and you can get to the bunker safely." I reached my Senses over the hill where the road split. At least a dozen lycans waited in an ambush with a couple of mages. "Make sure all of your people are restrained when I cut this stuff loose."

He jumped out of the vehicle. "Let's see what your friends back there think."

I took a deep breath and followed him in through the back hatch. I didn't get a lot of support, except from The Dag, who insisted on tagging along.

My chest was still tight after I convinced Wynn and Sonja that neither of them was fit for the assault. I had used a weak magical attack that left both of them unable to stand for a few minutes. Sonja cursed me and wished me luck in the same breath. Mike blessed me, and I'm pretty sure threw in last rites on top.

We locked Tinka, Leslie, and Davis in the back hatch. I hoped the gas masks would reduce their dosage of the pheromones if I had to use them. Sonja and Wynn rode with the driver. Mike, Irika, and Dyli took up positions in the back of the antique transport.

I tried to convince The Dagda to remain with the vehicle for protection. Instead, he turned his staff to me and gave me another healing charge.

The half-track crawled along the path as if stuck in the mire. Sonja was blasting out energy in an effort to mask our approach as The Dagda and I climbed the ridge.

The ambush was split between two groups, one on each side of the roadway. The groups were made up of a dozen lycans in human form and three mages in total. Rahm's citadel loomed in the nearby cliffside, a lot closer than I had expected.

"I wish to document in the histories that this is a questionable choice," The Dagda whispered.

"Does that mean you're ready to go back and sit in the car like I asked?"

He leaned back with a grin slicing from ear to ear. "There's no chance I'd give up a front-row seat for this."

"Just remember you said that." I drew back the arrow tipped with a vial of the lycan pheromones.

THE ARROW SAILED in a high arc toward one of the mages. It started to dip when I released the concussive blast from my hand.

The snap of the blast drew their faces skyward as a fine mist of splinters and love potion a la hound rained down. The mages glanced around, pointing their staves in the air.

The others rolled on the ground, howling and snarling at each other. Clothes shredded away as the lycans changed into their wolven forms with something other than ambush on their minds. A mage yelled, trying to restore order, and was rewarded with a claw through the throat.

The other two mages turned and ran for the citadel.

Enraged by the dose of pheromones, the males challenged each other for the attention of the few females in the pack, all of whom ran into the woods.

In the chaos, The Dagda pointed at the half-track nearly hidden inside of a cave. "Looks like they made it."

I slung my pack over my shoulder. "Good for them." I pointed at the citadel and the flood of black dots pouring out of the gate.

"Well, boy." He pounded his staff on the ground. "You might want to get out your new friend there."

"I thought you said—"

He stroked his beard. "That's before you sent every hound for a hundred miles into a frenzy."

I shifted the Leviskin to ready my weapons. Tellia's voice touched me as I drew the Anima Arca to shift its position.

I can help you. Tap my strength, my power, my knowledge.

As I slid the blade into place, I made sure it could touch my skin. Heph's gift, the stave, hung by a sling over my shoulder. "Let's try to sneak by while they all rush here."

He paused then shrugged. "We'll try it your way."

THE DAGDA CRACKED the skull of a raging Werewolf that swiped at him. We backed our way up the trail, trying to avoid the main flow of lycans, but we'd come across several stragglers cutting their own path, too driven to follow the pack.

From the number that poured out of the citadel, every Were in North America had to be within these few square miles of real estate.

To avoid a large pack in bloodlust, we cut along a path and emerged on the top of a spur, facing the main gate. We didn't have the gear to climb down and had to turn back down the hill. Enough passing lycans turned to face us, which told me we'd been splashed by enough pheromones to attract attention.

Between the number of lycans and the stress of sensory overload, I'd pulled my Senses back to barely scout what was in front of us.

A growl came from the woods behind us. Seven large Werewolves salivated as they stalked us.

I dropped the nearest with three rounds from my Colt. The Dagda brought his staff down onto the spine of another with a loud crack.

I'd dropped two more when The Dagda roared. A pair of lycans sprang from above us and knocked him to the ground. A flash of brown struck at me, but I was knocked to the ground by a small bundle of black fur with a white stripe before the blow could land.

I swung the silver blade in my hand upward to block the Werewolf above me as he reared back on his powerful legs. It drew back its lips to show me long canines.

My dog held me down and licked my face. "Unless you've swapped sides, get off me." I shoved at the tiny bundle that felt like it weighed something twenty times its size.

The lycan drew back its razor-sharp claw to strike and disappeared under a ton of gnarled flesh with red eyes as it slammed into the ground like a boulder.

The Dagda shoved one lycan away, which immediately disappeared into the jaws of the massive Hellhound before me, and crushed the skull of another with the swing of his staff.

The furball hopped off me and rubbed against The Dagda's leg in greeting. I held the silver blade between me and the descendant of Cerebos that had been on my heels for years, the one I'd nicknamed Scar.

The Hellhound sat on his haunches as if he was waiting for a treat.

"A friend of yours?" The Dagda quipped as he contemplated the creature.

"No." I tried to figure out why he was waiting, and locked my gaze onto him as I climbed to my feet, but the descendant of Cerberus seemed satisfied just to stand guard. "And it's kind of creepy."

The furball trotted between Scar and me, let out a little growl, and lay down.

I kept my eyes on Scar as I knelt down and scratched my mutt's head. "How the hell did you get here?"

The Dagda crossed his arms as he leaned against his staff. "I see what you mean."

"You really do know how to start a party." Eric Buci rode up on an Andalusian horse, wearing standard tactical gear, surrounded by the rest of Scar's pack. "I guess our invitation got lost in the FaeMail."

"Our?"

Another person in Amazonian armor trotted up beside Eric on a raven Friesian. I'd never seen their combat dress in black before. "Hello, Greyson."

"Onyx?"

"WE SHOULD TALK." Eric slid off his horse. "But not here. Not now."

The pack of Hellhounds wandered in a circle around us. A curious lycan came too far up the ridge and was torn apart by the hounds.

"I'm pretty sure I need some answers before we go anywhere else." I sat down on a rock, trying to understand everything that had happened in the last few minutes. I couldn't help but stare at Onyx. How could she be alive? Much less looking like she was out for a casual ride, if it wasn't for the sprays of blood on her and her horse showing how difficult their trip had been to get here.

Eric waved at the pack. "We will deal with the lycanthropes while you get into the citadel."

"I think I'm going to need more than that." My hand rested on the Colt. "How are you controlling them?"

"You wouldn't be their master, so they found me." He climbed back onto his horse. "When you started throwing around the scent, the pack became restless. Even my love sensed it, given the taint of her injuries. Color me shocked when I found you at the other end of the disturbance."

"We aren't done here."

Onyx turned her horse and rode down the hill.

"It seems we are for now." Eric snapped his fingers and barked a command. Scar stretched and let out a yawn then charged down the hill after Onyx, taking the rest of the pack with him. "Call me when you're done here."

The furball snorted as Eric followed the rest into battle.

The Dagda guffawed. "A boy and his dog. Who told Lassie you were at the bottom of the well?"

I rubbed my eyes and tried to focus. "Bite me."

THE MELEE RAGED in the valley below. Hundreds of lycans indiscriminately fought, frolicked, and mated under the influence of Heph's cocktail, unleashing a torrential accompaniment of yelps and mournful howls. Two riders on horseback surrounded by a pack of well-coordinated Hellhounds cut swaths through the otherwise-occupied and insanely driven beasts.

None had exited the citadel gates in several minutes.

I motioned to The Dagda. "Let's go."

Thirteen pounds of fury led the way and warned us of the lone Werewolf straggler. His own kind had already worked him over, and we gave him swift mercy.

The iron gates and inner wooden doors stood open as we passed underneath the incomplete stone gate. Construction materials littered the vacant courtyard, which was next to a firing range and an oversized cage large enough for half-court basketball. The discarded weapons and dried blood told of a different purpose.

"You would think someone would be left about." The Dag's voice echoed off the stone walls and granite cliff face.

I opened my Senses as much as I dared. "There are. Inside." The low pulse of magic blended with others. Some human, some not, wielded the power of magic.

Do you feel that?

Tellia's bond with me opened up telepathic communication. It was probably better that The Dagda not see me speak to myself then have to explain it. *Yes. What is it?*

Power. She Pushed an image into my mind. It looked a lot like the generator that the Erebites had used in the desert.

Here? There's one of those here?

You know the purpose of this?

I was overcome with a sense of heaviness and dread.

I think so. I nodded at The Dagda. "Lock and load. Things are about to get interesting."

His staff gave off an intense aura of power. "Good to know. Things have been dull up to now."

THE IRON PORTCULLIS shook the ground when it slammed down behind us.

"That's a good sign," I said.

The Dagda shrugged. "At least they left the door open for us to come in."

Braziers burst to life along the walls and climbed the wide staircase cut from the rock, rising into the inky darkness.

"I think they know we're here."

A low rumble came from the head of the stairs. In a strange way, the furball's growl was comforting. Five pairs of golden eyes bobbed as they stalked toward us.

Fireballs rained down from above and behind us.

We split up. I ran to my right and emptied the Colt's magazine into the balcony.

The first beast touched the sandy ground. It must have weighed four hundred pounds, even as its ribs outlined its body. I shot three silver-infused rounds into its flank, but they weren't enough to dissuade it from inviting me to be dinner.

Emptying the rest of the magazine into it only angered it more. It lowered its massive head and charged.

I dashed from left to right, trying to find any sort of cover as another shower of fire came from above. I was saved when the starved lycan took the hit from an errant fireball.

I drew back and pulled a small sun into existence between my hands, Pushing it outward in a wide arc. It doused my hunter in a finishing blow, as well as a second smaller one in a cleansing bath of flames.

A third lay with its skull crushed at the far end of the arena.

Where were the other two?

A shower of icy spikes rained down. I found The Dagda taking cover under the lip of a doorway. "What I said about your new staff?"

"Yeah?"

He deflected a fireball at the head of the staircase, illuminating the door. "You may wish to disregard my advice."

"Can you give me some cover?"

"Whenever you're ready."

I pulled out a standard fragmentation grenade and a couple of the latest versions of the holy hand grenades. They were loaded with a mixture of silver and holy water plus a few special herbs and spices.

"Now."

He batted away another fireball. I lobbed the frag into the balcony and followed up with a fireball of my own. The shower of stone and fire that rained down from my attack quieted the choir.

My night vision was temporarily gone. I'd spent too long waiting to check my handiwork. "Do you see the other two?"

"Straight ahead."

I relied on my Senses and threw the first blessed grenade in an underhanded toss. It exploded but did little more than enrage the creature.

It edged away until its partner flanked us.

The wounded one charged me, and I reached for a blade with each hand. I had a silver blade in my left that I planted in the beast's neck, and I sent a ceramic blade through its skull. But it kept coming. I held onto the hilts as the snapping jaws came within inches of my face, splashing me in hot saliva.

The ceramic blade snapped, and the hound's head flew past me into the wall. I grabbed another blade from my thigh and sliced straight through its neck.

The Anima Arca was covered in blood and glowing blue. My heart hammered in my chest.

Tellia whispered in my head. *I have purpose again. Use my power.*

"THEY'RE DIRE WOLVES. I haven't seen one of these since we landed in Eire." The Dagda held up the head I'd severed and stared at the jaws. "Dire wolves tainted with the lycan curse. A nasty combination."

A deep gash ran down his arm. "Are you?"

He tossed the head to the ground. "This? It's nothing. Their curse won't do anything worse to me than a cold is to you. Their kind has given me much worse before."

"The day is young."

My legs were rubbery by the time we reached the top of the 360 steps. Each was engraved with ancient sigils, and all were meant for legs much longer than mine. The Leviskin shifted to let the

343

frigid air flow through the suit and wick away the sweat. "Need a break?" I panted.

"No." He unhooked the horn from his belt and took a drink. "I needed that."

He handed me the drink next. Whatever elixir he was manifesting in the horn burned its way down before warming and soothing my extremities.

The archway was cut into the blue-green rock high above us. We wove though the pillars, which formed a regular obstacle course. Braziers cast their meager warmth, barely giving us enough light to navigate. Water dripped with a consistent sploosh into a distant pool.

A warm glow, similar to a late-spring midday sun, beckoned as we neared the end of the chamber. The air was getting warmer and more humid, and by the time we reached the gate, the chamber nearly felt like a sauna.

We stood at the top of a short staircase. Gold, bronze, and copper shields hung on the walls of an overgrown terraced garden. Waterfalls trailed into canals filled with fish. Birds chattered in a great caucus.

Braziers cradled jets of flame, but most of the light and heat came from a pair of jewel-encrusted dragons the size of cargo trains. They were crafted of precious metals that wrapped around half of the upper tier of the basin and spewed forth blossoming fountains of blue, orange, and red. The cascade splashed into a swimming-pool-sized globe and bathed the subterranean cathedral in a life-giving aura. A pair of phoenixes dove and played in the fire.

The Dagda slammed his staff to the ground. "By Gwydion's feat."

"This is creepy." I sat my pack on the ground and pulled out fresh magazines for the Colt. "I'm expecting a cartoon princess to come out singing."

He grinned, a faraway look in his eye. "In my day, we'd have had those maids a-milking."

THE GARDENS WOUND through a network of chambers, all heated and lit by eternal torches, fed by pockets of natural gas. I couldn't shake the feeling we were being watched.

It was almost impossible to gauge how large the cavern system was overall. Trails broke off in all directions, sometimes leading to a higher tier, other times into tunnels. I wasn't entirely sure we could find our way out the same way we'd come in.

"How about Slash?" The Dagda blurted out.

"What?"

"Your mutt."

The furball let out an indignant snort.

"I don't think he likes the name, or being called a mutt."

"He's got the whole lightning bolt scar down the side going for him." We had to duck under a partially fallen tree. "I mean, he

345

does need a name. He's obviously not smart enough to find someone else, so you're stuck with him."

"Kinda like me and you, huh?"

The Dag grunted. "I'll keep working on it."

"You do that."

We followed the widening pathway as it snaked along an artificial stream, ending in the gentle roar of a waterfall feeding an underground lake. A staircase cut into the stone led downward to a living wooden bridge, and across to an oval island platform.

From there, a number of wooden chairs circled a large table, but trees and overgrowth blocked most of our view.

"As I feared." The Dagda stopped. "We should turn back."

"Dead end?" As far as I could see, there was nothing past the platform.

"That depends on you." Aurelie Dube blocked the path we'd just traveled, with four lycans in human form.

From the terraced growths around us, a dozen Summer fae in various shades of yellow and green unfolded like blooms into archers around us.

A small boulder crashed to the ground a few feet in front of us. The minimal amount of magical energy in it made it crumble instead of fragmenting. A glance upward revealed four Earth elementals. Three still held stones larger than me.

We were surrounded by Summer fae.

I held the Colt in one hand and a blade in the other. Fire might help me with anyone in range, but I had nothing handy for the

346

elementals above. And that was just what we could see. My Senses told me these were just the beginning of the forces surrounding us.

Dube seemed unreasonably relaxed with a pleasant smile, as if she were inviting us for lemonade on the front porch. "Can we talk like reasonable beings?"

The Dag cut me a look that either meant "talking never hurt" or "I could use a drink before the bleeding starts."

I slipped the Colt and the blade into their homes. "Talk now, fight later. Works for me."

She motioned for us to follow her. "I believe you may come around to our way of thinking."

Like I haven't heard that before.

THE ROUND TABLE was nearly full. Sitting around the table were several lycans, a pair of dark elf mages in the robes of their high council, Summer fae in the gowns of the Seelie court, and an equal number of their counterparts from the UnSeelie of Winter.

A kobold with a collar around his neck stumbled around, serving drinks from a too-large tray.

An elemental held watch at each of the cardinal points. Other representatives of the Veiled peoples watched from the bushes that enclosed us.

I had to draw in my Senses because of the overwhelming amount of power around us. Dube took my pack and weapons then relieved The Dagda of his staff before guiding us to a dais where chairs were readied. As soon as we both were inside the circle, a field rose and sealed us inside. My dog curled up at my feet and waited for something to complain about.

The only thing Dube had missed was the Anima Arca, hidden by the Leviskin. Tellia gently probed our surroundings but wasn't able to tell me anything I didn't already know.

"Drink, master?" A kobold held up a tray.

Something about the little being was familiar. I remembered the night in the Vogt place. "Shmutzy?"

A hesitant grin formed. "You remember me?"

"Why are you here?"

"The master." The small creature shook. "He swept us all up and brought us here to serve him."

"I'm sorry. We'll get you out of here."

"The drinks are safe." He held up the tray and dropped it to the floor as he was whipped away and drawn into Rahm's hand by an unseen force.

"The refreshments are for our friends." He shook the kobold before dropping him to the floor. "It's yet to determine the intent of our unwelcome guests."

I Pushed against the field. It was solid. "Where are Priscilla and Abhile?"

"That's what you went through all this trouble for?" The crowd joined him in laughter. "They really have overestimated you."

348

"Is that a way to treat our newest converts?" The room fell still as an elven woman in an emerald cloak drifted in from the dense brush and lingered aside the ancient lycan.

Rahm bowed and held out his arm.

She drew back the hood and removed her cloak. Her lemon skin shone through the sheer material of a Summer Court elite.

"Swyn?" I exclaimed.

"No, boy." The Dagda rose from his chair. "Hello, Giranshee."

"Welcome, cousin."

"WHAT'S THE CRAIC?" The Dagda crossed his arms. "What's your game here?"

"What ever do you mean?" She laid her cloak across Rahm's outstretched arm and drifted across the floor to just outside our energetic cell. "I am continuing our mission, dear cousin."

"Nonsense." He retook his seat and closed his eyes.

She turned to me, stroking her chin with a lithe finger. "What about you?"

"What about me?"

"You see how many are gathered here. Traditional enemies, many of them."

I Sensed the subtle energies she was using to try to manipulate me. A nibble on her lip, the slight tilt of her head, the flexing of her bare leg. She was pulsing my senses with Summer's power of desire, heat, and ambrosia.

I felt myself slipping under her power, and I didn't care.

The Dagda must have felt it as well and nudged me with his foot. I discovered Tellia had been screaming in my head, drowned out by the powerful being across from me.

"What enchantment are you using to hold them?" I asked.

Her laugh was throaty. "I need no enchantment. They believe in our cause."

"Which is?"

"You saw it yourself. All of the forces staging in Los Diablos. Why do you think they are consolidating their power after tens of millennia? Where do you think they intend to come? The Veils are coming down. Hard. The floodgates will open." She dumped her drink onto the floor. "Who do you think will drown? Unless we control how it happens."

"And you're going to save the world?"

"The Divines spent their time feuding with each other, the obedient angelic and the rebellious Fallen. They had their chance to sculpt and mold the universe. They gave us the demonics, their bastardized experiments. Meddling with their hands just off the prize. They brought the power to create the generations that became the old gods, but even they eventually were abandoned by their followers."

The Dagda spoke without moving. "You *are* one of those old gods."

"And so are you, dear cousin. We are the top of the fae food chain. Royalty. And it's time we acted like it."

"We've had our time. The Veils were created between the realms as much for us as for them. Yes, some of us stayed behind, but the accords—"

"Are in tatters, dear cousin. Humanity has had its chance. It is time we retake our just place. This time, our hands shall not be bound. We will be the stewards we were meant to be."

The Dagda breathed a deep sigh. "And this motley bunch is how you wish to recreate the world in your image?"

"I had hoped more of you, dear cousin. Then again, I thought Priscilla would agree as well." Impossibly fast, Giranshee appeared just outside of the chamber of energy on the other side. "The Winter heir was on this path and has strayed. Where do you stand, Sorcerer?"

"In a cell next to a trusted friend, and on the other side is someone who did a lot to help me heal and recover my abilities." I stood to look her in the eye. "Or were Swyn's actions a ruse too?"

"I am not your enemy." She twirled her long golden hair between dexterous fingers. "It could be quite the opposite. We could unbind the last of your power. Imagine, you, Greyson, becoming the heir to Merlin at our table. The possibilities."

I winced at another kick from my cellmate. "Be careful, boy. You don't know where that's been."

THE GARDEN FADED away, a telluric cell exchanged for a solid stone one. The meager light filtered through a narrow opening blocked with iron bars. The Dagda hadn't moved from his chair, but now that we'd been transported deep underground in an instant, he looked around at our new surroundings.

Beyond the opening were three eternal torches and solid walls. The hall curved in both directions, and even though I couldn't see anyone, I Sensed a few other presences nearby and heard the rhythmic breathing of someone deep in slumber. "Who is this Giranshee?"

"Someone I haven't seen in a very long time." He grunted. "She was of the Tuatha for a time, and then she wasn't."

"Any idea why she'd be hanging out with Anraoi in Los Diablos as a healer?"

"Odd place for her to hide, but from the looks of it, that was a matter of convenience." He stood and stretched then waved his hand over the bars. "She always had a knack for unlocking people, usually for her own ends. Her ability as a healer would let her blend in quite well to whatever scheme she was working. The closer to a center of power, the better.

"When it came time for our people to cede and return across the Veil as it was in those days, she left with the Seelie in the Summer Court as an adviser. She was there for a few decades then disappeared. I'd thought she might have fallen during the War of Clementia, but then she surfaced for a time. Giran was against the Sovereign Accords giving humanity its reign, and the separation of the Veiled peoples."

"What does she want, then?"

"Isn't it obvious?" He planted himself in the chair and leaned against the wall before closing his eyes. "She wants to return us to the good old days."

THE DAGDA SNORED in his precarious position. I couldn't figure out how he could sleep while we were in the cell. In any case, the buzz saw rattling around in the small chamber ensured I wouldn't get much rest, even if the furball dozed without a problem.

I stretched my Senses to try to feel our surroundings. The enchantments hampered me from getting too much information, but I was able to figure out the hallway outside was a large circle with eight cells on the periphery. At least three were occupied.

Invisible to the naked eye, the sigils covering the floor, ceiling, and walls enforced protection and submissive feelings. They also obscured the short-range portal ring, which seemed to be linked only to the dais on the platform.

A soft shuffling followed by the regular squeak of a wheel came from outside. It took several minutes before the kobold dragging a cart came into view.

"Shmutzy, is that you?" I whispered.

His long, hairy ears flopped as he nodded. "I bring you food, master."

"Can you get us out of here?"

His head sunk. "The collar. I can do nothing the master does not order me to do."

I tried to be hopeful. "I order you to let us out?"

Tears welled in his eyes. "If only you were the master of this household."

"What if I could get the collar off?"

"I would be grateful. You have already fought for us once, but even if you could, I don't have the power to summon you."

The pit in my stomach grew. Even if we couldn't get out yet, I had to do what I could for the creature. I reached through the gap in the bars. "Come here."

He glanced around with his beady eyes and kicked up sand as he approached.

With a thought, the Anima Arca took form on my thigh. Tellia whispered a phrase in my ear, and I knew what to do.

"I'm sorry to have failed you, master." He froze, wide eyed and drooling. "What will you do with that? You would hurt me?"

"No. Never." I grabbed him by the arm and pulled him close as he struggled. I muttered the phrase the shaman had given me and nicked the collar, pulling it away.

He jerked away and reached for his neck. "You released me."

"Of course." The Anima Arca faded back into the Leviskin. "Let me clip it back on, but you'll be able to remove it at any time. They can't control you with it any longer, but you'll still feel their commands."

"Why?" He leaned forward and let me put the leather band around his neck, sealing my cut with a word. I gave him the one that would break its bond permanently. "If you see a way out, take it. But they can't suspect you're free of their control until then."

The kobold held his head a little higher as he dragged the cart to the next cell.

"That was damn good of you, boy." The Dag snorted. "But did he leave dinner?"

Damn. "Shmutzy?"

THE INCANTATION FORMED in my mind. I shared it with Tellia, and she made a few changes. I took the Anima Arca in hand and whispered the chant.

"What are you doing?" The Dagda asked.

I thought he'd been asleep. "Looking for a way out." The edge of the blade took on a red glow.

His voice was slow and hesitant. "How?"

I traced around the base of the iron bar with the blade.

"Stop, Greyson."

"It's cutting through."

The Dagda growled. "I said stop."

355

The blade sliced cleanly through the bottom of the bar.

"I. Said. Stop." Huge hands grabbed me by the shoulders and slammed me into the back wall. His eyes glowed a bloody red. He drew his hand back in a tight fist, one I'd seen crush skulls. "Why can't you ever listen?"

I mouthed the words Tellia whispered into my ear. "Reciprocum."

The Dagda brought down a killing blow but instead was launched backward, slamming into the wall.

"What's your problem?" I clutched the blade and prepared to strike the bar and remove it.

Great idea. Then I'll run it through the old god.

I started cutting into the top of the bar. The Dagda grabbed me by my neck and lifted me off the floor. He shoved me forward into the rails as I made a last cut through. The bar gave way, and I landed in the corridor.

I drug the bar off the floor and leveled it at The Dagda. He lay face down, unmoving, blood trickling from his head. His arm reached through the cleared gap.

The fury in my blood evaporated, and the bar clanged to the floor.

"Well, damn." I stepped back into the cell, using The Dagda as a step. My shoulders and neck ached where he'd grabbed me, but I struggled as I sat him up against the wall.

He gradually came around, confusion swirling in his eyes. I recognized the hangover of a defensive enchantment, and he'd taken the brunt of the effects.

Knowing what to look for, I modified the incantation to remove the rest of the steel rods keeping him inside the cell. For safety's sake, I finished it up while he was still dazed.

AN UNSPOKEN UNDERSTANDING hung between us. We both felt the same regret for having lost control even if it had been the result of an enchantment. The furball kept a wary eye on him and trotted between us.

The Dagda stood inside the cell and warily eyed the opening I'd created.

I pulled two Leviskin straps out of a side pocket. "Give me your hands."

He dabbed at the drying blood on his forehead. "Why?" he huffed.

"Just do it."

With a grunt, he shoved his hands at me. I wrapped a strap around each hand and Pushed a little Will into each one, forming gloves. I picked up two of the cold iron rods and handed them to him. "It's not your weapon, but it's better than nothing."

He stepped out of the cell and took my offering with a sniff. An unspoken apology flowed between us.

"I guess it'll do for now. Shall we find something to test it out on?" He dropped one of the rods. "I still need to hit something."

I nodded. I was good with the idea as long as he didn't hit me. "Let's find a way out of here."

The first cell we passed was empty. The next held two dead lycans. They looked as if they'd been there a while. From the appearance of the wounds, they'd torn each other apart.

The third held a barely clothed man reduced to skin and bone. I doubted he was alive until he let out a small moan.

"It's the claustritumus!" The Dagda bellowed.

"Who?"

He knelt low to the floor. "Edo. Are you still with us? Edoardo?"

Green-flecked eyes more alive that I'd thought possible flashed open and tried to focus.

"What are you doing in there, Edo?"

"They... they're trying to take it from me," the old man rasped. "They can't have it. I won't give it up. Not to them."

"What is it they want?" I asked.

"Get him out of there." The Dagda stood and tried to rip a bar out of the wall. "Open this thing up."

"Back up." I drew the Anima Arca from its sheath. "Give me room."

I couldn't be sure how these bars were enchanted, even though I could sense the power flowing through them was... different. I doubted the old man could do much, but I didn't want to deal with another bout of The Dagda's unchecked and magically fueled rage.

The edge of the black blade glowed a fiery red as I repeated the process at the top of the center bar and sliced through it cleanly. I was halfway through the bottom half of the bar when Edo's wandering gaze locked onto mine with a moment of terrifying clarity. "It's starting again," he said.

"Hurry," The Dagda shouted, grabbing the top half and pulling as I burned through the cold iron. We stood helpless as he vanished before our eyes just as the bar snapped free.

"What just happened?" I asked. "Who is he?"

"The Gatekeeper." The Dagda slumped against the wall and slid to the floor. "It's all making sense now."

"Would you mind cluing me in?"

"I know where we are." He took a deep breath and stared at the vacant cell. "And where we need to go."

THE NARROW STAIRCASE spiraled into the darkness in both directions. The steps were barely wide enough to support me, and The Dagda hugged the damp walls as we ascended.

He tested every one of the cantilevered bricks with a tamping of the rod he carried. One misstep, and we would find out how long it took to plummet to the bottom. I assumed there had to be one.

"Mind telling me where we're headed?" I asked.

Clang. "I want my staff back."

"And people in Hell want ice water." I tried to use the ache in my legs to shove aside the building vertigo as we climbed. "What's your point?"

"I know where she's at. I've never been this long away from that chunk of wood. I can feel her calling." *Clang.*

"Her?"

He snorted. "You'll know soon enough."

If people could name cars, and most vessels were "she," who was I to question?

I'd had to all but turn off my Senses. Something in the pit below was calling to me. I was afraid I would finally tip over from curiosity, or maybe just because I was tired of the trip.

It felt as if we climbed hundreds of feet, but I just stayed focused on the next step until The Dag stopped and tapped on the wall. "We're here."

"Where?" It looked like every other inch of the trip had.

"The entrance." He dug into the wall with the end of his rod. "It's been covered over."

In no time, a small entranceway emerged from the falling dirt and debris. I struck up a small fireball for light and gingerly kept it away from my tender hand. The small passageway was big enough to hold us both and give a little extra room, but not much more. The reinforced door at the far end was unmoving.

"Would you do the honors, lad?"

Happy to no longer be hanging over the bottomless pit, I opened my Senses again. Something moved on the far side of the door. Bars sealed the door shut. Others milled nearby. "There's six or seven beings nearby. Can't tell what or whom."

"Can you open the door?"

I traced the edge of the door with the Anima Arca. Its blade was burning hot. I kept it at the ready in my hand. "Brace yourself. Three, two, one." I loosed a wave of energy, blowing the door free.

Two shocked lycans stared at us, and a third was splattered against the wall.

I stepped through and freed one's head with the blade. The Dagda rammed the end of the post he held through the other's chest and yanked backward, pulling out its heart.

"Feel better?" I asked.

He shrugged with a snarl. "It's a start."

I felt a deep rumble coming from the other end of the hall. Three more lycans had shifted. The smallest one was over seven feet of fur, teeth, and claws.

I stepped back. "Knock yourself out."

The big man let out a growl of his own and charged down the hall. When it was done, two of the lycans had skulls crushed to the point of being split in half, and another's head had been knocked clean from its body.

"Let's find my girl," The Dag said.

"THERE YOU ARE." The Dagda's bellow drew the attention of the mage guarding the room, but The Dag's makeshift javelin flew in a short arc before pinning the sentry to the wall. He grinned gleefully and grabbed the knobby piece of wood. "Your stuff is over there."

The mage tried to pull together an attack, but the rod absorbed his power.

The Dag grabbed the elven practitioner by the throat. "You have a choice. Tell me what I want to know soon enough, and you might get to live. Where is Priscilla?"

My handle on the old fae tongue is rough, but he said something about where The Dag could plant his staff.

Dozens of shelves covered in mundane and magical objects surrounded the room. My pack and gear were in a loose pile. With a thought, the Leviskin made room for my weapons. I checked the Colt and loaded it with a fresh magazine.

The mage spat a curse. The Dagda shook his head and used the healing powers of his staff to meld the elf to the cold iron. The screams indicated a little discomfort, but they were short lived.

"What did you learn?"

The Dagda took his horn off the shelf, whispered a few words to it, and took a deep drink. "True believer. Or he didn't know anything."

We sorted through the shelves, looking for anything useful. Everything else we stacked to the side.

"Do you know nothing, lad?" He held up two objects. "You put a Santa Muerte idol next to a Xipe Totec fetish. Do you really want to unleash a curse to see who the better killer is?" He grinned and threw the objects in opposite directions.

A box contained two implements made of the same black metal as the Anima Arca. More items from the Armory of Abaddon. They looked like torches with holders where the crystals would fit. I tucked them into my pack and continued to search.

"Guess what I just found?" I held up the parchment with the key to open the portal to Phoenix Grove. "I thought it burned up. Wonder how she planned to use it?"

"You'd best make sure it doesn't fall into her hands again." He trembled and looked at a small object in his hand. It was a cameo brooch Priscilla usually wore. "Now we can go."

"DAGDA AND SORCERER." Rahm pounded his spear on the floor three times and roared in pleasure as bristling fur grew and covered his body. His limbs lengthened. His head stretched into a form that would make the Dire Wolves whimper.

Talons stretched from his feet, claws from his hands. Saber-like canines sliced downward.

His deep voice rumbled in my chest as he spoke. "And I thought I was going to have to come hunting for you."

363

I regretted thinking of the Pleistocene hound as a pack of them trotted forward. Behind them were more lycans and a half-dozen of the Summer fae archers.

"You remember when I suggested you leave that weapon be?" The Dagda growled.

I gripped the Colt in its holster. "Yeah."

"You may wish to ignore that advice."

Tellia whispered an assent with The Dag in my ear as I unslung my pack, keeping my eyes trained on the far end of the hall. I bent down and unhooked Heph's gift.

The staff snapped to triple its length, one end an etheric two-headed axe, and the other a spike.

"Someone has a new toy." Rahm motioned, and the archers loosed a volley of arrows. "Time to see if you can use it."

The etheric shield stretched from the axe head to the base, deflecting the bolts.

I drew the Colt and emptied the magazine. I lost sight as two archers fell and the Dire wolves charged.

The Dagda swung his staff, and I cleaved a wolf in two. Then another with a spike through his skull. For each one that fell, we backed down the hall, another wolf taking its fallen pack mate's place.

The furball raced between their legs. I caught a glimpse of him ripping open a wolf's throat and racing off.

A wolf slipped in the slick and sticky growing river of red and flew past me. Its claw caught my leg, bringing me down to my knee, and The Dagda shattered its back before it could try to bite me. He pulled me to my feet by my pack, and we beat back the onslaught.

One of the Werewolves leapt over the pack. The axe sang as it sliced through muscle and bone.

Claws sparked off the etheric shield, drawing my own energy away.

A spear point pounded against the blade, forcing me back. Rahm shoved his way between two of his pack and swung his spear again, transforming the point to a spiked mace. He swung again, knocking my axe aside. I blocked his next swing as it came in for my left side.

"You don't deserve that weapon." Rahm flashed his canines. "I'm going to take it from you."

The Dagda had gotten pushed away from me down the hall. He was battling three lycans, with more in reserve. I only had to face their Alpha.

Rahm lunged with his long, sharp point. The world grayed around me as I swept the attack aside, but the point sliced through the armor into my calf.

I swept the spike upward, but he blocked my attack and sidestepped my Push.

He lunged forward and snapped his jaws in my face. "Is that all you have in you?"

I pushed off my back foot and lunged forward. My blade drew a drop of blood from his chest when he turned right to avoid the attack.

He snarled, lunging forward and pinning me against the wall. My shield protested as he pressed against it. "Surrender, child. Join my pack."

Power flooded into my hand and exploded with a Push. Rahm slammed into the wall across from me. He jerked away as I brought the axe down, cleaving part of his snout and a canine.

He howled, ducked, and leapt over the rest of his pack.

All but three of the lycans and two archers lay in pieces as the rest fled behind their master.

I picked up Rahm's severed saber tooth and smiled. The darkness closed around me as I slipped to the floor, my blood mixing with the rest.

"THERE YOU ARE." I lay on top of my pack in the hallway. "Drink this."

Dull warmth spread though my limbs as I downed the ampule, amplified by the power The Dag was Pushing into me through his staff.

The furball tried to lick me clean. While his affection was welcome, it didn't help the pain. Maybe he'd refined his taste for blood. I couldn't be sure. "How bad is it?"

"The wound?" The Dag pursed his lips. "Just a scratch. It was your own weapon that dropped you."

The two-foot length of light wood lay next to me, bearing several new scars of battle. Traces of red seeped into the grain. I hefted it in my hand. "It feels... different. I don't know how to describe it."

"It's learning from you, taking from you. It's what a virgin enchanted weapon does." His brow furrowed as he examined it. "You shouldn't use it again for a while. You aren't strong enough. And it doesn't have enough power to not suck you dry."

I slipped it into a slot on my pack. "What?"

"That old gadget-head didn't tell you how these work." He held his own staff out. "The healing power in this comes from many years of work, the experience and lives it's absorbed. I'm as connected to it as I am my foot. That thing has never been wielded by anyone but its creator and has sat hungry for a long time."

"I... I don't understand."

"It must have taken more from you than I thought." He gave me another jolt from his staff. "Implements like these are alive. They have a soul. Yours has never fed, and it's like an infant. It has no identity. How you raise it will determine its future long after you're gone. But until it grows up some, you're feeding it, or more correctly, it's feeding off you. The more you ask it to exert, the more power it needs. As a weapon, it'll take some sustenance from those who fall under it, but you're the big food source until it learns."

"I need to get rid of this."

He snorted. "Good luck with that. It's bonded with you, and you it. Either you master it, or it will take everything from you, and your successor will benefit."

367

What felt different was I could hear its call. It had a taste of blood and wanted more. It had an unbounded will, an unbounded greed. Wrapping Leviskin around it muted the call but wasn't enough to block it or drown it out. "You're saying it will kill me."

"No. You'll live forever, melded with it, at the will of others." My hand disappeared in his outstretched paw. "Come on, lad, while the way is clear."

PRISCILLA'S MOUTH GAPED as she lay strapped to the articulated chunk of steel that passed for a chair. Her chest rose and fell in a shallow rhythm. I'd been seated in the corner, recovering, as The Dagda checked on her.

Whoever had been guarding her had either been in Rahm's pack or had run off when the remnants retreated.

He stroked her face with a light touch and whispered something in her ear.

Her eyes fluttered open. She was hoarse, but the corners of her mouth tilted slightly. "What took you so long?"

The straps holding her fell away under the blade of a small knife that appeared from his boot. She sat up and sipped at a bottle of water for a few minutes while she shook off the fugue state.

He leaned over and kissed the top of her head. It almost knocked me over when she leaned up and kissed him back.

He smiled. "Are you ready, darling?"

Her eyes glinted mirthfully as she saw my shock. I'd just been let in on a huge secret. "What are we facing to get out of here?"

He dangled the cameo in front of her eyes. "It might be *time*."

"That bad, huh?" Her face hardened. "I think it's time we took the boy to task."

I stiffened. "What did I do?"

"Not you." She pinned the brooch to the remains of the clothes she wore. "Romulus."

I couldn't believe it was that simple. "As in?"

"Romulus and Remus." The Dagda cocked his head. "Didn't you learn some history, boy?"

"They were raised by wolves, and when they decided to found Rome, Romulus killed his brother because they couldn't agree where to put the doghouse. I never heard about him being a Werewolf."

"My fault, I'm afraid." Strength returned to Priscilla as she got farther away from the interrogation table. "He was touched with the mark of Cain. It wasn't his fault, but he killed Remus in a fit. I punished him by trying to make him return to his childhood. He embraced the punishment rather well and found a way to enhance it with a curse. He found a way to pass it on."

"So he was the first Werewolf?"

"My, no. He was the first of the lycanthrope strain." She stared at me as if there was some greater message. "And it's time to end his curse."

I swallowed. I knew the answer before I asked. "Are you lifting the curse?"

"Permanently. And with extreme prejudice." She laid a gentle kiss on my forehead. "How is my granddaughter?"

PRISCILLA LAY QUIETLY on a mat in the corner. We'd retreated to a small room with a single door and a good view in each direction down the hall. The furball lay seemingly asleep, but his ears were perked up, belying his level of awareness.

Lines I'd never seen before creased The Dagda's usually jocular face. Even at the worst of times, he'd always been ready for the challenge. I sensed something was different, even if he wouldn't admit it.

In the quiet, I felt around and tried to Sense Abhile. I couldn't feel her exactly, but some part of her was nearby.

"What is this place?" I whispered to The Dagda. "It seemed like you figured something out back there."

He continued to polish his staff, ignoring that I'd spoken.

"What's it about this place that has you both so worked up?" I asked.

He rubbed his shoulder, massaging it as if doing so would take away an old ache. "This place. It was lost for a very long time. It never should have been found. It once was the one and only safe place in the world. Gods, Divines, fae, and man. Any and all could come here to meet in safety. No one dared break the bond. Later, it

370

was here the accords were struck. As it was the age of man, one was chosen to forever secure the Veils and control the portals between the worlds."

"The old man in the cell we tried to free."

"The Claustritumus, the gatekeeper of time." He closed his eyes. "Edo was a good friend. I felt for him when he was chosen. He was the best of men for the job. A terrible burden for one to carry."

"So why is it here? Now?"

"It rises when the need does. It's been almost seven hundred years since the last time. The conclave lasted almost half a century." He cut a sideways glance at me. "This place has always been one of sanctuary. Romulus's act is one of greatest treachery. We must discover how the accords were violated such that this could happen. More importantly, Giranshee and Romulus can't be allowed to hold this place. We must retake it at any cost."

PRISCILLA ROUSED SLOWLY, but I Sensed whatever effects had been cast upon her had worn off. There hadn't been any signs of life in hours. I was thankful for the chance to rest and heal. My hand had dulled to an angry red after casting the attack on Rahm… Romulus. The Dag had healed it further, but it was stiff and ached.

Priscilla came up and rubbed my sleeping dog's head. He responded with a happy sigh. The Dagda did the same when she rubbed his shoulder lovingly, but his sigh was much louder.

371

"I'm ready," she said. "And we need to act before we lose any more time."

The Dag stood facing her. "It's your decision, you know."

I had no idea what he was talking about, but her face grew stern. "I'm afraid the choice has been made for me."

The Dagda nodded and Pushed a jolt of power into her brooch. "We'll step outside."

"No." She grabbed my hand. "It's fine."

"Okay, then. I'm going outside." He looked at the furball. "Come on, hound. You don't want to be here for this."

He must have agreed, because he stood, stretched, and followed The Dagda outside.

"What is it you want me to see?"

She sat me in a corner and walked to the middle of the room. "The truth."

She ran her hands through her hair, turning it a golden color, then whispered to herself and stroked the brooch. The ancient pin shimmered, casting a wave that made her entire being semitransparent, like a crystal catching sunlight, growing brighter until it was blinding.

A loud snap echoed through the room, and the light died away, leaving me half-blinded and my ears ringing.

Priscilla had shed years and looked as though she might not even be legal to drink. Her light-olive skin was radiant, what could be seen under the heavy armor. She carried a shield emblazoned with the head of Medusa and a spear almost like my staff. A short sword rode on her hip, and an ash longbow was strapped to her back.

The Dagda stepped back into the room. "Athena. I never know whether to kiss you or get ready to fight."

She licked her lips. "I think it's time for both."

I WAS STUNNED. I hadn't fully recovered from the power released in her transformation. It was still her, but not her. It was something more. Something beautiful. Something wonderful. Something deadly.

I tried to sound intelligent, but all I could do was blurt out, "You're the goddess Athena?"

"The one and only." She strapped her shield around her back and closed to within inches of me. She stroked my face. "What do you think?"

The Dagda leaned against the wall. "How long has it been since you let the old girl out?"

She tapped him with the spear, and it snapped to a foot long with the spear point at the ready. "Shall we?"

The furball was on point, and I was the tail as we moved down the hall and emerged on a high terrace. All I could see were acres of greenery in every direction. With Athena's resurgence, The Dagda moved with a little more energy.

It was hard to keep up with the half sentences spoken between them, but I figured out they had both been there before. It felt as though we were moving with a purpose, as if we were headed to our destiny.

The underground jungle thinned out somewhat until all that was around us were cave walls. We'd gone absolutely quiet except for our footfalls softly echoing around us.

Odd clicks and whistles, almost inaudible at first, came from in front of us. The sounds grew, as did the warm glow from the chamber in the distance. We stopped at the threshold of a circular-domed cavern maybe thirty feet across.

Something about it was vaguely familiar. I'd never been there before, nor had I seen it exactly. The walls were paneled with copper plates and insulated with dark wood strips. A circular device made of various metals glinted under the torchlight as it jerkily crept along, floating about a foot in the air, and turned by unseen forces. Gemstones and crystals that had been seemingly placed at random flashed and dimmed at irregular intervals. One word came to mind. Contraption.

My heart pounded as I tried to enter the cave. I'd seen something like this before, but not as elaborate. The device was the ancestor of the portal ring devices, including the one we'd destroyed in the desert, sending chaos through all the Veiled realms.

"It's worse than I imagined." Athena stroked a translucent globe floating in midair. "We must get Edoardo back and on the job. Quickly."

The Dagda steadied her with his hand. "He was in pretty bad shape when we saw him."

374

I was dizzy the instant I entered the room. "Where are we?"

"The Glastonie." She took a deep breath. "The gatehouse. It controls the Veil between the realms. It's breaking down."

"What happens if it totally stops?"

"VERY BAD THINGS." That phrase echoed in my mind as we shuffled down another path. They believed it would continue going for a short time without the gatekeeper, but like all machinery, it needed maintenance and someone to control it.

They couldn't be sure, but believed if it just stopped, one of a couple of things could happen. The Veil would fall, and the realms would again merge, or they could become permanently impenetrable, and we would be forever separated.

Or all of time and space could be undone.

Where have I heard that before?

I couldn't shake the feeling I was missing something important. "Pri... Athena. Who built this? Why?"

Her eyes were closed, and her hands hovered around one of the metallic globes floating in the air. "It was built when the world was young. Your winged friend knows more than I. Melvin, Hephaestus, Nabataean, Seshat, myself, and others met at the table. Twelve of us in all. We came to do what had been decided by the highest gods, Divines, and human kings. We came to formalize the Veil and separate the realms."

The Dagda stood just outside in the hall. "I was not in favor of the agreement, but I was still only a demigod in those days." Something in her demeanor silenced him. "I'm going to scout around."

She turned away and faced me. "We imbued Edoardo with the power and the knowledge to be in essence the mind and the conscience of the engine. He replaced an ancestor of the fae queens to start the age of man. And here he has been for over ten thousand years, opening the great halls when the need arose."

"What was the need this time?"

She chewed on her manicured nail. "That's what bothers me most. I don't know who called for it."

Her faraway look told me from experience that she had nothing more to say. I tried to pull her back to the present. "What's the story with you and The Dagda?"

She bit her lip and glanced to the hall where he'd disappeared. "Let's just say it's been passionate but contentious. We've been as inclined to kill each other on the battlefield as to shag on Diana's temple steps, but we seem to have found a happy medium."

"And?"

She cocked her eyebrow like a derringer. "And we've done all we can here. Come on."

THE DRAGON'S BREATH roared just over our hiding spot in the terraces. A fine mist rained down from the condensation on the articulated metal beast.

The subtle clinks and clacks gave us cover as we moved through the low foliage, but we didn't need it. Lying in the grass and looking over the edge, I guessed we were looking at a thousand beings below us, if not more. Fae stood guard across from Fallen, perched on edges and railings, waiting for a careless creature to walk by. Two hundred lycans lined up in formation along the walkway to the bridge over to the artificial island. Mages and practitioners held positions as wardens among the assembled crowd, hoping to keep control.

Jets of water raised the irregular platform above the underground lake. The foliage had been shrunk down by the Summer fae to be replaced by lush grass and sparse shrubs. The round table was vacant, as was the marble altar resting on a weave of grapevines in the background.

A lone deep, rumbling howl echoed off the walls and quieted the crowd. The single-file procession started down the meandering path. Each time they reached another lycan, it broke out and added its voice to the choir.

A wooden cage on a cart was wheeled into sight. A wretched creature with a drooping head was strapped to a wooden plank.

"Edo," The Dagda whispered. "What have they done to him?"

"Look there." Athena pointed to the second cart just cresting the hill. Abhile was dressed in a flowing gown. The top half of the dress was a shimmering green and faded into an ice-blue train. The cart was a blending of both Summer and Winter fae symbols. She was standing but chained into an arboreal trellis. "Do you think?"

"It looks like they intend to try." The Dagda shook his head. "Look at the altar."

She rubbed on the bow in her hand. "She can't possibly have been prepared in that period of time."

The implements on the platform didn't mean much to me, but they did to them. "What are they doing?"

"They intend to transfer the power of the gatekeeper into the fae princess. The age of man will go into decline, and the fae will rise." She reached over and took my hand in hers. "I don't understand why they've chosen her."

In that moment, I knew. The pieces were coming together. Several years had passed since I stood in her room at the Underhill estate. A Fomorian warrior marched behind her cart, carrying a car-tire-sized version of the wheel from the copper chamber. A sigil made from hammered copper rode atop his breastplate. It was the key.

She'd studied the device. It had been in the scrolls in her room at the Underhills'. All over her notebooks. "She's been learning about this thing, this place for a very long time."

Athena dug her nails into me. "How do you know?"

"Does it matter?" The Dagda pushed back from the edge. "We must assume the boy is correct, and no matter what, we must put a stop to this."

Athena pushed away and leaned against the wall. "I assume you have a plan?"

"KILL THE PRINCESS." Athena pounded her head against the wall. "It's the only way. We can't let this happen, and we would never get anywhere close to pulling her and Edo out of here. If we kill her, they won't have another vessel with the knowledge. Your rescue plan simply won't work. We don't have the people, or the resources."

I couldn't believe what I was hearing. "You'll kill an innocent for this?"

"We cannot be sure she's without involvement here. You are the one who's seen evidence she's been into very arcane texts about the Veil." The Dagda took a deep drag from his horn. "Even so, I don't like it either. But we must stop this, even if it means taking a not-so-innocent life."

An icy hand wrapped around my heart and squeezed. All I could focus on were the jets of flame overhead as I flopped onto my back. Athena knelt over me, her hands grasping for a lifeline to give me. The curse was an electric eel swimming through my veins. I couldn't let her die. "I'll save her," I thought more than I groaned out.

I gasped and tried to sit up, but Athena pushed me back to the ground. I Sensed the power running through her hands and into me. "You're bound to protect her, still." She slammed me in the chest and backed away.

"Yeah." I rubbed my chest and pushed myself up. "I am."

"Why did you not tell me about this?" she hissed at me.

"I couldn't." Some part of the curse had broken within me. But not the part that would happily eat my soul. "It wouldn't let me. Until today, I'd hoped it was gone."

379

She grabbed me by the throat and pulled me close. "I cannot believe you were so foolish. I hope whatever you got in trade was worth it. Once that fae hag gets her claws into you, she will never let go." She shoved me away.

I rubbed the feeling back into my throat. "It was all your lives in the Winterlands. That's what I traded, and yeah, I'd take the deal again."

"Should we survive the next few hours, we are going to have a long reevaluation of our relationship." She pulled up fistfuls of sod and threw them into the trees below.

The Dagda dared to slide nearer and placed his hand on her back. "We act now. We hit them before they get to the island. I'll grab Edo, and he can grab the fae. Open the portal you recovered upstairs."

"It's just a key. I'd need several minutes to outline the portal." I dug into my pack and pulled out the tube. "Take it. I'll go alone. I can give you the inscription to use. If I fail, I'll make sure she can't use it."

The cart carrying Edo stopped. Four lycans pulled the frame carrying him down and laid him onto the route snaking over the bridge to the platform. Four more were preparing Abhile for her turn down the road.

"No." Athena chewed on her upper lip. "We will see this through. We need a distraction."

I glanced over at the honor guard of giant beasts lined up on the platform. The largest was over twenty feet tall and had the head of a ram. "How do Fomorians feel about lycans?"

THE TERRACE STRETCHED around the entire basin. My palms were sweating as I crawled along and approached the Fomorians. I'd pulled my Senses in as much as I could, and with Tellia's help, I'd masked myself well enough that the tribe of Menehune that scurried by paid me no attention.

I planted the device, which was made of a concussion grenade and one of the last vials of Heph's Werewolf love juice, where it would spray most of the Fomorian contingent. I wrapped a band of energy around the grenade that would dissipate over time, then pulled the pin. I had given myself about fifteen minutes to move out of the spray and into position.

Edo was two turns away from the entrance to the bridge. The beings nearest the path jeered, howled, and clucked at the unfortunate man being jostled in his bindings. Even more backed away, shrinking back from the spectacle.

Abhile was well behind them and moving much slower. She glassily looked around, seemingly confused and not entirely aware of where she was. Even from here, I could see her trembling and shaking in her restraints. Those who'd retreated rushed forward to rain down flowers and other adorations onto her.

I kept crawling forward. The furball crept along behind me, giving only the occasional low growl as a warning.

I stopped behind a herd of restless Satyrs. Two of them were facing off with harried blows and arguing in their native tongue. A few words floated over and hinted they weren't all in agreement with something about to happen.

I was prepared to cut past a cloister of harpies down to the next terrace when a pair of fully armored demons under Ba'al's standard shoved past them and kept working their way forward.

I stiffened my armor and pulled the Veil in tightly around me. The furball seemed to sense it and tucked himself next to me as we followed the soldiers.

Unlike the crowds gathered along the pathway, the different groups of entities along the top tier were much more stolid and severe. On edge. They were ready for something that the others didn't seem to know was coming, almost as if they were paranoid.

I was getting raw where my armor rubbed against my elbows and belly as I crawled along the ground, but I didn't dare rise up any more than necessary. Tellia was whispering in my ear about changes to make to my shroud and warning me any time someone seemed too curious about things in my general direction.

I coughed and almost gave myself away when I pushed around a corner too quickly and spied the demon general, Ba'al himself. I couldn't believe he had survived the blast in Los Diablos, but he did have visible scars from the experience. One of his great horns was cracked and being held on by what looked like black steel.

I had a little under ten minutes to get to my rendezvous point with The Dagda, and I had one more of the eau de hound bombs. The enemy of my enemy could still be helpful while they were my enemy. I decided to try to put it into practice.

Ba'al had his back to the wall I was atop of, scooting along. He was barking and grunting at the soldiers we'd followed. Either his latte hadn't been nonfat, or the two had messed up royally. I decided to help improve his day and added a vial of holy oil to the concussive device before I stuck it to the back of his armor. The band of energy would let loose in just minutes.

I decided one device wasn't enough and stuck more vials of holy oil to him, clipped a white phosphorous grenade to the other side of his armor, and set the energy holding it to trip if he flared his spikes again.

I prepared to back away when one of the general's aides approached. Ba'al switched from the demon's language to an ancient one I knew. I managed to catch a few phrases before I backed away, then had to fight the urge to run.

"If we lose the auction, you must take the girl by force. Once we have the key and the gatekeeper, we will be able to take seven billion servants home by the end of the week, and I will officially take the title as King of Hell. The rest will fall at our feet, and if Samael decides to try to return to his throne, I'll have it firmly in my hand."

THE DAGDA CROUCHED behind a boulder that hid him yet gave a good view of the procession route. If my timing was right, the distractions would be triggered about the time Edo reached the bridge.

Athena signaled from her high perch that she was ready to cover us with her bow. I would have felt better with a few more of the Amazons and some heavier weapons, but we had to go with what we had. The goal was a smash-and-grab—get Edo and Abhile while Werewolf potion number nine sent their pack into a frenzy.

I tapped The Dagda and told him what I'd heard on the ridge.

"It's worse than I thought, then." He took a big drink from his horn and offered it to me. "But maybe this is good as well. We thought this was a unification of the fae and Divine to overtake the world. If you're right, they'll all be fighting each other to see whose little faction controls the gatekeeper."

"Once we have them, doesn't that mean they'll be after us too?"

He shrugged. "That hasn't changed. We have to be the ones to win, lad. Whoever controls the gate controls everything."

Edo was almost to the bridge. On the platform, Giranshee's ten appointed counselors had taken their positions, standing behind their seats at the round table. Two more sat vacant. Giranshee was at the altar, dressed in a flowing sheer tunic. Romulus stood to one side and Dube the other, both dressed in decorative armor.

The Fomorian carrying the symbolic portal device was halfway across the bridge when they started carrying Edo across. Abhile was still surrounded by adoring fae when her caravan waited for Edo's to clear out of the way.

The Dagda was grinding his teeth. "How long before your plan kicks in? We're running out of time."

I was staring at the Fomorian enclave when the device went off. A small pop was barely audible through the chamber, but in the distance, the giants were looking at their leader and looking around for something to kill. I'd seen that look before. They'd been after me at the time.

Edo was halfway across the bridge when the first lycan let out a long, mournful howl. Abhile was starting her journey to the platform. The bridge was slowly dragging on the ground, retracting to the artificial island.

384

The Dagda pounded his staff. "We have to go, distraction or not."

"Just wait one more minute."

The furball let out a long howl and a battle cry—"Baaaa Wooooooo!"—and charged after the fae princess.

"AFTER YOUR DOG." The Dagda scowled. "Even your mutt is getting into the fight faster than I am."

I was last as we pushed through shocked fae and glassy-eyed lycans and leapt the small gap to the bridge. Four lycans turned to us with blood in their eyes as they shifted into their wolf forms. Any befuddling effects of the pheromones on Abhile dissipated when the first wolf guarding her dropped under three rounds from the Colt.

The furball sprang into the air, latched his jaws around the throat of another, kicked his paws, and swung back and forth twice then fell free, spitting the chunk of wolf meat out as he landed. He wagged his tail and gave me a look as if he wondered what was taking me so long, and what the lycan on top of me was trying to do.

I cut myself loose with two snaps of the Colt and slid the blade of the Anima Arca into its skull with a small moan from Tellia.

The bridge continued its slow withdrawal from the mainland. One of the lycans snapped out of the hormonal daze to transform and charge the bridge. He leapt with enough distance, but The

385

Dagda crushed it with one swing and sent the beast flying back to the shore in a much more misshapen form.

Abhile's cage leaned precariously against the bridge rail. She stared past me blankly as I freed her. The ropes fell away with a flick from my blade, but the locks on the chains took more. I aimed the black blade carefully at the lock on her hand, but the knife was repelled. It couldn't touch the lock.

Tellia's voice prodded me. *Use your staff.*

I unhooked the staff, and a thin etheric blade formed at the end of the short pole. I jammed the blade through the lock at her neck. It protested but finally shattered with a cry.

Mine.

The staff sapped me of my dwindling reserves. My head swam. Tellia's voice was a life preserver in the darkness.

The words were meaningless, but they were enough to guide my hand to the Anima Arca. A part of my mind protested as the blade touched the tip of the staff, but the words came out of my mouth.

When my head cleared, the crystal in the Anima Arca was clear. Tellia's voice came to me clearly from the staff in my hand. *Let's get to work.*

I sheathed the black blade and sliced into the restraint on Abhile's hand. Then the other. The ones at her ankles offered little protest. Free of the enchanted restraints, she slid to the ground.

The furball yapped with the incessant cry of small dog syndrome to get my attention. I snapped the handle, and the etheric blade grew into the two-handled axe with a spike at the bottom. When I held it in front of me, the shield took form.

The lycans guarding Edo were joined by backup from the platform. A human and two fae trotted to the bridge in the garb of high mages. Several others in the robes of their office tried to look menacing from their positions behind the lycans as they marched forward.

The mages unleashed a flurry of attacks at us, careful to avoid Abhile. The human threw darts that burst into fléchettes of cold iron. The way they popped against the shield told me they were magically charged. One fae mage threw splashy fireballs, and his partner held up a shield, blocking most of the bridge.

My bullets ricocheted off the mage's energy field. The blast of fire I unleashed did little more than push them back a few steps. The first shot from Athena's bow streaked down in a flash of lightning that turned the mage into a smoldering statue of ash and opened the path.

The reinforcements took control of Edo and freed up the remaining eight lycans to charge. When the shield fell, they made a run for Abhile. The two remaining mages launched volleys at The Dagda, who hid behind a flaming overturned cart, and I knelt behind the shield.

I emptied the magazine in the Colt, scratching another of the charging beasts.

I pulled power into my good hand and pitched a fireball at the human mage. He deflected it, but it still managed to catch his sleeve on fire. He cavorted in a spasmodic dance to free himself, giving me time to reload. He threw the garment to the ground with a triumphant smile and readied another projectile.

Mine reached him first.

The Dagda's hiding spot was fully engulfed in flames, and he glanced around for a new location. We were nearly hanging off the end of the bridge. We had no way to go but forward.

Three Werewolves were piles of ash from Athena's bows. She and the last mage were trading shots at each other. Though she had the high ground, she'd drawn the attention of the other attendees and was forced to move.

I hit the mage with an energy ball, blowing him into the waters below.

Abhile was coming around and flinging weak magic at the remaining Werewolves, barely holding them at bay.

Edo had been pulled onto the island and was being strapped to the altar by Romulus. Giranshee was making preparations for the ritual, paying the battle behind her no attention.

Dube led the remaining nine attendants from around the table to the far end of the bridge. The two remaining lycans limped as they were called back.

Abhile trembled as we pulled her behind our meager cover. Whatever they'd used on her was meant to tranquilize a god.

I'd have to get some for Melvin to have for his next party in the desert.

DUBE MARCHED FORWARD at the far end of the bridge just off the platform and planted herself solidly in the middle. The others held weapons at the ready but seemed just as happy for us to each stay at our own ends.

"Mr. Forrester." She sounded like a drill instructor as she shouted at me. "This is a foregone conclusion. We have the old man. Now give us the girl, and you and your friends can leave."

"That's an original line." I snuck a peek over the wagon, now more embers than anything. It wouldn't provide any protection if they threw anything our way. "Does it come in the villain handbook? Or did you pick it up from a movie?"

"Is it a piece of the deal you want? Is that it? We have three recent openings at the table."

Abhile shook her head and reached over to take my hand in a weak grip. The Dagda was trickling some of whatever he had in his horn down her throat.

Athena had disappeared into the melee that had overtaken the underground complex. The lycans outside of the artificial island had gone into a blood frenzy. The Fomorians were backed up into an alcove but were holding their own.

Ba'al was leading his troops in our direction, but at least a third of the lycans were swarming his men. Must have been his cologne.

The furball was letting out a low growl, vibrating on the pads of his paws.

"Hey, Dube."

"Yes."

"Do you have any spare dog biscuits or chew toys over there? You must, we've thinned out your pack."

The Dagda shook his head and refused to look at me as he grumbled about battlefield diplomacy.

"Have it your way, sorcerer."

Dube and her entourage backed away and headed for the altar.

GIRANSHEE'S MAGICALLY AMPLIFIED voice echoed through the cavern system, bringing all but the most determined brawls to a halt. Only the lycans and other combatant groups remained in sight. "Whoever brings the future gatekeeper to me will be assured the first rights."

Ba'al swatted aside the half-dozen lycans doing illicit acts against his armor and roared. He led his herd of demons on a charge down the hill. Anything crossing his path was quickly and mercilessly dispatched.

Demons stretched their leathery wings wide and prepared for the leap to the bridge.

I shouted back, "Ba'al, don't you want a rematch, or are you afraid I'll embarrass you in front of your boys?"

The Dagda grabbed me and pulled me close. "Have you totally gone over, boy?"

"I've already blown him up once. It's not like he's going to forget."

The Dagda swallowed the boulder-size lump in his throat and released me. "You're drunk with your meager power."

"Nope." I pulled energy into my hands and Pushed the concussive wave into the general who was barking orders to his troops. It knocked him forward but also shattered the vials of holy oil, showering the lower demons in a blessed spray. "Just prepared."

The general released a pained bellow as most of his men tried to put out the small flames eating through them where the oil landed. Ba'al ignored the flames raging and dripping off him and yelled across the chasm. "Challenge accepted."

The Dagda rose and readied his staff. I pulled myself up beside him, the axe between me and a very unhappy General of the Fallen.

The Dagda kept his eyes locked onto Ba'al as spikes shot out everywhere along his back, neck, and arms. "Now would be a good time to tell me if you have some trick up your sleeve."

"We'll know in just a second."

Leathery wings pocked with holes stretched from Ba'al's armored back. A crown of horns rose around his crest.

And the enchantment-enhanced thermite went off right on time.

He launched into a low orbit, trying to escape the unyielding white fire burning through armor, flesh, and anything else it touched. He splashed into the far side of the lake, leaving a sparkling trail of fire, and his few untouched soldiers fled into the caverns.

"Close your mouth, Dag." I patted him on the back. "You never know what might fly in."

THE FURBALL HOWLED as he zigzagged up the bridge.

I shook my head as he loped toward the artificial island. "It would be nice if he let me in before taking off."

The Dagda took a long draw from his horn and stashed it away. "Pot, Kettle. Do you need my phone?"

"Abhile"—I handed her a silver blade—"will you be okay here?"

She was pale and sweating. "I won't be good anywhere for a while."

"Shall we go get your dog?" The Dagda ran his hands through his long mane.

I swung the axe around and held it in front of me when the etheric blade vanished.

I need to recharge.

Damn it, Tellia. What timing. *Hurry up,* I thought back to her.

I hung the blade on my side, sheathing it in the Leviskin pocket to keep it from hitting me, and loaded a fresh magazine into the 1911. "Let's go."

My mutt was racing around the artificial island and had distracted most of Giranshee's people into trying to catch him.

"How about Chaos?" The Dag asked.

I leveled the 1911 at a lycan who was uncomfortably close to my dog. "What?"

"Call the mutt Chaos."

"Tempting." The Colt cracked in my hands, and the lycan ran a few more steps even though he was missing most of his head.

"Havoc?" The Dagda batted away a wounded lycan and swept it into the waters below.

I loaded a fresh magazine and caught a creature in the leg who had the bottom half of a kangaroo and the top half of a bearded lady. It stripped out of crimson robes, limped over to a fountain, dove in, and disappeared.

"Did you see that? It's a gateway."

"Yeah, let's make sure nothing is coming back through this way." He grabbed a Summer fae, throwing her into the lake. "How about Pandemonium?"

I loaded my last magazine. "Can't we do this later?"

Only Dube and Giranshee remained on the artificial island with us. The battle outside of the small floating island was either dying down or had spread to areas outside of the immediate chamber. I hadn't seen the flash from Athena's bow for several minutes.

My ears were ringing from the action, but I heard Tellia's warning that the Werewolf Dube was charging at me, her mottled gray fur unmistakable. She dodged all three rounds and looped back to the altar, shifting into her human form. Her claw hovered

393

just above Edo's chest. The old man struggled against the heavy bindings, trying to escape.

Giranshee held a glowing blue sphere of energy between her outstretched hands. "Dagda. You have fought valiantly, but we still win. The age of man ends tonight, one way or another. You can help decide if it is orderly or not. Take your place on the council."

"Giran." He held his arms out and stepped into the open. "Please reconsider this. We have been down this road before."

"Dear cousin, it can be different this time. We will be in charge, leading all with experienced hands and minds. Even your friend there shows promise and may have one of the seats of the humans."

He hung his great head, his beard flowing in the gentle breeze. "Not this way. There are ways and times for this to happen, and this is not it."

"Let me motivate you," Romulus bellowed from behind us.

I hadn't heard the bridge stretch to reconnect with the mainland. A dozen lycans, several mages, and other assorted beings eyed us hungrily.

Between them, Father Mike, Wynn, Sonja, and Irika were held with chains around their necks, and their hands were shackled to a belt around their waists. Each had a lycan behind them, holding them erect, with their heads tilted back and a claw to their throat.

Romulus, in his wolfen form, parted the crowd in the full glory. Athena was struggling against the same restraints, but the Alpha dangled her in one large claw by her neck. "An exchange. Take the offer. When she comes around, she too may have a seat at the table."

"Don't," Athena screamed.

The history of death and war reflected in The Dagda's eyes as he looked down to me. I Sensed the turmoil in him despite his calm, rhythmic breathing.

"You're not…"

"I must. You wouldn't understand." A lone tear rolled down the scars in his face and disappeared into his beard. He dropped his staff to the ground. "Stay here."

I couldn't move.

I couldn't breathe.

I had to watch one of the most trusted people in my world walk away to end it.

And there was nothing I could do to stop him.

GIRANSHEE STOOD ERECT behind the altar and motioned for Abhile to be brought forward. My all but useless Colt slipped from my hand to the ground. The few rounds remaining wouldn't have made a difference.

Three lycans loped forward, followed by a mage, to restrain me. I didn't have the energy or will left in me to fight as they grabbed my arms and pulled my head back.

Athena was swearing at The Dagda in at least a dozen languages.

As he approached the altar, he moved as if he swam in molasses.

The belt they wrapped around me tingled as the buckle was clasped. The first shackle bit into me as it locked around my wrist.

Irika was led next to me, and they joined the chain on her collar to my own then locked a chain to the belt and readied the clasp around my throat.

Abhile lay still as she was strapped down by Dube, who was assisted by a bloodied kobold. Like us, Shmutzy hadn't managed to escape and was knocked away by Dube as soon as the fae's restraints were locked.

The Dagda stepped onto the altar, and Giranshee thrust herself erect, wrapping her arm around him. "Dear cousin, I knew you could be trusted to come around."

"Yes, I can be trusted," he said.

Dube was cackling and didn't see his large hand shoot out and grab her by the scruff of her neck to throw her clear of Edo and the altar. His other hand thrust his small dirk through Giranshee's throat and into her skull.

No one else moved for seconds as they tried to understand what had just happened.

I'm here for you, Tellia screamed.

The Leviskin peeled away. The rough wood of the staff fell into my hand.

Irika shoved her head backward into the lycan holding her, causing a splash of blood and a baleful cry from him.

A thin, etheric blade shot up, slicing the chain of the wrist restraint loose. The double-bladed axe head formed at the other end as I dropped and spun the blade upward to my left, slicing through the arm and chest of a lycan and taking the head of the second.

The Dagda lowered Giranshee's body to the ground.

Irika shattered the knee of her captor to the left.

I brought the axe head down, slicing through the one on her right.

Irika's separated head rolled to the ground next to me, the lycan behind her dropping her body to the ground. Her eyes stared at me, uncomprehending, and her mouth moved as she tried to breathe.

"Enough!" Romulus jerked Athena high above him and held a talon to her throat. "One more move, and Athena's head joins the other one on the ground."

I backed away from my axe buried in a lycan. Sonja and Wynn were shoved forward into the middle next to me. Mike was thrown into the middle, where he lay on the ground, clutching his side. The remaining lycans surrounded us. Five mages scattered in an arc.

Romulus stared at Giranshee's body as he approached the altar. The Werewolf ignored her and locked his burning red eyes on The Dagda. "I would kill you where you stand if I didn't need you." He turned to us. "All of you."

The Dagda knelt on the ground and laced his fingers behind his head. "I will not help you."

"Maybe not voluntarily, but then I don't need you to." Romulus swept his claw down across Edo's chest, leaving four angry gashes. Blood dripped from the claw he pointed at The Dagda. "I told you the age of man would end tonight."

Athena fell from Romulus's grip as his arm exploded, his severed hand gripping her throat. She hit the ground at the same time the report from the rifle did. I took a look around to see where the shot had come from but couldn't pick anyone out in the melee filling the hills around us.

The Dagda sprang, plowing his shoulder into the wounded Werewolf, shoving him off the altar.

Power flowed from my hands in a stream of fire, clearing the way to my axe and charring the two lycans in my path.

A mage fell from the next crack of the sniper rifle.

Dyli stepped out of a shimmering light and knelt next to Wynn. Onyx and Eric stepped out and moved in opposite directions.

I grabbed the axe from the lycan's corpse then ran at a full sprint, cleaving another of the pack in two.

Freed of his collar, Shmutzy climbed back on top of Abhile, one arm hanging limply, and the other using dexterous fingers to free her.

Onyx was semitransparent, trailing a shimmering dark wake as she dashed past a mage summoning a turquoise sphere. He fell to the ground, his yellow-green skin turning brown. The sphere shot off aimlessly into the sky.

The Dagda had recovered his staff and was fending off the hurried blows from Romulus. His severed claw had regrown into a small human hand surrounded by a furry cuff.

Dube was on all fours, trying to get to Abhile, who huddled deep in a small hole. Her ice-blue eyes shined with power while Shmutzy used his small body to protect her. My hand burned as I loosed a daisy chain of bouncing silver lightning balls, but I grinned as two wrapped around Dube's hind leg. She yelped and rolled, trying to free herself from the dissipating blast.

Athena struggled to escape her restraints with her one free hand. I ran to her and used the bladed end of the staff to slice the chains. She ripped the collar free from her neck and dropped the belt at her waist.

With her veins pulsing, she shoved past me, bounced like a gymnast, and pounced onto Romulus's back. Her legs wrapped like a boa around his throat, and she grabbed his upper jaw. One hand held onto his remaining tusk, and the other onto his jaw that was still growing back where I'd sliced it off.

Her back arched as she leaned and pulled until she was rewarded with the tearing of muscle and the snap of bone. She rode the beast down, covered in a spray of blood and brains. The top half of his head flopped around, barely attached by his pelt, when they crashed to the ground.

MY COLT THUNDERED its last three rounds in Agent Wynn's steady hands. Former Agent Dube was having a rough day, but only one round found its mark as she vanished into the fountain portal.

Athena and The Dagda attended to Edo on the altar.

399

I went to Father Mike, who lay cradling his side. Sonja was bent over, checking him out.

I looked at her. "Is he?"

My aunt shook her head. "No blood. One of the bastards punched him in the side and shattered a few ribs. I'm doing what I can."

A quick look around told me the only one we'd lost was Irika.

Paul Tinka lumbered over the bridge. Leslie leaned against him, the rifle slung over her shoulder.

Shouting drew me back to the altar. The Dagda held his staff over Edo. Athena was holding the old man's head. I knew when I got closer, we were going to lose another one.

"He's changing." Sweat poured from The Dagda. "He'll change, or more likely die. This is what that bastard wanted. We'll have no choice but to make the ice princess the new gatekeeper."

Abhile was pale and shaking. "I won't do it. Not for them. Not for you."

Athena nodded. "We can't force her. That could be worse than letting the Veils fall and taking our chances."

"What do we need?" I blurted out. "I'll do it. I'll become the gatekeeper."

"Even worse idea. To restore the accords, we need a human with the proper knowledge and discipline." Athena laughed icily. "None of those would describe you."

Father Mike leaned on Sonja and limped over. "It does me. I've studied the old accords. I even know some about the mechanism that maintains the Veil."

Athena leaned against the altar and buried her face in her hands. With a heavy sigh, she looked up. "We need twelve volunteers to restore the accords, then do the ceremony. We've got nine now, but we need a representative from the lower fae, a Divine, and a Fallen."

I swallowed. "Should I?"

"May all the gods help and forgive us." She took a deep breath and shook her head as she let out a sigh. "What a mess. But we're desperate. Call Melvin."

"I DON'T KNOW." The angel paced in circles around the round table. A small black ball of fur and muscle trotted out, chewing on Romulus's severed ear, and flopped down to watch. "You want me to represent the Divine in the new accord?"

"Do you have another suggestion?"

"Anyone but me. Order and contracts and stability aren't really my thing." He walked around with his hands in the air. I couldn't tell if he was communing with the almighty or just stalling for time. He completed the next circuit and leveled a finger at me. "I know the perfect su—I'll be right back."

"Mel—" The angel wrapped his wings around himself and folded away into a dot before disappearing.

Athena stalked over to me. "What did the loon say?"

"That he'll be right back."

"Have you asked your little friend yet?"

"Let's do it now." I scanned the island and found the kobold sitting close behind the altar, staring at his loosed collar in his hands. "Hi, Shmutzy."

Sad brown eyes looked up at me. "Yes, Master."

"No more of that." I leaned down and gently took the collar from him. "You're free now."

"If you say so, Ma—. If you say so." He sniffed. "What do I do now?"

Athena crouched next to him. "That's what we'd like to talk to you about. How would you like to join us at the table? Join the new accords."

He looked around. "You need a servant for the proceedings? I'd be happy to."

"No." She took his small hand. "You would represent your people for the new accords. All of the lesser fae."

He pulled his limbs into himself. "No, I'm just a house servant."

"Now you can serve all of your people." She stood and offered her hand. "All peoples."

He let out a small squeak but did stretch out his thin hand. Athena pulled him to his feet before he could change his mind. "Very brave of you."

"We're baaacckkk." The smile on Melvin's face was blinding.

Inquisitor Delacroix came from behind the angel, rubbing the sleep from his eyes. He yawned. "Who wants to tell me what this is all about?"

"He'll do." Athena looped her arm through Delacroix's. "Melvin, do you think you can find a Fallen to assist us?"

"I think I can do a little fishing."

TWELVE BEINGS STOOD behind the chairs around the round stone table. Father Mike had given Edo last rites and now lay on the stone altar next to him.

Melvin stood behind an unhappy demon general. He'd pulled Ba'al out of the lake, and the two had a brief but intense discussion in the language only angels understood. The Fallen angel was still healing from the intense burns from the incendiary device, boosted by holy oil and Mike's blessings.

The hills and terraces around us were populated with timid but curious observers. Onyx and Eric had avoided us all thus far and stalked the hillside in case someone objected to what we were about to do.

Athena unrolled the scroll that had been sitting on the stone table, already prepared for the ceremony, even if it had been prepared for different participants. "We assemble to form an agreement between all sentient beings," she read. "One by which we agree and bind to our peoples until such a time as we are all dead, and someone willingly assembles a consensus to undo what we do today. Should anyone wish not to undertake this burden, now is the time to step away without penalty."

Ba'al let out a huff but stood his ground. Others moved subtly, but no one moved away.

"I, Athena, take this oath to uphold the accords until the moment of my death. My people shall also abide as long as this agreement exists, and I will see that it is done for the benefit of all." She looked at The Dagda to her left. "Your turn."

He repeated the oath and was followed by Dyli, Paul Tinka, Leslie, Wynn, Sonja, Abhile, Delacroix, Ba'al, Shmutzy, and I was last. We all sat in our places and began the painful process of reading the now voided accords. A few small changes later, we all sealed the document with a drop of blood, and it was done.

We gathered around the altar. Athena and The Dagda said a final good-bye to their old friend. She handed the document to Edo. His breathing was ragged, and he struggled to get his oath out.

Father Mike took the accords from Edo's trembling hand and repeated the oath. I Sensed the exchange of power on the table. A barely visible stream ran from Edo into Mike.

The old gatekeeper took a final breath, and it was over. The Dagda closed Edo's opaque eyes.

"After twelve thousand years, the age of man is over." Athena closed her eyes. "Long be the new age of man."

"EVERYTHING IS SECURE." Father Mike sat up on the altar. "I'll have to study to understand it all, but for now, this place is again sealed off from the world, and the Veils are stable. It'll take a while before traffic can resume between the realms, but it doesn't feel like too much damage was done."

Athena faced my old friend with a smirk. "Who'd have thought an old priest would be in a mountain, responsible for the clockwork of the seen and unseen?"

"Who indeed, lass, who indeed." Mike thickened his brogue. "I'm being called to check on the widgets in this place."

I hugged my old friend. "See you soon."

He pulled me in tight. "Check on Ephraim, would you? And let Jake know."

I followed him as he walked over the bridge and up the trail. My eye caught two forms watching in the distance. One wore cobalt blue, the other sported hunter green trimmed in gold. I was feeling my own call.

Athena was bent over Romulus's body.

"Hey." I knelt down next to her. "I need to borrow a piece of this."

She was feeling around his chest. "One moment." She plunged her hand into his chest cavity and ripped out a six-inch hexagon of clear crystal.

"What's that?"

She wiped it off and rolled it up in a piece of cloth before tucking it away. "I shouldn't tell you this, but you probably need to know. It's where gods draw their power from, a little like a piece of the soul of the Highest. Some of us were born with it. Others, like Romulus, were given one from a fallen god to give them

405

power for their mission. I'm the one who gave it to him, and it cost his brother his life. And a lot worse."

"What happens to it now?"

She shrugged. "It'll be put away until we find it a good home, and the need has arisen. But with what this one has been through, that will be a while. Go do what you need to do, and let's get out of here."

I flicked my knife and finished separating Romulus's head from his body then carried it to where Abhile rested. "Come with me."

She sighed. "I've seen her." She ignored my hand and pulled herself up.

As we crossed the bridge, she looped her arm through mine and rested against me. I couldn't be sure if it was for support, affection, or just exhaustion.

The figure in green and gold who'd been with Marsaile disappeared into the woods around us before I got a look at her face, but I Sensed something familiar about her. We reached the Winter Queen before I could figure it out, so I threw the skull at her feet in frustration. "One Werewolf, one daughter."

Her smile was cruel and her tone breathy. "Too bad you don't have all of my shopping list, but it's a good start. When we get home, I have such plans for you."

"Actually, Mother"—Abhile held up a piece of jerky in a sandwich bag and handed it to Marsaile—"he does."

The corners of her lips folded as she examined it. "What's this?"

"Drake." Abhile released me and folded her arms. "Or what's left of him."

The queen's eyes glowed as she shook her head. "Nice try, little one, but he didn't give it to me."

"As my consort, and as we were physically engaged when you took it from me, I had to be the one to present it to you."

Marsaile stretched herself and was nose-to-nose with me, her icy breath turning my skin blue. "Is this true? The two of you are now joined?"

My mind was swimming, and two sharks were circling in my chest, bumping against my heart. If I agreed, what did it mean? I had a pretty good idea of what would happen if I said no. Damn fae. I couldn't trust any of them. The lesser evil had to win. "Yeah. Snookums and me."

The Winter Queen drew back and folded her arms. Cold blue flames burned in her gaze. "I see. Well, then, I bind you to her. Her life is your responsibility. Her well-being is your only concern. Her happiness, your burden." She turned to Abhile. "Enjoy it while it lasts, dear daughter. Now I need something from you."

"No, Mother. You can't have it back."

"Tsk, daughter." She turned to me. "Maybe the mother-in-law needs to move in to help you set up your new home."

Someone could have kayaked in the pit in my stomach if it hadn't been frozen solid.

"Fine, Mother." She pulled the small wooden box out of her pocket and held it out to the queen.

"Open it," Marsaile said.

Abhile chewed her lip and glanced at me. Her fingers were a blur, sigils flashed to her touch, and the box popped open. "As you wish."

The queen plucked the box from Abhile's hands before I got a look at the contents. "Enjoy your honeymoon."

I folded my arms to blend into the indignation. "One question."

"As my gift to the happy couple, one question."

"Who were you with up here?"

"The Summer Queen, of course. We royals must stay in communication about major events to prevent misunderstandings."

"Dáiríne? Mave? Who?"

Her voice echoed as she faded into mist. "You only get the first one free."

Abhile hummed a haunting tune as we made our way back down the hill.

"It's not over, is it?" I asked.

"With Mother?" She took my hand. "It never is."

"What was in the box?"

"Something I was keeping from Mother." She squeezed my hand. "It doesn't matter now. You're free of her."

One icy chill had left me to be replaced by another. It wasn't as cold or as tight of a grip around my soul, but it was nonetheless there. "You set me up."

"I gave you a choice." She swung my hand and skipped down the path. "I'm certain Mother would be happy to come back for you."

I pushed the flash of rage down. I wasn't sure where it had come from. I'd brought all of these curses and burdens onto myself, and for the moment it was a reprieve. "How long have you been carrying Drake around? That's a little weird."

She looped her arm back through mine. "That's where you draw the line? You were carrying a Werewolf skull."

"Yeah, but not all the time."

A thin smile broke on her lips. "When they started making his body as much of a monster as his mind was, that gave me control over him. Sort of a panic button. He couldn't hurt me as long as I had it on me. I kept having the feeling he'd come back, so I held onto it."

The image of him being pulled into the Void flooded back to me. "I don't see that happening."

THE PORTAL KEY melded into the floor inside the circle. I could only imagine the flurry of activity back in the Grove for whoever was keeping watch, if they still were. It felt like months had gone by, but it had barely been two days.

Shmutzy decided to stay with Father Mike while he adapted to his new job. I promised to return soon and bring him supplies, but after we'd cleared out everyone who didn't belong, different lesser fae and magical beings came out of the woodwork. Also out of the rocks, rivers, and rainforest. He would have plenty of company and a new flock to oversee.

Onyx and Eric faded away with their pack of Hellhounds as if they'd never been there. Melvin dropped Ba'al off in some great nether-region.

Athena had become Priscilla again but was still shaking off some of the goddess's temperament. She joined The Dagda inside the circle, along with Dyli, Paul Tinka, Leslie, Wynn, Delacroix, and Davis, who was wrapped up like a lycan burrito.

"No pressure." Abhile kissed me on the cheek. "Things will be when they're meant to be. Until then…"

"Are you sure you won't come back with us?" I asked Sonja.

My aunt gave me a sideways hug. "I've spent enough time in that backwoods burg. We can make our own way out."

The fae princess took Sonja's hand and blew me a kiss. "See you soon, my consort." The pair faded away into an ice-blue mist. She really was her mother's wild child.

I stepped in and closed the circle. The furball leapt in behind me. It didn't really matter what was said, just the intention. "Get us the hell outta here."

Time froze, and a blinding light surrounded us. When it faded, we were in Underhill's production studio offices, surrounded by almost everyone I cared to know.

Except for two people.

I grabbed Josiah. "Where are they?"

MY GRANDFATHER SWALLOWED. "We did what we could. They're up at the house."

The door flew off the hinges as I raced to my grandfather's house. I could have shadow-walked, but my heart was pounding less from the exercise than what I feared I would find when I got there.

Rhea pushed herself out of the rocking chair on the porch as if rising from the depths in search of a breath. She blocked my path to the door. "Before you go in—"

I locked my jaw. "Are they alive?"

"There were… complications."

I was startled by the echo of my voice. "Where are they?"

She opened the door and stood aside before I pushed my way through. Drea leaned on a cane as she hobbled her way up the hall. She grabbed me and buried her head in my shoulder.

I stroked her hair. "Are you… you? Are you okay?

"I'll be fine. It'll take a while for my body to recover." She took my hand. "Come on. We need to talk."

She led me to the parlor. Brighid smiled softly from a wheelchair. I peeled away from Drea and kneeled next to her. She tried to stand, and her whole body trembled like a frightened

411

rabbit, so I gently pushed her back down. The tremor was worse as she reached out her small hand to take mine. "Hi."

I took a deep breath. They were both alive. Both were back in their own bodies. Even so, I Sensed a change. "How are you feeling?"

"They say I'll recover. I'll have to learn to be in my own body again. It'll be strange to be alone with my thoughts."

The furball finally caught up with me and trotted into the room, leaping into Brighid's lap. "Blitzen," she said. He curled up, and she stroked his fur.

"What? Like a reindeer?"

She shook her head. "Lightning." He leaned in as she traced the jag of white down his side. "Blitzen."

"Woof." He closed his eyes and gently snored.

"I guess he has a name now." I scratched his head. "So tell me, what's wrong?"

Her whole body shuddered, and tears streamed down her face. "I've lost my magic."

The journey of a thousand miles ends with a single step—into the Void.

412

Epilogue

MISS TEE RESTED her hand on Nora's shoulder. "Are you okay, dear?"

Nora's hand clamped over her mouth, subconsciously stopping her from blurting something out. Or screaming.

Her mother had always refused to tell her about that moment. She would only say that the cost had been high, but it was worth it. Nora wasn't so sure, even if it meant she would have never existed.

"Where's the next one?" Nora asked. "This one is incomplete."

Miss Tee took the thick tome from Nora's hands and placed it aside. "A few pieces are lost, it's true. He took them away himself. Wanted to forget."

Nora gripped the arms of the chair. "But you know what happened."

"Somewhat." The old woman grabbed her cane. "Walk with me in the garden."

At the center of the maze, a labyrinth was cut into tall thick bushes, a mosaic of tiles set in stone, weaving in four quadrants of narrow winding ribbons of a pathway. From experience, Nora knew to follow Miss Tee in silence until they exited the other end. The walk was an exercise in meditation and self-reflection, according to Miss Tee. Nora just thought it was a way of buying time to decide what she would say.

A block of highly polished obsidian lay in the center of the labyrinth, outlined in a braid of silver, gold, and copper. A sigil burned just under the surface, but Miss Tee refused to tell Nora

413

what it meant. Normally, they would make a short stop at the labyrinth in silence and walk on. Nora bowed her head.

"We are at a crossroads, child."

Nora snapped her head upward, unsure if she should speak.

"Greyson was a good man, and I miss him. He never fully knew how to control his power, and sometimes it controlled him. In hindsight, we can see events more clearly, but the picture you have, even through his own words, his own mind, is incomplete." She laid a carnation on the stone. "Your power is growing. You too will make decisions you believe are the right thing to do at the time."

"Did they know what they were doing when they reopened Saguenaya?"

"There was no good choice there." She stared at the eternally overcast skies. "You've read what happened. The refuge there was never closed, just hidden. It had always been populated by lesser fae looking for a better life."

Nora swallowed. "And the accords. Did they really think what they had done was legitimate? That the others would accept who committed to it on their behalf?"

Her head swung like a blade on a pendulum, lowering each swing to slice through the victim at the bottom. Nora felt its sting.

"It's not how we act in our everyday lives that really matters. It's those moments when the hard choices must be made. To step up or not. Like it or not, every being at that table swore to uphold the accords with their lives. And they have. Changing of the guard is always messy. Just think, if Giran had been the one to lead instead…"

"Things would have been different. There would have been a firm hand on things. The war wouldn't have happened."

"And you likely would never have been born."

"A small price." Nora looked away. It wasn't the first time she'd been told that. Her mother reminded her at every opportunity.

"Careful, child." Miss Tee smiled. "You might start sounding like someone willing to make the hard choice."

"I've not made many important ones in my life. In fact, most of my decisions were made for me before I was born."

Miss Tee chuckled. "Sound like anyone else we know?"

"Don't you compare me to him."

"You two are so alike, though."

Nora felt the tingling of power flow through her.

"There's no need for you to continue to make my point."

Nora released the building charge of magical energy. "What's your point?"

"As I said, you're at a crossroads." She pointed the way they had come. Go back that way, and your life is your own, and another will have to try to take your rightful place."

"Or?"

She pointed to the way out of the labyrinth. "You take on your destiny, both the good and bad. From here on out, you are committed, nae, bound to it. When the time comes, you will have to make these decisions and live with them. Or die because of them."

"Thanks for the pep talk, but you've said this before."

"I simply want you to understand the gravity of your situation." Miss Tee shuffled on the path to the exit. Nora stared at the back of her head as she walked away. "Stay here as long as you need to decide. Go back, and this place will be closed off to you forever. Go forward, and Lelia will meet you to start the next phase of your training."

"What about the rest of his story?"

Miss Tee clucked. "You are not ready for that. You'll have it soon enough."

MISS TEE EXHALED as she flopped down behind her desk. The girl wasn't yet ready for any of it, but as usual, events rarely waited for people to be prepared. You just had to be ready for whatever came.

If only Nora hadn't wasted all of that time avoiding her fate.

Then again, if she turned back, they only had to wait for the inevitable. It wouldn't be tomorrow, but soon. Miss Tee would know soon enough. For now, the girl still sat in the middle of the labyrinth. She'd been walking in circles around the center for several hours. She'd walked partway in one direction, then the other.

Miss Tee poured hot water on the tea infuser and pulled out a small wooden box from its hiding place. Moths made a home and fluttered about in her heart, yet she was thankful she wasn't the one having to contemplate her future. Either way would be a rough road for the poor girl.

She held up the last page, the one she hadn't given Nora. The one written in his own hand to his cousin, and not like the rest transcribed by Seshat's incantation.

Mari,

There's no place for me in the Grove. Even Josiah agrees that it's better if I'm not around while Brighid recovers, if she ever does.

Priscilla took Drea with her to whatever sanctuary the Amazons are holed up in. Priscilla held me tight and told me they'd find me when the time was right, but Drea needed to become herself again. Free of Brighid. Free of me.

She needed to go back to her roots as an Amazon. I Sensed there was something more, unlike anything I'd ever felt before. I had a suspicion, but if I was right, I'd probably never know. I'd served my purpose, and the Amazons have their own ways. Being their only son still gets me only so far.

I'm sitting in a little diner. Wynn is talking back to his crew at Longbow, but it's not looking good. LeGasse has me in her sights.

I'm going underground for a while. I'm going to spend time with Mike in his new home and get a grip on my building power. I'm having a hard time controlling it, and there, if something goes wrong, he can help me protect everyone else.

You'll be the only one who knows where I've gone. I'll leave the instructions on how to contact me.

Stay under the radar. Things are going to get worse before they get better.

I can feel it.

- G

She folded the letter and placed it back in the wooden box with some other keepsakes and hid it away. She said a little prayer to herself. "I hope you're well, boy, wherever you are."

Tea drained from the infuser into her cup. She sipped at the hibiscus tea and noticed Nora making her way along the path. "Godspeed and good luck."

NORA TURNED BACK and stalked to the center of the labyrinth. She rubbed her neck and stared at the sigil in the glassy stone. She paced in a circle, changed directions, then back again.

What would Mother say? she thought to herself.

That's a stupid question. Besides, this is all her fault. She pushed me here.

She stared at the way home. Could she give it up? Not know why it all happened?

She looked to the other end, and the archway in the bushes. What was on the other side?

The harsh realization set in. *You can never go home again.* She might walk away, but things would never be the same. Wondering what could be. What should be.

If she was ever going to get out of these ruins, there was only one chance.

She fidgeted with each step, crossing her arms, snapping her fingers, humming to herself. Now she needed only take the final step off the path and into the archway.

How many times had she done this in the past? Of course, she'd always been following Miss Tee. What an odd name. She giggled. *Miss Tee who drinks tea.*

The air got heavy. Her toes edged up to the line. Why couldn't she take that last step? She turned to go back to the middle.

"I do not have all night." A pair of stark white eyes stood out in the darkness. "I am leaving, with or without you."

Nora stepped forward. "Wait. I'm almost there."

"You have chosen."

"What?" She looked down. Her toe had broken the plane of the labyrinth.

A strong hand reached from the darkness and held out a silver pin. It was a pair of wings coming off the handguard of a sword. "Take them."

Nora flexed her hand, a fine tremor in her fingers as she reached out and plucked the pin away.

"Come forth, we have much to do."

Acknowledgements

Huge thanks to my friend and fellow author Calandra Usher, who has been on me to finish up this book, and give the furball a name. Check her out! Swing by http://homeoftheriders.com/ to get her series about the Four Horsemen of the Apocalypse, a love story.

Thanks John Hartness http://johnhartness.com/ for hooking me up with Nelia, who is a fantastic editor. He can feed your need for geeky vampires!

Thanks Nelia for all your work pulling me into line, and cleaning up all the things that made sense in my head.

And thanks to all my friends who keep supporting me and putting up with my ramblings.

About the Author

Jim has a long-standing love for and interest in history, anthropology, the sciences, and literature, which have been run through the blender of his twisted mind to produce this work. When not trying to get the strange ideas floating around in his head out in text, Jim lives in the central Carolinas with his wife, three dogs, and the occasional fish. When not clicking away on a laptop pretending to be the monkey writing Shakespeare, he is usually behind a different laptop adding to twenty-plus years on technology projects or playing with glass in fire.

To contact me with snarky comments, please visit

http://jim-mcdonald.net/ and sign up for the mailing list.

Or follow me on Facebook:
https://www.facebook.com/jimmacauth

Goodreads:
https://www.goodreads.com/author/show/8119076.James_McDonald

Twitter: @JimMacAuth

And eMail: jim@jim-mcdonald.net

Check out my fellow authors at: www.infinitylimitedgroup.com

Thank you for reading, and please watch for the next installment! And reviews are always appreciated —they let authors know what you think and what you loved so we can give you more of it.

Happy reading!

www.ingramcontent.com/pod-product-compliance
Lightning Source LLC
Chambersburg PA
CBHW030542260626
47157CB00006B/2150